ROBERT TANENBAUM

NO LESSER PLEA

Franklin Watts 1987 New York Toronto

FOR MARGE AND NORM FOR
ALL THEIR LOVE AND SUPPORT;
FOR RACHAEL, ROGER AND BILLY, MY ANGELS;
AND FOR PATTI, MY MOST SPECIAL LOVE.

My deepest gratitude to Michael Gruber for all his assistance;
to Eric Greenfeld for his enthusiasm during the book's pre-history;
to Marty Baum for encouraging me to focus my energies on Karp and all
the ensemble players; to Ari Makris for all her dedicated efforts.

Special thanks to Ed Breslin, my editor, who, like Henry Robbins
before him, has always been a faithful supporter and friend.

No Lesser Plea is entirely a work of fiction.
All names, characters, and situations are imaginary,
and any resemblance to persons living or dead is
unintended by the author and entirely coincidental.

Library of Congress Cataloging-in-Publication Data

Tanenbaum, Robert K.
No lesser plea.

I. Title.
PS3570.A52N6   1987   813'.54   86-28276
ISBN 0-531-09783-8

NO LESSER PLEA

CHAPTER ONE

Two men were leaning against the yellow Firebird talking quietly, ignoring the street life around them. The two men were professional criminals and they were plotting a crime. They were in upper Manhattan, on a mean street, one of the poor ones that smell like a barbecue party held in a garbage dump. It was noisy in the early twilight, with the shrieking of kids at play or in pain, and the contributions from half a dozen different radios drifting or blasting from the windows of parked cars or apartments. Frightened old men hurried home as the shadows deepened, past groups of idlers, past junkies, past staggering drunks, past poor folks chatting on steps and crates. It was late spring in New York, the first really mild day of the year, when New Yorkers are able to forget the hideous reality of both winter and summer in that city.

"We gonna use this car?" said the younger of the two. His name was Preston Elvis, twenty years old, recently out of Attica, where he did time on an armed robbery charge, thus making him a real man in his social circles.

"Yeah, man, we're gonna use this car. We gonna use *my* yellow Firebird, that everybody in the whole fucking neighborhood knows is my car, with *my* tags, and we're gonna drive it to a supermarket, and ace some dude and take his cash bag and then drive it back and park it in front of my building. That your plan, Pres?"

"Well, I mean . . ."

"Look, baby, when I say no connection between us and the deed, I mean *zero* connection. Different car. Different tags. After all, we don't hang out together, we don't know each other, dig?"

"So we steal a car?" Elvis was fascinated. He had been to crime school in Attica, of course, but the problem there, which even he could see, was that all the available teachers were failures—they'd been caught. This dude, now, this dude had never been caught. This was Mandeville Louis, by his own claim the most successful armed robber in New York. Elvis didn't know whether the claim was true. Certainly he'd never heard of him in prison or on the street. But the man had a definite style. Elvis liked the way he talked—this dude had brains, no question—liked his clothes, liked his car, liked his apartment and the women he hung out with. Fresh out of the slams, tap city, Elvis was a willing student. He'd fallen into conversation with Louis in a bar off 126th Street about two weeks ago, and since then he'd felt like a kid up from Triple A who'd been singled out by Pete Rose for special attention.

"No, baby, we don't steal no car. Cars is for car thieves and dumb kids. We steal a new car, we got eyes on us the whole way, especially in this here DE-prived environment. Then the owner squeals like a muthafucka to the cops and every pig wagon in the city got a description of our car pinned up on their visor. You wanna get stopped with a bag of money in your lap?

"We steal a old car, the bastard got a fucked-up fuel pump he forgot to tell us about. We break down in front of the Twenty-third Precinct. Forget it. No, little bro, we get a guy to *drive* us there, in his own wheels and *drive* us back. Then we pay him off and bye-bye. He don't know us, we don't know him."

"Hey, but what happens if he gets picked up," said Elvis. "I mean, you know . . ."

"Nothing happens. First, the dude don't know nothing. What he gonna say? Mister PO-lice, it wasn't me took the money, offed the dude, it was two other niggers, I don't know their names, don't know where they live. What they say? Bull-

2 —

shit, boy, we got *you,* you goin' up! Other thing is, the dude drive the car, he what they call a high-risk individual. You gotta find somebody maybe won't be round town too long."

"Won't be round town?" said Elvis. "What you mean? You mean we give him a ticket to somewhere?"

"Yeah, you could say that, Pres, we give him a ticket."

Elvis was drinking in criminal strategy like a sponge. Basically a smash and grab artist, he had pulled off no more than half a dozen crimes before being caught, all but one of them sneak thievery. They were crimes of opportunity, that required no more than a strong back, swift feet, and street sense. The best part of being a criminal to him was not so much the loot, which in his case had been petty—a couple of TV sets, a couple of purses, a pretty good stereo—but the feeling of power, of personal worth that went with being a bad dude on the street.

His desire for even more status led him to purchase a small caliber revolver for $20, and to try his hand at armed robbery. He stuck up a dry cleaner in his neighborhood, got away with $48 and was arrested the next day, on the information of the store owner, who had been robbed eleven times and made it his business to register every jitterbug in the district in his mind's eye.

Elvis's public defender spent twenty minutes on the case: Elvis was copped to a lesser—grand larceny and weapons—and went up for a bullet—a year, minus time served and good behavior. He had been in for nine months—not unpleasantly, since he was big, and looked tough, and as an armed robber was at the top of the pecking order in prison society.

Louis continued his lecture. "Deal is this. You ever meet a guy name of Donald Walker?"

"No, why?"

"You sure? Bout as big as me, bright colored, got a little Afro, little beard, they call him 'Snowball'?"

"No, Man, I don't know no dude like that. Who is he?"

"He our driver. He got a four-door Chevy sedan, I checked it out, he keep it up real good. Now, I got him set to meet us tomorrow night. We leave from here, take the subway downtown, get off at Fiftieth and Lex. He pick us up outside the subway station, ten-thirty on the dot. We drive nice and slow down to Thirty-ninth and Madison, shouldn't take us no more than fifteen minutes, tops.

"There's this supermarket there, closes at eleven. Bout ten minutes after, the manager comes out carrying two cash bags. He meet a guard from the guard service and they drive to the bank. We gonna be parked around the corner. When the man lock up, I get out of the car. I'm wearing my mean black suit, shirt, tie, carrying a little attaché case. You dig, I just been selling stocks or some shit, nobody scared of me, way I dressed. I get even with the car. The guard always stand outside the car and open the door for the manager. So, I pull out the shotgun from under my suit coat, off one, off the other, put the bags in the case and walk back to the car. We drive back to the subway station, and then we go our separate ways. Then, in a couple days, you call me, we get together, I give you your share, you give Snowball his. You got any questions."

Elvis had a million questions. This was the first he heard he was getting involved in a double murder. He stared at Louis, but the look of the other man dissuaded him from raising any serious objections. Louis was wearing his usual expression of friendly engagement, as if he had just invited an acquaintance to admire the wax job on his car. Elvis found it uncomfortable to meet his gaze. He dropped his eyes to the ground, and said, drawing on his ultimate reserves of cool: "Sound good, Man, sound good, but well, what about me, what I be doin' while you doin' that?"

"Glad you ask that, Pres. You got just the one job. When that gun go off, that little mutha Snowball gone shit his pants. Your job is, when I come round the corner, I expect my get-away vehicle be where I expect it to be, dig?"

"Yeah, that don't sound too hard."

"OK, that's cool. Well, Pres, see you around."

It was a dismissal. "OK, Man, see you tomorrow night."

"Oh, and Pres?"

The younger man stopped and turned to face Louis. "Yeah?"

4 —

"You got a suit coat and a tie?"

"Yeah, I guess, somewheres. Why you wanna know?"

"Wear them tomorrow night. And get rid of that do rag on your head. And the goddam shades, too. We gonna be three respectable colored folks drivin' a nice respectable Chevy Impala under the speed limit. Anybody look in the car I want them to think we goin' to your momma's funeral."

Elvis said, "Sure Man, I'm hip," and walked off. Man was hard to take sometimes, think he own your life, he thought. On the other hand, now, he sound like he *know* what he doin'. Suddenly, Elvis realized what was about to happen to him. Almost all his short life he had worked to convey an image of murderous villainy. Twenty-four hours from now he would be a murderous villain in fact, or at least a murderous villain's assistant. He gave a little skip of delight.

Man Louis watched the big youth turn the corner. He got into the Firebird and drove slowly down Lexington Avenue. At 135th Street, he spotted an open saloon, and cruised around until he found a legal parking space. In the saloon, he waited patiently until the man using the phone had finished placing a complicated bet, and then dialed a number.

Donald Walker jumped from his couch at the first ring of the telephone. "I'll get it. It's for me," he cried.

The voice on the phone was that of the man Walker knew as Stack.

"How you doin', Donald?"

"OK, just fine. What's happenin' ?"

"Everything set. How's the car? You got the new plates?"

"Yeah. The kid came and brought them over last night, just like you said. I gassed it up and changed the oil. Checked the brakes, everything. I done it myself. It runs real good."

"Yeah, that's real fine, Donald. Now listen up. At ten-thirty tomorrow night you gonna be at the Fiftieth Street Lexington station. I mean ten-thirty, Donald, not ten fuckin' thirty-one, we understand each other? Good. OK, me and my man Willy get in the car, and we drive real slow down Lex. We hang a right on Thirty-ninth and you park on the corner of

Thirty-ninth and Madison, on the side street. Eleven o'clock, I get out of the car and go 'round the corner. The whole thing'll be over in five.

"Then I get back in the car. We drive real slow again, back to the subway. Me and Willy get out. You drive to this hotel I got picked out, I'll give you the address tomorrow night."

"What's this shit! You never said nothing about no hotel."

"Donald, be cool—use your head. What if somebody see your car? You want to lead them right up your front walk? Wait a day, two days, see if there any heat . . ."

"What kinda heat? I don't like this, Stack. What the fuck I gonna tell my wife?"

"Goddam! What you worryin' about? You some kinda man can't even lie to a woman. Make up something."

"And you said I get paid right after. You said! When I'm gonna get my money?"

"You get it when I give it to you."

"No way, man. I want it then."

There was a pause on the line. When Louis began to speak again, it was in a low, whispery voice, slow and measured, like an adult recounting the crimes of a child to whom he is about to give a savage beating.

"Donald, let me explain something to you. You *in* this. You mind me now, cause if you crap out on me, if you mess with me now, you in more deep shit than you ever been in your whole life. Now you don't know me Donald, but I know you. I know your little house out there in Queens. I know your pretty little wife and your three pretty little children. What you want, Donald, is you want to keep old Stack real happy with you, and with your house and your little family. So how you gonna keep me happy? It real simple. You do what I say, when I say it, and you keep your fat mouth shut. Now, do we have an understanding?"

Walker's mouth was cotton-dry. He croaked out a sound.

"I didn't get that, Donald."

"Yeah, Stack, you know I didn't mean nothing. I just strung out, is all. You said you gonna get me some . . ."

"That's my man. I am gonna get you something to fix you

right up, Donald. I got some *bad* shit, Donald, and a big piece got your name right on it. Now you fix it with the wife, and you be there, hear?"

"I be there, Stack. Don't worry."

"I got nothin' to worry about, Donald."

The line went dead.

"Who was that on the phone, Donald?" his wife, Ella, called from the upstairs bedroom.

Walker shivered and wiped the sweat from his forehead with a dish towel. He walked slowly up the stairs.

"Donald?"

"It was Billy Cass, from the plant, he say they hiring up by that computer factory in Stamford. He say, maybe him and me should go up there, go for a job interview."

His wife was in her robe, sitting at her vanity table and applying face cream. Walker started to get undressed. He was a poor liar and he kept his face averted as he spoke.

"That sounds great, Don. When were you fixing to go?"

"Well, he say we should leave after work tomorrow and drive up. His sister live somewheres around there—he said we could spend the night there and be first in line the next morning."

Ella finished her face and got into bed. Walker joined her. "That sounds good, Donald. You be back Saturday, then?"

"Well, yeah, I guess. I'll call you from there and let you know how it comes out."

As he lay back and switched off the bedside light, Walker tried to compose his racing thoughts. Stack had promised him $500 for the job. That would be enough to pay off the two month's arrears on the mortgage. He had a letter from the bank that told him that unless they saw some money by the end of the month—in less than two weeks—they would start foreclosure proceedings. Walker had busted his hump, working double shifts at the commercial laundry, to get together the down payment, but it wasn't the thought of losing the house that bothered him as much as explaining to his wife where the mortgage money had gone.

Walker was an easygoing young man who had married

into a family of strivers. In six years of marriage it seemed to him that he had not drawn an easy breath. His wife had a year of college and his in-laws were all civil servants of one kind or another. He had not finished high school himself, and Ella was bound and determined to show her clan that she had not made a mistake in marrying the good-looking but feckless Donald Walker.

So he worked like a dog, and got pushed harder, until each demand seemed like a razor-toothed little animal chewing away inside his skull. But lately he had found a way out. He would drive out for an evening after dinner and go to a local pool hall, and shoot a few games of eight-ball or snooker. After a while, a man named Paradise would come in, and Walker would follow Paradise into the men's room and would give Paradise ten, or twenty, or fifty dollars, and Paradise would give Walker a glassine envelope filled with white powder. Then Walker would sit in his car and for a few hours he would be on top of things, in charge, together. He wasn't a junkie, hell no! He could kick it easy after things settled down a little. But that's where two months of mortgage had gone to, and that's why Mandeville Louis had picked him, with the mystical vulturelike radar that led him to the Donald Walkers of this world, to be his wheelman.

CHAPTER TWO

Walker had heard the expression "living hell" before, but he had never thought much about what it meant before the day he spent waiting for the night he was to debut as a wheelman for Mandeville Louis.

His environment helped. A commercial laundry would encourage even a soul washed white as snow to imagine the infernal realms. The air was gray with steam and thick with the sweetish reek of solvent. Periodically, there would occur a great hissing noise from the pressers, or someone would throw open a boiler hatch and release an even heavier cloud of vapor. Through this jellied air trudged indistinct figures dripping sweat, often stripped to their waists, bearing heavy loads or pushing carts heaped with bags. Urging them on were overseers in white, short-sleeved uniforms, with their names embroidered in red on their breasts.

"Hey, Walker, whaddya doin'? You been here two hours, you ain't done half a rack."

Walker looked across the steam presser at the foreman. "Sorry, Jack, I guess I don't feel so hot."

"Yeah? Well, be sick on your own time. You can't do the work, punch out, we'll get somebody else." He walked off and Walker cursed him vehemently under his breath.

Walker had been working at Ogden's Martinizing Dry Cleaners and Launderers for three years. The job required nothing but the ability to stand heat and endless boredom. Ordinarily Walker had the ability to shut his mind off and put his flesh on autopilot: remove the crumpled garment from the bin, arrange it according to its type, drop the cover, steam it, shift, steam, shift, steam, hanger it, next.

Now, however, he could not get away from his thoughts at all. He had to think about every motion; his body would not slip into its accustomed grooves. Walker was also extremely uncomfortable; every cell in his body was whining for a bath in smack. Heroin withdrawal symptoms are very similar to those of a bad case of flu: Walker's nose ran, his joints ached, he had the chills, and he was ferociously constipated. At first he cursed himself for a fool and a coward and swore that if he could only get past this night, he would never, *never* touch the stuff again, would never have to see Stack again, or hear his voice. After a while, he stopped thinking about anything but his next hit; that seemed enough to think about, the only thing worth thinking about.

So the day passed. Walker's noon-to-eight shift came to an end and he walked out into the evening toward his car. The air was cool, at least, and after what he had been breathing, almost pure. He made himself take deep breaths, hoping to calm his pounding heart and calm the tremor in his limbs. But his anxiety was deeper than he could reach with his own resources.

It took him half an hour to change the license plates; he kept dropping the bolts and skinning his knuckles. Afterward, he collapsed on the front seat of the car. He had intended to be straight for the drive, but he thought, "Gonna go off the goddam road if I keep shaking like this," and reached for the envelope taped to the roof of his glove compartment.

Ten minutes later, through the miracle of dope, Walker had to strain to remember what he was so worried about. It would be a piece of cake tonight—no different from driving the wife and kids to church, except he would be $500 richer. He thought about the money. Maybe he would give half to the mortgage company, keep them off his ass for a while, and see Paradise with the rest. Then he could get a little ahead, maybe taper off without too much trouble, be cool, clean up his act, and get a better job. Yeah, things were starting to look a lot better; it was amazing how every problem kind of fell into place when you got your head straightened out.

Thinking these and similar thoughts, Walker nodded off. He came to with a bolt of adrenaline shooting like a hot stake through his innards. He yanked his wristwatch out of his pocket, where he stashed it before starting work. It was 10:15.

Shaking and sick with fear, he cranked the car, almost flooded, started up, stalled, released the hand brake, started again, and peeled rubber out of the company lot. He whipped onto Queens Boulevard going fifty, heading west, sweating again, chanting, "Oh Jesus, clear the way, oh, Jesus mutha-fucka move your ass, you asshole move, oh no don' stop in the lane for no fare muthafuckin' cabbie oh Jesus don' make me be late, that man kill my ass for sure . . ."

Driving better than he ever imagined he could drive and with improbable luck, Walker reached 50th and Lex at 10:45. Stack and another man he didn't know were waiting by the subway entrance. They walked quickly over to the car; Stack got in the front seat and the other man got in the back.

Walker said, "Hey man, I got hung up. There was a wreck on Queens Boulevard."

Stack reached over and grabbed him by the front of his shirt and pulled him over so that their faces were inches apart. Walker noticed that his eyes were light-colored with yellow flecks, and burning.

"Shut the fuck up! I told you, mutha, I *told* you. You in trouble now, boy, I mean it. Now move this piece of shit, and don't make no more mistakes." He gestured to the backseat. "This here Willy Lee. He gonna make sure you don't."

Walker did as he was instructed, easing the car down the avenue. Out of the corner of his eye he saw Stack open his attaché case and take out a sawed-off shotgun. He put it on the seat next to him. "This here Thirty-ninth. Turn and pull up at the end of the block," he said.

As the car slowed to the curb, Louis stuck the shotgun down between his belt and his body on the left side. It was a 16 gauge Remington Standard Model 870 pump gun, which Louis had bought in a pawn shop in Passaic the week before and cut down himself from its normal length of forty-eight inches to slightly over sixteen inches. It had five double-aught shells in the magazine.

Louis also had a Smith & Wesson .38 caliber Bodyguard Airweight in an ankle holster on his right leg. He had never used this particular gun, since pawnshop shotguns had proved sufficiently deadly for all the killing he had ever done. Still, Louis didn't believe in taking unnecessary chances. There was always the possibility of pursuit after a job and the pistol was insurance.

"Wait," he said, as he picked up his case and swung out of the car and around the corner. Three minutes later he was back. He opened the door and got in. Walker said, "What happened. You do it?"

"What happened? You *shit!* What *happened?* I tell you what happened. Bullshit happened, that's what. They gone, boy, long gone. You made me late, and goddam Snowball, I call myself ready to tear your fuckin' junkie head right off."

"Shit, Stack, I said I couldn't help it," Walker whined.

"Ah, shut your mouth, just drive. Get goin' ."

"Where to now?"

Louis turned to Elvis. "Hear him, now. Think he a fuckin' cabbie. 'Where to?' my ass. Just go to the next robbery, Donald, you miss the first one. What the fuck I care, just move it."

Louis was blazing, not just because he had missed the robbery, but because he had built himself up as perfect to the kid in the back. For some reason he didn't quite understand, he wanted to impress Pres Elvis. He needed an acolyte to admire the perfection of his technique, to learn from him, and maybe set up in business on his own, using the same style. Louis also had in the back of his mind the idea of maybe starting a franchise. He'd show some likely youngsters how it was done, and then sit back and take a piece off the top each time they pulled a job. Let the younger dudes take the risks now. Louis was an avid reader of the business press and considered himself in the entrepreneurial mainstream of America.

Now it was turning to shit before his eyes. Louis, like most people in his line of work, had an extremely low tolerance for frustration. Since he spent most of his working life armed to the teeth, he did not need a high one.

The car had turned north on Madison. Walker was hoping Stack and Willy would get out and leave him alone, and he planned to loop back to Lex at 50th and maybe drop them off at the station again.

But at 48th Street he heard Stack say, "Right, turn right, dammit!" He turned the corner. "Park here now, I wanna check out that liquor store." Louis had spotted a lighted window with a figure standing behind the counter. He never pulled an impromptu job, but he was driven to bring something off tonight, to show Elvis he was a pro. To show himself, too.

Angelo Marchione, the proprietor of A&A Liquors, was spending the last few minutes of the night placing bottles of Chivas on the high-class Scotch shelf behind the register counter. His son, Randy, was working in the basement storeroom. The door ringer sounded and Marchione looked up to see a well-groomed coffee-colored man dressed in a black pinstriped three-piece suit, and wearing gold-rimmed glasses, walking toward him.

"Can I help you?" said Marchione.

Louis favored the classic approach. He pulled his shotgun out, stuck it in the other man's face and said, "OK, muthafucka, this is a stick-up. Let's have the cash drawer, NOW!"

Marchione did as ordered. He'd been robbed before and knew the routine. He pulled the cash drawer out and slid it across the counter.

"Now take out all the bills and put them in a bag," said Louis. "No, not no paper bag—use the cash bag from the bank."

Again Marchione complied, stuffing about $500 in bills from the drawer into the plastic zipper bag supplied by Bankers' Trust. (What was with this guy—did he want a deposit slip too?) The shotgun never wavered from his face.

"That's good," said Louis. "Now go and stand in the corner and be still."

The proprietor walked down the aisle behind his counter

and stood with his back to his high-priced cognac display. He watched the gunman open a leather attaché case and put the money bag inside. He seemed to be in no hurry.

"This your only store, hey?"

"No," said Marchione. "We got another one over on the West Side, Eighty-seventh and Broadway. My brother runs it, we're partners. That's where we get the name, A and A. I'm Angelo, he's Alfredo, we call him Al."

"You know anything about franchises?"

"What? What franchises?"

"I mean like franchising, somebody figure out a good way to sell liquor, do the overhead, buy the stock, then get a bunch of guys to run the stores for him. Like McDonald's and all."

Marchione stared at the other man, at the engaged, interested expression on his face and at the black circle of the shotgun barrel's mouth. (This is crazy, I'm having a business conversation with a robber. Only in New York.)

"Well, there's not much of that in the liquor business, not in New York. I hear they're starting it out of town."

"How come?"

"I don't know. I guess if you got a franchise operation everything has to be the same, so you can get your discount from the supplier. I mean you got to move a lot of the same product, and you got to have a limited inventory. In the city, it's all fashion, like clothes. One weeks it's Galliano, next it's Pernod, whatever. On the stuff that sells steady, well, it's hard to beat the department stores. A franchise operation would have to beat them on cost on the low end and beat the neighborhood stores on selection on the high end. Then you got the good will . . ." His voice tapered off. What was going on here? The thought entered his mind that this guy could be a real wacko instead of a regular out-and-out robber.

"I get it," said Louis. "It don't really apply to the operation I got in mind, though."

He closed and snapped his attaché case. "Well, time I was goin' ," he said briskly, and shot Marchione in the face from a range of about five feet. The blast exploded Marchione's head and a dozen bottles of fine cognac and hurled his dead body back against the shelves. Louis placed his shotgun on the counter and approached the body, being careful of the broken glass. He patted down the man's pockets and was rewarded with a thick roll of bills. The dead man had done a substantial cash business and routinely kept a good part of it outside his bank and out of view of the Internal Revenue Service. Louis smiled. He was something of an expert on the cash-diversion practices of dead storekeepers and never missed an opportunity to check in places other than the obvious cash register.

He walked out from behind the counter and placed the shotgun and the additional cash inside the attaché case. As he snapped it shut he was feeling good. The old man had about a grand in the roll, plus the $500 from the till—probably not as much as they would've got from the supermarket but sure as shit better than nothing, which it would have been on account of goddamn Walker being late. *That boy is not cut out for this business.*

Louis's hearing had been slightly impaired by the blast of his gun, so that he failed to hear the footsteps coming up the stairs from the cellar or the door opening behind him.

"Oh God! Dad . . . what, Oh, no!" Louis spun around and saw a good-sized kid of about seventeen in a tan shop apron and a college sweatshirt. The kid saw him at about the same time and for a heartbeat they just stared at one another. The stink of death and cognac was strong in the air.

Then Louis slammed his case down on the counter and began fumbling frantically at the snaps. The youth picked up a bottle of Scotch by the neck and with a bellow of rage came around the end of the counter, the bottle raised high over his head. Louis lifted the case to block the blow, but not quickly enough. The bottom of the bottle caught him a glancing blow above the ear. He dropped the case and went down on one knee, with hot stars exploding behind his eyes. The kid was on him then, trying to grab at his clothes to hold him steady so he could get a good blow in with the bottle, Louis squirming and trying to kick away across the rough wooden floor.

Louis was not much of a street fighter and the kid was big enough and mad enough to be very dangerous. Now he was trying to press Louis down with his knee, his hand wrapped tightly in the cloth of the other man's jacket. Enough of this shit, thought Louis, cocking his right leg to bring his ankle holster within reach. He heaved the middle of his body up and as the kid went over to one side Louis brought the Airweight out, stuck the muzzle in the kid's belly and fired three times.

Louis sat up. The kid was lying on his back not far from his feet. He was gasping and his hands were pressed into the widening stain of blood forming in the center of his body. Louis stood up and straightened his clothes. He was irritated to see that his suit-jacket lapel had been torn in the struggle. Walking over to the shelves behind the counter he inspected the stock and then selected a quart of J&B Scotch, bagging it neatly from the supply underneath the register. He picked up his attaché case, stuck the bottle under his arm, then walked over to the wounded youth and shot him twice in the forehead at point-blank range. Then he walked out of the store.

The ten minutes Louis was away were the longest ten minutes in Walker's life. He was itching and shivering. The last hit was hardly enough to keep him calm; after this, he deserved another, but damn, that was his absolutely last stone empty bag of dope. He glanced up and looked at the man in the backseat through the rear-view mirror. Pres was leaning back in his seat, eyes half closed, a faint smile on his lips. Walker studied his face. The dude was cool, no lie. Walker said, "Say, Stack been gone a long while, ain't he?" The other man's eyes came open a fraction and he met Walker's gaze in the rear-view mirror.

"No, it's just a couple of minutes. Take it easy."

"Maybe we should drive around the corner, maybe something went wrong."

"We staying right here. Jus' be cool."

There was a muffled bang from around the corner. Walker jumped.

"Uhnnh . . . ooh, shit, what was that?" he said, although he knew very well what it was. Walker's legs were twitching uncontrollably by now, like a four year old who needs to go potty.

There were three more popping sounds, sharper this time, and then two more.

"What the fuck he doin' in there, playin' shootin' gallery? Oh, come on, les go, les go!" he moaned, banging the heel of his hand against the steering wheel.

In the back Pres thought, "This boy comin' apart, now. Might have to whap his head a couple times, settle him down." The idea gave him some small pleasure. He felt in charge, cool, a little tingly. It's wonderful to find one's metier while one is still young.

Then the car door was opening and Louis was getting in. He had recovered his composure, and flashed a grin at Elvis. "Alright, my man! Nice score." He turned to Walker. "Damn, Snowball! You look like death eatin' a sandwich. Was you worried about your Uncle Stack?"

"No, Stack, it jus' like . . . seem like you took a long time an all."

"Yeah, right, now Donald, I want you to start drivin' up-town on Madison. The speed limit is thirty-five, red mean stop, green mean go. Fiftieth, cut over to Lex an drop us off. Now, move."

Walker did as he was told, driving like an old lady on the way to church. The night was cool and the traffic fairly light. He made it to the subway station in a little over eight minutes and pulled up to the curb.

The two other men got out. Louis came around to the driver's side. He said, "Listen here, Snowball. You goin' to drive to the Olympia Hotel, that's at Tenth Avenue, 'round 23rd Street. There's an all-night garage across the street. Put the car in there. *Before* you do that, pull over somewheres and change the plates. You got that? You got a screwdriver, don't you?"

"Yeah, but Stack, I sick now. I'm fucking crawlin', don't you got anything to fix me up?" He snuffled back his running nose.

"Oh, I got some *good* stuff for you, Snowball, but I gotta go back to my place for it. Tell you what—take this here bottle and put yourself to sleep tonight. When you wake up I be there with your money an what you need."

"You sure, Stack? I be bouncin' off the walls come mornin' ."

Louis reached in and patted Walker on the cheek. "Yeah, Snowball, I be there, you my man, you part of my gang, ain't you?"

Like the fly fisherman or the duck hunter, Man Louis had a solid practical understanding of the psychology of his particular prey, which in his case was the dope addict. He knew that junkies owned only two psychic states: fixed and looking for it. At a certain stage of looking, he knew, they were the most suggestible beings on earth, the promise of dope being enough to cancel any normal sense of suspicion or caution. He needed Walker in a certain place, alone, for at least twenty-four hours, and experience had shown him that a scared junkie would hold still that long on the expectation of a freebie hit of *good* dope.

Walker put the car in gear and drove off. Louis watched him go and then turned to Elvis.

"That asshole. Pres, my man, let me tell you. Some people they just tools, oughta have a damn on-off switch top their head. This Snowball, now, I meet him two weeks ago, hangin' around Stacy's out in Queens? I know this dude pushes shit round there. Lil Donald's one of his prime clients. Anyway, I ask around, the man's in trouble, got a fifty dollar Jones on him, in hock up to his ass. We get to talkin' , me and Donald, an I slip him something from my private stash. He's flying, man, I his momma and his poppa. I tell you, Pres, you want to *own* a dude, get you a smackhead. I tell you somethin' else. When you done, they got that switch on 'em, you jus reach up and switch it off. Dig?"

Elvis dug. "How you gonna do it?"

Louis looked pained. "*I* ain gonna do nothin' . *He* gonna do it. We jus gotta set up the situation, hey. That's the other part of your job. Now let's go home."

As the two men descended into the steam-smelling passages, united as they were in the camaraderie of the deed, their minds held quite different thoughts. Elvis was elated, but at the same time calm with the sense that his immediate future was safely in someone else's hands, that the awful necessity for daily choices was in abeyance. In this he was like a monk or a woman who has just become pregnant. To him, the reality of the murder, the horror that was about to descend on Mrs. Marchione and her family, was utterly opaque. He had no imagination, or rather, his imagination was suspended at the level of a child who can say, "Bang, bang, you're dead," without being able, in fact, to grasp the nature of death.

Louis, on the other hand, had plenty of imagination and his mind was continually writhing with plans and contingencies. Although he affected the style and speech of a bad street thug, he was in fact the product of a comfortable middle-class home, his mother a schoolteacher, his father an undertaker and part-time preacher. Strait had been the gate and narrow the way in the Louis household: Mandeville's two older brothers and younger sister had grown up strong in the church and, riding the crest of the civil-rights movement, had risen well in the world—dentist, lawyer, high-school principal.

But in one of those quirks of human development that confounds liberal philosophy, Mandeville, at eight, had had an illumination, or rather its opposite. It suddenly occurred to him that the complexities of the moral life—thinking of others, giving rather than receiving, following the commandments— and the plaguing guilt and conscience that enforced them, could be dispensed with. If one was clever enough to avoid detection and capture, one could do anything, *anything.* You could curse God in church and nothing would happen. You could sneak into the church and pee on the altar cloth and the minister's robes. You could steal a kitchen knife and dismember your sister's kitten. And if you slipped and got caught (and this was almost the best part), you could wail and beg forgiveness, and promise never to do it again and quote the gospel about the prodigal son and all that bullshit, and *they believed it!*

Of course, one does get a reputation. By fifteen, Mandeville was known around his suburban Philadelphia neighborhood as a bad boy, although he was protected from major consequences by the mighty respectability of his family, by the inability of the community to believe that so sterling a house could bring forth such a monster, and by the belief, sadly strained by the passage of years, that he "was young yet," and would "grow out of it."

Mandeville by this time had discovered his talent for armed robbery. He was a highwayman in the lanes behind the elementary school, growing rich on the lunch money and allowances of his terrified victims; lacking sword and pistol he made do with an ice pick. So effective was this instrument, when applied gently to the eyelids, at producing instant compliance, that Mandeville was unprepared when an unusually spunky eleven-year-old girl had not only refused him her lunch money, but had called him a dumb asshole and kicked him painfully in the shins.

He felt he had no choice but to chase her down and work her over a little with the ice pick, thus discovering both the limits of his community's tolerance and the foolishness of leaving witnesses.

The girl had staggered home, bleeding from dozens of wounds, with a piece of Mandeville's windbreaker clutched in her hand. The police were called, Mandeville was arrested while trying to burn the torn and bloody windbreaker in his backyard, and at the juvenile hearing scores of children and their parents came forward to accuse him. For his part, Mandeville was outraged that his sincere repentance, his neat suit and polished shoes, and the reputation of his family cut no ice with the presiding judge. He was sentenced to a year in the state reformatory.

On the evening of his first day on the inside he was given the obligatory beating by the boss kid of his cottage, a huge and brutal redneck youth who had by no means enjoyed Mandeville's advantages in life, and knew it, and was looking forward to making the thin, scholarly looking black boy's life hell on earth.

This was an error. Simple brutality is rarely a match for evil. Mandeville scrounged around under the cottages the next day until he found a foot and a half of siding with a rusted tenpenny nail sticking through it. He twisted the nail out of its hole, put it in his pocket and shoved the slat into his belt under his shirt. He also picked up a small chunk of cinder block.

That night, Mandeville was beaten again and forced to perform a sexual act upon the body of the boss kid. This gave him the opportunity to crawl under his blanket and sob, the sound of which provided a cover for what he was really doing, which was putting a needle point on his nail by rubbing it against the cinder block.

Around three in the morning, Mandeville forced the nail back into the hole in the slat, and carrying the slat and the chunk of cinder block, padded over to where the big youth lay sleeping. By the moonlight filtering in through the wire-meshed window he carefully positioned the nail over the youth's eye and drove it home with a powerful blow of the cinder block. Then he went back to bed.

Things like this happen often at reformatories. The big kid had many enemies and the investigation was desultory, as Mandeville had calculated. Nobody bothered him for the rest of his stay. He also became a model prisoner. He was polite to the staff, attended lectures dutifully, and worked on his reading. He was employed in the library. Here he delved deeply into whatever books it possessed on the law and the workings of the criminal justice system. He read *Crime and Punishment* with great interest, as a text. He followed Raskolnikov's rap at the beginning with approval, and was confused and annoyed when the dumb-ass turned himself in.

Mandeville got out in eight months. On returning home, he found not the prodigal's welcome he expected as his due, but a destroyed family. His father had died—of shame mostly—and his mother had withdrawn into an impenetrable melancholia. With his brothers away at college it fell to his sister to inform him that he need no longer consider himself a member of the Louis family. This was fine with Mandeville, but, he figured, they owed him something for not sticking by him in his hour of need. After all, what was a family for?

In fact, he figured they owed him all the money in the house, his father's gold watch and his mother's tiny hoard of jewelry. His sister was foolish enough to try to stop him and got knocked down and kicked in the head a couple of times. There was enough to get him set up in the big city, which he reached in late 1965. The times and the man conspired—there has hardly ever been a better milieu to begin business as an armed robber than a large American city in the period between the assassination of John F. Kennedy and the resignation of Richard Nixon—"the sixties." The citizens were rich and disinclined to divert from their private use the monies necessary to run a criminal justice system remotely adequate for the scale of the problem, a problem that stemmed from the vast increase in the number of unemployed young men and the disappearance from most big cities of anything for all those young men to do for an honest living.

Then there was the guilt. The political movements of the time had taught the middle classes something about their complicity in injustice and brutality. Perhaps people who committed crimes were simply responding to irresistible social forces. Perhaps crime was a form of political protest. Look what we were doing in Vietnam. . . .

Thus, as London at the end of the sixteenth century was a hot place to be a literary genius, and France at the end of the eighteenth century was a hot place to be a military genius, New York in the sixties was made for a murderous psychopath like young Mandeville Louis. He thrived.

Even Louis himself understood this. As he swayed in his seat on the uptown Lexington Avenue local, with the murder weapons and the profits from his most recent crime on his person, he knew how slim his chances were of being caught, tried, and punished.

Still, there was something wrong. Something niggled at the back of his mind. Walker was wrong, for one thing. He didn't like a junkie with a family—people could ask questions if something happened to him, and Louis's career was founded on only the most shallow level of questions ever being asked about his criminal activities. Even Elvis, sitting happily next to him in his simple and murderous innocence, was a little wrong. Louis had never had a real accomplice—patsies, yes, but nobody who was really *in* with him. This need for some human contact shamed him; it was a blemish on the polished and icy globe of his perfection. Perhaps he would have to get rid of the kid, too.

But deeper than these disturbing thoughts, something else was starting to stir through the mind of Mandeville Louis, almost imperceptibly, like the flutterings of a small moth. Though he could not know it, it was in fact an intimation of the moral order of the universe, which dwells somewhere in all conscious beings, even those far gone in evil, even—the theologians tell us—within the demons in the lowest hell. It is told often proverbially: "God is not mocked," we say, or "The mills of God grind slowly, but they grind exceeding small."

A shiver ran through Louis's body. "Somebody walked on my grave," he thought. But it was not that. It was the first shadow of something that would have been recognized instantly in the ancient world, which understood these matters rather better than we do today. They called it nemesis.

CHAPTER THREE

Nemesis was six-five and a bit, well-muscled, with a bad left knee. At seven o'clock on the morning after the Marchione killings, Roger Karp, called "Butch," an assistant district attorney for New York County, was slowly rising from what was literally the sleep of the just. As he awakened he experienced, as usual, a moment of disorientation. He was not in the bedroom of the comfortable apartment he had shared with Susan. Susan was in California, with the furniture. He was in a renovated two-room apartment on West 10th Street off Sixth Avenue, with no furniture. Actually, he had a Door Store platform bed and a rowing machine; everything else he owned was in storage or at the office. The place had a kitchen, which he never used. The range and refrigerator were new and still had their packing slips and little instructional booklets tucked inside. Not a domestic guy, Karp. The bed and the rowing machine didn't fit in the office, or he would not have needed an apartment at all.

Karp stretched, swung his legs out of bed and stood up. By habit, he bounced a little on his left leg. The knee neither locked nor collapsed. Dr. Marvin Rosenwasser, orthoped of Palo Alto, was not God (except in the opinion of his mother) but his patellar re-creation seemed to be functioning approximately as well as the original—on a light-duty basis, of course. It would not stand a pounding dash down the length of a basketball court or a leap for a rebound, which is why Karp was an attorney, rather than a professional basketball player, in New York.

In his faded Berkeley sweatpants, of which he had retained a prodigious supply, Karp walked over to his rowing machine, sat in its seat, put his feet in the stirrups and pulled boldly into the current. The room was cool. The windows were open and the morning air was touched with the smell of rain. Still, after ten minutes Karp was running a sweat and after twenty he was dripping. He had the tension on the rowing machine set to its highest level. Karp didn't believe in taking it easy. At thirty-two he had managed to retain a body that, legs aside, could still have started in the NBA: big shoulders, a hard slab of torso, sinewy arms, thick wrists.

He rose from the machine, stripped and went into the bathroom. It was the best thing about the tiny apartment, being one of the original bathrooms from the days when each story of the apartment house had only four flats instead of ten. It had a patterned tile floor in three shades of tan against black and white, an alcove behind the door housing an ornate cast-iron radiator where you could heat towels, high ceilings, sculpted cornices covered with three inches of yellowing paint, a huge cast-iron bathtub with ball-and-claw feet, with a chrome shower ring, and one of those old-fashioned flat shower heads.

Karp turned on the cold water almost full and then goosed the hot faucet gingerly. The room was immediately filled with steam. Karp had retained his athlete's taste for hot showers, but the old building, equipped with boilers on the scale of those that drove the *Carinthia* to win the Atlantic Blue Ribbon, often supplied too much of a good thing.

After finishing in the bathroom, Karp dressed in a lawyer's dark blue pinstriped suit, black shoes and socks. He made the bed, picked up his briefcase, and left the apartment.

The Manhattan DA's office was at Foley Square, about two miles away; when it didn't rain, Karp walked the distance. He walked down Sixth, over to Broadway and then straight south, moving fast, with long powerful strides. Every ten steps or so Dr. Rosenwasser's magic knee would give a little soundless pop, just to let everybody know it was still on the job. Most people would have felt it as a jab of pain, but Karp had been playing hurt since he was twelve years old. "No pain, no gain," had been drummed into him by a succession of beefy older men, until he had grown up into a perfect little masochist. Winning made the difference; it was the balm beyond compare, the incomparable analgesic. So that when, playing hurt, Karp had received the injury that ended his athletic career, and the beefy older men had no more time for him, it was natural to switch to criminal law, a field that presented many of the same conditions and offered many of the same rewards as top-flight athletics.

It had the same elements of intense preparation and concentration, of confrontation in a circumscribed arena, where passion and aggression were bound by elaborate rules, of the final decision, and the emotional charge that went with it: won, lost, guilty, not guilty. He had done well at law school—Berkeley—and had earned a place on what was generally agreed to be the Celtics or the Knicks of the prosecutorial league—the Manhattan District Attorney's office, then in its last years under the direction of the legendary, the incorruptible, the incomparable Francis P. Garrahy.

In fact, as he walked that morning past the lower fringes of Greenwich Village, past the faded commercial streets of lower Broadway, the chic squalor of Soho, the tacky circus of Canal Street, and into the gray ramparts that held the administrative heart of New York, he felt again that little turmoil in the belly that for years had signaled for him the start of competition. His shoulders flexed, his jaw tightened, his face, which when relaxed was fairly pleasant—broad forehead, slightly crumpled largish nose, full mouth, gray eyes—became grim, even predatory. He began to look like what they tell you to look like in New York—if you don't want to get mugged.

By the time Karp rolled into Foley Square, he had worked up a mild sweat and an appetite. He cut across Chambers Street and went into Sam's to take on fuel. Sam's was a lunch-eonette, one of the thousands of such establishments, all different and all the same, that had been dispensing fast and semi-fast food to New Yorkers for generations before the appearance of the first Golden Arch. Nobody remembered when Sam's had come to Foley Square; probably Foley used to stop by for a prune Danish and a container of coffee before going out to collect graft. Sam's had a street window that was opened for knishes and egg creams in mild weather, a counter, four booths, six tables, tile floors, a stamped tin ceiling and a pay phone.

Karp was greeted by the current proprietor, Gus.

"Two?"

"Yeah," said Karp. "One butter, one cream cheese." As Gus sliced and toasted the bagels, Karp glanced around the breakfast-crowded store. Mostly courtroom types, lower-level bureaucrats, a couple of hard cases with their lawyers, getting the story straight before the trial.

"Hey, Butch."

Karp saw Ray Guma, another assistant district attorney, waving from a rear booth, and waved back. Gus was about to wrap the bagels in waxed paper and put them in a bag, but Karp stopped him.

"Don't bother with that, I'll eat them here."

"I already put the coffee in a container, I'll get a cup."

"No, that's alright," said Karp, "I like the cardboard."

He paid and walked back to where Guma was sitting, balancing his bagels on top of his coffee container and clutching his briefcase under his arm.

"Hey, Goom," he said. "Hey, V.T.! I didn't see you. This adds a tone of unwonted elegance to my breakfast."

"Good morning, Roger," said V.T. Newbury. "Do join us."

The two men were both assistant DA's like Butch Karp, and like Karp were both athletes and both smart and aggressive men. Besides that the three had little in common. V.T. (for Vinson Talcott) Newbury was Old New York Money, Yale, Harvard Law, and an intercollegiate single sculls champion two years in a row. He was an extraordinarily handsome man: straight blond hair, worn long and swept back from a widow's peak, large blue eyes, even, chiseled features, and a lithe well-proportioned body. He looked like the kind of man that cigarette ads in the 1920s depicted to show that their products had class. Luckily for envious souls, he was quite short, a hair under five-seven. He was sensitive about this modest flaw and had adopted—as a matter of self-protection—a sardonic mien, often describing himself as "a perfect little gentleman."

Ray Guma was short too, but with no obvious compensating physical virtues. He had a funny, swarthy, gargoylish face in constant, extravagant motion, mounted on a stocky and hairy body, with big ears and a little neck. He had grown up rough and tough in the Bath Beach section of Brooklyn, one of six children of an Italian plumber. He'd gone to Fordham on a baseball scholarship (shortstop), played a season in the Yankee farm system, batted .268 (he had trouble with inside curves), and then had worked his way through NYU Law.

Guma slid over and Karp sat down next to him. V.T. said, "I'm glad you stopped by, my boy. Perhaps you can settle a fine point of discussion for us. My learned friend here was just speculating on the sexual proclivities of our colleague, the divine Ms. Ciampi."

"Definitely a dyke," said Guma.

"It's true," said Newbury. "The evidence is overwhelming, especially from one for whom the laws of evidence are life itself. Consider the facts: one, we know that Ray Guma, *Mad Dog* Guma, is irresistible to women . . ."

"Awww, V.T., I didn't say that . . ."

"Irresistible, I say, and two, the luscious Ciampi, undeniably a woman, has succeeded where all women before her have failed, in resisting his fabled blandishments. Not even a *cheap feel* can he cop in the dingy corridors of justice. What do we conclude, gentlemen of the jury? That Guma is losing his touch? That the technique to which legions of cocktail waitresses and singles-bar secretaries have succumbed no longer works? Never, I say! The explanation, the *only* explanation that will stand the test of reason is that Ciampi is queer, a bull-dagger in fact."

"You're really a shit, V.T., you know that?" said Guma, flushing in discomfort.

"Just trying to state your case, Goom. Let's ask Karp, who is a true man of the world, and from San Francisco besides, which should make him an expert witness."

Karp washed down the last of his bagels with coffee and dabbed his lips. "I can't believe I'm hearing this," he said. "This conversation sounds like a cross between *Screw Magazine* and *Archie Comics.*"

"No, really, Butch. This chick is driving me crazy. Look, I'm a nice Italian boy from Brooklyn. She's a nice Italian girl from Queens. I try to talk to her, I get nothing but bullshit."

"Goom," said Karp, sliding out of the booth, "I got to go, but let me suggest a change in approach. You're trying to interest an individual who made Law Review at Yale, you don't yell 'Hey Champ, sit on my face, I'll guess your weight' across the bullpen. Which is, I think, the most endearing thing I ever heard you say to her. Meanwhile, if Veronica won't put out, try Betty. See you guys."

Karp left the luncheonette to Guma's despairing wail: "I don't want her fucking law degree, I want her *body!*" He moved across Foley Square, at this hour already full of civil servants and their victims, and strode briskly up the steps of 100 Centre Street, the Manhattan Criminal Courts Building.

This was a massive sandstone cube, Mussolini-modern in style, occupying a full square block. Stuck on to its left side was a similarly massive structure: the Manhattan House of Detention, New York's jail, known as the Tombs. The first four floors of the Criminal Courts Building were packed with room after featureless room, each packed with paper, pink, blue, yellow, and white, on which were inscribed the names of New York City's criminals, and those of their victims, and a history of their crimes and punishments. The men in the Tombs might come and go, but here, at least, they had achieved immortality.

Four floors above the street, balanced on their midden of paperwork, sat the Criminal Court and the Supreme Court. In New York, Supreme Court was the name given to the top tier of courts in the judicial system, where felony trials were conducted. The Criminal Court was for arraignments, felony hearings, and motions and trials for misdemeanor crimes, such as shoplifting, indecent exposure, and possession of stolen property. The Criminal Court was also the place where young

ADAs were initiated into the art of trying criminal cases, and was where Roger Karp worked. Above the courtrooms were the offices of the Manhattan District Attorney.

As Karp trotted up the broad steps, he passed by and under a set of legal homilies engraved in the building's imperishable stone. One of them, "Justice is denied no one," leaped out at him. At one time these had been engraved in Karp, too. And, though the atmosphere of the judicial system was far more corrosive than New York air, he could still read them on the tablets in his mind. Karp was an innocent and he believed in justice. That made him one of the most dangerous men in the building.

He got off the elevator at the fourth floor and entered the area known to everyone who worked at 100 Centre as the Streets of Calcutta. The hallways outside the courtrooms were thronged with people of every caste, race, class, and moral dimension, with poor blacks and Puerto Ricans being somewhat overrepresented. Some were desperate, others sneering and cynical, or sleepy with drugs or exhaustion. They were waiting their turn in the Criminal Court system and were packed here in the murmuring corridors because all the seats, all the standing room, in the courtrooms proper were similarly packed.

These were the friends and families of criminals and victims. Many were witnesses for the prosecution or defense. There were a substantial number of people with swollen or bandaged faces, or with limbs in casts, the walking wounded of New York's perpetual civil war. Defendants out on bail or their own recognizance lounged amid the victims and witnesses who would shortly testify against them. The defendants who were still jailed were kept in holding pens beside the courtrooms as they awaited their hearings or trials. An informal order was maintained by police officers, also waiting to testify, identifiable by their uniforms or—if off-duty—by the shields pinned to their clothing, but even more by the air of world-weariness and contemptuous humor they exuded as they stood chatting in little knots.

Four courtrooms sat along each corridor and each of these had between 100 and 150 cases on its calendar each day. The system commanded all those with business before it to appear either at 9:00 A.M. or 1:30 P.M., which meant hours upon hours of waiting for most of them. Some courtrooms had seating for about sixty people, but others were merely converted cloakrooms or judges' robing rooms. In these, justice was done in what amounted to the anteroom to the latrines; the Men's Room and Ladies' Room signs were taped over, a desk was squeezed between the flags of state and nation, and the system was ready for business. There was barely room for the defendant.

In the standard courtrooms, furnished with heavy wood and dusty grandeur, people would rush in and scramble for seats like subway commuters. The overflow occupied the Streets of Calcutta. Here the experienced ones brought food and pillows, toys for the kiddies, playing cards, and plenty of smoking material. They sat on hard wooden benches and on the floor. The air soon became a dense fog of smoke, disinfectant, old paint, and too many people.

Through this dismal village strode Butch Karp, like a prince, toward the courtroom to which he had been assigned for the past eleven months. Supplicants surrounded him, plucking at his sleeves like true Calcutta beggars: "Ey Señor, my son's case, Hector Sanchez, wha time it is?" "Hey man, what you done wit ma property?" "Mister, mister, can I tell you something. . . ?"

Pushing through, Karp opened the oak doors to Part 2-A of the Criminal Courts. Within, a similar crowd was seated, but more quietly. There was a dull, coughing chatter here and the sounds of rustling newspapers and discarded paper vending machine cups.

The spectators from whom this noise arose sat on blond oak varnished benches arranged like church pews in the back of the room. A wide aisle dividing the rows of benches ran from the rear of the courtroom to a low barrier and a swinging, saloon-style gate. Beyond the gate sat the long oak tables for the prosecutor, on the left, and the defendant, on the right. Beyond these, the judge's presidium rose like a squat wooden tower, with a table for the clerk at its base.

This was the courtroom of Judge Edward Yergin. Its business was misdemeanor trials and felony hearings. Each day's schedule typically included a mix of petty larceny, burglary, possession of a weapon, possession of narcotics, rape, indecent exposure, resisting arrest, assault, picking pockets, and mugging. A little shoplifting. A little murder. The felony hearings were held to determine whether for each felony charge there was reasonable cause to believe that a crime had been committed and that the defendant had committed it.

Karp swung through the swinging door, Wyatt Earp entering the Last Chance Saloon, and dropped a six-inch-thick stack of papers bound with rubber bands onto the prosecutor's table. Jim McFarley, the court clerk, looked up from his desk. "Hey Karp! Them Yankees, huh?" he said.

"Unbelievable," Karp replied. "Definitely their year. All the way." Karp gestured at the crowd. "What's going on, Jim? You passing out tickets? What're you giving away today?"

McFarley grinned. "Was up to me I'd give 'em all three to five. Nah, nothing special, just the usual hunnert 'n fifty."

The clerk was a cone-shaped man with a huge, gelatinous chin that seemed to flow into his shoulders with no need for a neck. He had ruddy cheeks and had played Santa at the annual Christmas parties for as long as anyone could remember. You rarely saw McFarley outside his wooden swivel chair; both of them were permanent fixtures of the court. McFarley dressed in polyester sport jackets and double-knit slacks of unlikely shade, and toted at his side a .38 caliber revolver he had never used. McFarley was strong against crime. The presumption of innocence did not carry a lot of weight with him. The people he saw accused in court every day must have done something wrong or the cops wouldn't have arrested them, for cryin' out loud. For that reason he liked ADAs (they put the dirt balls behind bars) and mistrusted the Legal Aid lawyers (they got the dirt balls off).

A simple philosophy, but one that had served McFarley well for nearly thirty years of providing the only continuity the New York criminal justice system would ever know. He and his colleague clerks ran the courtrooms; they were the traffic cops for a city without stoplights or signposts. They controlled the mountain of paperwork and determined what cases would be heard in what order on the daily calendar. Piss off McFarley and you sat in the Streets of Calcutta for days on end.

McFarley said, "Butch, the judge wants to see you before he takes the bench. He's at an administrative meeting, should be here in about a half an hour." He waved at the courtroom. "Better get this moving."

"What does he want to see me for? Oh no! He finally found out I never passed the bar."

"We all knew that when you tried your first case."

"Thanks, Jim, I love you too." Karp turned to the crowd and began the morning ritual of learning about the cases he would have to prosecute in just a few minutes. The first step was finding out which witnesses were present in the crowd. He had, of course, never met any of them before.

Karp walked to the gate and scanned the crowd. Pitching his voice to cut through the chattering, he said, "Excuse me! May I have your attention, please! All private defense attorneys, please check in with the clerk. Would all civilian witnesses, all witnesses who are not police officers and are here to testify, please come forward."

One by one, the witnesses snapped out of their lethargy and began gathering in the well of the court. Quickly the space around Karp's desk became crowded. He picked up a clipboard holding his copy of the day's calendar. "People, listen up a minute. When I point to you, I want you to tell me what case you're here for. And, if you know it, tell me the calendar number of your case. Then I may ask you a couple of brief questions. The important thing is for me to find out who is here and who isn't. Does everyone understand?" Murmurs of comprehension. "Fine. OK, what are you here for?" Karp asked the man nearest to him, a balding, thin black man with thick glasses.

"Ballroy. He assaulted me."

"What's the number on the calendar?"

"Thirty-seven."

Karp found the number on his calendar and saw that it had been circled in red by the clerk, indicating that he was supposed to have the case complaint in his stack. He riffled through the stack and found the complaint, making a notation on it to remind himself that the witness was present.

"You must be Alan Simms," he said, reading the name off the top of the affidavit."

"That's right."

"Fine. Have a seat, and I'll be calling you as a witness." Karp repeated this sequence with the rest of the two dozen or so people in the crowd.

After he checked through these, there was only one person, a tall, thin woman in her thirties, left standing by the table.

"What are you here for," asked Karp.

"Mancusi, attempted murder. I'm his sister and I saw the whole thing. He's innocent."

"Excuse me?"

"He's innocent, I don't care what the bitch says."

"I think you're here as a defense witness. You'll have to . . ."

"Yeah, defense."

"Well I'm speaking with witnesses for the prosecution. Does your brother have an attorney?"

"No. Just Legal Aid."

"That's an attorney, lady. Look, when the Legal Aid lawyer comes he'll speak with you. Now go sit down."

Karp went back to the railing and called out, "All police officers who are the principal complainants, please step up here now." Nine cops, some off duty, some in dark blue, some detectives in street clothes, came up to the prosecutor's table. Some had physical evidence connected with the crime, which they had retrieved from the police property clerk before coming to court.

"What d'you got?" Karp asked the first cop, a young off-duty patrol officer with dark, close-cropped hair and a bushy mustache.

"Resisting arrest. Defendant's name is Marshall, a real scumbag." He glanced at the pink slip in his hand. "It's case one thirty-seven on the calendar."

Karp found the case on his calendar, circled it, picked up his yellow pad. "OK, shoot. Start with your name."

"Collingsworth, Ansel. I'm with the one-seven. This guy Marshall we collared maybe half a dozen times on burglaries on the East Side."

As Collingsworth spoke, Karp was searching his stack for the case's paper work. He found the complaint, which had the defendant's jacket clipped to it.

"Yeah, I see he's got nine burglary convictions and some trespasses."

"That's what I mean," the cop went on. "So I'm walking along the alley, on foot patrol. It's about one in the afternoon and I see this guy get off the fire escape from an apartment building. He's carrying one of those big, heavy color TVs. I sorta recognize him, so I say, 'Hey, where ya goin'?' So he walks right up to me and starts throwing some bullshit about how he's a TV repairman and had to come down the escape because the front door's too narrow? So I look him in the eyes and say, 'Repairman, my ass. I seen you before, sucker.' So the shithead drops the TV on my foot."

The other cops laughed. Karp looked down and saw that the young cop's foot was in a cast and covered with a white sock.

"He resisted arrest with a TV set?" Karp asked.

"Fuck no! The scumbag punched me in the mouth and took off. I had to chase him down with a busted toe."

"All right, have a seat," said Karp, putting a star next to the defendant's name on top of the affidavit, to remind himself that this case was to be prosecuted to the fullest extent, with no plea bargaining. Then he went through the remaining eight cases, jotting down brief notes in anticipation of the arguments that might be made by the defense.

Looking up, he noticed a small, sixtyish woman in a gray suit sitting in the row of benches directly behind the prosecutor's table. He noticed her because she was scared, her face stiff, her body twitching like a cornered mouse. She kept glancing over to her left and then sharply looking away. Karp followed her glance and spotted a skinny kid with a turned-up porkpie hat jammed low over his eyes. He wore tight, black pants and a cream-leather sport coat, and every time the old lady glanced at him he grinned and shook his head slightly, no-no. He had a gold front tooth.

Karp went over and spoke quietly to the woman. "Excuse me, my name is Roger Karp and I'm the assistant district attorney in this courtroom. Is anything wrong?"

"That man," she said in a whisper, eyes darting to her left. "He's the one. He hit me and took my purse."

Karp glared at the kid, who returned the stare for an instant and then, smirking, dropped his eyes.

"And you're here to testify against him?"

"Yes. But he's trying to scare me."

"OK, let me tell you something, Mrs. . . ."

"Murcovitch, Edith Murcovitch. Look, mister I don't want no more trouble . . ."

"Mrs. Murcovitch, you're not in trouble. *He's* in trouble. Now come right through here and sit next to me, at this table."

Mrs. Murcovitch came through the gate and sat down. Karp went through his affidavits until he found her case. "This guy's name is Jenkins?"

"That's right. He hit me in the face."

"Ma'am, I don't want you to worry anymore. When the case is called I'm going to ask you to testify and I don't want you to be scared of him. Just tell the judge what happened."

He motioned to one of the cops he had just interviewed, the biggest and meanest-looking of the lot. When the cop came up to the railing, Karp said, "Doug, see that scumbag with the hat? He's hassling my witness. Do me a favor, could you go sit by him and make him be nice?"

"Glad to, Chief," said the cop. He sat down next to the kid and gave him the New York's Finest cop glare. The kid decided to take a nap.

Karp went up to the clerk's desk. "Jim, I'm about set. One thing, this case eighty-nine, could you call it first? The defendant is hassling my witness and I want to move her out of here as soon as possible."

"I already promised first to one of the private attorneys, but I'll slide her in sometime after that."

"Great. Thanks, Jim."

"It's OK. Hey, Yergin's in his chambers. Why don't you see him now. I want to get the show on the road."

"Whenever."

McFarley picked up the receiver on his ancient black phone and dialed one number. "Judge, Karp is here. . . . Fine, will do." He hung up and pointed his thumb over his shoulder. Karp walked behind the clerk's desk, went through a door, and entered Judge Yergin's chambers.

It was a room just a little bigger than a walk-in closet, with a government green two-seat leather couch on one wall facing a small desk, behind which sat the judge.

Edward Yergin was black, one of New York's first black Criminal Court judges and before that one of the first black assistant DAs. He had spent seventeen years prosecuting murder cases in the Homicide Bureau. He had convicted a hundred murderers and sent thirty of them to the death house. It showed on his face. He was a good judge and he liked Karp. The younger man had worked his courtroom for nearly a year and the two men had become sociable. They often had lunch together, sometimes with other ADAs or Legal Aid lawyers, sometimes alone. Away from the bench, Yergin never talked about court cases or the law, only about the old days in Homicide, city politics, or sports.

Yergin rose from behind his desk and shook Karp's hand. The judge was a tall, strong man, strong-featured, with close-cropped gray-black hair. He had a black nylon robe over a snappy sky-blue suit. His face shone with a wide grin as he pumped Karp's hand. "Congratulations, Butch."

"Thanks, Judge," said Karp, who had no idea what was going on. "What for? I usually show up for work on Friday."

Yergin laughed. "What do you mean, 'What for?' I think it's great. You're going where you belong."

"Sorry, Judge, you've lost me. Where do I *belong?*"

Yergin laughed again and slapped Karp on the back. "Homicide, Butch. You're being transferred to the Homicide Bureau. There's probably a message from John Conlin on your desk right now. I wanted to be the first to congratulate you."

Karp felt his face flush. "Judge, are you sure about this? I mean . . ."

"Of course I'm sure. I had it from Mr. Garrahy himself, last night. He called up and said it was evaluation time. He asked about you, said they'd been checking out some of the younger fellas for a new slot in the bureau. I told him you were a pretty fair trial lawyer. I also told him you probably wouldn't let your old granny cop to a lesser on littering the sidewalk if you had a good witness. And that was that."

Karp was still stunned. He found his voice and said, "Thanks, Judge, I just don't know what to say. I mean, Homicide . . ."

Yergin noted the younger man's discomposure, and said, "Butch, sit down there for a minute. I want to tell you something."

Karp plopped down on the leather couch. Yergin leaned against his desk. "Butch, look here. I've been in this system, God help me, it must be close to thirty years. Believe me when I tell you we're close to losing it. Plea bargaining! It's not a convenience any more, it's a necessity. And the crooks know it, believe you me. That's the real value of the Homicide Bureau. It tries cases and it wins them and murderers get put away, for murder one, for a long time. Every time there's a big murder trial and Homicide wins it, it's got to send a little jolt through every crook in the city. I don't mean the crazies. God, they're like car crashes, you can't do anything about them. But the cold-blooded little bastards with their pistols: they think they might actually have to do a long stretch, they might not shoot that old lady for four dollars and twenty cents.

"And there's another thing. Trials reverberate throughout the whole system. I truly believe this. The crooks have to learn that they can't just waltz out of here with an easy plea. They have to learn that when they turn down the prosecutor's offer, they *will* go to trial and they *will* lose and they *will* go to prison. That's the way the system's supposed to work. About the only place it *does* work anymore is in the Homicide Bureau. But if the bureau starts to slip, if the number of trials gets too small in relation to the number of pleas, then criminals won't have to think about facing trial. They'll know it's an empty bluff. That can't ever happen, Butch. If it does, the whole justice system becomes a . . . a. . . ." He gestured expansively with his hand and fell silent, as if unable to conjure up a word appropriate to such an enormity.

The silence hung for a moment in the little room. Karp cleared his throat nervously but couldn't think of anything to say. Then the judge straightened up, and smiled. "Why am I telling you all this? You know it, or they wouldn't have picked you. Besides that, it's the best legal team in the world. You're going to work your buns off and love it."

Karp got up, shook the judge's big, brown hand again, murmured some more words of thanks and left. He sat down in his chair, shrugged off McFarley's inquiring glance, and began arranging his papers in calendar order.

His mind was still a blur, the waiting courtroom unreal. He wasn't thinking about the stack of petty offenses before him. He was thinking about homicide: the *New York Daily News* front page type of homicide, mousy-looking ax murderers snapped as they walked handcuffed between burly cops, partially covered corpses of gangland honchos riddled with bullets—the Big Time. He was going to be part of that, he was going to be on the First Team. It is very hard for someone who has been a star to stop being one while still young. Karp believed in justice. He felt for the victim. But what he loved was what he had just been given; the chance to shine, the chance to bend every element of his mind and spirit to some great end, and for everybody to know it. He had lost that chance on a hardwood floor in Palo Alto fourteen years ago, and now the carousel had brought him around to the brass ring again. He shut his eyes and took deep, calming breaths.

The clerk snapped him out of it with his "All rise!" as the judge entered. "HearyehearyehearyeallthosewhohavebusinessbeforethishonorablecourtdrawnearandyeshallbeheardthehonorableJudgeEdwardYerginpresiding," boomed Jim McFarley. The fabled wheels of the law began to grind.

CHAPTER FOUR

On the morning after the killings, Donald Walker awakened in a reversal of the usual order of things— from a rather pleasant dream into a living nightmare. In the dream he had actually gone to a job interview instead of to a robbery. A nice man had shaken his hand and told him he was exactly the kind of fellow the firm had been looking for. He would have a big office and sit behind a desk and wear a sharp suit and talk on the telephone and have lunch at fancy restaurants. In the dream he was just telling his wife about the job and receiving her praises, when the cockroach walked across his face.

He sat up with a stifled scream, clawing at his face with both hands. Junkies often have the experience of cockroaches crawling over their skin and often—at a particular stage of withdrawal—it is difficult to determine which are real and which are not. Walker leaped off the bed. He had fallen, fully dressed, into a drunken stupor the night before. He yanked off one sneaker and held it high, then pulled the grayish sheets and tatty chenille coverlet off the bed and shook them. No target appeared. Then he felt the tiny legs crawling down the back of his neck. Cursing, he began swatting at his back with the sneaker but the maddening tickle continued. Now it started on his legs. He was crawling with them. He dropped the sneaker, tore off his pants and fell to the floor on his back, swatting at his legs and writhing, soaked with foul sweat, until he resembled a dying roach himself.

The violent motion was too much for his stomach. It had taken half the quart of Scotch to knock him out last night, and a sour bile now rose into his throat. He staggered to the washbasin and vomited. Now the chills started. He wrapped himself in the sheets, bedspread and thin blanket, and shivered. He was entering deep withdrawal, freezing and burning at the same time, itching, sniveling, bowels frozen. Yet the physical agony was nothing compared to what was going on in Donald Walker's mind. It was reality, seen for the first time in many months without the intervention of heroin. Such a view is grim enough for the upright citizen, which is why they sell beer, Valium, and Gothic romances. But the reality that junkies make for themselves is unspeakable.

Donald Walker, now. He was going to lose his house. His wife would probably kick him out when she found out about his habit. He'd told somebody at the plant—he didn't remember who—he would take his shift, because the guy took his last week when Walker was too stoned to work, but no way was he going to work today, and maybe have to take Monday off too. Oh shit, he promised Emma he would take the boy for asthma shots today, but the doctor probably wouldn't see him. Walker had been taking the money Ella gave him for the doctor, money she got from her mother, and giving about half, well maybe a little more than half, to Paradise for smack. He had just helped a crazy man rob a store and probably kill somebody. The crazy man was going to kill him, his wife and his kids if Walker didn't do exactly what he said, which was stay put in this shitty little room crawling with roaches and stinking of vomit, whisky, and Walker's desperate fear.

On the other hand, every cloud has a silver lining. Stack had money and dope for him. Junkies may have lots of problems, but junk cures them all. This thought struck Walker with the force of revelation. He leaped to his feet, splashed water on his face, dressed, and stumbled down three flights of stairs to the peeling cave that served the Olympia Hotel as a lobby. There was a pay phone against one wall. Walker fumbled a quarter in the slot. A dial tone! Maybe his luck was changing.

He dialed the number written on the scrap of paper Stack had given him last night.

A woman's voice answered. "Is Stack there?" he asked.

"Stack? There ain't no . . ." Her voice cut off, and after a few seconds of silence, Walker heard Stack's whispery voice.

"This is Stack. Who's there?"

"It's me, Stack, Donald. Stack, when you gonna get here? I need some help, man."

"Yeah, well Donald, help is on the way."

"No, I'm really sick, man. You gotta help me, like you said. I gotta get out of this shit hole . . ."

"Don't you go nowhere, boy! You go back to your room, have a little drink. I'll get something 'round to you before you know it. Just stay put, hear? Now, Donald, what room you in?"

"Uh, Ten. You gonna be here soon? Stack, they got roaches here, I can't stand it much more, you *got* to come soon. . . . I need some help, Stack . . ."

The voice in Louis's ear degenerated into an inarticulate whine. He broke the connection and dialed a number.

"Elvis? Listen here. It's going down, now. Get over to my place, we gonna make a delivery. OK, man, see you soon."

This business accomplished, Man Louis hung up the phone and resumed what he had been doing before Walker called. He lay back on his king-sized waterbed, naked. "Girl, get busy," he said. The woman on the bed, also naked, obediently lowered her mouth to his groin. Louis's sexual activities were ordinarily restricted to the periods immediately following his robberies. At such times he would call up this particular woman, DeVonne Carter, who would come to his apartment on Amsterdam Avenue, remove her clothes and put herself at his disposal for from three days to a week. She was a big woman, with the hard rounded body of a nineteenth-century fountain statue, and she felt she had found a good deal. Louis paid her rent and gave her spending money, in return for which she had to come when called, leave when bidden, keep her body clean and free of venereal disease, and her mouth shut. Louis's tastes were odd, but bearable; at least they didn't draw blood. Remaining silent was something of a burden, since she was a naturally friendly and gregarious person, but this too could be borne. She was used to men making the rules.

DeVonne had scarcely finished her latest service when the door buzzer sounded. Louis rolled away from her, got off the bed, put on a terry cloth bathrobe, and strode through the living room to his front door. He peered through the fish-eye lens set in the door and observed Elvis's distorted image. He opened the door, admitted his accomplice, and then relocked it elaborately, two dead bolts and a police lock.

Elvis glanced around the living room with pleasure. It had deep white shag rugs, pale leather couches facing across a wood and glass coffee table. Big color TV, big stereo. The most fascinating thing about the room, however, was the bookcase, which covered the entire wall facing the windows. Elvis had never seen so many books in a private residence; there were hundreds of them, neatly racked and arranged by subject and author. The first time he had visited the apartment he blurted out, "Shee-it, man! You read all them books?"

To which Louis had replied with a superior smile, "Yeah, I read them. Some of 'em twice."

Louis was at the bookcase now, taking down a hardbound copy of *The Shame of Our Prisons*. He carried it over to the coffee table and sat down on one of the couches, motioning Elvis to take a seat opposite him. Louis opened the book, to reveal a cut-out section in its center. In the cutout was a plastic bag, a package of glassine envelopes of the type used by stamp dealers, and a pair of surgical gloves. Louis pulled on the gloves and unrolled the plastic bag. He tapped a teaspoonful of white powder into one of the glassine envelopes.

"What's all this, Man?"

"It's headache powder, what you think?" Louis held the envelope up to the light and tapped it so that the powder fell into a corner and then folded it into quarters. "This is gonna get rid of our little headache. Come on, I'll get the rest of the stuff."

Louis went into the bedroom. He left the door open for a moment and Elvis caught a glimpse of a chocolate-brown woman sitting naked on the bed. She caught him staring and flashed a broad and antic grin over Louis's shoulder as he re-emerged. He was carrying the attaché case. Opening it on the coffee table, with the rubber gloves still on, he removed the bank cash bag he had taken from the liquor store. He took out all the cash except a dozen miscellaneous small bills and put in the packet of white powder. He placed the bank bag inside a paper bag and handed it to Elvis.

He said, "Take this down to that hotel where that Snowball's stayin' and give it to him. Olympia Hotel, Room Ten. He won't ask no questions when he see that bag o' shit. Make sure he shoot up, then get out of there and go back to your own place. And don't touch nothin' , especially not the damn cash bag. Let him take it, and then take the paper bag with you."

"What, you put some rat poison in the shit?"

Louis grinned. "No baby, there's nothing in that bag but shit. Pure shit, that's all it is. No quinine, no milk sugar, no nothin' . He shoot up what he usually do, figures maybe it be bumped six, seven, ten times—but this ain't been bumped at all. Cost me a fuckin' load but it's worth it, you dig? That boy go out like a light. The cops find him, coupla days, maybe a week, all swole up with the needle still in his arm, what they gonna think? Hey, what the goddam medical examiner gonna think? Heroin overdose, open and shut."

Elvis was slow, but he could follow this. "And he got the bag from the store on him, so they gonna think . . ."

Louis's grin widened. "You got it, Pres. You caught on, good for you. Now look, here's the most important thing. He got a little piece of paper with my phone number on it. Get that from him before you give him the bag. *Before,* dig? Don't worry, he give you the key to his momma to get his hands on what you holdin' . OK, take off. I don't want him jumpin' out no windows or goin' nowhere." He reached into the attaché case again and brought out a roll of cash. "Oh yeah, here's your share of the job." He counted off five hundred dollars.

Elvis had never had five hundred dollars in his life. It took all the cool he could muster not to giggle like a schoolboy. He pocketed the loot without a word, gave Louis what he imagined was a gangsterish sort of nod, took the bag and left the apartment. As he left, he thought of what he had seen in Louis's bedroom. Fine set of jugs on that girl, he thought. Got to get me one, get some kinda fine setup to put her in. That Louis, now he some kinda dude, he thought. So he strolled toward the subway, money in his jeans, the future bright before him, on his way to commit his very first murder, innocent as a clam.

It took Elvis nearly two hours to get to Tenth Avenue and 23rd Street. He ran into some guys he knew from the street on the way to 137th Street IRT station, and had to jive with them awhile. Then they walked up the avenue a little way, scoping out the girls, and then went into a hat store and tried on some hats. Elvis finally bought a Borsalino for sixty dollars, got to flash his roll, show some class. Sincere, but not efficient, was Elvis.

Two hours was too much for Donald Walker, though. Two *minutes* was too much, if it came to that. The insides of his veins were twitching like poison ivy. He knew he was going to die. Lying on the tangled sheets, looking at the spotted ceiling, his mind lost all comprehension of time; he was a hungry infant at 3:00 A.M. He might have been in that room for a week or a month. Like an infant, he now thought of his mother. Once again, he made his wracked body leave the foul room and move down to the pay phone in the lobby. He dialed his mother's number; no answer. He was abandoned. He snuffled back his runny nose as tears of frustration ran down his face and bathed the mouthpiece of the telephone.

No mother. Poor Donald! Then he thought of his wife. Same difference. He dialed again, the number of the real estate office in Jackson Heights where his wife worked as a secretary-receptionist. Contact.

"Hello?"

"Ella," he croaked, "Ella, I . . ."

"Hello? Donald, is that you? Is something wrong?"

"Ella, I need . . . I'm sick, baby."

"Oh no! What's wrong? Are you in Stamford? Where's Billy?"

After a chilling silence, the croaking voice resumed.

"Ella, I didn't go to Stamford. Shit, Ella, I'm in big trouble, I need help!"

"Trouble? What are you talking about, Donald? What kind of trouble? What did you do?"

"Can't tell you, baby, he kill me. I need . . . I need some, uh, money."

"What? Who's going to kill you? Oh, Donald, Jesus, you didn't do anything stupid, did you?"

"Ella, don't ask no questions, just get over here with some money."

"Money! Donald, you come home this minute, you hear! I want to know what you've been doing. I can't believe this . . ."

"I can't, dammit! He gonna kill me. I'm sick, godammit to hell!"

Here he gave a groan of such mortal agony that even over the wires his wife realized that whatever her husband had gotten into was outside the zone of ordinary domestic troubles.

"OK, Donnie, be calm, honey. What do you want me to do?"

"Bring some money, anything, and some clothes. I'm at the Olympia Hotel on Tenth Avenue. Room Ten. And hurry, Ella, huh?" The line went dead. After that, Ella Walker went to the ladies' room, sat in a booth and cried for a while. Then she washed her face and returned to her desk. As she had learned to do from earliest childhood, she now turned to her family in time of trouble. With trembling hand she punched out the number of the Midtown South Precinct and asked to speak with her brother, Detective Second Class Emerson Dunbar, Homicide.

When his sister called, Sonny Dunbar was walking down Eighth Avenue in the lower Forties, with the beginnings of a nasty headache, doing his job, but not liking it very much. His job at that moment was looking for a skell named Dingleberry, who, according to a snitch named Rufus, had been seen lately in the company of a prostitute named Booey Starr, or (if you were her mother), Francine Williams, now deceased. Since Booey had probably not hit herself in the head with a claw hammer twenty or so times, her death had been duly judged a homicide and added to the 153 open cases that were Dunbar's particular responsibility.

Dunbar had been a New York cop for fifteen years, a detective for ten. Before that he had jumped out of some airplanes for the U.S. Army and before that he had gone to high school in Queens, about two miles from where he now lived, in St. Albans. His high-school career had been undistinguished, except on the football field, where he turned out to be very good at stopping other players from catching footballs, or if they did catch them, stopping them from running very far. He was an All-State safety on two teams, got the usual offers from faraway schools and turned them all down.

This was remarkable, but Sonny Dunbar had always taken the long view. He hated classrooms, and knew he wasn't good enough for a sure slot in the pros. He didn't care to be another Big Ten black jock with a meaningless B.A. in phys ed. So he enlisted, spent three years with the airborne as an MP, figured he was tough enough for anything after that, and joined the cops.

He had put on about ten pounds in the years since, which hardly showed on his wide-shouldered, six-two, two-hundred-pound frame. He didn't like the way some cops let themselves get sloppy, and he had a reputation on the squad as something of a dude, not as splendid, perhaps, as the members of the special narcotics squads, but his wardrobe came out of his own pocket. It helped that his wife was an executive with a restaurant chain.

Today he was wearing a cream-linen jacket, tan slacks, lemon-yellow shirt, and a dark-blue silk tie. He had cordovan tassel loafers (no gumshoes for him) on his feet and a cream fedora on his head. And sunglasses; Sonny Dunbar was definitely Broadway. He had left his car at a cab stand on 43rd and was cutting across Eighth to a drug store for an Alka-Seltzer. Moving fast, he was just about to enter its doorway when the thought hit him that he had a roll of film in the car that he had promised to bring in for developing two days ago. Almost without any conscious effort, he hit the pivot and began moving in the opposite direction, and a kid in sneakers carrying a large leather handbag crashed into him at full speed.

Dunbar staggered, but the kid went sprawling and banged his head on a parking meter. Dunbar was about to apologize and help the kid to his feet, when he noticed the big handbag. Although many young men in that area of New York carried handbags, this particular young man did not look like that kind of young man. He was wearing a dirty brown jacket, jeans, and the expensive athletic footwear that street cops call "perp shoes."

Dunbar's impression that the kid was a Times Square bandit was soon confirmed by a distraught woman, blonde, and well dressed in an arty way, who came dashing unsteadily up the street in heeled boots. "There he is! He took my bag," she shouted. "Somebody get a cop! Oh, thank God!" She addressed this last remark not to heaven but to her handbag, which she clutched to her breast like a lost child. "Thank God! My entire LIFE is in this bag." She noticed Dunbar, who was staring glumly at the fallen robber. "Say, mister, did you catch him? Listen, can you hold onto him while I go and call the cops?"

Dunbar thought, just my luck, a solid citizen. He said, "Well, Miss, that won't be necessary. I happen to be a police officer." He pulled out his gold shield and showed it to her.

The woman laughed. "Unbelievable!"

"Yeah, ain't it, though," answered Dunbar, with very little enthusiasm. He wrote down the woman's name and address and then hauled the young robber to his feet. The kid tried to shake off Dunbar's grip.

"Hey, man, wha chu doin'? I din do nothin'." Dunbar pushed him against a wall, back cuffed him in one smooth motion and then patted him down, extracting a large sheath knife from his jacket pocket.

"Right, mutt, you din do nothin', but I'm going to arrest you for purse snatching anyway. Let's go."

Half an hour later, after the perp had been booked and caged at the Midtown South Precinct, Dunbar was rummaging through his desk for a package of Alka-Seltzer, when Petromani, the desk sergeant, came into the squad room. "Sonny, call your sister Ella. What're you looking for?"

"Alka-Seltzer. My head's coming off. You got any?"

"I got aspirin and Tylenol. I got Empirin and I think I got something for menstrual cramps. Listen, you should call your sister, she sounded really uptight."

"Yeah, the toilet probably won't flush. My brother-in-law is not what you call a take-charge individual, so she still calls me when something goes wrong." He reached for the phone.

"Petromani said, "I heard the story on that collar you made. It's great the way you detectives track down criminals by putting together all these tiny clues . . .""

Dunbar grinned. "Aww, it was just perseverance, solid old-fashioned police work, and fucking bad luck. I'm going to waste half tonight in the complaint room." Petromani waved and left. Dunbar dialed his sister's office. The phone rang just once and his sister's voice said, "Barnes and Franklin, good morning."

"It's Sonny. What's up, girl?"

"Oh, Sonny, thank God! I'm worried out of my head."

"What is it, the kids?"

"No, they're fine. It's Donnie. I got the scariest phone call from him. He says he's in this hotel, and he's sick, and he told me to bring him money and clothes. Sonny, I never heard him sound like that before."

"Was he drunk? Did you tell him to come home?"

"That's the first thing I told him. But he said somebody was going to kill him if he left the hotel. I didn't know what to do." She started to cry.

"OK, calm down, sugar. It's probably nothing much. Maybe he got fired and wants to soften you up. You know how Donnie is." Dunbar had little respect for his brother-in-law, but he was grateful to him for paying attention to the youngest and least attractive of the four Dunbar sisters, marrying her, and giving her the home and children she had always wanted. He sort of liked the little jerk in spite of himself. Donnie was a baby, but he could be funny and charming, in his way.

Ella blew her nose and said, "No, he sounded *bad,* Sonny. I hate to bother you and all, but could you go over and see him?"

"Sure, fine. Where's he at?"

"It's the Olympia Hotel, Room Ten. It's on . . ."

"I know where it is. Listen, don't worry about a thing. I'll take care of it. And I'll call you when I find out what's going on. OK? Good. So long, baby."

Dunbar hung up and ran his hand over his face. If Donnie was holed up in a skell joint and shooting gallery like the Olympia, something might be very wrong indeed. He rose and left the precinct, first stopping off to hit up Petromani for three Tylenols.

The lobby of the Olympia Hotel smelled exactly like those pink cakes of disinfectant they clip into urinals in gas station toilets, but stronger. It was furnished with two patched orange plastic lounges and a kidney-shaped gold Formica coffee table. Nobody was lounging over coffee though. The desk clerk was sacked out in the space behind his little barred window.

Room 10 was on the second floor. Dunbar knocked on the door, which was immediately flung open. The detective had some difficulty in recognizing the rattled creature in the doorway as his brother-in-law; but Donald recognized the cop. He cried out "No!" and attempted to slam the door in Dunbar's face, but the bigger man blocked it with his shoulder and easily pushed his way into the room.

"Donnie, cut that out! What the hell is going on here? Ella's worried sick."

But Dunbar knew what was going on. He had been in innumerable little stinking rooms like this. Donald was crumpled on the bed, moaning. Dunbar sat down beside him, grabbed Donald's wrist and looked at the inside of his arm. "How long you been shooting dope, Donald?"

"She shouldna called you. I tol her . . ."

"Answer me!"

Donald raised his head. "Not long, not long. I swear it, Sonny. I ain't hooked, I just pop some now and again, I swear . . ."

"Shit you ain't hooked. You a smackhead, boy. You *were,* I mean, cause starting now you are *off.* Now get up and wash that snot off your face. I'm taking you home. We'll figure out something to tell Ella." Dunbar got off the bed.

Donald shrank away. "No! I can't, he kill me for sure. He said he gonna kill the kids, he . . ."

"What're you talking about? Who said?"

"Nobody! Nothin' . . . I can't tell you."

Dunbar reached down and grabbed Donald by the front of his T-shirt, pulling his face close to his own. Donald's breath was fetid. "Goddamit! Don't give me that shit! Who's gonna kill you? What you been up to, huh? Talk!" He threw Walker back on the bed like a rag doll, hard enough to rattle his teeth.

Slowly, in disconnected sentences, the story emerged, helped by sharp questions from Dunbar. "Alright, you drive these two guys to the supermarket. Then what?"

"Well . . . I was late, and the supermarket guy was gone, so I thought, that's it, we can go home. But then Stack, he sees this liquor store, an he makes me park, then he takes his case an. . . ."

"Wait! Where was this liquor store?" Dunbar had a sickening feeling that he knew what the answer would be.

"I dunno, Madison, I think, around Fiftieth."

"Madison, between Forty-seventh and Forty-eighth?"

"Yeah, that's the one."

"Oh, Donnie, you dumb asshole! Do you know your friend wasted two people in that store? Blew one guy's head off with a shotgun and killed a seventeen-year-old kid."

"I din do nothin! I swear, Jesus, I never even touched the gun. Sonny, as God is my secret judge, all I done was drive the car."

"Donnie, let me explain something. The law don't care about that. The law says that if a murder is committed in the course of a crime, everybody involved in the crime can be charged with murder, just the same as whoever did the killing itself. You understand what I'm saying?"

"Sonny, hey, that ain't right! I tol you I din do nothin' ."

"Yeah, baby, but that's the way it is. Now look, Donnie,

we're in a bad situation here. You just told me about being hooked up in a crime. I'm a cop, right? That means I got to do something . . ."

"You gonna arrest me!"

"No, but I got to get you to somebody who *is* gonna arrest you. It's hard to explain, but my ass'll be in sling, if you don't do what I say."

"*Your* ass! What about me? Shit, I thought you was gonna help me get away."

"Oh, shit, Donnie! Think for once! I can't cover up two fucking murders. I'm a goddamn *homicide* detective. Somebody else catches you, and they will, Donnie, and this comes out, and it will, I'm out of a job. Then who's gonna watch out for you and Ella and the kids, with you in jail? Tell me that!"

Donald was silent at this. Then he let out a long shuddering sigh and got unsteadily to his feet. In a dull, small voice he said, "OK, Sonny, tell me what you want me to do."

"First, get yourself cleaned up. Then I'll take you up to Midtown South. You walk in and tell the desk you want to talk to Detective Slocum. Tell him everything you told me, and whatever else he wants to know. He's a good guy. I'll take care of Ella and getting you a lawyer."

"Will I go to jail?"

"Well, for a while. But we can probably swing bail."

"No. I don't want to be out." He looked straight at Dunbar with red-rimmed eyes. "I'm scared, Sonny. That man scares the livin' shit out of me. I better stay in jail."

Elvis missed them by about ten minutes. He strolled into the lobby with his new Borsalino cocked over one eye and went directly to Room 10. He knocked a couple of times, and when nobody answered he slipped the lock with a piece of celluloid that had come, conveniently, with his new hat. Look like old Snowball went out for a while, he thought. This was definitely the right room, though. He recognized the bottle of Scotch that Louis had given Walker. He was not inclined to wait around in the smelly room for Walker's return, however, and so he left the cash bag on the little shelf above the sink. He was about to close the door, when he remembered Louis's lecture on finger-prints. OK, he had the paper bag, he hadn't touched anything in the room, not even the inside doorknob. He shoved the door closed with his foot and carefully wiped the outside knob with his shirttail. Whistling as he walked off, he felt very clever indeed.

CHAPTER FIVE

Good morning, gentlemen," said Judge Edward Yergin. He glanced over at the defendant's table and saw that it was empty. "Mr. McFarley, have we no defendants this morning?"

McFarley laughed. "Your Honor, the Legal Aid lawyers are still down in the holding pens."

"Well, invite them in," said Yergin.

"Your Honor, the first cases on this morning's calendar are represented by private counsel," the clerk replied.

Yergin said, "Call the first case," and McFarley read from a sheet of paper, "People versus Hutch. Burglary and criminal possession of stolen property. Defendant Willard C. Hutch, please come forward." As McFarley read the change, the defendant, who had been out on bail, came forward with his attorney. Karp searched through his stack of files. In theory, each case on the calendar should have been represented by a complaint in the stack. As each case progressed through the courts, each Assistant DA was supposed to keep the file current and then return it to a clerk, who was supposed to pass the file on to the assistant DA who would be handling the case next.

But by the time each case came to trial, it could have passed through the hands of half-a-dozen assistant DAs and as many clerks. The files were often misplaced, in which case the ADA could either muddle through without it, or ask for a delay. This morning there were seventy-five cases on the calendar and Karp had fifty-three files.

The file for the Hutch case was there, however, and Karp

scanned the complaint form rapidly. This form had been prepared in the DA's Office Complaint Room weeks before. Occasionally, Karp could pick up complaints the night before so that he could look them over before going to court. More often, the stack of cases was not prepared until he arrived at 100 Centre Street in the morning. When that happened, as it had this morning, Karp's total preparation time for a case ran to about two minutes.

The Hutch case included a sworn affidavit given to an assistant DA in the complaint room by the arresting officer, a detective. The detective stated that he had received information from a tenant in a housing project that Hutch—also a tenant—was burglarizing apartments. The follow-up investigation found another tenant who said he saw a man fitting Hutch's description leave an apartment—not his own—carrying a stereo. The detective had obtained a search warrant and found stolen stereo components in Hutch's apartment. Hutch was arrested, but the witness was unable to pick him out of a lineup.

The file also included Hutch's yellow sheet, which showed numerous burglary, breaking and entering, and possession convictions. OK, Mr. Hutch is a career burglar. He's pleading innocent to the burglary charges. This is a hearing to determine whether there is probable cause to charge him with the crime. We have physical evidence to prove that Hutch was holding stolen goods, but no evidence to show that Hutch stole them.

As Karp scanned the file and considered what to do, the judge said to the defendant's counsel, "What's your motion, Mister Steinberg?"

Marty Steinberg was a typical small-time defense lawyer, who represented dozens of petty and professional criminals every week, and who was as much a fixture of the Criminal Court as Jim McFarley. Graying, sixty-odd, slightly shabby, he cruised the Streets of Calcutta like a pretzel vendor, occasionally stopping at a pay phone to dictate a motion to his secretary, whom he rarely saw.

"We are now ready to proceed, Your Honor."

"Are the People ready?" the judge asked Roger Karp.

Karp asked "Your Honor, may I approach the bench?"

Karp and Steinberg now stepped outside the record and into the dark and oily crankcase of the criminal justice system, where the real work was done. They spoke in low voices. "Judge, the People feel we can make a disposition on this case right now," Karp said.

"How so?" asked Yergin.

"We'd be willing to drop the burglary charge, if, and only if, the defendant agrees to take a guilty plea on the charge of criminal possession."

"Sounds OK," said Steinberg.

"Hold on, Marty," said Karp. "The defendant must also agree to maximum time. We're talking a year in the pen."

"What? Why maximum?" complained the defense attorney.

"Because if it's not max, we'll go to trial on both burglary and possession, and we'll win on possession at least, and get max time from the judge anyway. We could also get lucky and win on burglary, in which case you're looking at a lot more time."

Yergin's eyes met Karp's in understanding. This was what the judge had been talking about. The threat of trial greased the system and made it possible to render justice in fact, if not in form. "Counsel, this sounds reasonable to me," Yergin said.

"Let me discuss it with my client," said Steinberg, and went back to his table to confer with Hutch for a few minutes. He returned to the bench and said, "Your Honor, I'm ready to proceed."

Yergin now spoke out loud. "Mister Karp, do you have any motions?"

"Your Honor, the People wish to drop the charge of burglary against the defendant."

"Charge dismissed."

Steinberg spoke now. "Your Honor, my client wishes to change his previously entered plea of not guilty to guilty of the crime of criminal possession of stolen property."

With that, Judge Yergin sentenced Hutch to a year in prison. The gavel came down. Bang. Next case.

The morning wore on. The wheels creaked. Assault, one year. Assault, no defendant, bench warrant. Larceny, assault, no defendant, bench warrant. Shoplifting, sentenced to time served. Assault, no witnesses. Where are the witnesses? Not here, Your Honor. Move to dismiss. Witness has appeared five times, Your Honor. Each time, the defense has requested adjournment. Request case be put on the bottom of today's calendar, Your Honor. Granted, next case. Mrs. Murcovitch whispers her testimony. The kid with the hat goes up for a bullet, still smirking. The cop with the broken toe speaks his testimony in the stilted copspeak they all used—"the perpetrator then proceeded . . ." Next case. Next case. Next case.

Karp was shuffling papers, looking again for a file that obviously was not there, when Ray Guma tapped his shoulder.

"Hey, Butch," he said with a grin, "what's with all these rumors I'm hearing about you moving up to the big time?"

"What rumors are those, Ray?"

McFarley said, "The People versus Lasser. Defendant Adrienne Lasser, please step forward. Charged with possession of marijuana."

Guma said, "Cut the crap, Butchie. They picked you for one of the new slots in Homicide."

The judge asked, "What is the defendant's motion?"

The Legal Aid lawyer, a chubby blonde kid about six weeks out of law school, scanned the bleachers for his client, then turned to Yergin in embarrassment. "Ah . . . Your Honor, Your Honor . . . my client, ah, the defendant was here just a minute ago."

Karp said, "The People are ready, Your Honor."

"Thank you, Mister Karp," replied Yergin. He peered down at the defense attorney. "Do we have a defendant yet?"

"No, Your Honor, ah . . . I believe she may have gone to the bathroom."

"I see. Would the clerk kindly find the defendant?" Before McFarley could move, however, the Legal Aid man had dashed full-speed down the center aisle, crying: "No, I'll get her, I'll get her."

Guma cupped his hands around his mouth to imitate a

crowd's chanting: "DE-fense, DE-fense, DE-fense." The court-room rippled with giggles.

Two sharp raps came from Yergin's gavel. "Mister Guma, do you have any business in this court? Part Two A of the Criminal Court? Of New York?"

"Your Honor, my colleague has solicited my advice on a fine point of criminal law," Guma replied.

"I find that most unlikely, Mr. Guma," and then, turning to McFarley, "It appears that our defendant has released her-self on her own recognizance. Bench warrant issued. Next case."

Karp said, "Look, Ray, I'm working . . ."

"OK, Butch, just two things: first, Conlin wants to see you after court today—hey, hey, hey!" He raised his elbow and swung his hand vigorously from the wrist—the classic New Yorker's gesture for striking it rich. "Second thing is, we are all going out for dinner at Cella's tonight, to celebrate." He flung a salute at Karp, and at the frowning Yergin, then trotted off.

John Conlin was the Homicide Bureau chief, and a re-puted ball-buster. That was OK. Karp wasn't afraid of work and knew he was good. He looked forward to the interview.

McFarley called the next case and Karp slipped back into gear. Assault, no priors, steady job, released on own recogni-zance. Maybe the guy would show for the trial, maybe not. You had to play the odds if you were a judge. You had to keep the jail space free for the real bastards, which meant that the average lawbreaker was in small jeopardy of spending any time locked up. Each year tens of thousands of people were re-leased on their own recognizance; thousands were never heard from again, unless they were arrested on another charge. It was every judge's secret fear that he would walk some bozo who would later turn up on the front page of the *Daily News* as a gently smiling mass murderer. It happened, but there was nothing you could do about it. ROR was the Drāno of the criminal justice system.

Thirty-two cases later it was noon, and Yergin recessed the court for two hours. Karp gathered his stack of papers and left the courtroom. It was lunchtime in the Streets of Calcutta.

People were eating snack-bar specials out of greasy paper containers. An immense Puerto Rican woman was feeding her three children on Twinkies and Pepsi. Karp steered through the mob to a bank of pay phones and called a couple of witnesses who hadn't shown that morning. One of them was the woman who had appeared five times and had been sent home five times when the defense had asked for an adjournment. Karp convinced her that this time she would get to testify, and arranged for a cop to pick her up at her office. The other one had left town; they didn't know when he would be back. Scratch that case.

After dumping his papers in his cubicle, Karp took the elevator down to the ground floor and walked out of the courthouse into the real world. It was still spring. Foley Square was full of lunchtime strollers.

Karp walked across the square to a food vendor and joined the line of customers. He was something of a connoisseur of New York street food, since he bought most of his weekday meals off wheeled vehicles of one kind or another. He knew that all Sabrett carts were not equal. He sought out the ones that grilled the hot dogs before putting them in the steam box, so that the skin became crisp and chewy; the ones that had fresh, steam-soft buns, and crisp hot sauerkraut, and real deli mustard. He knew one guy who sold real potato knishes with paper-thin layers of pastry over peppery filling, not the usual hard square kind that looked and tasted like brake pads for a heavy truck.

Today he ordered three hot dogs, mustard and kraut, a salted pretzel, also with mustard, and a can of orange soda. He ate standing at the curb, his fellow citizens flowing past him like breakers around a jetty. Karp ate the hot dogs with four chomps each. Garbage, but good garbage. He drank his soda and walked back up to the courthouse chewing on the pretzel. Elapsed time for lunch: fifteen minutes.

He went back to his office to familiarize himself with the afternoon's cases. The offices given to assistant district attorneys in the Criminal Courts Bureau were not elegant; strictly speaking, they were not offices either, just glassed-in cubicles, each containing a file cabinet, a gray metal desk, a swivel chair designed to produce hemorrhoids as quickly as possible, and a wooden chair for visitors. Karp had just begun reading when a knock on the frosted glass made him look up. It was Tom Pagano, the Legal Aid bureau chief for the Criminal Court and responsible for the hundred-odd public defenders who were Karp's usual adversaries. Karp tried to think of what case on the day's calendar would merit a personal visit from the captain of the opposing team.

"Hello, Tom. Hey, if this is about the Rankin mugging, I told your boy we're going for trial on the armed charge. No copping to larceny anymore for this baby . . ."

Pagano waved his hands to shut Karp off. "Stop, stop, this has nothing to do with any defense case. Can I sit down for a sec?"

"Sure, what's it about?"

Pagano sat down in the hard wooden chair. He was a stocky, well-groomed man of about forty, with short dark hair, swarthy skin, and high cheekbones. He stared at Karp for a moment with large, intelligent eyes, as if undecided about whether to proceed. Finally he said, "I've got a case for you."

Karp grinned. "Sure. You have a hundred and fifty cases for me every day. So what else is new?"

Pagano didn't return the smile. "No, this is serious, and frankly I'm coming to you personally, rather than going through the system, because you seem like somebody who cares about people getting fucked over, which is what we have here."

"I'm listening," said Karp.

The other man took a folded sheet—from a yellow legal pad—out of his breast pocket and consulted it.

"Four kids—Sheldon Goldstein, Victor Cruz, Willie Martinez, and Tony Ocha—were remanded to the Narcotics Addiction Control Commission Center in West Harlem in December of last year. Two weeks ago they tried to escape, unsuccessfully. They want to press charges against the guards who captured them."

"Brutality? Against guards in the course of an escape attempt? Tom, give me a break."

"Yeah, I know, I know, but this is a real one. Look, do one thing for me. I've got them in a pen on the fourth floor. Come down and listen to their story."

A few minutes later, Karp, feeling like a sucker, was sitting in a questioning room across a battered oak table from Sheldon Goldstein. Pagano was leaning against the wall near the door. In a corner sat Hal Dooley, a detective assigned to the DA's office for investigations. Karp had worked with Dooley before; the two men respected one another, but Dooley was the kind of cop who trusted only cops, preferably those over forty-five. He thought the country was going to the dogs. It was obvious from the expression on his face that he thought Goldstein was one of the dogs.

Karp looked at the nineteen year old across from him. He was a weasely faced, skinny kid with acne and bad teeth. As a junkie, at nineteen, he had a life expectancy of approximately three years—and looked it. He wore a Grateful Dead black T-shirt and tattered jeans and kept picking nervously at a scab on his forearm. His face was covered with bruises, his lip had stitches in it and a white bandage covered his left eye.

After introducing himself and Dooley, Karp said, "Alright, Mr. Goldstein, please tell us what happened in the Drug Center on the night of, let's see . . . Saturday, February Twenty-eighth, Nineteen-seventy. Take your time. I want to hear the whole story."

Goldstein began in a reedy voice that grew louder as he warmed to his tale. "See, we was all watching this movie on TV in the Rec Room. Tony says, 'Fuck this shit, let's get outa here. Who's comin'?' So we all said OK. Tony had this plan, an' all. Before the show, fuckin' guy rips off a fire extinguisher from the hallway by the bedrooms and stashes it in the can by the Rec Room.

"So we all go to the can. One by one, see. Tony gives me the fire extinguisher. Him an' Willie got these pennies rolled up tight in paper in their hands. Victor goes out to where these two screws are sitting, you know, watchin' TV, an' says the toilet's stopped up, shit all over the place, an' all. So one of the screws comes in to check and I blast him inna face with the foam. He's blind. Willie clocks him a couple of times and he goes down. Tony grabs his billy club an' we all run out into the hall.

"OK, so Victor runs down the hall and gets another fire extinguisher. The other screw comes toward him, gonna bat him with his stick, but Victor blasts him inna face an' Tony coldcocks him with the stick he took offa the other screw. So he goes down.

"Then we run through the kitchen. There's another screw there an' he goes for his piece. Victor and me we both blast him with the foam inna face, same like before. Willie knocks his piece outta his hand with the stick an' we run past him out to the foyer. The alarm's ringin', everybody's yellin' like a muthafucka, two more screws jump us. Me an' Victor bust our way through and get out the door. Then two cars of pigs pull up an' grab us."

Goldstein stopped and Karp looked a sharp question at Pagano, who said, "Wait, the best is yet to come."

Dooley lost it at this point, and bellowed at Goldstein, "You little shit! You beat up three guards, trying to escape, and you have the fucking nerve to press charges? You wish!"

"Hold on, Dooley," Karp said. "Let's hear the whole story first. Well, is that it, Mister Goldstein? You tried to escape, pounded on some guards and picked up some lumps in return?"

"No, that *ain't* all," said Goldstein indignantly. "It's the *next* day we're complainin' about. The next day!"

"What are you talking about?" Karp asked, more alert now.

"The next day. Two guards came into our cell and beat the living shit outta us. They handcuffed me and Victor and kicked us around the floor." He pointed to his bandage. "They kicked my fuckin' *eye* out, man."

There was a moment of silence. Dooley cursed. "Those goddam assholes," he said. Pagano added, "Ocha has three cracked ribs and a broken jaw, Martinez has a cracked vertebra, and Goldstein, as you see, has lost his eye." He looked at Karp. "Well, Counselor, you going to take the case?"

Karp took a deep breath. "What do you think, Pagano, I'm

going to bury this shit?" He turned to Dooley. "Hal, I'm going to write up the guards involved for felonious assault. Go up to the Drug Center and look around. Talk to the guards. See what kind of cover-up they've got going. Tom, I'll get Goldstein's story down on paper and signed and then get the statements of the others in the next couple of days, alright? Good. See you guys, I'm in court in about twenty seconds."

Karp worked for the remainder of the afternoon with the knowledge that this might be one of his last days in the criminal court system. A grin kept breaking out on his face, so it was hard to maintain the correct prosecutorial mien, which was grim and full of righteous indignation. His last case involved Dickie Waver, an exhibitionist, a graying pleasant-faced little man who had been arrested twenty times before—and probably would be many times again—who enjoyed being arrested almost as much as he enjoyed showing his penis to schoolgirls. Another little psychological service of the criminal court system. The defendant pleaded guilty and was fined. Bang. Justice triumphed. But soon, soon, without Butch Karp.

He went back to his office, dumped his stuff. The phone rang. It was Lannie Kimple, secretary to Doyle Cheeseborough, the chief of the Criminal Courts Bureau and Karp's immediate (and, he prayed, soon to be former) boss. Lannie was a thin, thirtyish lady who wore horn-rimmed glasses, and translucent blouses over plain slips. She wanted to marry a lawyer and wore a tiny gold cross around her neck to show her sincerity.

"Butch, the boss wants to see you—now."

"I've got something I've got to do. How late will he be there?"

"Uh-uh, he said *now,* and he's all bent out of shape about something."

"What else is new? Tell him I'll be there in about five minutes."

"Five minutes ain't now, Butch."

"For Crissakes, Lannie, I'm going to pee first, alright?"

There was a silence on the line; then Lannie said, "Five minutes," and hung up.

True to his word, Karp went to the men's room, relieved himself, then washed his hands and face. There were no paper towels; there rarely were. Karp dried himself with his pocket handkerchief, then smoothed his hair into place in front of the mirror with a damp hand. He examined the reflected face. He went through a repertoire of expressions. Stern—eyes narrowed, brow furrowed, lips compressed; sterner—eyes staring intensely, brows rolling in knots, jaw tight, lower lip bent under, tense, chin protruding; sternest—(maximum-time-bad-mutha-put-your-ass-in-jail-for-a-thousand-years) eyes popping from sockets, nostrils flared, lips in a snarl, teeth bared and grinding. "Is this the face of a HOMICIDE DA?" said Karp, the words whistling through his clenched teeth. "IS IT? IS IT? YOU BET YOUR ASS IT IS! You'll talk, Rocky, you'll talk. Your pal ratted on you, Rocky, it's all over . . ." Then, a switch to Sincere—eyes large and almost brimming, face relaxed, big shit-eating smile. "Hi," he said, in a passable imitation of Liberace, "My name is Karp. I'm with the Homicide Bureau. I'd just like to ask you a few questions. But first, are you comfortable? Can I get you anything? Cigarette? Sandwich? Coffee? A hit of smack? A piece of ass?"

Karp stopped suddenly with a jolt of panic. What if there was somebody in one of the booths listening to all this? He checked. All empty. He returned to the mirror, tightened his tie, put his official face on and left for the Criminal Court Bureau Chief's Office.

This was not going to be pleasant, thought Karp. Doyle Cheeseborough was a twenty-nine-year veteran of the DA's office. His tenure had given him dyspepsia, piles, and a rampaging intolerance for anyone who disagreed with him, or for anyone who differed from him in any aspect of philosophy, personal taste, or physical appearance. This intolerance included virtually all of the human race, but it was especially focused on minorities, Jews, tall people, and anybody at 100 Centre Street who appeared to be having a good time.

Karp entered Cheeseborough's outer office and nodded to Lannie Kimple.

"What happened, did you fall in?" she asked.

"No, it took me a while to coil it up. Cut the shit, Kimple, what's this about?"

"I don't know, and to be perfectly honest, I don't care. I am out of here in two weeks."

"Oh, when did this happen?"

"I gave him my notice today. I'm going over to work for Judge Calabrese in Appeals."

"Good for you. You get a better class of people over there."

She regarded him coldly. "I'll say. It wouldn't be hard either. You'd better go in."

Cheeseborough was sitting behind a massive wooden desk as Karp entered. As usual, he made the visitor wait while he shuffled papers. He had a round head perched on a round body, with skinny arms and legs and white, papery skin. He was nearly bald, but kept a patch of graying hair combed up over his dome, which, by day's end, was usually pointing straight up, specked with dandruff. Because of this appearance and his personality, he was universally known around 100 Centre Street as the Mad Onion.

Karp was not invited to sit down. Eventually, the Onion looked up, took in Karp's unpleasant height with his small and malevolent blue eyes, and said, "Who do you think you are?"

"What do you mean?"

Color began to rise in the Onion's papery cheeks. "You know damn well what I mean. All of you. Who do you think you are, seducing my secretary? She's leaving. Quitting, and she was just learning where everything was. I won't have it!"

"Um . . . Mister Cheeseborough, have you spoken to Miss Kimple about this?"

"Of course I've spoken with Miss Kimple. She won't say anything. Oh, no! She's leaving for 'personal reasons.' My Aunt Fanny! One of you seduced her and then you dumped her, she's probably knocked up in the bargain, and *that's* why she's leaving." The Onion was on a roll now, waggling his roots about and filling the air above his head with tiny white flakes. "And I'll tell you something else. One of you seduced my last secretary, too. She left. Oh, you think I don't know what goes on. I've seen you all making goo-goo eyes at her, and filthy remarks." He glared at Karp and clenched his tiny fists.

"Mister Cheeseborough, when you say 'you,' to whom are you referring? Me, personally, or some larger group?"

"Don't give me that! You're all in it together. You, and that clown, Guma, and that wise-ass Newbury, and that what's-his-name, that goddam Hungarian . . ."

"Hrcany?"

"Yeah, him."

"Well, Mister Cheeseborough, I don't know what to say. As you point out, we have no evidence that Miss Kimple is pregnant, still less that any staff attorneys have, ah, interfered with her. I can only give you my personal assurances . . ."

The Onion interrupted with a snarl, "Oh cut out this legalistic bullshit! I know what I know. I been around a long time, and let me warn all of you—I don't get mad, I get even."

More jiggling, more dandruff. The shoulders of the Onion's blue serge suit were covered with a dusting of it, like the windowsills of a building being sandblasted. Karp glanced discreetly at his watch.

"I'm sorry you feel that way, Mister Cheeseborough. Perhaps you could file a complaint of statutory rape on the grounds that Miss Kimple has the mind of a four-year-old girl. And now, I have to go. I have an appointment with Mister Conlin in five minutes."

The Onion gaped like a fish. Karp nodded curtly and left at a fair rate of speed. Through the closed door he heard the Onion's cry, "Hey, wait you, wait . . ." As Karp took the stairs to the sixth floor two at a time, he considered that he had substantially singed his bridges behind him. The Onion could make things nasty for him. If the fix was in for the homicide job, there wasn't a hell of a lot he could do, except screw up paperwork and delay things a bit. If it wasn't, Karp was dead meat.

"You must be Roger Karp," said John Conlin's secretary. "Mister Conlin is expecting you. I'll tell him you're here." She picked up her phone and did so, then smiled and motioned Karp through the anteroom. "Down the hall, first left, then to the end of the hallway. Good luck." Friendly. Efficient. Not pregnant by attorney or attorneys unknown. Class.

John Conlin's office was not quite as large or luxurious as the offices of officials are in the movies, but it was a good start. The desk was made of dark wood, as was the long boardroom table. There were two large windows, with blinds and curtains. If you looked out, you could see Chinatown. One wall had built-in bookcases filled with law books and bound transcripts of trials. The other wall was almost solid with framed plaques and letters commemorating twenty-five years of good deeds and useful connections; also pictures of Conlin at various stages of his life, in association with the great or notorious. There was one newspaper picture of Conlin—looking about as old as Karp now was—in the company of two uniformed cops and a gentleman who was trying hard not to be photographed. With a shock, Karp recognized him as one of the founders of Murder, Incorporated.

The present-day Conlin was moving around his big desk, hand outstretched. "Hi. I'm Jack Conlin. They call you Butch, right? Thanks for coming by. Sit."

They shook hands and sat at opposite ends of a black Chesterfield couch set along the wall under the frames. Conlin was a large man with high coloring and longish silvery hair swept back from a broad forehead. He had pale-blue eyes that crinkled when he smiled and perfect small white teeth, which he flashed a lot. He looked like a movie version of a slick Irish pol. In fact, he *was* a slick Irish pol, but he also was one of the smartest prosecuting attorneys in the United States.

He gestured to the news photograph. "You know who that is?" he asked. Karp nodded. "My first big one," Conlin said. "He used to put them under the asphalt while they were building the Belt Parkway. I think about him every time I drive to Brooklyn." He gave Karp an appraising stare. "I hear you used to play some ball."

"Some."

"That's good. You'll find a lot of the best DAs are former athletes. The competitive instinct." He smiled some teeth.

Karp knew he was supposed to ask if Conlin had played

ball and where, and he did, and got Conlin's version of what football was like at Fordham back in the forties. Then the conversation got around to sports in general and how the Knicks were doing great that year, and whether the Yankees had a chance, and what was wrong with college basketball in the city, and then drifted imperceptibly from winning games to winning cases.

Somewhere in the middle of the conversation Conlin started using phrases like, "now that you're part of the team here," and "after you've been working homicide awhile." Karp began to realize, with some irritation creeping into his original delight, that everything had been arranged on the unseen levels of power. He was not sure he liked being moved around like a piece on a game board.

"Umm . . . Mister Conlin, are you telling me that you want me to work in Homicide?"

Conlin seemed surprised. "Hell, yes. It's all set up. You *do* want the job, don't you?"

"Oh, sure, of course. I just wanted to know the details, and all."

"Nothing to worry about, we'll take care of the paper shuffling from this end. We'll be having our regular meeting next Thursday; that'll be a good time for you to start." Conlin stood up. Karp stood up. They shook hands. Conlin said he looked forward to working with Karp. Karp made an appropriate parting mumble and found himself once more in the outer office.

Karp said to no one in particular, "Holy Shit, I'm in." A stifled laugh made him turn around. Conlin's secretary said, "Congratulations. However, it seems your former boss is not so anxious to let you go. He called while you were in there and said for you to report to the Complaint Room for duty tonight."

"Oh, crap!"

"Have a heavy date?"

"No, just dinner with some friends. Screw it, I'll eat fast."

CHAPTER SIX

It was just a short walk from Foley Square to Mulberry Street in Little Italy, but Karp found himself in a different world, one of the last remnants of the European ethnic neighborhoods that once dominated the social and political life of Manhattan. Karp's own parents had been born in similar neighborhoods; Ray Guma's parents had been raised along these very streets.

The air itself was exotic, perfumed with anise, strong cheese, and frying garlic. On this temperate evening, chatting old ladies dressed in black sat on folding chairs on the sidewalk outside their apartment houses. The dusty storefront social clubs were brightly lit, each one with its handful of old men. Grocery stores displayed enormous rope-bound cheeses and great rectangular cans of olive oil covered with rococo inscriptions.

There were also a fair number of import-export firms which seemed never to have any business, their display windows always showing the same espresso machines and tarantella-dancing dolls, on tattered red crepe paper. Oddly enough, they were extremely profitable, although the source of their profit was not espresso machines. In some of their back rooms Sicilian assassins, lately smuggled in, sat waiting for their assignments. In others, men guarded suitcases full of cash. This had been going on for eighty years. The Mob clung to its roots.

Karp pushed past the door with the white, green, and red wooden cut-out map of Italy and entered Villa Cella Ristorante Italiano. Guma and V.T. Newbury were waiting at the center table, the one Italian family restaurants usually reserved for regulars. It was set for four places. When they saw him they gave a round of applause. "Sit down, kid," said Guma. "How'd it go with Conlin?"

"OK, I guess. The fix was in. I'm starting at Homicide next Thursday."

"Hot shit," said Guma, "we can drink the night away."

"Maybe you can," Karp replied glumly. "The Onion put me in the Complaint Room tonight, the asshole."

"What! I thought I was the only one he had a hard-on for."

"Don't flatter yourself. No, he was all bent out of shape because he thinks one of us has been screwing his secretary, and she's leaving. I wised off to him about it and he put it to me." A strange expression came over Guma's face as Karp said this. Karp suddenly caught on. "It was *you*! Goddamit! Hey, V.T., the Goom is dorking Miss Kimple and I get the shit for it. You owe me one, Mad Dog."

"Honest, Butch, how did I know she would fall in love? Christ, I only balled her a couple of times."

V.T. looked up from his study of the wine list. "Guma, we are going to have to start a collection and hire one of your Sicilian relatives to castrate you. You're a positive menace to the peace of the Manhattan District Attorney's Office."

"Fuck you too, V.T."

"Or," V.T. continued, "we could turn your ass in to Conrad Wharton, the scourge of porn. Why should he content himself with dirty pictures and tapes when pornography incarnate stalks the halls of 100 Centre Street." The other two men laughed.

"Wharton, my ass," said Guma. "I can't figure out why Garrahy keeps him right there in his office. The fucker is scared shitless of courtrooms, one, and two, he's an incredible schmuck. A schmuck from Schmuckland." He kissed his pinched fingers in a gesture of connoisseurship.

"True," said V.T., "but Conrad has attached himself to the boss's pet project, which is one way that weasels get on in the world. Deep in Francis P. Garrahy's Irish-Catholic soul is an abhorrence of public pornography. In the old days, when he was coming up, you couldn't see pussy until you were married.

In fact, where Garrahy came from, you couldn't see it even *after* you were married. Now he has to look at snatch every time he goes in to buy cigars.

"Conrad observes this and sells his all-out campaign against smut to the DA. Now he's got a private office next to Garrahy's and an army of twerps just like him to drag two-bit magazine publishers into court for five grand fines, like we have space on the calendars for that shit. No, Conrad is going places. He knows how to exploit the foibles of great men."

"Bullshit. He's an empty suit," said Karp.

"As a prosecutor? No question. But Conrad isn't interested in being a prosecutor and putting asses in jail. He's interested in power. You know, Butch, there are two kinds of people in the world: people who are interested in doing real things—growing gardens, or inventing, or trying cases—and people who are interested in making other people jump through hoops. Conrad is one of those. And they're hard to stop because while the rest of us are learning how to do the things we want to do, they're spending all their time collecting power. Watch the guys who volunteer to do the secretarial and bureaucratic bullshit that nobody else wants to do. They usually wind up running the show."

"Let 'em," said Karp. "As long as they leave me alone."

"Ah, but that's just the point. They can't leave you alone. Anything real—passion, excellence, skill—is a reproach to them. It's a source of satisfaction that they can't control. They have to destroy it. Look at Stalin and Trotsky. Trotsky ran the Russian Revolution almost single-handed. Stalin was the Communist Party's administrative boss. Look who won. And I'll tell you something else. Conrad's got you targeted, Butch. He mooches around me a lot because he thinks my old man has pull, which he does, and the little piss-ant doesn't miss an occasion to put you down."

"Fuck him, he can't touch me."

Guma broke in. "Hey, what is all this Trotsky bullshit? This is supposed to be a party. Hey, Margo!" He gestured to the waitress, who came out from behind the bar and over to their table. She was a good-looking woman of about twenty-five, plump, with heavy eye makeup and a blond streak in her dark hair.

She pulled out her pad and smiled. "How are you all tonight? Ready to order?"

Guma said, "No, we're still waiting for someone. But bring us a bottle of Barolo, the Fontanafredda. And the big antipasto, for nibbles."

She scratched on her pad. "OK. Hey, Ray, classes are starting in two weeks." She flashed a smile at Guma, who got red in the face and looked away with a sickly grin.

"Going back to law school, Goom?" V.T. asked.

"No, I am," said Margo. "Well, paralegal anyway. Ray says he can get me a job."

"Oh, really?" said Karp. "You're a helluva guy, Guma."

"Yeah, he sure is," said Margo, the light of love, or at least opportunism, gleaming in her eyes. "I'll go get your wine."

She left. Guma said, "OK, guys . . ."

"Very tacky, Mad Dog, *very* tacky," said Newbury.

"Yeah, Goom, is that the same technique you used on Kimple? Maybe you promised her a job in Villa Cella," Karp said.

"Hey, what the fuck. She's a bright kid, why shouldn't I encourage her?" Guma protested.

"To quote you, Goom, 'It's not her mind I want, it's her body.' Tell the truth, Margo *is* more your speed than Ciampi," said V.T.

"Don't remind me. God, *that's* an ass I'd love to get a piece of. What a body! Hard, tight—knishy little tits. She can probably yank nails with her snatch. By the way, where is she? You invited her, didn't you, V.T.?"

"I did, and I believe she's here now."

The door opened and Marlene Ciampi breezed in, in blazer, knee-length gray flannel skirt and high boots, a Marlboro gripped between her teeth like a stogie. Her thick, kinky, coal-colored hair was parted in the middle and drawn into a bun, getting a little ragged this late in the day. She had a heart-shaped face and the conventionally regular features of a cosmetics model, which she downplayed by keeping her eyebrows thick and her expression tight and belligerent.

"Sorry I'm late, guys," she said, yanking the empty chair out with the toe of her boot and slamming her rear down on the leather. "I've had an un-fucking-believable whorehouse of a day."

"That's OK, Champ, we waited. As a matter of fact, we were just talking about you. Ray here was saying . . ."

Guma gave a strangled yelp. "Newbury, you're dead!"

"Yes," V.T. continued blandly, "he was speculating that your vaginal musculature was capable of ripping a nail out of a board, weren't you, Ray?"

Ciampi didn't blink. "Oh yeah? Did he elaborate? I mean sticking up, pounded flush, or countersunk?"

"A corpse, Newbury."

"All flesh is grass, Goom," said Newbury with a dazzling smile. "Ah, here's our Margo. Let's drink to Butch." They poured the rich, pungent wine. "To homicide," said Newbury, glass raised. They all drank and then Margo took their orders.

Karp said, "You got any pizza, Margo?"

Guma sputtered. "Pizza! Give me a break, Karp. Pizza in Villa Cella? Margo, don't listen to him. Look, this is my party, I'm the head guinea, and I'll order. First, bring a big plate of trigliette allo zaffrano, then the special canneloni, with veal piccata all around, OK?"

"I'm not eating veal," said Marlene.

"Why not?" asked Guma.

"Because they nail the poor animals' feet to the floor so they can't move around and their flesh will be white. Yuck!"

"Marlene, they only do that to geese in Strasbourg," said V.T.

"Well, I read that they lock them up in dark rooms, or something. Anyway, they have a horrible life, the little veals."

"Shit, Marlene, so what! *I* have a horrible life," said Guma.

"Yeah, but I'm not eating you, schmuck."

"I only wish," replied Guma, rolling his eyes to heaven.

"Guma, will you get off my case for one fucking minute? Christ, give me another glass of that stuff." Karp poured and she picked the glass up and drained it in a gulp. She gasped and color rose high on her cheeks. "OK, I'm not going to get pissed off and screw up Butch's party. But you will not believe my day."

"What happened, Champ?" Karp asked.

"OK, first of all, you know the Ruddy Child Center case? This scumbag who runs the place is diddling the kids, and one of them tells the parents. It turns out that living on the same floor is our own Rick Pearl. He's got his own two daughters in the place. So the parents go to their friendly, neighborhood assistant DA and Rick goes apeshit, gets a detective, goes down to the center and braces the scumbag. Who cracks in about four seconds and spills his guts.

"OK, it's tainted, right? Rick didn't read him his rights. Granted, he should have turned it over immediately to somebody else. But we had solid testimony from a dozen kids, other workers in the center, other people who had quit working there because they didn't like what was going on. What does the judge do, Albert "The Asshole" Albinoli? He dismisses all the charges, on the grounds that Rick's mistake tainted all subsequent evidence. Can you fucking believe it?"

"That's a tough one. It happens, though," said Karp.

"No! No, that's just for starters. OK, the hearing's over, it's the last case of the day, everybody's riding down in the elevator—it's packed solid—me, the witnesses, kids, parents, lawyers, and the defendant. He's standing behind me. I still can't believe this. All of a sudden, I feel a hand clamped on my ass. I look around, and there's the fucking shit-face cocksucker slime dirt-ball pimp *defendant* with this little smarmy smile on his face and his hand on *my ass*."

"What did you do?" asked Karp.

"What could I do? I jammed the heel of my boot down as hard as I could on his arch, and I said, in a loud clear voice, 'Mr. Ruddy, kindly remove your hand. I already have an asshole down there.' "

The three men by this time were convulsed with laughter.

"Why are you laughing?" said Marlene. "It's not funny. And that's not the end! OK, I drop off my files, and head out of the building, and catch this—he's waiting for me. He asks me for a fucking *date!*"

"You accepted, of course," said V.T.

"Of course. He has terrific acne. We're going out for an evening of dinner and dancing and then he's going to set me up with a groovy six-year-old. Supposed to be hung like a horse."

The food came and they dug in. The espresso had just been poured when Karp glanced at his watch. "Shit, guys, I got to run."

Guma said, "Well, Butch, the Complaint Room sucks, but if you have to be there, tonight is the right night. It's going to be a party."

"What party?"

"The Two-Three Precinct just pulled in a whole house full of high-class hookers who say they've been kidnapped. Can you believe that? The detective told me that some pimp with a lot of muscle got the idea that there was a plot by this other pimp to move onto his turf, so he snatched the girls and locked them up for four days in a basement.

"The girls' pimp is a law-abiding citizen—his property's been ripped off. So where does he go? The fucking Two-Three, right, and he tells them that this maniacal hooker-killer is on the loose. OK, now this particular pimp is like the sorriest pimp in New York . . ."

"Present company excepted, of course," V.T. put in.

"Of course, V.T. And, of course, the cops take one look at this guy, who they know very well, and tell him to get fucked. So he leaves the precinct and a block away he gets jumped by the other pimp and three of his torpedoes and they beat the shit out of him and leave him in a trash can."

"Is this for real, Guma?" asked Marlene.

"Honest. I got it from the cops just before I left for dinner. Anyway, the detective who took the original statement from the pimp—he's a friend of mine, the detective, not the pimp—

gets off work a few minutes later and finds the pimp. 'Ah tol'
you muthafuckas sompin' goin' down. Ah tol' you!' says the
pimp."

"What the hell does this have to do with the Complaint
Room?"

"Wait, Butch, this is the best part. The detective figures
there might be something in the pimp's story after all—not the
Jack-the-Ripper bullshit, but some kind of fucked-up pimp
war. Maybe the wise guys are involved, who knows? So he puts
a call out for the SWAT team. The pimp leads them to where
the girls are, they blow down the door and make another he-
roic rescue. So now we have a gaggle of hookers on our
hands—they'll all be down at the Complaint Room tonight to
press charges."

"Jesus, Guma, big fucking deal. You think I'm going to
accept tips? Just sign the form right here, madam. Oh, you'd
like to give me a blow-job? How generous, thank you so
much."

"Karp, you're a great lawyer, but you have no sexual imagination. I got to take you under my wing."

V.T. said, "A truly fascinating story, Guma. However, I
don't believe 'a gaggle of hookers' is the correct term of ven-
ery."

"What is it, then, wise-ass?"

"How about, an anthology of pros?"

"No, a tray of tarts," said Marlene.

"I'm gone," said Karp, dropping his napkin on the table
and pushing back his chair.

"No, wait, Butch, you haven't received your present yet,"
said Newbury.

"What present?"

"A decoration for your new palatial office." He handed
Karp a flat package wrapped in brown paper. "We've all
signed it."

Karp unwrapped the package. It was a framed photograph,
grainy, as if it had been copied from a newspaper. It showed a
group of horsemen in odd, square hats galloping into the plane
of the picture. They wore white gloves and carried pennanted

spears. Under a smoke-filled sky, they were heading toward several squat black shapes that close inspection revealed to be tanks. It was the famous photograph of the last charge of the Polish Lancers, September 1939. Beneath the picture, V.T. had written, *"C'est magnifique, mais c'est ne pas la loi."*

"Thanks, guys," said Karp. He shook hands all around, got a quick kiss from Ciampi, and walked out into the dark streets toward Foley Square and the Complaint Room.

The Complaint Room was the gateway to the criminal justice system, just as those little grates set into the curbs are the gateways to the sewage system. It had a similar ambience.

About fifty by one-hundred feet in size, it was painted with peeling green and ochre paint, lit by dull and flickering fluorescent lights, and overheated. The floor was covered with the evening's trash and the air smelled of the losing battle Lysol was fighting with urine, vomit, sweaty bodies, and smoke. It looked like the second-class bus station in a third-world country. Half its area was partitioned into eight small booths, in each of which sat a typist with the appropriate equipment, a filing cabinet full of forms, and two chairs, one for the cop and one for the civilian witness if there was one. The cops took turns going into the booth and giving the typist the facts: the time, nature, and location of the alleged crime.

The ADAs—three by day and two at night—traveled from booth to booth, questioning the arresting officer, dictating the complaint to the typist, then moving on to the next booth. It was a slow process, which meant that the police officers had to sit waiting their turn, sometimes for hours. Once inside the booth, the cop had to wait for the ADA to come around and dictate, and for the typist to type and proofread. Then he signed the affidavit and took the complaint to the docket desk in the corner of the Complaint Room, had the complaint stamped with the docket number, and then went to court for the defendant's arraignment. A single arrest might thus take up five or six hours of police time, which is one reason why you can never find a cop when you need one.

Karp walked into the Complaint Room at seven o'clock, to find more-than-usual chaos in progress. There were at least fifty people crowded into the waiting area and spilling out into the hall. Voices were raised in irritation and in the hallway some cops were breaking up a fight between two drunk witnesses. He turned to a woman seated at a desk in the front of the Complaint Room.

"Debra, what the hell is going on here? And what are you doing here? It's past seven."

Debra Tiel was a tough lady from South Philly who started in the DA's Office as a typist. Now she ran the Complaint Room. Sharp and commanding, she knew how to get people to do things efficiently and like it; she was one of the indispensable, if unsung, trench soldiers of the bureaucratic state. After almost eleven hours in the pits, settling arguments between typists and cops and typists and ADAs and ADAs and cops and cops and cops, her coffee-colored face was visibly drawn, but her white blouse still retained its perpetual crispness. At the sight of Karp, she hoisted her silver-colored reading glasses from her nose and jammed them into her Afro like the visor of a knight.

"Sugar, am I glad to see you! We're short a typist and an ADA and I've got sixty people to get into booths. Most of 'em are holdovers from the afternoon, before we closed up for dinner. I mean. . . !"

"Who's working?"

"Hunk's in Booth Six, doing good. Ehrengard never showed."

"It figures, that shithead! OK, we'll clean the place out."

He walked into the room and scanned the seats. A tall black woman wearing fuchsia hotpants, a red satin camisole and a blond wig was using the pay phone. An elderly woman, her head bandaged, and her face bruised was sitting in a chair looking dazed. Next to her a young cop read the sports page of the *Daily News*. Two other cops were bringing a wino out of the men's room and setting him down with some gentleness on a chair. The person next to him, a middle-aged shopkeeper in a checked sportscoat, said "Sheeesh!" and immediately vacated his chair. Karp caught a whiff and sympathized. The wino must have witnessed some significant crime. The cops would dry him out, keep him dry through his testimony and then toss him back into the gutter, where the person whom he had testified against would probably cut his throat some night. Right now, though, he was the safest wino in New York. The rest of the crowd reflected the city's population—all races, the two major sexes, several of the minor ones, and most social classes were represented, united for once in boredom and irritation.

Karp took off his jacket, rolled up his shirt-sleeves and climbed up on Debra Tiel's desk. Pitching his voice to carry, he said, "Alright, may I have your attention please! Everyone, may I have your attention! Hey, you want to shut off the radio?" Martha and the Vandellas vanished and the crowd turned to face the source of the voice booming down from eleven feet up.

"OK, we're going to speed things up here a little." (A few claps and sarcastic cheers from the cops.) Everybody with homicide, rape, or sex cases raise your hands."

"Does that include Dickie Wavers?"

"Tonight it does—flashing to fondling. All of you, go to Booth Three and get in line. All prostitution charges and all violations, including public intoxication, disorderly conduct and harassment go to Booth Four and line up. All robberies and assaults, go to Booth One on my right; all burglary, trespass, go to Booth Two; all larceny, theft, auto theft, go to Booth Five, also anyone with bad-check arrests; all narcotics or gambling charges . . ."

"Does that include bookie collars?" a detective called out.

"Sure does. Go to Booth Six. Now, anyone left?"

"Just me, man." Karp looked down from his tower and saw a black detective in a cream-linen jacket.

"Could I talk to you? I gotta get out of here, like now."

Karp had worked with Sonny Dunbar before and liked him. He stepped down from the wastebasket and walked over to the detective. "What's the problem, you got tickets to the Yankees tonight?"

Dunbar grimaced and ran his hand across his face. "I only

wish, man. No, I got this shitty little purse-snatch collar, I've been waiting three hours, and I got serious family troubles, no lie." He looked at Karp expectantly.

"Sure, Sonny, no problem. Let's go into Eight."

They went into the booth and Dunbar shot the basic facts to the typist: his name, defendant's name, victim's name, witness's name, time, and location of the crime. Then he described the events in front of the drug store. Karp chuckled. "You wish they were all that easy, right?"

"Yeah, sure. I thought I was through with that garbage when I transfered to homicide. Anyway, I vouchered the purse, the chick says she'll testify. The perp has a long sheet already; he'll probably cop to petty with no trouble. Have you got that?"

Karp had been jotting notes on a yellow legal pad. He looked up and said, "Sure, Sonny, take off." Dunbar flashed a smile.

"Thanks, Butch. I owe you one."

Dunbar ran out and Karp dictated the language of the formal complaint to the typist. As he did so, he walked out of the booth to check on his handiwork. The Disneyland Principle had worked again. People were always happier on short lines, even if the waiting time was nearly the same as it would have been on longer ones. Much of the chaos and irritation had drained from the atmosphere in the Complaint Room; it now resembled a first-class bus station. Within an hour, there were scarcely a dozen people left on line.

Karp moved among the booths, listening to cops and victims, organizing the histories of human suffering and viciousness into the colorless language of the law. As always, he was torn between the natural impulse to sympathize and the requirement to keep the gears rolling. The gears had to win, of course, and not for the first time he reflected on the damage that continuous exposure to these experiences worked on the spirits of the people who made up the criminal justice system. This old lady now, telling him about being beaten bloody and robbed in the elevator of her building. It was the worst thing that ever happened to her. There was no way he could ever make her whole again. Certainly, putting the miserable kid junkie who had done it behind bars for—what, six months?—would hardly put her world back into balance. But he had heard it a hundred times. The cop had seen it fifty times. He looked at the face of the cop who had made the arrest. Young, curly-haired, wispy mustache, with a cynical old-man's eyes. Armor, like Karp's armor. He shook himself. He was letting the old lady ramble.

"Just a minute, Missus McGregor, let's go over what the man actually said to you. Can you recall his words?"

As Karp dictated the tale of the mugging he heard a commotion at the front of the Complaint Room, loud female voices, and above them Ray Guma's unmistakable barrelhouse laugh. Karp finished his dictation, left the booth, and went into the waiting area. Guma was standing in the center of a group of attractive young women waving his cigar and snapping off Groucho Marx one-liners. The women and the cops who were with them were cracking up. "Alright, ladies, I'd like you to remove your outer garments and go into the various booths we got here according to speciality. Booth One, fellatio. Booth Two, lesbian orgies. Booth Three, rim jobs. Booth Four, eyyahh-hah-hah, UNSPEAKABLE PRACTICES! Booth Five ..." He caught sight of Karp. "Hey, Butch, the party's on! What'd I tell you, hey?"

"Goom, what the fuck is going on here?"

"It's the girls from the Two-Three Precinct. The kidnap victims I told you about at dinner. They're here to make their complaint. I'm directing traffic." He rolled his eyes, waggled his cigar in his mouth and grabbed handfuls of buttock from the two women on either side of him. They squealed girlishly, like chorus girls in a Marx Brothers' movie, being trained to pick up quickly on sexual fantasies.

"Goddam, Guma, this isn't a whorehouse."

Guma put a puzzled expression on his face. "It's not? Gosh, I'm sorry, I thought this was One hundred Centre Street."

"Hey, what's going on?" said a new voice. "Guma! My man! You finally brought your sisters around to meet me."

Roland Hrcany was the other ADA working the Complaint Room. He looked less like a New York lawyer than a refugee from Muscle Beach; he was in fact a serious weight lifter, with a weight lifter's big shoulders, broad chest, and wasp waist. He had white-blond hair, no stranger to Clairol, swept back to fall below his collar, baby-blue eyes and a ferocious cavalry mustache under a large nose.

Guma clapped Hrcany on his massive shoulder. "Girls, this is it! Allow me to introduce Hunk Hrcany, the Hungarian Hustler and Heartbreaker. He will be servicing your every need in Booth Six tonight, for those who desire the crude and violent approach. And . . ." with a leer, "he has agreed to waive his usual fee. How about that?" Giggles. A few claps.

Karp broke in, "Guma, as long as you're here, you might as well work. Take your little friends to Booth Eight and get their statements, OK? I'd like to get out of here before dawn."

"Oh, no, Butch, do I hafta? OK, ladies, follow me."

Guma led the call girls away. Hrcany looked after them with a laugh. "Fuckin' guy! *I'm* a sex maniac. He's off the charts. Hey, Butch, I heard about homicide. Good for you, baby."

"Yeah, thanks, if I live through tonight."

As they turned back to work, the bomb exploded.

Out of the large number of people opposed to American involvement in the Vietnam War a small proportion had become convinced that the only way to stop it was to bring down the entire structure of the state—literally—with explosives. A good place to start was the criminal justice system, and so that day a former cheerleader from Larchmont had dropped off a package containing a dynamite bomb in the fifth floor women's toilet at 100 Centre Street. The bomb was not powerful enough to bring down the American state, but it sufficed to bring down the ceiling of the Complaint Room, a good beginning.

Karp was still on his feet, but bent over with his arms over his head. Plaster chunks and bits of masonry rained down on the room and the air was opaque with steam and gray dust. The lights had gone, except for the battery-operated emergency lanterns over the exit. Screams of dismay were coming from the direction of Booth Eight. A figure stumbled toward Karp through the murk. Blinking the dust out of his eyes, Karp saw that it was Debra Tiel.

"Butch! You OK? What the hell happened?"

"Damned if I know, but I think it was a bomb. Look, Debra, stand over by the exit and start yelling for people to come to you. I'll check the booths and make sure nobody's hurt. Good thing this didn't happen two hours ago." She moved off and began to call people to the exit. Karp picked his way through the wreckage, passing stumbling people made anonymous by the pall of dust that covered their faces and clothes. He bumped into Guma leaning against a wall, trying to get the dust out of his eyes.

"Goom, you OK?"

"Butch, what the fuck! I can't see for shit." Karp gave him his still-damp handkerchief, and Guma cleaned his eyes.

"Goddam, justice is blind, but this is too much!" He called out to his prostitutes, "Let's move it, girls. Next stop my place and a nice shower." They followed him in a bunch, looking now like so many pillars of salt.

There seemed to be no panic and few serious injuries. Karp saw two cops carrying the mugged Missus McGregor, who was out cold and bleeding from another head wound. Not her day, thought Karp. In the last booth, he found a typist, still sitting at her table, staring at a chunk of masonry and tile that had crushed her machine and missed her head by inches.

"Miss Park, time to go. Miss Park . . . ?"

She was frozen, like a rabbit mesmerized by a snake. There was a rumbling sound and more bits of plaster fell down. Karp could hear sirens in the distance. He kicked the typing table away, swept the typist up in his arms, and walked out of the Complaint Room, down the corridor and down the stairs.

The stairway was full of smoke and the smell of drains. Two men, from the Bomb Squad judging by their flak jackets, raced past him. Then came three masked firemen carrying hoses. Karp yelled, "Fifth floor, I think," to their backs and then continued down the four flights to the street.

The square was full of fire engines, police cars and ambulances, and lit with flashing red and blue lights. He deposited his burden with one of the ambulance crews and then began to walk home. A perfect end to a perfect day, he thought. He'd lost his suit jacket and the evening was getting chilly. He began to jog up Broadway. At Canal Street, he stopped at Dave's, an all-night sidewalk-service joint for a knish and an egg cream. The counterman gave him an odd look. "What happened to you, man?"

"I was bombed," said Karp. He felt giddy with the release of tension. He related the story of the bombing to the counterman, who was unimpressed.

"That's New York," he said.

Later, back in his apartment, after a long hot bath, he called his wife at her parents' home in Los Angeles. He told her about his transfer to the Homicide Bureau.

"That's very nice, Butch."

"It's more than that, Susan. I don't think anybody has ever made homicide with as little time in the office as I've had."

"OK, it's great, cosmic. What do you want me to say, Butch? I guess this means you have no immediate plans to change what you're doing?"

"Come on, Susan, don't start all that again." He thought of telling her about the bomb. He knew she was frightened of New York, and ordinarily he would not miss a chance to play on her natural sympathy for him. But he let it pass, and said instead, "How are you getting along?"

"OK. Still a little confused, I guess. My mother's driving me batty, trying to find a villain in my marriage. I keep telling her we both needed some space. She says, 'What space? You're married, you're married, you live with your husband. You're not married, you're not married, you get a divorce.' "

Karp laughed at his wife's imitation of her mother's characteristic tone. "Well, I just wanted to tell you that I miss you and I wish you were back here."

"For what, Butch? Tell me for what? You're never home. You never talk to me. I have no friends . . ."

"We had friends."

"*You* had friends. Cops and ADAs, sitting around drinking beer and talking hard-boiled about all the nasty things that happened to you that week. And *you're* hard-boiled—that's the worst part. You're getting, I don't know . . . brutal. We stopped talking, you know that? We had about four conversations the whole time I was with you in New York. Three about furniture and one about lamb versus roast chicken. I'm not going to live my life that way."

"How are you going to live your life, Susan?"

"I don't know. I went up to Stanford the other day and saw Phil at the Poli Sci Department. He says he can get me a research assistantship starting next month. Maybe I can get back to work on my thesis."

She talked on for a while about her plans, and mutual friends, but Karp wasn't really listening. There was a pause on the line. She had asked him a question and he had no idea what it was.

"Butch, are you still there?"

"Yeah, I'm here." Another pause.

"No, you're not. Good night, Butch."

He stared at the receiver for a moment after she had hung up. He almost called her again, but couldn't think of what he could say that would extract them from the knot they were in. He replaced the telephone and slipped under the covers of the bed.

He had built a wall around himself. It was part of his working equipment, like his legal pads. He couldn't survive without it, and he couldn't leave the job that required him to build it. Susan didn't understand that part. He was not sure he did either. In his mind, he started to rehearse the conversation that would finally, convincingly explain to her why things had to be the way they were and why, despite that, she ought to come back to him. But he fell asleep.

CHAPTER SEVEN

Monday was the first of April and Karp kept expecting somebody to yell "April Fool" in his ear and tell him that the homicide appointment had been a big joke. On his arrival at Centre Street he discovered that he was still scheduled to take a full load of cases in Criminal Court. The dead hand of the Mad Onion was evident in this, Karp thought.

His weekend, in contrast, had been not that bad, not the usual restless, boring intermissions they usually were. He'd awakened that Saturday missing Susan intensely, remembering their conversation with shame. His head was of course full of heartfelt, logical, and compelling arguments which would have been marvelously appropos last night, but which now cluttered up his head like a stack of dusty magazines that don't get thrown out because you might want to read one of the articles again, someday.

He lay in bed as long as he could stand it, then had a scalding long bath and got ready for playing softball with the DA office team, the season's first game. He spent two minutes dressing in old blue sweats and high-top sneakers, after spending twenty minutes wrapping his knee in layers of wide tape and Ace bandage.

It felt fairly robust as he began walking up Sixth Avenue to Central Park, with his big glove tucked under his arm and his old-fashioned all-wool Yankee cap on his head. Playing first base he didn't have to run much, but he ran—so it seemed to him—like a camel on eggs. And he still couldn't risk any dramatic slides on the base paths. But maybe it was getting better.

For breakfast he stopped at the sidewalk window of a Greek joint on 14th Street for a sausage sandwich with peppers and onions and a Diet Pepsi, which he consumed while walking north. The day had clouded over and turned chilly. Spring, scheduled to appear the previous week, had reneged. At 43rd Street he bought a couple of egg rolls and an orange soda from an Oriental lady with a push wagon. He ate one and drank the soda while walking, and kept the other one in the front pouch of his sweatshirt, as a temporary hand warmer and for later snacking.

It was not a bad game. The DA's team was called the Bullets, after the slang for a year in the pen, and because the DA liked to hire athletes, it was a good one. Today they were playing a tough team from the New York City Department of Sanitation, officially named the White Knights, but known to the city leagues as the New York Stinkees.

Pitching for the Bullets was Big Joe Lerner, the Homicide Bureau's star trial lawyer. Lerner was taller even than Karp, and about as ferocious a competitor as one can be in slow-pitch softball. Guma at short, naturally; Karp at first; Hrcany caught and played the outfield. As they flipped the ball around the diamond before the game, Karp felt centered again. Sometimes it seemed to him that his real life was just this: leaping around on a patch of ground with ruled lines, flinging a ball around with a bunch of other guys. Everything else—marriage, family, work—was to a greater or lesser degree merely a pain in the ass.

Garrahy was there. He came to the ball field in the bottom of the first, during the Bullet's at-bat and watched the game intently, like a major-league owner in his private box. Karp thought he looked ill and shrunken, and mentioned this to Guma on the bench. "Him?" Guma retorted. "He's made of rock. He'll last forever. I guarantee you, he'll bury us all."

"No, really, Goom. You ever think of what'll happen to the DA's office when he goes?"

"I don't know, but it'll be a helluva wake. We'll all be drunk for a month." A bat cracked and Guma leaped to his feet. "Way ta sock it, Jamesy baby! No pitcher, no pitcher!"

Karp glanced again at Garrahy. The old man was sitting in the small set of bleachers behind the players' bench, hunched in a camel hair coat, his thin white hair covered by a grayish green loden hat. His nose was red and he looked cold, but his eyes were clear.

Karp did not see much of Garrahy in the normal course of work and it was always a thrill to be in his presence. Karp was an unashamed hero-worshipper. As a schoolboy athlete, he had once sat next to Mickey Mantle at an awards dinner and been speechless with awe. (He eats! He drinks! He wipes his mouth with a napkin.) Karp stole the napkin afterward; he thought he still had it somewhere. The iconoclasm of the sixties—"don't follow leaders, avoid parking meters"—had barely touched him. In his soul Karp loved being coached. Besides his obvious physical skills, that was the one thing that made him an extraordinary player, his willingness to make himself an instrument of a larger, grander design. As they say in basketball circles—and this is a high compliment—he moved well without the ball.

Garrahy caught him staring, smiled, and gave a nod and a little wave of his gloved hand. Karp smiled back. The Bullets had a little rally going—two men on—and when Karp came up to bat, his head was full of the kind of romantic hero drivel usually found only in the kind of sports books written for ten-year-old boys. Karp was not that great a hitter, having too much of a strike zone and the wrong kind of body and reflexes, but this time he whacked the second pitch into deep center field and made it to third standing up. He scored on the next play and—as it turned out—that was the winning margin, as the Bullets took it, six to four. Garrahy shook his hand. Lerner shook his hand and said if he needed any thing when he got to homicide to be sure and look him up. After the game the whole team went as usual to McGonnigle's on Third Avenue. They drank beer and ate corned beef and told lies and watched the

Knicks win another on their march to the playoffs. A perfect day.

Sunday he went to the NYU law library and read, and didn't think of Susan until he was in bed that night. He called, but her mother answered and he hung up without saying anything. He was hyped for the new job and didn't want anything bringing him down.

Which was why another day in Yergin's courtroom amid the petty miseries of New York was too much to bear. At the lunch recess he called John Conlin, and the smiling secretary told him he was out. He called Lerner, a triple ought to be good for a little information, but Lerner was out too. Or maybe they were just saying that. Not ordinarily paranoid, Karp started to get antsy. Friday the fix was on; maybe it was off again. Standing in Calcutta at lunchtime he had a horrifying vision of permanent entrapment. What did he know, after all, of the deals that went down at the upper reaches of the DA's office. Maybe he should call Garrahy? He shook himself. Don't be an asshole, Karp. This joint is Kafkaesque, right on, but not actually Kafka itself. He went to find V.T., who usually had the inside poop, or if not, some words of what passed for wisdom on Centre Street.

A man touched his arm. "Mister Karp? I'd like to introduce myself. I'm Mervyn Stein. Representing DeLillo, Brant, Billings, and Coker? Could we talk for a moment?"

Karp had his hand taken and shaken vigorously by a large man in a three-piece banker's gray pinstripe. The man had frizzy pepper-and-salt hair, thick tortoiseshell glasses, and the ingratiating hand-rubbing manner of a maitre d' or an undertaker.

"What about? What's Delilla et cetera, a law firm?"

Stein gave a little giggle. "DeLillo, Brant, Billings, and Coker are the four correctional officers at the Drug Center against whom you filed assault charges. You recall, do you not?"

"Yeah, I recall. You their lawyer?"

"I am indeed. I am also counsel to and cochairman of the

Narcotic Addiction Control Center. Now, Mister Karp, or Butch, isn't it? I thought we might have a little talk, if it's convenient, to see if we can clear this matter up."

"Clear what up, Mister Stein?"

"This case, Butch. You know this kind of case isn't the kind of case that gets taken to trial, so why kid around?" He smiled broadly, except around the eyes.

"I don't see why not."

"Look, Butch, I used to work here, yeah, seven years. I could tell you stories you wouldn't believe. So take my advice: save yourself a lot of trouble, because as sure as we're standing here, the Supreme Court will never hear this case."

"Well, you could be right, Mister Stein—"

"Please, Mervyn . . ."

"—Mister Stein, in that there won't be a trial if your clients plead guilty to the top count of the indictment. If not, the case will be tried. I'm taking it to the Grand Jury myself."

"You must be joking. Young man, you're stirring up a hornet's nest here, and I expect you will get more than your share of stings. All I ask is that you reconsider this precipitous action. Look at this case! Four decent young men, working under considerable pressure at a job that is vital to this city. They are brutally assaulted by a gang of depraved drug fiends, and then, before their wounds are even healed, you charge them with assault. How do you expect the city to run narcotics centers . . ."

"Without maiming prisoners is how. Look Mister Stein, we could stand out here and bullshit all day about how sad, how sad, but the fact is that these guys, your clients, are going to trial. If the jury thinks that three guys holding a seventeen-year-old kid down while a fourth guy kicks his eye out of its socket is a legitimate part of narcotics rehab, that's fine with me. Meanwhile . . ." Karp moved to leave, but Stein placed a hand on his arm. He had stopped smiling.

"Wait just one minute, you. Look, Butch, you're a young man. You have a fine career in front of you. What you don't need is the kind of trouble this case is going to stir up. You know the kind, the caliber, of the people who sit on the Narcotics Control Commission? These are people you want as friends, not enemies. Now are you absolutely sure that Phil wants you to go ahead with this case?"

Karp knew that there was a small circle of intimates who called Francis P. Garrahy "Phil." He doubted that this bozo was included in it though.

"I haven't spoken with Mr. Garrahy about this case, Mister Stein, but as usual his name will be on the indictment." Karp broke away and started for the stairs.

"Well, perhaps *I* should," boomed Stein.

"His office is still on the eighth floor, *Mervyn*. Ask anybody for directions," Karp snapped over his shoulder.

It was raining outside, so Karp bought two jelly doughnuts and a pint of coffee at the ground floor snackbar. He went back to his cubicle to eat and ran into Guma in the hallway.

"Hey, Butch, what's happening?" Guma was wearing a dripping dark-blue raincoat and a plastic cap and was carrying a large, damp paper bag.

"Not much, Goom. You know, making powerful enemies. The usual."

"Great! Hey, you want some lo mein? I just went over to Chinatown, I got a ton." So they went into Karp's cubicle and divided the quart of greasy noodles between them, with the jelly doughnuts for dessert. "I see you're still here," said Guma around a mouthful. "I thought you'd be up on the sixth floor today. What's happening?"

"Damn if I know. They scheduled me for Criminal Court this morning, as usual. My guess is the Onion's behind it, or maybe Wharton." He ran his big hand over his eyes. "At this point I don't particularly give a shit."

"Ah cut it out, you'd trade your left nut to get Homicide. But meanwhile don't worry, it's just the usual sand in the gears—I guarantee you'll be there this week. Hey, look at this, this'll cheer you up." Guma reached across the desk to the paper bag and spread it open. "Fireworks! I picked them up in Chinatown from a guy I know. I got ten packs of ladyfingers, cherry bombs, M-Eighties, Whiz-Bang Flying Bomb Rockets. Hey, I got a Triple Royal Star Salute too, the whole schmeer. All illegal, of course."

"Of course. What're you going to do with them?"

"I'll think of something. Right now I got to go to court. I got a victim—marone!—got a set of jugs that won't quit."

"Are you going to impound them as evidence?"

"I wish, any kind of pounding. I'm gone, see ya."

Guma breezed out with his fireworks and, after cleaning up the debris, Karp went to court. It was not a good court in which to be a petty felon that day. The Legal Aid attorneys were dumbfounded as Karp held out for trial—on what were ordinarily bargainable offenses—in case after case. Finally, Yergin called him to the bench. "Butch, what's wrong with you? This is a domestic. You really want to try this man for aggravated assault?"

"He used a pipe wrench. It's a deadly weapon, Judge. The law makes it clear . . ."

"I know the law, Counselor," said the judge, his voice rising, "and I'm telling you to lighten up. I don't know what put the hair up your ass today, but don't take it out on my calendar. Let's just get through today in an expeditious manner, and save the trial slots for the bad guys. Understood?"

Karp mumbled assent and walked away. Yergin had never dressed him down before, and he felt his face burning. He tightened his jaw and tried to ignore the smirks from the defense table. He finished the calendar in an expeditious manner.

Then he went back to his cubicle and kicked his desk a couple of times, hard, so that the tin walls of the cubicle rattled like the cage of a psychotic hamster. He called Conlin, but the smiling secretary said he was in a meeting. He slammed down the phone, which immediately rang. He picked it back up and Lannie Kimple's South Brooklyn soprano sang into his ear, "Hello. Guess who's in trouble again?"

"Lannie, why don't you tell the Onion it was Guma who porked you so he'll get off my case?" A pause.

"He doesn't need an excuse, Mister Karp. Nobody likes a wise-ass. I think you'd better get down here right away. He has

Mister Wharton in with him and they're both waiting to see you."

"Great! That makes my day. OK, Lannie, tell them I'll be over as soon as I've filled my enema bag."

When Karp got to Cheeseborough's office, he walked right past Lannie, gave a perfunctory knock on the frosted glass of the inner office door, and entered without being asked. The Onion and Conrad Wharton were sitting with their heads together; the Onion planted behind his large wooden desk as usual, Wharton in the green, studded-leather visitors' chair to the right of the desk. They both looked up sharply when Karp came in, like startled geese.

"You wanted to see me, Mister Cheeseborough?"

The Onion frowned. "Yes, Karp, we did. You know Chip Wharton here, of course." Nobody but the Onion and a few sycophants called Conrad Wharton "Chip," a name he was trying to cultivate because of its clean-cut, horsey-set, masculine connotations. Everybody else referred to him as "Corncob" because of his peculiar walk, a sort of rapid waddle with the thighs of his short legs pressed close together, which suggested that he had secreted such an object in an intimate recess, and was trying to keep it from falling out.

Wharton was about thirty-five, plump, with a round face, wide-set blue eyes and a red cupid-bow mouth. He had fine, almost white-blond hair, which he wore long, razor cut and blow-dried. He looked like a mean, animated Kewpie doll in a three-piece suit.

Wharton shifted his chair so he could look directly at Karp. Cheeseborough went on. "Chip has brought something to my attention that requires an explanation from you. Chip?"

Wharton consulted a folder on his lap. He spoke in a rich, fruity voice, of the type that was popular among radio announcers in the forties. "This case you've filed, Butch, against these four guards at the Narcotics Center? I'm afraid it is in serious violation of our Trial Screening Profile. Not only that, we, that is the district attorney and I, have received numerous complaints from several highly placed . . ."

Karp broke in. "What the hell is this, Wharton? Since

when are you reviewing Criminal Court actions? I thought you were supposed to be chasing jerk-off movies."

Wharton glanced at the Onion and the two men traded supercilious smiles. "Ah . . . the Pornography Campaign is just one of my duties. I'm also responsible for seeing that our resources are appropriately targeted so as to produce the maximum benefit to the taxpayer."

"Very noble, Wharton. What has this got to do with my case?"

"Well, to gain maximum efficiency, we have to view the entire criminal justice system as a whole, and adjust the inputs of resources at each node so as to optimize throughput. Now, as you know, Butch, trial time is one of our scarcest resources. It hardly makes sense for one part of the criminal justice system—us—to spend that resource trying to penalize representatives of the Drug Center, which is another part of the same system. So we have developed a Trial Screening Profile that assigns priorities to different sorts of cases and generates scores. Then we can observe the trial dispositions of various ADAs and bureaus and see whose scores diverge from the optimum, and take corrective action. Am I making myself clear?"

"Um, I'm not sure, Conrad. This is a little new to me. You seem to be saying that people who work for the criminal justice system, if they break the law, well, they can get a sort of special deal from the DA's office, maybe cop an easier plea because the whatsit, the Trial Screening Profile, gives a low score to those particular crimes."

"I wouldn't say a 'special deal,' actually. It's a . . . more subtle ordering of priorities type of thing . . ."

"No, I think I got it now. So it would mean that, if I were a cop sitting here, and you were to go over to Mister Cheeseborough there and start sucking his cock, and he said, 'Let go of my hose, you little faggot,' and then I arrested you for sexual battery, in such a case, because you were part of the criminal justice system, the Honorable Francis P. Garrahy or his representatives would be more inclined to let you plead to say, consensual sodomy. Is that how it would work, Conrad?"

The Onion came up out of his chair so fast that his anti-hemorrhoid Komfort-Kushion squawked. "Damn you, Karp. You're offensive!"

"Not as offensive as what I'm hearing from him." Karp jerked his thumb at Wharton, who was silent, with an expression of superior resignation on his cherubic face. "The law doesn't say diddly-squat about goddam *priorities,* Mister Cheeseborough. It says everybody gets the same shake, the same day in court, and if we spend more time nailing a multiple killer than a sidewalk spitter, that's part of the discretion of the assistant district attorney in charge—which is me—subject to the concurrence of the district attorney, from whom I have heard not one word on this matter—"

"Karp, you're way out of line now," sputtered the Onion, his top knot lashing about like a palm in a typhoon. "I am . . ."

"—and furthermore, behind all this happy horseshit about 'optimizing throughput' I detect just a taste of old-fashioned politics. You wouldn't have gotten a call from a guy named Mervyn Stein, hey Conrad?"

"That has nothing whatever to do with it," said Wharton, coloring slightly.

"Oh, Conrad, is that a blush of shame on your cheek, naughty boy! Does Mr. Garrahy know you've been using his office to make important friends for yourself on the Narcotics Control Commission?"

Wharton sighed. "Karp, you're getting carried away. This case has nothing. You have the word of four teenaged addicts, who were regrettably injured during an escape attempt, against the testimony of four reputable guards. In my view, you're wasting the office's resources because of some private vendetta that . . ."

"In your view! The courtroom wizard speaks. When was the last time you tried a case, Wharton? In moot court?"

"He's right, Karp," the Onion said nastily. "You haven't got any evidence besides those scumbags' testimony."

"You're wrong there. I have complete documentary proof that the guards lied about their whereabouts during the time the inmates were beaten."

This was bluff. Karp had sent Hal Dooley up to the Drug

95 —

Center to check on the movements of the guards on the day in question, but so far, he had come up with nothing. But there *had* to be that evidence.

"Oh?" said Wharton, "what sort of proof?"

"Come to court, you'll find out."

"No way, Karp," the Onion put in. "I'm still running this bureau, and I won't have . . ."

But they never found out what the Onion wouldn't have, because at that instant there was a loud explosion from the direction of the outer office, followed by two more in quick succession.

"Jesus! What the hell is that?" cried the Onion. And then several more sharp reports.

Wharton's pink face blanched and he croaked, "We're under attack by radicals! That's automatic weapons fire!"

All three men rushed into the outer office, where Miss Kimple was crossing herself nonstop and begging forgiveness for her sins. Lurid flashes could be seen through the frosted glass of the hallway door.

Luckily Wharton was there to take charge. He had spent four years in the ROTC and nine months in a logistic-support unit in Saigon. On two occasions he had flown in a helicopter over paddies where there were reliable reports of Vietcong sightings, for which exploit he had received a Bronze Star.

"Miss Kimple!" he barked, "get down behind the desk! Everybody, take cover!" They all got down on their knees behind the secretary's desk, Kimple half dead with terror, the Onion red faced with rage (this was not covered under Civil Service regulations), and Karp feeling foolish. Wharton pulled the phone down and dialed 911. For a wonder he was connected at once and began shooting vital information down the line in clipped military tones: "This is the DA's office, One hundred Centre Street, fourth floor. We're under attack by a group of armed radicals. They have automatic weapons, probably Kalashnikovs, grenades, and rocket launchers . . ." Suitable background noises for this dramatic report continued to come from outside: explosions, the sound of breaking glass and now a woman's voice screaming hysterically and a man's hoarse shouts.

Wharton concluded his report: ". . . my name is Conrad Wharton, I'm Mister Garrahy's special assistant. For God's sake, hurry! They're getting closer. Send the SWAT team!" As he hung up the telephone there was an unusually loud BANG–WHOOOOSH–BANG! outside the door and the room was lit with a hellish red glare, which died and was then replaced with a blue light and then a green one. Finally, the loudest explosion of all went off, the door shook, its glass rattled and a wave of harsh actinic white light, like a welder's torch, came through the door glass. Miss Kimple screwed her fists into her ears, shut her eyes, and commenced to scream at the top of her voice.

Green light? Karp had never seen combat, but he doubted that light shows were part of the standard repertoire of the militant left. He rose to his feet and walked toward the hallway door. "Get down, you fool! You'll draw their fire," croaked Wharton, still prone. "Doyle! Can't you shut her up!" The Onion grabbed Miss Kimple's shoulder and shook her. The screams continued. Then he made his big mistake. Trained by dozens of B-movies as to the appropriate masculine behavior in such situations, he sat up and slapped Miss Kimple across the face. It stopped her screaming. She opened her eyes wide, brought down her fists and delivered a right cross that would not have embarrassed Willy Pep smack on the Onion's nose. He fell back across Wharton's body gushing blood. Kimple closed her eyes, plugged her ears and began screaming again.

Karp left the office and walked out into the hallway. He already had a pretty good idea of what had happened, and it was confirmed by the charred and glowing cardboard cylinders that littered the floor. The passage was smokey and thick with the acrid fumes that recalled childhood summers and Tuesday night fireworks at Coney Island. People were beginning to emerge cautiously from the other offices in the hall. Karp spotted Roland Hrcany and waved.

"Karp? We have to stop meeting like this. What the fuck's happening, man? Another bombing?"

"I doubt it. It seems to be coming from Guma's." Karp pointed to Guma's door, two doors down from the Onion's and across the hall. As one of the senior ADA's in the bureau,

Guma had his own office. Its door glass was shattered and it now appeared to be the source of the smoke, the continuing red glow, an occasional BANG! and the noise of a violent argument between a woman shrieking in a foreign tongue and a man speaking Low Middle Brooklynese.

Now there was a rumble of footsteps on the fire stairs. The fire door burst open and half a dozen big men dressed in black uniforms and helmets and carrying riot guns and Armalite rifles charged into the hallway. The office workers backed against the walls to let them by. The SWAT sergeant shouted, "Where are they?" Silence from the crowd. "OK, you three men check the offices on this floor. Camello, Rasmussen, check the fifth. What the hell is all that screaming?"

Karp stepped forward. "Uh, Sergeant, I think there's been a mistake."

"Who're you?"

"My name's Karp. I'm a DA. Look, I think what we've got here is an accidental explosion of some fireworks." Karp held up a large cardboard tube on which still fluttered some colorful tissue paper printed with Chinese characters. The sergeant swore. "Alright, but what's going on in there?" He gestured to Guma's office. "It sounds like a broad getting raped by a wild pig."

Karp said, "You could be right, Sarge. Let's check it out."

The two men went over to Guma's door. Hrcany and a dozen or so spectators followed and crowded around. Meanwhile, one of the SWAT officers had liberated the Onion's fortress. Miss Kimple was being ministered to on the office couch by another secretary. The Onion and Wharton had come out into the hallway, both spattered with blood from the Onion's nose. The Onion still held a red-sodden handkerchief to his face and leaned on Wharton for support.

"Holy shit," said Hrcany, noticing them. "This looks like the relief of Khe Sanh. Butch, what the fuck . . ."

"Wait, wait" said Karp, "here comes the payoff."

The SWAT sergeant rattled the knob to Guma's door. It was locked. The shouts from inside ceased. "Open up!" shouted the sergeant. More silence. The SWAT man then knocked the rest of the glass out of the door with the butt of his shotgun, reached in, and released the lock. The door swung open and the spectators leaned forward and peered through the smoke still rushing out through the doorway.

Guma was standing in the middle of the small room. He held up his pants with his left hand and with his right held the arm of a very large, very angry, very blonde, and very naked woman. The surface of his desk was cleared of everything except a green blotter and a gooseneck lamp. Smoke still poured from the waste can near the desk. A black lace brassiere hung from the lamp. When the woman saw the crowd she cried out something incomprehensible and slapped Guma's face with her free hand. She broke free, snatched various items of clothing off the floor, and, clutching them to her middle, bent over double to shoot out through the doorway and down the hall before anyone could stop her. The last part of her they saw was a set of generous white buttocks twinkling away through the swirling smoke.

Karp spoke first. "Sergeant, this is obviously not a job for the SWAT team."

The sergeant laughed. "I guess you could say that. But what'll I do about my report? I gotta say something."

"Just say it was . . . a case of DHE, that's detonative hysterical ecdysiasm."

"What?"

"Here, I'll write it down for you. Detonative hysterical ecdysiasm is an uncontrollable desire to undress in front of lawyers while setting off fireworks. We have two or three cases of it every week."

"Yeah?"

"Sure, Sarge," said Hrcany. "We usually handle it quietly, but this was worse than usual. That poor woman! I'll see that she gets the appropriate treatment."

The sergeant appeared satisfied with this explanation. He had once worked in the East Village and had heard a hundred stranger stories. He gathered his commandos together and left. The crowd began to disperse; it was after five and most of them were on their way home anyway. Karp and Hrcany went into Guma's office. Guma was straightening his clothes.

"OK, Mad Dog, spill!" said Karp.

"Holy shit, Karp, what the fuck am I going to do about this office?"

"More to the point, what are you going to do about the Onion?" said Hrcany.

"He won't do shit," said Karp. "Corncob Wharton will convince him to keep it quiet because he won't want it known that he called out the SWAT for some firecrackers. It might prejudice his machismo, and the Onion won't want the world to know he was cold-cocked by his secretary."

In fact, they could hear the Onion bellowing in the corridor, a bellow transmuted by the tissue jammed into his nostrils: "I wonk to know the meanbing of this! What is gonking ong here?" They also heard Wharton talking rapidly to him and then the closing of the Onion's office door.

"See?" said Karp. "OK, Guma, what *is* gonking on here? Who was that bimbo?"

Guma collapsed in his swivel chair and sighed deeply. "That was no bimbo, that was my witness, Christa Spirotekas. She's a Greek, runs a bar on Eighth Avenue. I just nailed some guy who burgled her place and she wanted to show her appreciation. So I let her. I sat in my chair smoking a cigar and she did the horniest strip act I ever saw in my life. Then she sat on my lap and started torquing my tool. What could I do?"

"What, indeed?" said Hrcany.

"So she cleared off the desk—"

"Except for the blotter."

"—except for the blotter and lay down on her back, and I dropped my drawers and got to work. Mama mia! What a piece of ass! Did you catch those mazoomas?"

Karp said, "I can see it coming."

"Right. I tossed my cigar into the shit can. I guess I forgot that's where I stashed my fireworks."

"And the rest is history," said Hrcany. "One thing, Goom, since me and Karp saved your butt with our quick thinking, I figure you owe us something."

"Oh, yeah?" said Guma suspiciously. "Like what?"

"Goom," said Hrcany, "I don't know what Karp wants, but I want that blotter. I'm going to have it framed."

"Terrific, you can have it."

Karp went to the door. "Guys, it's been real, but I gotta go."

"Stay, Butch, we'll go for beer and pizza. You're not gonna work now, are you?"

"Yeah, Goom, I got to clear up some stuff."

Karp went directly to his cubicle and dumped the contents of his desk drawers into a waste basket and stuffed all his books and papers into his briefcase. He went out into the hall, found a janitorial cart and took a couple of brown plastic trash bags. These he filled with the rest of his things and the briefcase. Then, burdened like a pack mule, he staggered to the elevator and rode it up to the sixth floor.

He went directly to Joe Lerner's office. The secretary had gone home, but he knew Lerner would be there. The man was famous for working late. He was also famous for not tolerating bureaucratic bullshit. Twenty minutes later Karp was unpacking his stuff in a tiny office—tiny, but with a real door and walls that reached to the ceiling. He had just hung up his Polish picture, when Lerner came in with a fat sheaf of papers and dropped them on the desk.

"What's that?" asked Karp.

"*Coram nobis* petitions."

"Oh, crap." *Coram nobis* are postconviction appeals filed by people in prison demanding retrial on the grounds that a witness had changed testimony or that evidence had been illegally seized. Answering them is a boring, thankless, endless, and necessary task—and the job was always given to the lowest scullion in the bureau's kitchen, which at this point, was Karp.

"You'll love it," said Lerner. "No, really, I know you're a hotshot, but Homicide is a slightly different league than what you've been doing. You'll see. You'll come to the meetings, go on call, see the way we do things. Then, after a while, they'll let you second-seat on a case. Unless they stop killing each other out there, you'll be up to your ass soon enough."

Karp gestured around. "No, it's OK. I like the office. Thanks."

"Yeah, it used to be a supply closet in the old days. When

it gets damp, you can still smell the Lysol. By the way, what was all that commotion downstairs a little while ago?"

"Nothing much," said Karp. "One of the DAs was fucking a witness on his desk and set off a bunch of fireworks."

"Oh," said Lerner. "The usual."

CHAPTER EIGHT

Two weeks later, Karp was still in the little office, answering *coram nobis* petitions. It used to be, somebody got caught, and convicted, they went to prison and, mostly, stayed there for the time they were sentenced, or until paroled. "If you can't do the time, don't do the crime," the cons said, and in a weird way, they were proud of it. But now, as Karp realized more and more, wading through the piles of petitions, that subtle agreement between the bad guys and the good guys had entirely vanished. Although very few of the thousands of felons in New York City were ever caught, and although few of those few were ever sentenced to long stretches in prison, and although it was absurdly easy to cop a plea to a lesser offense, the small number of people actually sentenced for killing somebody seemed to be spending their entire lives behind bars looking for legal technicalities that would free them.

In general, there was no question here that these people were killers. Here was a guy, for instance, who quarreled with his neighbor about a gambling debt, went home, brooded about it, got liquored up, took a steak knife from the kitchen, went next door, stabbed his neighbor four times through the heart, went back home, rinsed off the knife, and went to sleep. Next day, the cops come. Hey, there's a trail of blood leading from the corpse to the house next door. The cops go in, brace the dude ("I din do nothin' "), they find the knife—he washed the blood off the blade, forgot about the handle, also forgot about his shirt and pants. The blood's a ten-point match with the victim's. Case closed, right? Wrong. On the advice of his cellmate, the guy does a *coram nobis* on the grounds that the evidence was illegally obtained, because the cops did not have probable cause to enter his castle.

There were a lot of them like that. Law was a game, sure, but there used to at least be agreement on the rules. Now it was as if, at a basketball game, one side would argue about whether the court or the ball was exactly the right size until the other team got pissed off and left, giving them the win on a forfeit.

Karp soldiered on through most of the morning, with the sunlight from the bright day moving slowly across the piles of forms on his desk, making jagged shadows like springtime in the Rockies. He was starting to think about breaking for lunch, when he heard a couple of taps on his door and Lerner came in.

"How's it going, kiddo?"

"I'm dying. How about yourself, Joe?"

Lerner chuckled. "This too shall pass. Actually, I'm bringing you some relief. How would you like to do something for me?"

"I left the Johnnie-Mop home, so I can't clean the toilets, but besides that I'm at your disposal."

"That's it, keep your sense of humor." Lerner sat down in Karp's visitors' chair and stretched his long legs almost to the opposite wall. "No, this is an interview with a homicide suspect over at the Tombs—the Marchione killings."

"They got the guy for those?"

"Not exactly. A guy turned himself in, says he was driving the car, he never pulled the trigger. Says there were two other guys involved, one of them did the job."

"Shit, what else is he going to say?"

"Sure, but it's not that simple. You know Sonny Dunbar, works out of Midtown South? OK, it turns out this guy's his brother-in-law, name's Donald Walker. Kid's never been in much trouble, but apparently he started using junk, fell in with some bad guys, and they got him to drive for the Marchione job. Anyway, apparently the kid panicked and got in touch with Dunbar and spilled his guts."

"Spontaneous statement?"

"Ah, that's the catch. Dunbar seems to have put the fear of God into the boy, like you would if somebody in your family was screwing up. That's before he knew what Walker had done. So that whole part of it is tainted rotten. Then he told Walker to turn himself in and tell his story for the record. The problem is, by the time he got to the cops—Dunbar sent him to Fred Slocum—he was frozen up, looked to be half out of his skull with coming down off of the junk. I talked to Slocum. He thinks the kid made the other two guys up."

Karp was scribbling rapidly on a yellow legal pad. "What do *you* think? Any other evidence linking this Walker to the crime?"

"Some. We have an eyewitness, on the car, at least. Woman named Kolka was sitting in a car on Forty-eighth Street the night of the murders, waiting for her husband to come down from their apartment. He's a retired cop. She sees a white car come around from Madison and park a couple of cars down and across the street. She sees a light-skinned Negro male leave the car from the passenger door, carrying some kind of briefcase. About ten minutes later she hears what she described as 'firecracker noises' coming from Madison. Couple of minutes after that, the same guy comes back, gets in the passenger door and drives off."

"Did she do an ID on Walker?"

"Yeah, she says close but no cigars. She's pretty sure this guy was clean shaven. Walker's got a beard."

"She spot anybody else in the car?"

"She thought she saw a head in the backseat, but she couldn't swear to it. The angle was wrong to see the driver's seat. *But*, when the car pulled out, she got a good look at the plates, and that nice old lady wrote down the tag number."

"Which was Walker's number?"

"Which was *not* Walker's number. But from what we can figure, it *was* indeed Walker's Nineteen-sixty-four Chevy Impala. The plates on it that night were reported stolen in East Harlem the week before."

"Pretty clever."

"Yeah, real pros we got here. But there's something else.

The morning after the murders, an anonymous caller rings up the cops and tells them that he saw the whole thing, describes the car, and gives the tag number."

"Confirming Mrs. Kolka?"

"*Not* confirming Mrs. Kolka. This guy gives Walker's real plate number, the plates that were on the car when the cops picked it up."

"Uh-oh."

"Uh-oh is right. It looks like somebody is trying to stick Walker with the whole bag. That tends to confirm Walker's story about other guys being involved. Oh, they also checked the hotel room where he went after the crime. In the trash can there, they found an empty J&B bottle with three good sets of prints: Walker's, the room clerk's and Angelo Marchione's, and nobody else's. That tends to put Walker in the store, unless one, he was a regular patron of A&A Liquors, or two, he had been there earlier, maybe checking the place out, or three, somebody else, who was careful not to leave any prints, took the bottle and gave it to Walker. Which, of course, is Walker's story. In any case, we booked him for the double murders. He's been in the Tombs since last Friday."

"So what do you want me to do?"

"Our basic problem is that Walker clammed up with Slocum. He hasn't wanted to talk at all. I think Slocum came down too hard on him, and he thinks he's being railroaded to take the whole rap for the murders. I figured to let him cook in the Tombs for a while. If he is telling the truth, I got to have that gunman. Yesterday evening, Walker called his brother-in-law and said he was ready to spill, if he could make a deal. Dunbar called me. He's scared too, for his brother-in-law, and also because he doesn't want to be blamed for fucking up a big case."

"How big is it?"

"Biggish, for a retail store rip-off and killing. The old man was a pillar-of-the-community type, the kid was popular and good-looking. But mostly it's the brother, Alfredo Marchione. He's a *macher* on the West Side; big in the Knights, active in the Party. The kind of guy elected officials like to be nice to. He's jerking chains all over town."

"I think you're going to tell me I'm not handling this case all by myself."

Lerner smiled broadly. "Smart boy! No, you're going to second-seat Jack on this. I'd love the case myself, but I'm starting a trial on Monday. Anyway, I told the cops somebody would meet them over at the Tombs at one o'clock."

It was 12:40. Karp got up and said, "I'll be there. It still sounds great."

Lerner said, "Enthusiasm, that's what we like. Oh, to be fifty again! Good luck." He patted Karp on the shoulder and left.

Karp took his yellow pad and his suit jacket, left his office and picked up the case folder from the smiling secretary. He went down the hall and, on his way out, told Walter Leonard to meet him at the Tombs at one. Leonard was in his late fifties, a gray, quiet civil servant, who as a stenographer for the Homicide Bureau during the last twenty-five years had recorded more tales of illicit slaughter than Agatha Christie.

The Tombs was in the building next door. Karp picked up a couple of hot dogs and a root beer from a Sabrett cart and sat down on a bench across the street to read the case folder. It was thin and told him little he did not already know from Joe Lerner's briefing.

After lunch he went into the Tombs, a noble institution serving New Yorkers badly since 1838, met Leonard, went through a series of clanging doors, smelt the smell, heard the noise, felt the feelings that most visitors feel in jail (how horrible to cage men like beasts, how marvelous that they're in here and not out on the street) and arrived at the interview room at just one o'clock.

The room was about ten by twelve, city green, furnished with a battered long table and hard chairs, like the boardroom of a long-bankrupt corporation. Slocum and Dunbar were already there. Fred Slocum was a beefy, florid man in a plaid blazer and sky-blue polyester pants. He had one of the last crew cuts in New York, a reddish fuzz like an unusually hairy peach. He was smoking a Tampa Nugget.

Karp shook hands all around and in a few moments a guard brought Donald Walker into the room. Walker looked shrunken in his yellow prisoners' jumpsuit; he'd lost the touch of baby fat in his face and his tan complexion was grayish. He nodded at Dunbar and sat down. When everyone was seated, Karp began.

"Mister Walker, my name is Roger Karp, and I'm an assistant district attorney here in New York County. I am about to ask you some questions about the shooting deaths of Angelo Marchione and Randolph Marchione, which occurred between ten-thirty and eleven o'clock on the night of March Twenty-sixth, Nineteen-seventy, at A&A Liquors, located at Madison Avenue and Forty-ninth Street." Karp then introduced everyone in the room—for the record—and told Walker that Leonard would be taking down on the stenotype machine everything that was said.

Then he advised Walker of his right to remain silent, of his right to have a lawyer present. Walker had had these rights read to him at the precinct, but Karp was establishing for the record that Walker was confessing voluntarily, in full knowledge of these rights, and without coercion. It was not enough to find out the truth. If Walker had killed fifty people on a live broadcast of the "Johnny Carson Show" it would still be necessary to go through this ritual before he could be brought to justice.

Karp went on. "Now, Mister Walker, having been advised of your rights, are you willing to tell us what you know about the shooting deaths of Angelo and Randolph Marchione, without a lawyer being present?"

Walker raised his head and tugged at his sparse beard. "I din see no shooting."

At this Slocum gave a disbelieving snort. Karp shot him a sharp look. The detective rolled his eyes and looked away.

"Could we have your full name and address, please," asked Karp. Walker gave it. Speaking his address made him think about the missed mortgage payments, about his family losing their home, about his failure. He started to weep. "Take it easy, Donny . . ." Dunbar began, but Karp cut him off with a gesture of his hand, and said, "Mister Walker, just tell us what you *do* know; that's all we want."

Then the story emerged, Walker speaking in a monotone, broken by sniffling and long silences. Karp let him tell his tale at his own pace, scrupulously avoiding any leading questions. After a while, Walker began to enjoy the confession; here, after all, were four serious, grown men listening attentively to what he had to say. It was a unique experience in his life.

Walker finished his confession by describing how he had dropped the two other men off at the 50th Street subway station. The sound of the stenotype machine echoed his last words, and after a brief silence, Karp said, "Mister Walker, I want you to know that I appreciate you coming forward like this and giving us this information. I also want you to know that while I can't promise that it will have any effect on your own case, I would very much like your help in finding the two men you say were with you on the night of the crime. Are you willing to help us do that?"

"Yeah, sure, but I done already tol you everythin' I know."

"OK, but let's go over some of the details once more. This man you call Stack—you met him at a pool hall near where you live?"

"Yeah, Torry's, on Queens Boulevard."

"More than once, right?"

"Yeah, a couple times."

"And he supplied you with heroin?"

"Yeah, just one hit."

"And he gave you the phony plates for your car?"

"Yeah, the last time I saw him, it was a couple days before the, you know, the robbery."

"And where did he give you these plates?"

"In the parkin' lot outside of Torry's. I open my trunk an he toss 'em in."

"So he had the opportunity to see your real plate numbers?"

"Yeah, I guess."

109 —

"Mister Walker, are you aware that on the morning after the robbery, an unidentified man called the police and said that he had witnessed the crime at A&A Liquors, described your car in some detail, and gave your plate numbers?"

"No, I din. But so what? I already tol you I was there in my car."

Karp paused for effect. "Not the phony plate numbers. The real ones."

It took Walker a long minute to catch on. He jumped to his feet, and for the first time an animated emotion appeared on his face. "That muthafucka! He never . . . he never was gonna . . . that fuckin' lyin' bastard!"

Karp put a hand on Walker's shoulder and eased him back into his chair. Karp believed Walker's story, and thought him to be what he seemed—a patsy with his ass in a sling. He asked, "Mister Walker, do you have any idea who could have made that call?"

"Who! You know damn well who. It hadda be him, that Stack, him or his damn buddy, Willy Lee. Who the fuck else knew my damn plate numbers?"

"You did," said Fred Slocum.

"What! You think I call the cops to turn my own self in?"

"Take it easy, Mister Walker," said Karp, "nobody's implying anything of the kind." He gave Slocum another look.

"But here's our problem, Mister Walker. You say there were two other men involved in the robbery, but all you've given us are two names, without any indication of where we could find these men. Somebody who knew your real plate numbers called the police. But if you were frightened about what you had done, and you wanted to paint yourself as a relatively innocent wheelman and not as the cold-blooded killer of two people, it is at least possible that you could have invented a couple of partners and made that call to make it seem like somebody else was involved in the crime."

Walker looked at Karp as if he were speaking Ukrainian. He turned from one man to another and settled on Sonny Dunbar. Waving his hands, he cried, "I tol you! They don believe me. I bein' set up for this. Damn, Sonny, you gotta tell them. How could I make up some story like that?"

"Donny, it's OK, I believe you. But you gotta give us something. Are you sure neither of these guys ever mentioned where they lived or worked, nothing we could use to find them?"

"Shit, Sonny, I tol you that. I don know nothin' about who he is, where he live. I jus call him at this number he give me an . . ."

"Number? You have a phone number?" shot back Karp.

"Shit, Donny," said Dunbar, smacking the table, "why in the hell didn't you tell me you had the dude's number?"

Karp leaned closer to the bewildered Walker. "Look, this is very important. Can you remember the phone number?"

"Remember? Hell, I jus call it a coupla times. It was . . . eight, five, three or two, or eight one five, somepin like that."

Dunbar rubbed his face and gritted his teeth. Slocum smiled an innocent smile. Karp tapped a pencil on the table. Walker looked like a man trying to remember something. "Shit, I can' recall it. I was readin' it offa this piece of paper he give me on the night . . ."

"What paper? What did you do with it?" snapped Karp.

"I din do nothin' with it. Jus put it in my pocket."

Karp said to Slocum, "Fred, was there a piece of paper with a phone number found on him when you arrested him?"

"Not that I recall. But it's no big thing to check with prisoners' property."

"Could you?"

"No problem, but we're getting our cranks yanked." The red-haired detective got up and left.

Dunbar said, "Donny, if we have a number we can trace where the phone is installed. That means we have a chance to pick up the guy Stack, or the other guy. OK, let's say we find out where he is. You know the guy. Is he gonna give us trouble?"

"Shit, trouble? That dude nothin' *but* trouble. Guy look like a fuckin' schoolteacher, I know he kill somebody like you squash a fly. That other dude, that Willy Lee? A big, strong-lookin' guy, look like he could bust Stack in two? He scared shit of him."

"How do you know?"

"I jus know. I done smell it, man. You go after Stack, you better take a fuckin' tank."

They waited in the little room, tense, for fifteen minutes. Karp sent Leonard out to get the confession typed for Walker's signature. Slocum returned first, with a bemused expression arranged around his cigar.

"So? What did you find?" asked Dunbar.

"Sonuvabitch if it don't check out. There *was* a phone number on a scrap of paper in his pants pocket. I ran it through the phone company. It's registered to a guy named M. Louis, Apartment Five-fifteen, Thirty-six-oh-two Amsterdam."

Dunbar jumped up and headed for the door. "Let's get him."

"Sonny, calm down," said his partner. "Let's think this through."

Dunbar looked narrowly at the other detective. "Don't tell me. You still think it's a scam. Shit, Freddy . . ."

"You're wrong there, kiddo. I'm converted. But look here. One, this is a big collar. We don't want to screw it up. Two, we got a mutt with a handgun and a shotgun, maybe two mutts, come to that, who killed two people in cold blood and then calmly pinned the rap on this kid here. I'm thinking, these guys are smart, not just some street jitterbugs, you know. I mean, let's give it some thought before we go stepping on our jocks."

Dunbar let out his breath in a rush and relaxed against the table. "OK, Freddy, I'm listening. You got a plan?"

When Slocum didn't say anything Karp spoke up. "I do."

The two cops looked at him, surprise showing on both their faces. Karp was surprised himself.

The object of their discussion was at that moment reclining on his couch, dressed in a bathrobe of blue silk with Chinese figures, reading *Forbes*. He liked to read about big deals and the kind of people that the business press in the sixties called "corporate gunslingers." He considered these people kindred spirits. Louis was a calculator rather than a fantasist, but occasionally he let himself imagine what it would be like to move through the Lear-jet world of high finance. He felt ready for a change; he was almost forty, and he did not look forward to cleaning out tills and knocking off payrolls at fifty.

In fact, Louis was quite well-off at this point. For nearly a decade he had been taking in thirty to fifty thousand dollars a year, tax-free, naturally, and without thinking about it very much had stashed it in gold collectors' coins. A quantity of these now sat in the safe deposit vault of a downtown bank. He would have liked to play the go-go market along with everybody else, but wisely decided that his source of income could not bear the scrutiny that a complicated tax return would entail.

But like most men of action, Louis was short on self-knowledge. He increasingly saw himself as an executive, although he utterly lacked the premiere quality of a good executive, which is the ability to choose and inspire good subordinates. Nobody really existed for Mandeville Louis except Mandeville Louis. The rest of humanity was a sort of animated Kleenex, to be used when needed and then thrown away. This was no problem as long as he remained a lone-wolf robber, but it was inevitable that, when he decided to obtain a true accomplice, his choice would fall on someone like Preston Elvis, who was a jackass.

Louis put down his magazine, yawned, arose, stretched, and consulted his gold Rolex, the kind all the corporate gunslingers wore. It was 2:30. DeVonne was due back from the beauty parlor at 4:00. He had time for some work. Louis had a legitimate job, which he felt he needed as a cover for the straight aspects of his life—his car, his apartment, and so on. He worked as a free-lance proofreader for the Claremont Press, a Harlem weekly newspaper and book publisher in the black liberationist vanguard. Louis rather enjoyed mingling with the sincere young people on the paper, although he was, of course, quite indifferent to black political aspirations, radical or otherwise. He enjoyed it because he liked pulling the wool over peoples' eyes; it was another version of pissing on the altar. When the talk ran to revolutionary action and trashing the system, Louis always cautioned against violence, for which reason he was considered something of a Tom.

In his real career, Louis was perfectly oblivious to racial issues. Most of the people he had robbed and killed were white, while all of the people he had killed to cover his tracks were—naturally—black and as close to Louis himself in physical appearance as possible, since there was always the chance of an unexpected witness. He was an equal opportunity murderer.

As Louis sat down at his desk to check galley proofs, this career, and the whole elaborate structure of deception that supported it, came to an abrupt end. The phone rang. Louis picked it up and when he heard and recognized the voice on the line a jolt of pure terror ran through his body. His brow broke out in sweat and his mouth dried up so that he could barely speak.

"Stack? Hey, Stack, you still there?"

"Ahhh ... ckk ... S ... Snowball? Snowball, what you doin'?"

"What I'm doin' is I'm in deep shit. Nobody show at that goddam hotel so I come home. Now there's cops swarmin' all around the front yard. What I spose to tell 'em?"

"Be cool, Donald. You don't tell em nothin', hear? I take care of you."

"But Stack ..."

"Just keep yo lip buttoned, everything gonna be all right."

Louis heard a pounding noise in the background over the phone.

"Stack, they's beatin' on the door. I gotta go open up or they gonna bust it down."

"Donald? Goddamn, Donald, hear me now! I'm talkin' bout yo family now, you hear!"

Louis shouted this into the mouthpiece, but his ear told him that the line had gone dead. He drew a deep breath and struggled for control. He cursed himself for his mistakes. Elvis had screwed up, that was obvious; and Walker had possessed a home to go to, which had broken the pattern of perfect junkie dependence that was at the heart of Louis's strategy.

He got up and went to his closet. No point in sticking around here. The cops would crack Donald Walker in about four minutes flat. Donald still had his phone number, which meant they could trace it to his Amsterdam Avenue apartment. As he dressed, he was already planning his next setup. First of all, Elvis would have to go. That whole move was a mistake. Then, no more phone numbers. He'd have to work out some other system of keeping junkies on ice until he was ready to zap them. In any case, he had plenty of resources. It was time to get out of town for a while; he could get in touch with De-Vonne, leave her to watch the place. The cops would soon give up looking for someone who wasn't there. They had plenty else to do.

By the time he was dressed in slacks, a light sweater, and a raincoat he felt calm again. He pulled his attaché case from under the bed and flipped it open. He took out all the cash and stuffed it in his wallet, then threw a change of clothes on top of the shotgun and the pistol. The pistol! HOLY SHIT! Louis ground his teeth and trembled in a paroxysm of self-contempt. He'd forgotten to ditch the pistol that tied him to the liquor store killings. Damn! He should have given it to Elvis and then wasted the asshole. But who could have figured that Elvis would fuck it all up like this? Weirdly, one of his mother's sayings passed through his mind: "Oh, what a tangled web we weave, when first we practice to deceive."

He shook his head. I'm going batshit, he thought. He closed the attaché case and made for the front door. He decided to go down the fire stairs and ditch the gun in the trash can out back. He went out the door and slammed it behind him.

He turned right toward the fire stairs. A white man in a plaid jacket was leaning against the fire door. Before Louis could register what this meant, a voice behind him said, "Don't move." He snapped his head around and looked into the barrel of Sonny Dunbar's revolver, pointed at his head, three feet away. Then, as he stood frozen, the white man was by his side, he was pushed against the wall, his attaché case was taken, and he was thoroughly frisked. His hands were cuffed behind his back. Dunbar told him he had a warrant for his arrest for murder and read him his rights. He took his right to remain silent seriously. The two detectives got not a single word out of him during the long ride downtown.

Nor did Karp do any better. He was still jazzed up from the excitement of the last hour: the ride to the precinct and the operation of his plan to catch Louis without violence, the positioning of the two detectives by radio, Walker's phone call, and the successful capture of the desperado. His first sight of Mandeville Louis had been a letdown. It was difficult to believe that this calm, slight, almost scholarly looking man could be a cold-blooded murderer. The thought flashed through Karp's mind that a mistake was being made—but then he recalled the guns in the attaché case. The pistol was already on its way to police ballistics to be test-fired.

After Louis had been booked and fingerprinted at Midtown South, and after Walker had identified him as Stack, Karp had him brought to an interrogation room. Karp found the man disturbing, his preternatural calm, something almost reptilian about the way he sat erect in his chair, hands folded on the table, as if waiting for a rabbit to emerge from a hole.

Karp introduced himself, Dunbar, and the stenographer for the record and said, "Mister Louis, I want to ask you some questions concerning the shooting deaths of Angelo Marchione and Randolph Marchione at A&A Liquors, located at Madison Avenue and Forty-ninth Street, which took place on the night of March Twenty-sixth, Nineteen-seventy, between 10:30 and 11:00 P.M. Before I ask you any questions, I want to advise you of your rights. You have the right to remain silent and to refuse to answer any of my questions. Do you understand that?"

"Yes."

"And anything you do or say can and will be used against you in court. Do you understand that?"

"Yes."

"And you have a right to consult a lawyer now, before any

questioning, and to have a lawyer present during any subsequent questioning. If you cannot afford a lawyer, one will be provided free of charge. Do you understand that?"

"Yes."

"Fine. Now, do you wish to make a voluntary statement concerning the shooting deaths I have described?"

"No, I do not. I wish to remain silent and I wish to consult a lawyer at this time."

And that was that. Any information obtained through questioning after such a statement would be tainted. Karp knew it, and obviously Louis knew that Karp knew it. He gave Karp a little smile. Karp tightened his jaw and called the prisoner duty officer to take Louis back to one of the precinct cells.

But after some reflection, Karp felt he had done pretty well. With Walker as a prosecution witness, and if the gun checked out, he felt he had a tight enough case. There was also the chance that Mrs. Kolka had gotten a good enough look at Louis to pick him out of a lineup. As Karp gathered his papers and prepared to return to Centre Street to write up the case, he began to feel happy—champagne-silly happy. He thought, I caught a killer!

But Karp was not the happiest person concerned with this particular case. The happiest person was a prostitute named Violet Buttons. She had checked into Room 10 of the Olympia Hotel with a trick about ten minutes after Preston Elvis had left. As she entered the room her quick eyes spotted the blue plastic bank envelope on the shelf above the sink. In an instant it was buried in her oversized handbag. Twenty minutes later, in a booth in the ladies' room of a cafeteria on Tenth Avenue, she inspected her prize. Cash! Jesus! And what was this? Smack? It couldn't be! But it was. She looked at the bank envelope. Uh-oh, better get shut of this. She took a straight razor out of her bag, reduced the envelope to confetti in seconds, and flushed the pieces away.

She got out her works and shot the stuff into a vein on the top of her foot. Goddamn, she thought, this is fine shit. And free, too. I have died and gone to heaven, she thought. And she was half right.

CHAPTER NINE

Twenty of the best prosecuting attorneys in the Western world sat in Jack Conlin's office for the Homicide Bureau's weekly meeting. It was the next Monday. Karp had been working nonstop on the Marchione case in preparation for this weekly event.

The meetings usually took place on Thursday, but somebody in the mayor's office had scheduled a Bullets softball game with the Bronx DA's office on the previous Thursday, in Yankee Stadium no less, which of course took precedence. The point of these meetings was to allow the assistant DAs to present their cases, and for the other assistant DAs, especially the half dozen or so senior ones, to tear them to shreds. This was done with acid wit and without pity.

Karp sat in the rearmost of two rows of straight chairs that had been set up behind the leather banker's chairs around Conlin's big table. The senior guys sat around the table, with Conlin himself, looking now like a large pink shark, at the head. The man presenting the case would stand or sit by the door at the foot end of the table. This was where Karp would be in a few minutes and present the liquor store murder case, after the bureau got through with chewing up poor Terry Courtney.

Karp was fibrillating with nervous energy. The room was overheated and he was sweating like a pig and hoping it wouldn't show. Every few minutes, he casually wiped the heel of his hand across his face like a squeegee and wiped the collected sweat on his trousers. He thought, I can do this, the case is in my head, I did everything right, it's OK to be nervous, this is just like before a game. Like a game, he thought, grimly, but I never played against Bill Russell.

Courtney was a good lawyer who had come to the bureau six weeks ago from Felony Trial; this was only his second homicide case. He'd won his first and had gotten cocky. Now he was meat.

Courtney felt as he imagined Angel Ramirez, the deceased in this particular case, must have felt, when the 4.3-inch blade wielded by his rival in love, Hector (Kid Benny) Benvenista sliced through his anterior abdominal musculature, inflicting a 2.1-inch perforating wound in the inferior vena cava, causing death by exsanguination and shock at approximately 11:30 P.M. on March 4, 1970 at 78 East 129th Street in New York County in the State of New York.

Angel was dead. Kid Benny had killed him. Courtney knew it. The crowd of witnesses who had observed the deed knew it. God knew it. But Courtney could not *prove* it, in the eyes of the law—and what was vastly more important—to the satisfaction of his colleagues in the Homicide Bureau.

Chuck Walsh and Sean Flaherty, who between them had nearly a half century in the bureau, were now taking turns exposing his incompetence.

"Wait a minute!" said Walsh. "How many witnesses did you say there were?"

"Ah . . . eight or ten."

"Eight or ten? Eight or ten! Which was it? Eight? Or ten? You sure it wasn't fourteen and a half?"

"No . . . ten. It was ten."

"And of these ten, how many did you depose?"

"Um . . . three."

"Three? Good work! What happened to the other seven? Did they die?"

"No, but ah . . . the three, the three that I got statements from, they ah, all agreed, and so I thought . . ."

Flaherty broke in. "You thought! You thought you could cut corners, save yourself a little time, right? But you didn't think, did you, that maybe those other seven people saw something different. That maybe the defense is going to march in with evidence from those other seven people, who happen all to be solid citizens, while your three people turn out to be—surprise, surprise—asshole buddies of the deceased from birth and sworn enemies of the accused. How about that?"

Courtney opened his mouth to speak, or maybe to vomit, such was his expression, but neither words nor bile emerged. He had been caught being sloppy, the unforgivable sin in the Homicide Bureau. It was worse to be sloppy than to make a mistake. But Courtney, in his unthinking zeal, had also made a mistake.

It now turned out that he had botched the most important part of his work: the interview with the accused. Karp noticed, as Courtney stumbled through the close of his presentation, a pronounced tightening of jaws and tapping of fingers around the big table. Flaherty puffed his pipe like a locomotive getting up steam for a mountain run, always a bad sign. At last he removed the pipe and slammed his hand down on the table.

"You said what? What did you ask him?"

"I, ah, asked him if the victim had a knife, too?"

"And what did he answer, dear boy?"

"He said yes."

Flaherty slammed his hand down again. "Jesus! What the hell did you expect him to say, you ninny? Don't you realize you put the idea in his head and that you've established the possibility that he killed Ramirez in self-defense?"

Flaherty threw up his hands in a gesture of disgust and Walsh took over. "Did you establish in the witness statements that the victim was unarmed? Did you at least do that?"

Courtney shook his head, his mouth gaping in shock.

"How about defensive wounds. Did you check with the M.E. report to see if there were any? Were there any wounds or evidence of a fight on the person of the accused?"

Courtney looked from stony face to stony face around the table. Of course, he hadn't done any of these things. He flapped his hands and made inarticulate noises. Nothing like this had happened to him in law school. His brain was numb. He began to think about how nice it would be to have a quiet real estate practice in Rahway.

Walsh turned to Conlin. "Jack, this man is wasting our time. The case stinks."

Conlin nodded. "It does that. Courtney, this preparation is a disgrace to the bureau. More than that, you may have prevented us from trying a dangerous criminal for first degree murder. I'll see you in my office after this meeting. Sit down. Karp, let's hear from you next."

Courtney took his papers in shaking hands and went to a seat in the rearmost row. Karp replaced him at the foot of the table, and opened his notes. He looked out at the faces before him and met Joe Lerner's dark gaze. It was blank and uncommunicative. Although Lerner was the closest thing to a mentor Karp had in the bureau, it was clear that he would not budge to help if Karp floundered.

Karp cleared his throat and began. As he progressed, he became more confident and he did not falter even when the questions began. Chris Conover, Conlin's head crony and the Homicide Bureau's administrative chief, asked, "The two victims, do we know who was killed first?"

"Yes, we do. It was the older man, the store owner."

"How do you know?"

"Because Angelo Marchione was killed with a shotgun at close range in a store full of bottles. There were bits of glass from those bottles and traces of his blood on his son's shoes. I have copies of the police lab reports here."

"OK. Go on."

"The son was shot three times with a .38 caliber Smith & Wesson Airweight, once in the abdomen and twice in the forehead. Any one of the shots would have been fatal."

"Did you check with the M.E.?"

"Yes. I read the transcript and listened to the tape from both autopsies. They check. No problem."

Conover grunted and sat back, waving at Karp to continue.

"The M.E. says he was shot in the abdomen first, at point-blank range. The slug went right through the victim and lodged in the wall of the store. Trajectory evidence, as well as deep embedded glass in the victim's knees shows that he was most likely astride the killer when he was shot."

Karp then proceeded to elucidate the strands of evidence that linked Mandeville Louis to the crime. The police ballistics evidence that connected the gun found in Louis's attaché case—after a duly warranted search—with the slugs that killed Randolph Marchione. His fingerprints on the very cartridge cases that had held the slugs dug out of the victim. The fragments of cloth in the victim's fingernails, that matched the cloth in the suit jacket found—again after a duly warranted search—in Louis's apartment. The fragments of glass, shown to be the same as the kind of glass shattered by the shotgun blast that shattered Angelo Marchione's head, in the trouser cuffs of the same suit. The eyewitness testimony of Mrs. Kolka, who had picked Louis out of a lineup. The testimony of Donald Walker.

When Karp had finished, Walsh said, "Very fancy, Karp. The Walker evidence is the key to the case, as I'm sure you're aware. But tell me, did you promise Walker any leniency in his own case? Does he know about felony murder?"

"He didn't get any promises. The officer who interrogated him first didn't even believe there were any accomplices. I established that in my interview. Let's see, it's right here." Karp read from the transcript of his interview. "OK, I say, 'Mister Walker, as regards your own prosecution for this crime, we will inform the court of your cooperation in the investigation, but I want you to understand before you offer any answers to my questions that I make no promise whatsoever about any case that the District Attorney's Office may make against you. Is that clear.' Then he says, 'yes.' And I say, 'Have any promises in this regard ever been made to you by any member of the District Attorney's Office or any police officer or any other person in authority regarding this case?' And he says, 'No, nobody ain't promised me nothing.' "

There was no comment when Karp finished speaking. I rest my case, he thought. He looked at Lerner, who at last cracked a broad smile. Lerner began to clap and the rest of the members of the bureau joined him in a brief round of applause. As always, Conlin asked for a show of hands on whether the case should be sent to the Grand Jury with a recommendation for indictment. All hands went up. The Grand Jury's decision was largely a formality. On a recommendation over Francis P. Garrahy's signature they would have sent George Washington to trial for the murder of Abe Lincoln.

Then the cases resumed. As Karp sat down, Terry Courtney whispered out of the side of his mouth, "Nice job, Karp. My first one went OK too." This sour remark did nothing to dismay Karp, who was the next thing to floating. But by the end of the meeting, he was considerably brought down.

The trouble was too many cases. The discipline and morale of the bureau, of which the weekly meetings were the living symbol, rested on the assumption that the bureau had the resources to give each case the attention that homicide cases deserved. This was no longer true. New Yorkers were killing each other at a rate four times that of thirty years ago. As the crime rate rose, people clamored for more police. More police they got, but the courts, the prisons, the DA's office did not grow apace.

As the meeting wore along toward noon, Karp noticed that the questions were both less numerous and less sharp. The aging heroes wanted their lunches. Karp realized he was seeing the early stages of what was already rampant in the lower reaches of the system. The house Garrahy had built was rock-solid when each bureau member was handling ten or fifteen cases. Now the caseload was closer to forty. Dry rot was creeping in and the foundations were cracking. Karp knew in his heart he had done as well as he had today because he had only one case to prepare. Could he do the same with forty? Probably not. He thought of what had just happened to Courtney and shuddered. Even worse, he realized that being picked at the beginning of a meeting insured tougher questioning. For him it had been an advantage, since it gave him the chance to show off his brilliant prep. For Courtney, struggling with dozens of cases, it had been a disaster. He felt again the same disquieting sense that he was being manipulated.

That afternoon, around two, Conlin summoned Karp to his office. When Karp knocked and stuck his head in the door Conlin was on the phone, but he waved Karp in and motioned him to take a seat on the couch. Conlin was reclining in his gray-green leather judge's chair, in shirt-sleeves and unbuttoned pinstripe vest. Karp waited while his boss poured charm over the line, punctuated by hearty laughs.

He hung up and turned his chair around to face Karp.

"The county chairman. An asshole, but he's *our* asshole." He smiled deprecatingly. "Politics ... unfortunately, part of the job. Butch, I just wanted to tell you personally what a fine job I think you did on the Marchione thing. This is an important case to me, to the bureau, and while I don't mind telling you that I was a little worried when Joe told me he was handing the prep over to you, I have to say that his confidence was well-placed."

Karp mumbled a thank-you and waited for the other shoe. Bureau chiefs in Homicide did not call junior DA's in for personal congratulations on case preps.

Conlin lifted a La Corona from a walnut humidor on his desk and lit it as he spoke. "You know, I feel that development of young prosecutors is one of the most important things we have to do here. It's good for the bureau and it's good for them. Take a young tiger with a good head, a couple three years in Homicide, hell, there's no limit to where a man like that could go. Tell me, do you know anything about politics?"

"Not much. I was president of my senior class in college. Does that count?"

"Sure it does, sure it does. Stanford, right?"

"Um, Berkeley, actually."

"Right, well, there's an election year coming up. You have any thoughts about that?"

"Nationally? I don't know. With Nixon in there the Republicans ..."

"No, not the national bullshit. I mean here. The DA's office."

"The DA's office?" Karp shrugged. "What's to think? Mr. Garrahy will run and be elected by ninety-eight percent of the vote, as usual."

Conlin regarded the younger man inquiringly through a cloud of cigar smoke. "He's seventy-three. Have you looked at him lately?"

Karp remembered the day at the Bullets' game and what he had seen, and what he had said to Guma and what Guma had answered.

"Yeah, but somehow it's hard to think of the New York District Attorney's Office without the . . . well, without the *DA*. Are you suggesting he might not run?"

Conlin leaned back in the judge's chair and blew a stream of smoke at his high ceiling. "He's been making noises in that direction. The question is, who replaces him if he decides to retire?"

Karp waited. This was obviously the other shoe. Conlin resumed.

"There's what's-his-name, Bill Vierick in the Mayor's Office: lawyer, very big with the liberals; never argued a criminal case as far as I know, but ran the Mayor's Task Force on Criminal Justice. I know he'd like to be DA. Like JFK said about Bobby when he made him attorney general, give him a little legal training before he goes into private practice.

"Then we have Bloom over in the Southern District. Good political connections on the state level, hard charger, ambitious as sin. Rich fucker, too. On the other hand, he comes on like a nun. Our party leaders don't like that, so that could be trouble for Mister Sanford L. Bloom."

"O.K., who else . . . ?" Conlin mused, as if to no one in particular.

My cue, thought Karp. "There's you," he said. And it was true. Jack Conlin would make a fine DA, but Karp could not help resenting the manipulation.

Conlin pursed his lips and drew on his cigar, as if this notion had never occurred to him before. Then he laughed, a short bark. "I guess you do know something about politics, Butch. OK, let me cut out the blarney. I want to be the DA. But not at Phil Garrahy's expense, and not at the expense of splitting the Party vote. I happen to know Vierick has already organized a committee and that the mayor will support him, whether Garrahy runs or not."

"What! Garrahy will blow his doors off. Who gives a damn

who the mayor endorses for DA? The only endorsement worth squat in an open DA race would be the one from Francis P. Garrahy himself."

"Assuming he doesn't run, in which case I can't see him endorsing anyone but me."

Karp did not like the way the conversation was going. He did not care to examine that closely what went on under the hood in the DA's office. As long as it let him get on with putting bad guys in jail, he was content to let others get greasy hands. He was also a little confused about what Conlin wanted of him.

"Yeah, but he is going to run, isn't he? I mean, nobody is telling him not to, right?"

"Of course not. I've been asking him to declare as a candidate at every bureau chief meeting for the past six months. No, he's just being cagey. I think he's feeling his age and wants everybody to tell him he's still the man he used to be, and all."

"Hell, *I'll* tell him that."

Conlin chuckled. "Well, you may get the opportunity some day. Meanwhile, if he doesn't run, and it does come to a primary fight, I'd like to be able to count on your support."

"Uh, sure. I mean, for what it's worth . . ."

"No, don't go undervaluing yourself. You happen to be among the most respected of the younger men in this office. People listen to you. They think you've got a good head on your shoulders." Conlin let go a flashy smile. Karp smiled back. An inane song of the period rattled through his head— "I'm in with the In Crowd, I know what the In Crowd knows." Conlin was looking through some papers on his desk. Karp sensed the meeting was over and got up to leave.

"Oh, couple more things, Butch," Conlin said. He consulted a piece of paper on his desk. "This Marlene Ciampi. You ever work with her?"

"Yeah, some. She's hard to miss."

"The bureau has been getting some pressure about hiring a woman. Abondini's leaving next month, so we've got a slot. What d'you think?"

126 —

"I think she's a great lawyer. Works hard, knows her procedure, plenty of guts."

Conlin grunted. "Yeah, well Phil is a little uneasy. You know how old-fashioned he is. Thinks maybe a woman might have, how did he put it? Sensibilities too delicate for the rough-and-tumble of the Homicide Bureau. What about that?"

Karp barely restrained a giggle. "Ah . . . I think Mr. Garrahy can put his mind at ease in the sensibilities department."

Conlin made a few notes and then turned to Karp again.

"Oh, and on the Marchione case? You'll be happy to learn that our defendant has hired Leonard Sussman."

Karp whistled. If you were a society matron and you found your husband in the rack with the upstairs maid and shot him five times in the head with your pearl-handled .32, you might hire Leonard Sussman to get you off, or if you were a Mafia chieftain and a number of your business associates had died under circumstances so unusual that the police suspected foul play, then you would definitely want Sussman to be your man in court. But Sussman did not work for armed robbers who shot liquor store owners.

"Sussman is doing *pro bono*? Stop the presses!"

"Nope. The little shit is paying regular rates. Where's it coming from, I wonder? What do we know about this Louis guy, anyway?"

"Next to zip. No record, for one thing—that's unusual as hell. No family in the city. Apparently works as a proofreader when he's not shooting. Just a guy who decided to be an armed robber, it looks like. Say, is Sussman going to be any trouble on this case?"

Conlin said with a laugh, "Oh, he's always trouble, some way or another. But, really, we built a great case. It's a lock. I mean, what can he do?"

Which was precisely what Leonard Sussman was wondering at this moment.

Seated across from Mandeville Louis in the small lawyers' meeting room in the Tombs, Sussman radiated the solid confidence that was his great professional tool. What he felt was irrelevant and invisible. He was a silver man: curly silvery hair, pale eyes, silver-rimmed half glasses, silvery-gray pinstriped suit, and silk tie. His skin might have been pale and silvery too, had it not been bronzed by a recent week of skiing in Gstaad.

Sussman was about to become annoyed with his client, something he never did. He considered it bad for business. But, of course, Louis was not part of his usual clientele. He was black, for one thing, and he wasn't frightened, for another. In fact, he was maddeningly confident. Sussman tried again.

"Mister Louis, I seem to be having a great deal of difficulty communicating to you the gravity of your present situation. You're being charged with murder in the first degree. Walker places you at the scene with a loaded shotgun. Another witness also places you at the scene. Your pistol killed one of the victims. I am a very good criminal lawyer, as you know, but I doubt that even I will be able to fix in the mind of a jury the possibility that in the fifteen or so minutes you were gone from the car somebody else killed the Marchiones with your weapons. Yet in spite of the strength of this evidence, you refuse to countenance negotiating a plea to a lesser offence, nor have you been forthcoming in offering me any extenuation, any scrap of . . ."

Louis broke in, saying, "Mister Sussman, I am not going to prison. Not now. Not ever."

Sussman regarded his client coldly. Louis was dressed in a yellow jail uniform too large for his thin frame. His hazel eyes, discomfortingly odd in a black man's face, glittered back at the lawyer from behind round, gold-framed glasses. Sussman felt himself becoming unsettled under this gaze and glanced down at his papers. Rich and recently widowed women did not treat him this way.

"Yes, yes, of course, that's what I'm here for. Now I can of course delay the date to some extent, and I have in fact taken the liberty of entering a number of motions to that effect, but at some time we will undoubtedly have to go to trial, and I can assure you that . . ."

"There will be no trial."

"No trial?"

"That is correct."

Sussman stared at Louis over his half glasses. "Mister Louis, are you, ah, *planning* something?"

"Yes," said Louis.

"Don't you think you should discuss it with your attorney?"

"No, I do not."

"You're being impossibly difficult, Mister Louis."

"Yes. That's why I hired you," said Louis with a cold smile. He rose and knocked on the door for the guard. "Good day, Mister Sussman. See you in court."

Some weeks later Karp was having breakfast at Sam's with V.T. Newbury.

"Anyhow," said Karp, "I love the work, you know, but I'm getting nervous. Conlin makes me nervous. I mean I've always had a lot of respect for the guy, and all, a great lawyer, but this political shit is making everything wacky. I mean, he leaks stuff to the press all the time, stuff about cases that shouldn't get out. But if it makes him look good, there it is on the front page. And, there's cases he won't go to trial on, cases we have good chances to win, but no, he's thinking about the track record. It's got to be a sure thing or he lets them cop to a lesser. This is *homicide* I'm talking about now . . ."

"And Homicide should be above reproach—and immune to the sort of corruption the rest of us are sunk in?"

Newbury finished his soft-boiled egg and dabbed his lips with a napkin. "I think you're learning that the bureau is not King Arthur's Round Table, is that it?"

Karp bridled. "I never expected that."

"Yes you did. But the bureau is made up of human beings. Human beings are fallible, frightened and prone to corruption. 'In Adam's fall, we sinned all.' Conlin wants Garrahy's job; why shouldn't he jerk chains to get it?"

"It isn't right."

"Yes, that's the correct Old Testament position. But look, how long did you expect Homicide to survive as an elite unit when the rest of the system is crumbling like cheese? The cops are rotten, the jails are rotten, the lower courts are rotten: it's got to touch everything—Conlin, Garrahy . . ."

"Never. Not Garrahy."

"No? There are different kinds of corruption, you know. There are sins of omission."

"What are you talking about?"

"Look around you, damn it! The criminal justice system of this city is operated like a third-class whorehouse. It would be a scandal in Venezuela. Not enough prosecutors, not enough office or courtroom space, not enough judges, not enough jails. Police corruption? I see cops wearing clothes and driving cars *I* can't afford and I'm pig rich. And when was the last time you saw Garrahy making a stink about any of that on television or the front page?"

"Hell, V.T., you can't blame the whole bad business on one man."

"No? Who else is there? He doesn't have the clout? The man's got more political power than God Almighty, and as far as I can see he does fuck-all with it."

"Jesus, Newbury, calm down! Would you prefer Jack Conlin in there? Or Bloom?"

Newbury drew a couple of deep breaths and then grinned sheepishly. "God help us! No, I guess it's eight generations of outraged civic virtue. Good government DNA is in my genes. Look, Butch, it's not that I don't respect him, I mean as a person. Sure, who wouldn't, he walks on water. But, I mean, look at the institution. Why hasn't he groomed somebody to take over? Why does he tolerate that total shit, Wharton?"

"How should I know, V.T.? Maybe he doesn't know what's going on . . ."

"Oh, yeah. If only the czar knew how his people suffered, surely he would do something! Did I ever tell you about my Uncle Parker? A crucial event in my young life. Actually he was my great-uncle. Had a big place out in Sag Harbor where I used to spend the summers. I was crazy about that man. He had a room full of toys for all the cousins, and he would actually spend hours, playing with us down on the carpet. He was, I don't know, everything you want your parents to be, but they never are: wise, kind, patient, unbelievably funny. A marvelous man. I was his absolute dog.

"He died when I was fourteen. I cried for a week. They thought I was bonkers—nobody cries in my family. OK, the scene switches to Newbury in college. I'm in American studies. I'm doing my senior thesis on labor organization in West Virginia in the twenties. You ever hear of the Highland Coal War? No? Not many people have. It was a little bit of Vietnam in our own dear land. For three years the Highland Coal Company carried on what amounted to a war of extermination against striking miners, their union, and their families.

"The miners fought back—dynamite, ambushes, sabotage—but Highland Coal had the county and state governments in their pocket and they had a private army of goons who used to whip through the hollows up there on fucking search-and-destroy missions. Finally, they imported blacks as scabs and kept them in locked stockades under unbelievable conditions—practically slavery. That broke the strike, but the hatred those people had—there are even songs about it—'P. C. Highland, you got blood on both your hands. You done starve my children, you done shot down my good man.' And so on. OK, here's the kicker. You know who P. C. Highland was?"

"No, who?"

"My Uncle Parker, that's who! It almost killed me when I found out."

Karp was confused. "So he was a hypocrite; how could you know, you were just a . . ."

"No! He *wasn't* a hypocrite. He hadn't the faintest notion of where his money came from. That's just the point. It was his *responsibility* to know, to know what was being done there in his name."

"And you're saying that Garrahy is like your uncle? That's bullshit, V.T."

Newbury sighed. "O.K. Butch, whatever you say. Maybe the job is getting to me. Maybe I should take my father's advice and go work for Mitchell in Washington." He glanced at his watch. "Hey, I love to linger, but it's getting late."

Both men slid out of the booth and went to the door. It was raining, a fine, warm April rain.

Karp said, "You ever think about a Washington career? God knows, you have the connections."

Newbury looked surprised. "Washington? Oh, it'd be fun for a couple of years, but, I mean New York is . . . where we *live*." He waved his hand in a global gesture to encompass Sam's, Foley Square, Manhattan, the entire great, wet, smelly metropolis. "I mean, we've been here over three hundred years. I'm related to half the people the streets around here are named after."

"Yeah? Like Izzy Chambers and Morris Broadway?"

Newbury laughed. "Up yours, Karp. No, really," he said, gesturing again, "this is our . . . I don't know, our . . . fief."

This conversation disturbed Karp more than he understood at the time. Newbury's attack on Garrahy had irritated him for reasons he could not quite fathom. It was all stuff he knew. Why did he so resist acknowledging it? Then there was Newbury's confidence and security. His fief! Karp's fief was an eight by eight office and a pile of papers, a job, and his brains. Family? His wife had flown off in her own orbit and who knew if she would ever come around again? His mother had died when Karp was a child, his father made corrugated boxes, and was not interested in a son who was not interested in sweating Puerto Ricans to make even more corrugated boxes. His two brothers consisted of annual phone calls.

Karp compared himself to his friends. They all seemed to have a center—aside from work—around which their lives revolved. Guma chased women. Hrcany immersed himself in the social life of his vast Hungarian family. V.T. had noblesse oblige and was engaged to a young lady of suitable background. He looked out of his window at the gray slanting rain over Chinatown. He felt the walls closing in. He shook himself and crumpled up the sheet of yellow legal paper he was writing on and threw it across the room to join half a dozen other sheets in the wastebasket. Two points. He thought, there's someone in my head, but it's not me. He got up and took his jacket off the hook and went out of the office.

There was a greasy snack bar on the ground floor of 100 Centre Street. Guma called it the Cancer Ward. Karp went in and had a cup of coffee and a cheese Danish. Then he stood in the lobby and looked out at the rain. The crowds in the Streets of Calcutta were damp and ill-tempered. The noise level was higher than usual. The fresh smell rain gave to New York's streets did not penetrate here; it stank of damp dishrags.

Without thinking about it, he found himself at the door to his old office bay in the Criminal Courts Bureau. "Hey, look who's slumming," said a voice behind him. He turned and looked into the black eyes of Marlene Ciampi.

"Hi, Champ. No, just wandering." She smiled and made to go past him into the office, but he stopped her by saying, "Say, has Conlin or anybody from Homicide called you yet?"

She frowned. "No—is there any reason why they should?"

"Oh, it's just that I was talking to Jack Conlin the other day and he asked my opinion about you. I think they're thinking about you for Abondini's slot."

Her eyes went wide and her mouth dropped in astonishment.

"What! What did you tell him?"

"What could I tell him? I said you had a great ass and liked to talk dirty."

Marlene jabbed him in the belly with a rigid forefinger. "Goddamit, Karp, are you pulling my pork about this?"

"So to speak. No, really, he asked me and I told him you were a sharp little lawyer . . ."

"Little!" Poke.

"Ouch, Marlene! No, I told him the truth: I said you worked hard, knew what was what, and had plenty of guts. Then he said Garrahy was worried that your sensibilities might be offended by the rough-and-tumble of the Homicide Bureau, and I said he didn't have to worry about that. That's it."

Marlene let out a shriek of delight. "I can't believe it. I'm throwing up. Butch, this is great! Oh, God, what time is it? I'm late for court." She ran two steps down the corridor, then stopped, turned, ran back to Karp, gave him a solid hug and planted a firm kiss on the side of his neck. "Thanks, Butch, I owe you," she said, and then broke loose and ran off, weaving through the crowd like a racehorse breaking for daylight.

Karp stood still and waited for his groin to rejoin the rest of him. He thought, for the first time in many months, no wonder my head's fucked up. I'm horny.

CHAPTER TEN

Conlin said, "Look at that Sussman. That's what you get if you call Central Casting and order somebody to play a lawyer. Looks like he could blow Perry Mason out of the box. It's a long way from Bensonhurst for Lennie Sussman."

Conlin said this softly to Karp as the two men waited at the prosecution table for the trial of Mandeville Louis to begin. The courtroom was crowded. It was an important case, and the press was there in some strength. It was in fact why Conlin was there. Nothing like a nice homicide conviction at primary time.

Nearly six months had passed from the time Louis had been captured to the day the case had been called. It had taken another week to select the jury, with each side questioning, challenging, selecting the veniremen, throwing out those who might lean the wrong way, according to an arcane set of rules, which had as little to do with the desire to see justice triumph as the choosing of a team lineup had with the desire of a coach to see a good game. Winning counted, nothing else.

So there they sat, twelve citizens of Fun City, nine men, three women, a little whiter than a stratified random sample of New Yorkers, but reasonably representative. Some were pissed off at missing work, but most were mildly excited to be doing in reality—so they naively supposed—what they had read about in high-school civics texts, and seen represented on television shows. None of them were lawyers; none of them had ever been on a jury before.

Karp did look at Sussman. The defense attorney was arranging papers from his briefcase precisely, like a fortune-teller setting out the Tarot deck. A clean yellow legal pad and sharpened pencils were on the long table in front of him. He observed Karp staring at him and nodded pleasantly. Karp nodded back. They were gentlemen about their serious work. Conlin was right; it was a long way from Bensonhurst for Lennie, a long way from Calcutta for Karp.

At 9:05, Judge Frederick Braker entered the courtroom. He was sixty-eight, frail and bent with scoliosis under the shelter of his black robes. His eyes were bright blue, his nose long and sharp, his forehead domed and running back into close-cropped silvery hair. He still had—as he would say himself, if you asked him—all his marbles.

All rose. All sat. Braker discussed some details of the court calendar with the lawyers, and then two guards escorted Mandeville Louis into the courtroom and delivered him to the chair next to Sussman's. Karp was startled by the change in Louis's demeanor. He was clearly distraught. He kept removing and replacing his glasses and plucking at his yellow jumpsuit. He swept his head from side to side rapidly, as if searching the room for an enemy. His eyes were bulging, and every few seconds his tongue would protrude for a long, unnatural swipe at his lips.

Karp nudged Conlin, and whispered. "Jack, catch the defendant. This guy was an ice cube the last time I saw him. Now he looks like a basket case."

Conlin glanced over. "It happens sometimes. Some guys, it takes a while for the penny to drop—that he's really in a courtroom looking at Murder One."

Braker cleared his throat. "Are the People ready, Mr. Conlin?"

"Ready, Your Honor."

"Is the defendant ready?"

Sussman rose, removed his half-glasses, looked carefully at each member of the jury and then at the judge. He was not going to be tricked into a careless admission. "Ready, Your Honor."

136 —

"Then please begin, Mister Conlin."

Conlin rose gracefully, his suit jacket already neatly buttoned, and strode into the well of the court to face the jury. He met each of twelve pairs of eyes.

"Good morning," he said. "May it please this Honorable Court, Mister Justice Braker, Mister Sussman, Mister Karp, Mister Foreman, and members of the jury.

"At this point in the trial, as the assistant district attorney in charge of presenting the evidence in this case on behalf of the People of the State of New York, the law imposes on me the duty of making an opening statement. Its purpose is to outline for you what the People expect to prove by way of the evidence in this case. Now, you should know that there is no corresponding duty for the defense." He gestured casually toward Sussman's table. "They may make an opening or they may not, as they see fit."

Conlin paused and moved closer to the jury box, almost belly up to the rail. He resumed, in his rich baritone, a little more intensely. "You may consider this opening as a preview of what we plan to present as evidence, like the table of contents of a book, so that you can follow the testimony more easily.

"Ladies and gentlemen of the jury, the People will prove that this man," (here he pivoted sharply, and pointed the classic accusing finger directly at Louis) "this man, the defendant, Mandeville Louis, during the night of March Twenty-sixth of this year, while committing an armed robbery of A&A Liquors, in Manhattan, at 423 Madison Avenue, brutally and callously snuffed out the life of the proprietor, Angelo Marchione, by shooting him in the head with a sawed-off shotgun."

Karp watched in fascination, taking professional note of the way Conlin held himself, the way he modulated and pitched his voice. This was the reality, worth twenty years of law-school lectures. But as Conlin launched into a gripping description of how Randy Marchione had been done to death, Karp was distracted by a whining sound, a low "uh-heh, uh-heh, uh-heh" like a child getting set to throw a tantrum, from the direction of the defense table. He turned his head and observed Louis bouncing up and down in his seat. The defendant held his arms bent at the elbow, rigid, his hands like blades, moving them in a chopping motion in time with each bounce.

The jury was distracted from Conlin's speech. Conlin himself stopped talking and turned around, fury and confusion on his face. All eyes were on Mandeville Louis. Sussman plucked at his sleeve; Louis yanked his arm away and rose to his feet, jerking like a puppet. His glasses hung askew from one earpiece, his mouth gaped wide and from it now came a dribble of saliva and a loud inarticulate wail.

The judge tapped his gavel. The wail grew louder, reached a crescendo and stopped. A confused babble from the spectators; more banging of the gavel. Louis pointed a finger at the judge. "You hurt my momma," he shrieked, and with that he overturned the heavy defense table, climbed over it and jumped the rail. The two court officers were stunned; in the seconds it took them to react, Louis had cleared the well of the court and thrown himself at the judge's high presidium, which he attempted to scale like a commando on an obstacle course. A woman began screaming. A man yelled, "Stop him! Stop him!"

Judge Braker had seen many odd things during his forty years on the bench, but these barely prepared him for the sight of a foam-flecked, raving lunatic face heaving over the cliff-edge of his domain. "Ah get you, ah get you, you hurt mah momma," said Louis, with accompanying groans and shrieks. The judge rolled his chair away as far as he could, and prepared to defend himself with his gavel, returning that symbolic instrument, for perhaps the first time in six hundred years, to its literal role as the defender of the physical security of the judiciary.

Fortunately, he did not have to defend himself against the defendant. To his relief, the grotesque face and clutching hands were yanked away. Two court officers and a police officer fell on Louis, cuffed his hands and his ankles, and carried him feet first through the door to the holding pen.

Judge Braker wiped his face with his handkerchief and

waited for the unaccustomed, but not entirely unwelcome, flood of adrenaline to dissipate from his system. The murmurs in the courtroom died away. "Mister Conlin," he said wryly, "it appears to me that your opening statement has upset the defendant." Conlin said nothing. What could he say?

The judge turned to the jury. "Ladies and gentlemen, I am going to adjourn this court for a few moments. In the meantime, I ask that you not discuss what you have just witnessed among yourselves, and that you do not draw any conclusions from it." To the lawyers he said, "I would like to see all counsel in my chambers—right now."

In Braker's chambers it was neat Chivas all around, except for Karp, who declined. Conlin was wary and silent, Sussman looked genuinely stunned, Braker looked exhausted as he knocked down his first belt in a single gulp, and poured himself another.

Sussman said, "Fred, I honestly had no idea . . . I mean, the man gave no indication . . ."

Braker smiled. "Relax, Lennie, nobody thinks you're putting on an act. Everybody knows it's not your style. But, we obviously . . ."

Sussman nodded vigorously. "Obviously, I will move to declare him unfit to stand trial."

The judge choked on a swallow of his Scotch, recovered, gave Sussman a bleak look. "No shit, Lennie, no shit." He turned to Conlin. "No objection from the People?" Conlin seemed about to say something, then shook his head. "Then I will have the orders drawn up and send him to Bellevue." Braker sat back in his chair with a sigh. "See you in court, gentlemen."

"Jack," said Karp, "didn't anything strike you as odd about that scene?" Conlin and Karp were walking in the corridor toward the bureau offices after the dismissal of the jury.

"Odd? Yeah, I guess it would strike me as odd when a defendant goes off his nut and attacks the judge. What the hell are you talking about, odd?"

"No, no, not what happened—I mean the details. Did you spot that Louis sort of stopped fighting when the court officers had him? I always thought that maniacs—I don't know— fought like maniacs. None of the officers even had their hair mussed."

Conlin snorted. "Hey, how should I know? Am I a shrink?"

"And another thing. His glasses. When he threw over the table they were hanging off his face. When the guards carried him out he had them in his hand. That's what I mean by odd. Protecting eyeglasses is not something you expect a psychotic to do."

"What are you getting at? You think he pulled a scam on us?"

"It's a possibility."

Conlin made a contemptuous noise. "Boy, have you got a lot to learn! Listen, forensic psychiatry is *the* biggest tar pit in this business. Go near it, and you get dirty." He started to walk away.

"But . . ."

"No buts, Karp. Hey, don't you think I'm pissed off? This was a perfect trial—did you see the press in the courtroom? Now we'll be lucky to get three inches of ink back by the car ads. But there's fuck-all we can do now. They'll examine him at Bellevue, they'll give us their report. Then we'll know where we stand. Meanwhile, we've got other things to do."

He left Karp alone in the hallway, confused, feeling like a fool, clutching his meticulously prepared case file, now trans- formed by the morning's events into so much scrap paper.

He still couldn't believe it. He thought, this asshole walks into a store, heavily armed, kills two people in cold blood, throws a patently phony crazy fit in court, and walks away from his trial. Karp knew that delay almost always favored the defense, and he was pretty sure Louis knew it too. Once again Karp thought about how society in its happy idiocy continued to believe that murderers would play the game by the rules, and assist in their own conviction. He also thought about the calm and rational Louis he had met in the Tombs, the man who knew his rights. There was no way that person could have become the flaming lunatic of the courtroom except by way of the underworld equivalent of the Actors' Studio. But Karp reckoned without the marvelous explanatory power of modern psychiatry.

Dr. Edmund Stone, plump, balding, owlish, thirty-three, a second year resident in psychiatry at Bellevue Hospital, was dictating his initial report on Mandeville Louis. Stone found court interviews an unpleasant task. They made it necessary for him to spend time in the presence of crazy people, whom he detested. Stone had not become a psychiatrist to talk to crazy people. That was better left to Freudians and other nincompoops. Stone had become a psychiatrist because that was the only way they would let him give experimental drugs to human beings.

"Patient is thirty-eight-year-old Negro male, referred to Bellevue as a result of a violent outburst in court during his trial for murder," Stone said to his Dictaphone. "I have had one thirty-minute consultation with patient, and this was patient's first consultation with a psychiatrist since being admitted to hospital yesterday."

This interview, Dr. Stone reflected, had been more than usually unpleasant. Louis was black, in the first place, and violent. He had thrown a plastic chair across the office, causing in Dr. Stone a disturbing and unprofessional rush of fear. Dr. Stone was not prejudiced. He considered himself a liberal, in that he believed that when black people were violent and committed crimes it was not really their fault. Nothing, in fact, was anybody's fault. Behavior, so Dr. Stone believed, was merely the result of differences in the flavor of the rich soup that everyone kept in the cauldron on top of their neck. One flavor was Albert Schweitzer, another was Jack the Ripper. When he met a violent black person like Mandeville Louis, something which, as a psychiatric resident at Bellevue, he could hardly avoid, Dr. Stone always thought how wonderful it would be if such people could be given to science, for experimental purposes, drugs or implants or surgical procedures, so we could at last discover the real causes of violence and antisocial behavior, and cure them, and so people like Dr. Stone could walk the streets without fear.

Dr. Stone pulled himself away from these thoughts, and from his perpetual fantasy that one day he would be the scientist to discover the secret of the soup, and resumed his dictation.

"Psychiatric nurses on patient's hall state patient has been calm. They state patient has been generally lucid, but with three recorded episodes of incoherent shouting, with delusional aspects. On these occasions patient received standard dose of one hundred milligrams of Thorazine, i.m. Response to this medication normal and satisfactory.

"When I first entered the consulting room, patient was seated and appeared calm. I introduced myself but patient did not respond. I asked him if he knew why he was in hospital. Patient sighed and nodded his head. I asked him if he remembered what had transpired in the courtroom. At the word 'courtroom' the patient leaped to his feet, shouted 'No!' and began to pace the room. Affect agitated and fearful. He began to mumble something about 'someone telling him to do it' and the judge 'trying to get his momma.' Patient then became violent and threw his chair at the wall. This episode similar to those observed by ward nurses.

"Violent episode lasted about three minutes, after which patient appeared confused, disoriented, and subdued. He picked up chair and sat in it when asked to. Patient responded well to reality-testing questions: name, current date, present location, common facts. On questioning, patient gave lucid responses as to subjective state during 'seizure.' He believes something is taking control of his body against his will. He says he 'feels it coming' but is powerless to stop it.

"General impressions: Patient appears to be suffering from some acute, episodic, delusional syndrome associated with courtroom proceedings. During these episodes, patient is uncontrollably violent. After them, he appears confused and states that he lacks all recollection of what occurred during the episodes. Recommend patient be retained for further observation. Referred case to Doctor Werner."

Dr. Stone flipped off his Dictaphone. He picked up Louis's case file and wrote out a medication order for a daily dose of 400 mg. of Thorazine, orally, four times a day. That should hold the little bastard, he thought.

Dr. Werner, unlike Dr. Stone, was delighted to have Mandeville Louis as a patient. Unlike Dr. Stone, Dr. Werner was not just passing through forensic psychiatry on the way to the Nobel Prize for Physiology and Medicine. The study of the criminal mind was his whole life. Dr. Werner was a portly man in late and comfortable middle age, heavy of jowl, beetled of brow. He wore black horn-rims and a white coat over his vest, which sported a gold watch chain and a Phi Beta Kappa key. Although born and raised in the Bronx, Werner cultivated a middle-European manner. When he spoke on a professional matter, for example, he might occasionally look up to the ceiling and wave his hand as if hard-pressed to ferret out, from among his many languages, the correct English idiom.

As he read Dr. Stone's report, Dr. Werner became increasingly excited. The purity of the reaction! Here was a man whose insanity was triggered exclusively by the prospect of trial and punishment. Louis was a living representation of everything Werner thought was wrong with the way society treated criminals. It was perfectly clear to him that criminals, especially violent ones, were mentally ill. Take such a person and place him in an environment in which everyone assumed he was mentally competent—in, say a courtroom—and the mental disease could not help but get worse. Dr. Werner had observed the most extreme form of this reaction once before, in a rapist named Ganser, and had written a paper about it. Now, to his delight, he was observing the Ganser syndrome once again, in Mandeville Louis. He regarded it as a confirmation of his theory.

Dr. Werner continued to be delighted when he met Louis in person. In an interview he set up the following day, Louis was intelligent and articulate about his mental and emotional states. In this he resembled the people seen by Dr. Werner's Park Avenue colleagues more than he did the typical rubbish of the Bellevue criminal ward. All Dr. Werner had to do was to hint at some aspect of the Ganser syndrome and in a short while Louis would confirm it in extravagant and inventive detail. Dr. Werner saw a major journal article developing.

Louis was even more delighted with Dr. Werner. He had studied forensic psychiatry as he had the Bible in his father's house, as an aid to exculpation, his abiding and lifelong interest. Becoming an exemplar of Ganser's syndrome was in fact much easier than accepting Jesus as your personal savior. For starters, you didn't have to kneel and spend a lot of time praying. Also, those church ladies, some of them, were pretty sharp, and it took a bit of doing to jerk them around to the proper Christian forgiveness. Werner, on the other hand, did half the work for you.

As Louis spun out the fantasy of his mental incompetence, his mind drifted. It was pleasant in Bellevue Hospital, far more so than the Tombs. It was less noisy and the food was better. As a violent patient under observation, he had a room of his own. He expected they would send him to Matteawan for a while, and he didn't mind that either. As a mental patient, he had better access to the phone, for example. He had already called DeVonne Carter and got her to stay in his apartment, so the place wouldn't get ripped off while he was away. He would lay low in Matteawan for a while, let the case get stale. Maybe something would happen to the witnesses. He made a mental note: in a couple of weeks, maybe call up old Elvis. He'll be anxious to get back on my good side after the way he fucked up his delivery.

Louis figured he had experienced an unusual run of good luck during his years as a robber and was not particularly surprised that he had at last been caught. Now it seemed his luck had changed back. How else could you account for falling into the care of such a perfect asshole as Dr. Milton C. Werner?

When Karp had finished reading Dr. Werner's report on Mandeville Louis, he was almost nauseated with fury. He called Conlin.

"Jack, have you read this incredible bullshit they sent us on Louis?"

"Yeah, what about it?"

"What about it? What about it? It sucks, that's what! They, this Werner character, they want to send him to Matteawan until he's competent to stand trial. The guy's a fraud, him and the shrink both."

"Karp, I've explained to you about Bellevue. What do you expect me to do?"

"Fight the report, that's what. Jack, this guy is gaming the system, he's malingering. We can't let him get away with it."

"He's off the streets, Butch."

"Until when? Hey, they do some marvelous cures up in Matteawan. One of our witnesses is seventy-six. The other one is a junkie who's probably going up for three-to-five. What if somebody knifes him in prison? His porch light is a little dim in the first place. Give him a year or two and he won't remember shit, and Sussman will eat him up on the stand. Come on, Jack, this bastard is setting himself up to stale the case and walk."

Karp listened to Conlin breathe on the line for a few moments. "Butch, let me tell you straight out, I'm not going to get caught in a pissing contest with Bellevue on this case. It's not worth it to the bureau."

"Why not? Look, Jack, we can win on this. I got the transcript of the *voir dire* here. Louis was participating in his own defense like a son of a bitch on practically every page. We can blow Werner away in two minutes on the stand. Did you read this crap he wrote? Ganser syndrome, my ass! Listen to this, on page three: 'Mister Louis shows all the signs of sanity, because, ironically, he is generally sane.' Get that 'ironically?' And it gets worse.

Karp continued, " 'However, the defendant suffers from delusional constellation of pathogenic paranoia arising from his fear of impending imprisonment. Given the proper stimulus, the defendant invariably exhibits psychotic behavior. In the present case this stimulus may be seen to be a courtroom during a trial. Mister Louis can be expected to maintain appropriate affect and rational behavior absent this stimulus.'

"Jesus, Jack, this is like, like a criminal saying we can't incarcerate him because he suffers from claustrophobia. This asshole is saying that Louis will never be competent to stand trial because he goes crazy when we try him. No judge in the world will fall for that."

Conlin sighed. "You're wrong there, Butch. No judge is going to take on Werner within his field. It ain't done."

"Then let's get another shrink to say that all this Ganser business is bullshit."

"Uh-uh. Butch, it's not just Louis. I'm not, the bureau is not, taking on the mental health establishment to nail one scumbag. We've got thousands of psycho reports every year. There's one for just about every other damn homicide. You got any idea of how badly they could fuck up the criminal justice system if they thought we were second-guessing their professional expertise? They'd go batshit. And the bastard is black— that's the cherry on top. Can you see the papers? DA's office persecutes poor mentally ill nigger, hospital administrators fight to get underprivileged shithead the treatment he needs. No thank you!"

Conlin's voice had turned loud and gravelly, a sign the bully in him had emerged and the courtly and distinguished public servant had taken a hike. Karp realized there was no way Conlin was going to court negative publicity while he still entertained the notion of running for DA. Karp thought of his Polish lancers picture. Time to cut and run, he thought. Hey, great, I'm getting corrupt.

"Fine, OK Jack, whatever you say. You want the case file back?"

"Nah, just give it to my girl. Hey, Butch chin up now— there'll be other cases."

After Karp had hung up, he sat in a frozen rage for about twenty seconds, then flung Werner's report as hard as he could at his open window. It sailed out into the warm spring air and fluttered down on to Foley Square, where it was snatched up by a passing bag lady. At last, she thought, my message from God.

Karp grabbed up the Marchione murder case file and stormed out of his office. As usual when he was angry—which occurred more and more often recently—he had to move.

Maybe I'll run over to the East Side, to Yonah Schimmel's and get a kashe knish. I haven't had a kashe knish in months—no wonder I'm depressed.

He was about to trot down the stairs when on impulse he stuck his head through the door of an office, which had been recently constructed out of painted plywood, in what used to be waste space in the hallway past the fire stairs. It was Marlene Ciampi's, and she was in, sitting behind her desk, frowning and answering *coram nobis* petitions. She had been in Homicide a month.

"Champ, you want a kashe knish? I got to get out of here."

"God, that's the best offer I've had in weeks. I'll give you some money." She reached into a desk drawer for her handbag.

"Hell, no. My treat. Don't you love those petitions?"

"Yes, indeedy. I was just thinking that I gave up the opportunity to be a plumber in a Tijuana whorehouse to come to work in the New York DA's office and sort through this garbage."

"A plumber?"

"A figure of speech. That's what they call the girl who does the stuff that nobody else will touch for any amount of money."

"Champ, how do you know all this shit?"

She gave him an evil grin. "It's my Ivy League background. So what's with you? Getting any?"

Karp laughed. "Only up the ass. Conlin just put it to me."

He related the story of Louis's trial and the Werner report.

"Poor Butch! I always thought our fearless leader was just a tiny bit of a slime ball. However, things will be different when I run the bureau, which I will not get to do if we sit here bullshitting all day. I promised myself that if I got through two more of these, I would treat myself to a cigarette and a trip to the ladies' room for a nice pee and, perhaps, a vomit."

"See you, Marlene."

"Knish me, big boy."

Karp left her office and was about to go down the stairs when he realized he was still holding the Louis case file. He walked back to the big room where the Homicide clerk kept the bureau's files. The clerk, a largish black woman of immense civil service seniority, was sitting at her desk, and Karp dropped the folder like a dead rat in front of her.

"Wrap that in plastic, please, and refrigerate it," he said.

"Why, what's wrong with it?"

A light went off in Karp's head. "What's wrong with it? Cora, it's just missing one little detail. Have you got a red pen?"

She rummaged in her desk and pulled out a red ballpoint. "That do?"

"No, something bigger."

"I got a Magic Marker."

"Great, let's have it."

Karp had realized that there was a way to scam Louis's scam. The criminal had read the system too well. He knew that delay worked in his favor because the system was so overloaded that there was no continuity. Judges changed, prosecutors changed. He expected that when he came out of Matteawan in six or eight months, "cured," he would face a cast of characters for whom his case was just another unit to move along the assembly line, people who would be more than willing to let a poor sick man from a mental institution cop a plea to a lesser crime than murder in the first degree. Karp thought, you scumbag, nice try, but no cigar.

He opened the file. On the first page he wrote, for all future prosecutors to see, in letters three inches high: "CALL KARP— ACCEPT NO LESSER PLEA!"

CHAPTER ELEVEN

So far, so good, was what Mandeville Louis thought, upon waking up in his little room in the Matteawan State Hospital for the Criminally Insane. They put him in a private room because he was a potentially violent case, which was fine with Louis. He figured he might have to stay here for six months, let things cool down, maybe see what could be done about fixing the witnesses. Six months—certainly not more; then a change of scene, permanently. He figured he was washed up in New York. The cops, the system, had his name, and since his way of life depended on complete anonymity, it followed that he had to get out of town and change his identity. He had no desire to be known as a criminal, to be rounded up whenever there was an armed robbery, to have cops intruding on his private life. He did not regret having to leave. Hell, he had had a damn good run anyhow. But he was not going to go to prison.

Louis lay with his hands behind his head and thought about places to go. He also tried out new names. Maurice Pemberton of Los Angeles. Lewis Pemberton. Forrest Stanton. Of Detroit. Of Philadelphia. Of D.C. Louis smiled. In his confinement, he was beginning to feel liberated. He thought, that's why I got into trouble. I was getting in a rut. No more.

He heard the key turn in the lock. He put his glasses on and sat up. The door opened and a big, beefy male ward nurse filled the doorway. He was carrying a tray filled with little white paper cups.

"Medication," he said. He had a farmer's face, decorated

with pockmarks. Louis gave his most winning smile, and got a cold stare back. "What is it?" he asked.

"Just take it, huh."

Louis swallowed the spoonful of red liquid.

Later he went to the dining room and had breakfast. He observed his fellow inmates. They did not look particularly crazy. He suspected a fair proportion of them were pulling the same sort of scam he was to get off some crime. In all, a better class of people than you might expect in a loony bin. Nobody screaming or jerking off, like you read about. Everybody nice and calm, he thought as he looked around the room. He felt calm himself. He was sure everything was going to be just fine.

After breakfast, he found himself in the dayroom, although he did not remember walking there. A large television set was on in one corner, and vinyl couches were grouped around it, all occupied by men in bathrobes. They watched the gray flicker, their eyes dull, their faces slack—soap operas and situation comedies. Nobody laughed.

Louis watched, too. There seemed no reason not to, although he rarely had watched television on the outside. He noticed the man next to him was urinating on the floor, the pool slowly spreading toward Louis's foot. He got up.

He found himself walking across the dayroom to the terrace. Two male nurses stood talking near the door to the terrace. Louis thought he should tell them about the man peeing on the floor, but when he got to them it didn't seem that important. He went out on the terrace, which was furnished with steel and plastic chairs in primary colors.

He sat down and faced the sun, which was full and warm. An elderly white man with scarlet rashes all over his face sat down in a chair across from Louis. He stared at Louis for a moment and then put his face through an elaborate grimace, eyes screwed up, tongue thickly protruding. He smiled at Louis, as if nothing odd had passed.

"You're new here?"

"Yes, this week."

"I've been here for months and months. I'm the oldest inhabitant." Again he let loose a spectacular grimace.

Louis wanted to ask why the man was making faces. Then he remembered he was in a booby hatch. A ripple of discomfort passed across his mind, but soon faded.

"I killed them, you know," the Oldest Inhabitant said. "But it wasn't my fault." Another grimace. Louis thought the man was doing a good imitation of a crazy person. He recalled doing a very similar thing with his face in Judge Braker's courtroom. In fact, the grimaces had nothing to do with the man's mental state. They were the result of a condition called tardive dyskinesia, one of the unhappy side effects of fifteen years of maximum dosages of Thorazine. Thorazine gave quiet wards to the people who ran mental hospitals. It gave the people in the wards blotched faces, facial spasms, tremors, incontinence, and massive deterioration of just those portions of the brain that distinguish us all from the turtles. Also impotence, not that people with tardive dyskinesia got a lot of nooky.

"I had to," said the man. "Doris, Jennifer, and little Edgar, and the maid. It was the Holy Ghost. It didn't say anything about the maid. You understand, I wouldn't have done anything to the maid if she had stopped yelling. But she wouldn't, and I couldn't hear the Voice. So what could I do?"

Louis nodded agreeably, and said that no, there was nothing he could have done.

"I have been washed in the Blood of the Lamb, did you know that?" said the elderly man. "The Holy Ghost told me, I should wash them in the Blood of the Lamb, too, Doris, Jennifer, and little Edgar. But afterwards, not the maid." He cocked his ear as if listening to a distant sound. Grimace. Smile. "Thank you, thank you very much. Thank you."

Part of Louis wanted to get up and walk away from this nut, and another part of him wanted to invite the nut for a walk, and beat his brains out with a rock. But these parts of Louis were separated from the part of Louis that actually did things by the thick, pleasant buffer of the psychoactive drug.

Then it was noon, and time for more of the red liquid. Then it was evening, and tucking-in time and more medication. Then it was tomorrow. And the next day. On Thursday, Louis saw the psychiatrist, Dr. Ghope.

"How are you feeling?" Dr. Ghope wanted to know. Actually, Dr. Ghope had a pretty good idea of how Louis was feeling, since it was he who prescribed the Thorazine. Dr. Ghope did not like trouble. When planning his medical career, years ago in his native Bangladesh, he never imagined himself in charge of a ward full of homicidal maniacs. He had specialized in psychiatry—a field of medicine his young nation needed about as much as it needed fashion models—so that upon finishing his studies, he could emigrate to the United States, to New York, and listen to the troubles of wealthy matrons at one hundred dollars an hour.

But it had not worked out that way for Dr. Ghope. There was some difficulty about his diploma, and more difficulty about his license to practice. He had assiduously sought out the correct person to bribe, but had been unsuccessful, probably because, so he believed, of his problems with idiomatic English.

He felt himself lucky to have landed this job. It was hardly any work at all, consisting mainly of regular interviews with patients who were either perfectly sane or incurably crazy. His colleagues were largely drawn from the subcontinent or the various corners of the developing world, so he did not feel isolated, as he might otherwise have in the upstate backwater in which the mental hospital was situated.

Every so often, Dr. Ghope would meet with several of his colleagues to decide if any of the crazy people had become sane. How this could have happened as a result of weekly interviews with a psychiatrist who barely spoke English and massive doses of tranquilizers was a question beyond the theoretical grasp of Dr. Ghope. But lacking theory, Dr. Ghope had developed a technique. Upon arrival, each new patient would be slammed with a dose of Thorazine, the chemical equivalent of the maul that slaughterhouse workers use to drop steers. Thereafter, the dose would gradually be reduced. If the patient did not show any obvious signs of mental disturbance during his interviews with the psychiatrist during a certain period, he would be pronounced cured, and ready to rejoin society. It was a simple technique, but effective. It had earned him the nickname "Dr. Dope" throughout every level of the hospital.

The period necessary to obtain a cure varied with the number of intakes from the outside. The more people sent in from the courts, the more people became sane. Dr. Ghope and his colleagues did not want crowded wards, which meant trouble, budget problems, and more work. The only restriction on this system was the notoriety of the patient. They knew better than to let an infamous ax murderer out on the street while the memory of the crime was still fresh. They did this as infrequently as they could, but after all, they were only human. In short, the hospital was part of the criminal justice system.

Dr. Ghope consulted Louis's case file. He read what Dr. Werner had written. It was always a pleasure to read Dr. Werner's notes. Such a learned man! And his referrals seemed never to give much trouble. He, Ghope, had cured so many of them. Dr. Ghope looked across his desk at the thin, yellowish-skinned man slumped in the plastic chair. He certainly didn't look violent now. Perhaps he would be an easy cure.

"How are you feeling?" he asked again.

Louis raised his eyes. "Feel fine. Sleepy."

"Excellent! Well, let us see. Mandeville, your name is? What an unusual name! Yes, indeed. Well, Mandeville, have you experienced any delusions this week? Have you acted out?"

"Wha'?"

"Excellent. First-rate! Any problems with your medication?"

"Medi'shum."

"Oh, very good. Very good, indeed. Well, Mandeville, you seem to be progressing splendidly. Steady progress is our rule here, as you shall find." Dr. Ghope made some notes with his fountain pen, capped the pen, replaced it in the breast pocket of his white lab coat and closed the folder. "I will see you next Thursday. Until then, please do continue your excellent progress," he said, and rang the buzzer for the nurse to come and lead Louis away.

Louis was in the Arts and Crafts room, coiling a clay candy dish, trying to remember what he had to do that was important. His dosage had been reduced over the last few months, but he still felt like there was a concrete block tied to his higher mental functions. Louis was extremely sensitive to drugs, which was why he had never used any himself on the outside; and of course nobody paid enough attention to him on the inside to find this out. Had he not met Fallon he might have continued inexorably declining into carrothood, and so truly have reached that state—for which the hospital had been designed—of not being a danger to himself or others.

He stopped coiling the clay and glanced idly around the big, light-filled room. Most of the inmates were busy with clay or rubber band and wooden toy boats. In the corner, by the window, one man was painting at a large easel. Louis wandered over to see what he was doing.

"Holy shit!" said Louis, when he saw the painting.

"Ah, a connoisseur," said the man, with a friendly smile. He was a big, soft, moon-faced man, pasty of complexion, with a hooked nose, thick moist lips, longish, thinning black hair and a fringe of dark beard, like Henry VIII.

He held out a large, long-fingered hand, blackened with paint. "Robert Fallon," he said. Louis shook the hand and said his name. He could not take his eyes off the painting. Its subject was a scene of sadistic pornography brilliantly executed, explicit, and suggestive at the same time. It was as full a realization of the lower reaches of the human spirit as Rembrandt or Monet were of the higher.

Louis watched Fallon paint for a while. Fallon didn't mind. He enjoyed adulation. At one time Fallon was considered one of the most promising artists of his generation. Were it not for his unfortunate desire to rape, murder, and mutilate little girls—a desire to which he had given full vent some six years before in the art colony of Millbrook, New York—he might have continued as an ornament of the Manhattan salons forever. He had got himself put into Matteawan, after being arrested, by his version of the same scam Louis had used. He had just gone semi-catatonic and refused to admit that he remembered anything at all about the four little girls, the sink in the basement, the plastic bags, and the box of blood-clotted industrial razor blades.

The hospital was really his only choice, since he understood that his life span—had he been sent to Attica—would have been no more than a few weeks. Thugs have their standards, too. He was happy in the hospital, although, as the Millbrook Ripper, Fallon was on Dr. Ghope's list of unreleasable inmates. He painted, he sold his paintings at premium prices to a small group of wealthy admirers, and saved his money in a numbered account in the Cayman Islands. One day he planned to escape and live out his days in a less effete country, perhaps in South America, where they still appreciated extraordinary men, and where little girls could be purchased like bananas.

The light began to fade and Fallon got ready to put away his work. As he cleaned his brushes he fixed his companion with his huge and shining blue eyes, and said, "You're the shotgun artist, right?"

"What're you talking about, shotgun artist?" said Louis coldly.

Fallon chuckled. "Hey, it's OK. I know everything that goes on here. No, really, just making conversation—why should I care if you slaughter a hundred shopkeepers? Let me just finish up here and we'll go into the lounge and have a nice chat."

Louis let himself be towed by the big man into the dayroom. He had little enough will in any case, and the painter seemed to be the only inmate he had met so far who was not a zombie. He thought maybe Fallon would be able to help him remember what he had to do.

"Friend," said Fallon, "the first thing is, we've got to get you off the dope. You see, decadent societies always try to clip the wings of their superior men. Three centuries ago it was the stake and torture. Now it's tranquilizers. You understand what I'm saying? The sheep can't handle wolves like us and they haven't got the balls to kill us any more. So they send us to so-called hospitals to 'cure' us. And what's the cure? Slow poison. Hey, you can barely understand what I'm saying, you're so doped up. Listen, next time that asshole with meds comes by, do what I do. Give him a dumb smile, take the drink, hold it in your mouth and then spit it out into some toilet paper. Here, take some of mine."

Louis did as he was told. By that evening, his head was

clearer. The feeling of being wrapped in a warm blanket was fading. The next day he spat out all three doses. The day after that, he remembered what he was supposed to do.

Elvis almost fell out of bed when he heard the voice on the phone. What made it especially unnerving was that the bed he was in belonged to the voice on the phone, as did, in a manner of speaking, the woman who shared it with him.

"Elvis, my man! How you doin', bro? You comfortable an' all?"

"Man? Hey, that really you, huh? Where you at, Man?"

"Where I at? Where the fuck you think I at, asshole? I'm in the goddam nuthouse, where I got to be to keep from goin' to the slams for about a thousand years, cause goddam Snowball Walker snitched on my ass, instead of bein' dead in his grave, where you was supposed to put him. Now what the fuck happened?"

Elvis explained about leaving the package in Room 10.

"You *left* the shit! Goddam, Pres! If I wanted to leave the fuckin' package I coulda hired a goddam *white* man from the Railway Express Company to *leave* the package. You suppose to watch the muthafucka take the stuff. An' since Snowball wasn't there you didn't get the damn paper with my phone number on it, did you? No, you sure as shit didn't.

"Now listen to me, little bro. You fuck up once, OK, you jus' learnin'. You fuck up again, you dead. You dig what I'm sayin'?"

Elvis dug. And resented it. He had moved into Louis's apartment, which apparently included, as an appliance, the occasional favors of the luscious DeVonne. He told himself he would keep an eye on things until Louis's situation cleared up, which, he hoped, would not be for a long time. Meanwhile, he could live damn good on Louis's stash, and after that was gone, he was pretty sure he could, with a solid base like Louis's pad, figure out some ways of bringing in easy money. Elvis had big plans.

Which was why the voice on the phone had come as such a shock. Elvis tried to get his thoughts together. There was obviously no need for panic. Louis was behind bars, prison or crazy house didn't make no never mind, and Elvis was outside. Shit, Louis needed *him,* right?

"Now wait a second, Man," said Elvis, putting a little sass into his voice, "don't go comin' at me like that. I ain't your nigger."

"You ain't?" said Louis after a long pause. "I think you wrong there, little bro. But I see how you could maybe think that, I do indeed. Now say if I go wrong now, but you thinkin' 'Shit, Louis in the can now, I get to play with his toys, play his fine stereo, an' all, sleep on his soft bed, nothing can't touch old Pres.' That right? Yeah.

"But the problem with that, see, is if it turns out I gotta do time in Attica, well then it'd be my duty to stand up in court and tell them all 'bout you, boy, how you help me plan the crime, how you stood right by me when I blew those two dudes away. That make you guilty, same as me, the law funny that way. So we both be in Attica at the same time. You gonna love that, Pres, I promise you that. Shit, Pres, there's dudes in there, they'd shove goddam broken glass up your asshole for 'bout fifty dollars apiece."

"Ah, Man, I din mean . . ."

"No, lemme go on, Pres," said the soft voice on the line. "It hurt me you not doin' all you can to help me out, especially since it was your own self got me into this. Anyway, let's say I don't go to Attica, let's say I stay here in Matteawan. Shit, Pres, this place—a fuckin' blind man could walk outa here. So you see, Pres, I figure we friends, you gonna help me outa the fine affection you feel for your main man, but if not, you know I'm gonna come after you, one way or the other. I'm up on murder one already, so I don't have shit to lose, you dig? An' when I catch you, an' I *will* catch you, cause you a dumb muthafucka, I will cut your black ass into tiny little pieces. Now, you dig how you might of been wrong about you not bein' my nigger anymore?"

Elvis was bathed in sweat, both from fear and from the effort of having ventured to suggest an independent course of action for himself. Elvis did not fear the law; there were thousands of ways of avoiding it, and even if it caught you it was no big deal. But he was pretty sure there was no way on earth of avoiding Mandeville Louis, and he was absolutely sure that if Louis caught him, it would be a big deal.

"Hey, Man, hey be cool. Jus bullshittin', that's all. Shit."

"Good. I like your attitude, Pres. Now, listen, here's what I want you to do."

"The problem," Karp was saying to V.T. Newbury, "is that he only has two weeks to get certified as a candidate. Vierick's been campaigning for months. Every time somebody gets mugged, the mayor puts Vierick on TV, with the implication that the city needs a war on crime under a new general, which is him.

"Meanwhile, Conlin is going batshit. He can't come out publicly as long as Garrahy is hanging fire, but short of that he sure as shit is acting like a candidate. Hogging press? Fucking guy is now inviting *reporters* from the *Times* and the *News* to sit in on Homicide Bureau meetings. It's unbelievable. Morale is in the toilet."

The two men were sitting on a bench in Foley Square. It was spring again. The Marchiones had been in their graves for over a year. Karp was carrying a full load in Homicide, as was Ciampi. Hrcany was in Felony Trial. Newbury was in Frauds, conducting interminable and arcane investigations of the financial markets, most of which involved, according to him, jailing his relatives and their friends. He loved it. Guma was in the new Narcotics Bureau, also, presumably, jailing his relatives. Conrad Wharton had been named chief administrative officer of the District Attorney's Office.

"Something's wacky there, Butch," said Newbury. "Why doesn't Conlin get together with the other bureau chiefs and tell Garrahy he's either got to run or to declare for a successor, you know, for the sake of the glorious DA's Office? I mean, the thought of Vierick in there ought to shake him up. Or, dare I say it, a Republican."

Karp laughed. "Bite your tongue. Yeah, I can't figure it out either. I've heard some weird rumors, but Conlin assures me that he's been pushing Garrahy to run for a year."

"What does he say Garrahy says?"

"That he'll see how he feels when the time comes. Anyway, the time has come. I'll tell you though: I wish I was a fly on the wall at the next bureau chiefs' meeting."

They were silent for a while. Then V.T. said, "We couldn't bug his conference room, could we? I mean, that would be wrong."

"Oh, very wrong, and besides there isn't time. The meeting's today at four-thirty. However, talking about 'flies on the wall' and 'bugs' has got me thinking. You know that big wooden wardrobe at one end of Garrahy's conference room? If somebody was standing in it, he could hear everything that was going on at the meeting."

"Yes, he could. But surely you're not suggesting that you or I . . ."

"Of course not, V.T. I'm way too big and you're way too couth. No, for this venture we need somebody small, slimy, utterly devoid of moral discrimination, yet possessed of a kind of animal cunning, and most of all, somebody who has absolutely nothing to lose as far as career goes."

"I believe you're right, Butch. But where are we to find a colleague so utterly devovid of professional ethics, so desperate a villain that he would stoop to spying on our esteemed leaders? I mean, where in the New York District Attorney's Office would we find a creature so vile?"

"Where indeed?" said Karp.

"No fucking way!" said Guma. "You guys are crazy."

Karp, Newbury, and Marlene Ciampi were ranged around Guma's desk, like detectives around the suspect in an old-time movie. Karp had been inspired to drag Ciampi along on the theory that the presence of a woman would turn Guma's brain to mush, a necessary preamble to the plot. She came, but was not amused.

"Come on, Goom," said Karp. "There's nothing to it. We

got to find out what Conlin's been feeding Garrahy about the election, and this is the only way. There won't be another chiefs' meeting until it's too late."

"You do it, then!"

V.T. said, "Raymond, where's your spirit of adventure? What happened to the Mad Dog we used to know? You lost your nerve?"

Guma scowled like a sulky Pekinese. "Up yours, V.T.! Look folks, I'm a busy man—got places to go, people to see. Let's have lunch sometime . . ."

"Guma, we got to have you in on this. Name your price."

"Fuck you too, Karp. What d'you think, I'm some kinda sleaze bag? 'Name your price,' my ass! It's unprincipled, that's why I'm not gonna do it, and nothing you can say is gonna make me change my mind."

At this, Ciampi leaned forward from where she was perched on the corner of Guma's desk and looped her finger through one of Guma's curly locks.

"Guma," she said, "this is the final offer. Do the job and I promise that when we ride up on the elevator when it's crowded and you accidentally-on-purpose brush my bazoom with your arm, I won't kick you in the ankle anymore."

"Yeah? And you won't yell out, 'Guma, stop mashing my tits!' anymore?"

"You got it. I'll pretend it was an accident and back away."

Guma looked at his wristwatch. "When's the goddam meeting?" he said.

Outside Guma's office Ciampi spoke to Karp with some heat, "OK, I owed you one, and I consider us even, with interest." She began to walk off.

Karp said, "Hey Champ, it's all for the cause. Where you going? Aren't you going to wait around for the payoff?"

"Sorry fellas, I got to get into my hot pants and get down to Times Square. Leroy gonna whup my ass if I be late."

At 5:30 that afternoon, Karp and Newbury entered Guma's office to get the dirt. They found him seated at his desk, smoking a White Owl and reading the *Post*. The office coat rack was propped up against the sill of the wide-open window. A pair of navy-blue trousers and a pair of jockey shorts fluttered in the breeze like ignoble flags over Foley Square.

"Guma, what's going on?" asked V.T. "You know, you don't really have to undress in order to jerk off, but let me say I admire your delicacy."

Guma dropped his paper and gave the two other men a sour look. "Shut the fuck up, Newbury. I swear I'll never forgive you guys for this. I was in that goddam closet for two and a half hours. It was like a fucking bad dream."

"What happened," said Karp, "what did you hear?"

"I should've gone before I went in there, but who knew the meeting was gonna take so long?"

"What are you talking about, Goom?"

"I peed in my pants, for Chrissake, a fucking drop at a time. It was murder. Then I had to wash my stuff out in the men's room and come back here buck naked. Hey, V.T., feel that stuff and see if it's dry, willya? Jesus, talk about embarrassment . . ."

V.T. said, "Anything, Guma. I will be your personal laundress, but for God's sake tell us what happened!"

"What happened was that Conlin did a big bullshit number about how while he, Conlin, supported the old man to the limit, the support just wasn't there in the office. He said the younger attorneys respected Garrahy, but wanted new leadership. Oh, he was rare, made you want to cry."

Karp was astounded. "And nobody else said anything?"

"Nope. It was Conlin's show. Oh yeah, he brought out a poll he said he had done, that showed Garrahy splitting the Democratic vote with Vierick thirty points apiece. If Vierick runs as an independent, which he says he's going to do, that means a turnover in the general election. He had all the figures."

"What a piece of crap, that bastard!" cried Karp. "How the hell can Garrahy believe that?"

"Maybe he wants to believe it, Butch," said V.T. "Maybe he's tired and looking for an excuse to quit."

"He can't quit. I need, I mean the office needs him."

"Then what do you intend to do about it?"

"I'll think of something," said Karp.

That weekend the Bullets clinched the city-wide Lawyer's League title for the fifth straight year. Which meant a party for the team in Garrahy's office, which meant that Karp could sneak in for five minutes with Garrahy alone, when the DA was likely to be in as good a mood as he would attain at any time—and without having to get on his official calendar, of which Conrad Wharton had become the virtual master.

The party was scheduled for twelve o'clock on Monday. At a quarter to, Karp entered the DA's outer office. Ida, Garrahy's secretary, who had been with him for thirty years and was one of the last Ida's in New York, looked up and smiled.

"So early, Butch? You must really love chicken salad."

"Ida, I could say that I came up here to bask in your youthful beauty, but the fact is I'm in a jam and I need five minutes with Mister G."

"Oh? Nothing serious, I hope."

"No, just a personal matter."

Ida nodded and spoke briefly into her intercom. Then she gestured Karp into the inner office.

Garrahy was sitting behind his desk in an office that was a large and airier version of Conlin's, with even more impressive memorabilia. A good proportion of the photographs covering one wall antedated Karp's birth; the man had been the Manhattan District Attorney since before Pearl Harbor.

He was starting to look it. Garrahy had aged visibly during the past year and grown smaller than his clothes, in the way of old men.

"Sit down, Butch, sit. What a season, hey? What is this now, four, five in a row for the Bullets? If the Yanks could do the same this year, oh boy!"

Karp allowed as how that would be a good thing, and the two men spoke about baseball for a few minutes, as any strangers might do. Karp was nervous, not because he was speaking to one of the most powerful men in the city, but because he could not take his eyes off the inch of space between Garrahy's neck and the collar of his shirt, or take his mind away from the thought that he was about to ask for something that could not be delivered.

They reached the end of baseball talk and there was a silence. Garrahy glanced at his watch. Karp plunged in.

"Mister Garrahy, I hope you won't think I'm sticking my nose in where it doesn't belong, but I, I mean I and the other attorneys in the office are, well, concerned is the word, I guess about what your plans are for running for another term."

Garrahy drew on his pipe and looked bleakly at Karp through the woody smoke. "Well, well. Are you concerned that I'll run or concerned that I won't?"

"That you won't, of course. Everybody I know wants you to continue as DA."

Garrahy leaned back in his tall swivel chair and appeared to consider this. "That's very interesting. But that's not what I'm being told. I'm being told that there's a mighty yearning for a fresh face at the top of this office. I'm also being told that if I run, I'll split the party vote. What do you think of that?"

"I think it's nonsense, sir. If you announced, you'd win the primary and the election both, in a walk."

"In a walk, hey? It'd have to be. I don't have the energy to do anything else. No, Butch, I've just about decided to let it slip away. Mary's got her heart set on spending half the year at our place in Florida, and I tell you the thought of another winter in the city . . ." He waved his hand.

"Mister Garrahy, look, I'm just a kid, wet behind the ears, what do I know? I've got some nerve coming in here presuming to tell you how to run your life, but Florida? I mean, that's for, for *appliance salesmen.* You're the DA! You stand for something in this city and we need you to keep on standing for it."

Garrahy grinned around his pipe. "That's quite a speech, Butch. I hope you're that good in court." But like all politicians, he liked to be wooed, and wooing had been scarce for some time. "So you don't think I'm too old?"

Karp felt himself blushing. "No, I don't," he said in as firm a voice as he could muster. Which was a lie. Of course you're too old, he thought. You're old and weak and probably ill, and you've let the office go down the drain. But it'll go down the drain about ten times faster if you're not around.

"I don't know," Garrahy mused. "But in any case, this discussion is probably moot. With the time left I couldn't possibly put together the organization to get the signatures for a nominating petition."

Gotcha, thought Karp. "Forgive me, sir, but there you're wrong. There are about two hundred attorneys in this office. I will personally guarantee that if you give the word, every one of them will be out on the street pulling in signatures. We could get five thousand signatures in a week. I'll organize the whole thing myself."

"Hah! You will, will you? A children's crusade for Phil Garrahy? You almost make me want to run, just to see that."

There was a discreet knock at the door, and Ida entered, carrying sandwiches on a huge caterer's tray wrapped in yellow plastic. Behind her trooped the Bullets. Before turning to greet the team, Garrahy said to Karp, "I'm glad we had this talk, Butch, and I'll keep what you said in mind. And I'll get back to you."

"What was that all about?"

Karp and Joe Lerner were loading their paper plates with delicatessen. "What was what all about, Joe?"

"I got big ears, Butch. What is the boss going to let you know?"

"Oh, nothing much. We were just discussing his political plans. Hey, is there any pastrami on that side?"

"Yeah, here's a pastrami with Swiss cheese. So tell me, when did you get to be Phil Garrahy's political adviser?"

Karp looked up and met Lerner's gaze. The older man looked worried.

"Oh, crap, Joe. I just told him that everybody in the office wanted him to stay DA and ... uh ..."

"And what?"

"And I said I would organize the ADAs to hit the streets and campaign for him."

Lerner's chicken salad sandwich halted halfway to his mouth, which hung open for a long moment and then snapped shut in a grim line.

"Goddamn, Butch, why in hell did you want to do something like that?"

"Because nobody else wanted to. Our great boss, Jack Conlin, was feeding him a line of bullshit about how nobody wanted him, and how he couldn't win, et cetera. I just told him the truth."

"Oh, you did, did you? Well, good for you. But let me tell you something you might not have thought of in your pursuit of truth. Let's say Garrahy runs. If he runs, he wins, we all know that. That gives us at best four more years of the half-assed leadership we've got now. At worst ... ah shit, Butch, look at the man! He's a walking corpse. You think he's going to last four years? And when he goes, the governor gets to appoint his replacement, which means sure as hell we're going to get some Republican dickhead in there, instead of Jack Conlin, who whatever you think about him, at least knows his way around a fucking courtroom."

"Conlin can't fill Garrahy's shoes."

"Did I say he could? Do you know *anybody* who could? But Jack's the best we got, and you might have taken away his chance to get the office and maybe grow in it. Fill his shoes! We'll be lucky to get somebody fit to *kiss* his shoes. Wake up, Butch! It's Nineteen Seventy-one and there aren't any heroes anymore. Why the hell didn't you come to me and talk about it instead of weaseling around like this?"

"I wasn't weaseling! I'm going to go down and see Jack and tell him what I did."

"Oh, that's sweet of you. Hey, Jack, I just put twenty-five years of your life in the shit can—just thought you'd like to know."

"Dammit, Joe, I figured you of all people would understand. I mean Jack lied to him. He lied!"

"So he lied. In his place, I would have done exactly the same thing. What do you think we're running here, a convent?

God, Butch, you're a damn fine lawyer and you've got—you *had*—a hell of a career in front of you, but you sure can be an insufferable, self-righteous prick!"

Lerner turned on his heel and strode away. Karp put his plate down. He wasn't hungry and he had a cold feeling in his belly. He thought, Joe's full of shit. I did the right thing. Then he walked out of the party and down the stairs to see Jack Conlin.

CHAPTER TWELVE

Mister Bloom, please. Chip Wharton here. Thank you. Sandy? I've got some good news for you. The old man is definitely going to run. Of course I'm sure. Yeah, Conlin must have gone through the roof. No, Sandy, I can assure you, there's absolutely no possibility that he'll survive until the end of this next term. If I had any doubts about that, I wouldn't have urged you not to run, and I wouldn't have pushed him *to* run. No, Conlin won't do a thing, I guarantee, he'll be out of here in a month. Look, you just work on the governor and his people and I'll nail down things around here. Karp? Don't make me laugh! He's a nobody, a Boy Scout. Yeah, it's ironic alright. Yeah, it might be a nice gesture if you called Phil and offered him your warm support. Thanks, Sandy. And, Sandy? Just sit tight, I'll be in touch."

"Susan, it's me. I just wanted to call you and let you know. Remember I told you about the primary and what I was doing? Yeah, well, I'm sitting here in the Hilton, election headquarters, it's a madhouse. I think we're going to win big, twenty-five, thirty points. Well, yeah, it's no big surprise, but still . . . he probably wouldn't have run it if wasn't for me and the rest of the gang in the office, so I guess I feel personally responsible, you know? Susan, it was incredible, I mean just about every attorney in the office, the secretaries, the whole staff practically, out on the street, getting signatures for the petition, and then getting the election committee set up, then back on the streets, putting up posters, talking to groups. I still can't believe

167 —

it—Garrahy let me run the whole thing. God, I've got so much to tell you.

"Anyway, I've been running off my feet the past three weeks and it looks like we did it, and, well, the reason I called is, I thought I'd take a couple of weeks off and fly out, and, I thought we could go up the coast to Monterey and stay at that place on the beach we used to go to. You don't? Why not? I don't understand, what kind of plans? You're what? What do you mean you're *seeing* somebody? What the fuck does that mean? A *relationship!* You mean you're *fucking* somebody! You're goddam right I wouldn't understand.

"Listen, this is bullshit, Susan. I'm flying out there tonight ... don't tell me you're leaving, uh-uh, baby, we're going to have this right out, you, me and your bozo, whoever he is. What? It's not a *he?* What are you, kidding me? Susan, this is sick. I can't believe I'm hearing this. OK, OK, I'll listen, go ahead, tell me.

"Great, Susan, what can I say? You told your parents? No, why should I? No, I realize you don't want to hurt me, it just takes a little getting used to, you know? No, I'm fine, really. Listen, I got to do some thinking, so, ah, I'll see you, whenever, right? Right. Good-bye, Susan."

Karp hung up the pay phone. He walked down the hallway in a daze and went into the Hilton Hotel ballroom that served as primary-night headquarters for the Garrahy campaign. People were clapping and cheering, which probably meant that Vierick had conceded, which meant Garrahy had the Democratic nomination, which meant that unless he was found naked in the Bryant Park public toilet with a thirteen-year-old Republican male prostitute, he had another term as DA locked up.

People surrounded Karp and clapped him on the back and said nice things. An elderly man was pumping his hand; vaguely Karp recognized him as Garrahy's campaign manager. Karp felt a smile appear on his face spontaneously, like the twitching of a dead frog's leg or the rictus of recent death. The cheering increased. Garrahy had entered the room. The old man stood before a microphone and made a short speech. Karp couldn't focus his mind on the words. He felt as if his head was about to explode. He couldn't catch his breath. Something slammed into his shoulder, rocking him. He turned toward the blow and saw Guma, pop-eyed, sweating, wearing a huge tricorn hat made of a Garrahy poster. The picture of Garrahy contrasted weirdly with the actual face below it, which looked depraved.

"Butchie baby! We did it! *L'chaim!*" He took a deep drink from a plastic cup full of Scotch and ice. "Hey, where's your drink. Hey, get a drink for my man here!" A plastic cup was pressed into Karp's hand.

Karp said, "Guma, my wife is a lesbian."

"No shit? Will she let you watch?"

"Guma! I'm not kidding. This is serious."

"What serious, it's California. OK, it's serious. Your wife is a dyke. My wife is an asshole. We both got problems. Luckily our problems are easily solved by two easily available items, booze, one, and two, pussy."

"Goom, be serious! What am I gonna do?"

Guma looked at him hard and popped him in the chest with a stubby finger. "Serious? What're you talkin' about? I'm serious. Booze is real. Pussy is real. You're in fuckin' Oz, in comparison. Wise up, Butch! Start living, for Chrissake. Now listen! What you need is to get drunk and laid, which is going to be easy where we're going, because you are the man of the hour, and the bitches'll be crawling all over you. I'm going to get my car from the garage here and I'll meet you on the Sixth Avenue side in ten minutes. It's bring your own, so hit the joint across the street and pick something up. See you."

Guma trotted off. People were leaving the ballroom now and Karp drifted with them. He knew he was losing his mind. My life is falling apart, he thought, and I'm blabbing the intimate details of my married life to Ray Guma, drunk, wearing a funny hat. He walked through the crowded lobby, out into the summer night. The air was soft, and smelled of roasted peanuts for some reason, the way air in New York will often carry odd and unexplained smells. In the food market he bought a six-pack of Schaeffer's; that amount of beer represented approximately one half of his annual intake of alcohol.

"What did you get, a *whole six-pack?*" asked Guma, when Karp slid into the front seat of his car outside the Hilton. Guma had half a case of Teacher's in the trunk. "Jesus, Karp, we're talking oblivion here. What's wrong with you?"

"Come on, Goom, you know I can't stand the taste."

"Who can? Schmuck! You drink it *in spite of* the taste."

"Fine, fine, stop hocking me!" snarled Karp. Then, after a while: "Where're you driving? What's this party we're going to?"

"You're joking! This is not just a party. This is a classic, guaranteed. We're having a Dance at the Gym."

"Oh," said Karp glumly, and thought about oblivion, heretofore a scarce commodity in his life, but looking better.

The Gym was the one good part of one of Conrad Wharton's worst ideas. For decades one wing of the fourth floor of 100 Centre Street, where the Felony Trial Bureau was quartered, had been divided into tiny bathroom-sized offices for the ADAs. For most of them, coming from the squad bays of Criminal Court, it was their first real office-with-a-door, and prized accordingly.

But Wharton had read something about the latest thing in efficiency being open space plans with individual "work-stations," divided by colorful foam partitions. He therefore ordered the razing of the entire area and the replacement of the cozy old offices with an immense echoing space filled with flimsy tin furniture and cloth-covered panels in earth tones and primary colors. As a functional office it was a disaster, since Wharton had not thought it necessary to buy the sound baffles and special flooring that prevent such offices from sounding like what they resemble—cheap day-care centers for the retarded.

On the other hand, the "modules" were easily shifted. Half an hour's work produced an open hall with eight big windows that would easily hold 200 people—presto, the Gym.

When Guma and Karp arrived there were only about a dozen people in the room, mostly secretaries and clerks arranging platters of food on desks covered with paper tablecloths. The secretaries supplied the food, the professional staff supplied the drink. The overhead lights had been doused and the room was lit by candles stuck in ashtrays and cardboard coffee cups. Guma deposited his half case of Scotch and Karp his six-pack on the pair of desks designated as the bar. Jugs of wine were cooling in ice-filled trash baskets. Towers of paper cups were arranged around them.

A short, red-haired, pug-nosed man was standing at one end of the "bar," pouring pineapple juice from a can into a huge galvanized washtub, the type used to bathe the heroine by candlelight in western movies.

"Denny! How they hanging, my friend?" said Guma.

"Not so bad, Goom. A couple more cans and this will be ready to taste."

"What is it? Oh, hey Butch, you know Denny Maher, from the M.E.'s office?"

"Yeah, sure, hi."

Maher cracked another can and poured it into the foaming, creamy mixture. "Butch, you look like shit. I believe you are low on potassium, the inevitable result of excessive masturbation. Therefore, as your personal physician I will insist that you swallow at least twelve ounces of this here punch." Maher finished pouring and filled a paper cup from the tub. Karp eyed it suspiciously.

"What's in it?"

"Nothing but the purest tropical ingredients. It's a piña colada, or pina colitis, as we used to call it in medical school. C'mon, taste it."

Karp took a swallow. The drink was sweet and icy. "Hey, it's all right. Is it spiked?"

Maher and Guma exchanged glances. "Spiked? No, not really, just enough to prevent bacterial contamination. I mean, I wouldn't want any of the guests to come down with salmonella."

"Hey Butch, come over here and help me with the meat."

Hrcany, dressed in a Hawaiian shirt and cutoffs, was tending half a dozen smoldering hibachis set up on the window ledges. He was taking shish kebabs out of a cooler and placing them on the grills. Karp took his drink and walked over, glad of something to do to get his mind off his troubles.

Maher stirred his tub and gestured in Karp's direction. "Spiked? Is he kidding, or what?"

"Ah, Karp's OK, he's just a little new to physical depravity. What did you put in it anyway."

"Oh, the usual twelve pints of Olde Medical Examiner." Maher reached under the desk and held up a squat bottle with a black and silver label. The label said "Ethyl Alcohol $-C_{2H}40H-$(Absolute)."

"Is that all?" asked Guma. "No exotic aphrodisiacs?"

"Is that all, he asks! Listen, friend of mine, by the time the bottom of this old tub sees the light of day there won't be a functional higher brain in this room. The lowest animal reflexes will rule all."

Guma laughed. "You're an evil man, Maher, and I love you for it. But isn't this a violation of your Hippocratic oath?"

"Oh, that. It's sad, but sometimes we physicians must appear to cause pain in order to work our miracles of healing." He poured a cup of punch and offered it to Guma. "No thanks, I'll stick to Scotch, Denny."

"You're a fool. That stuff'll kill you. I speak as your personal physician." He took a deep drink himself. "Ahh . . . healthful and refreshing!"

"Better you than me, pal. Oh, and Denny, we're trying to get Butch to loosen up. Why don't you see that his cup stays full, hey?"

"A duty and a pleasure," said Denny Maher.

For the next hour Karp cooked fifty pounds of skewered beef. It was a warm, humid night and the grills were blazing hot. He took off his jacket, then his tie. He unbuttoned his shirt and rolled up his sleeves. Then he wrapped his tie around his forehead. Every so often somebody would appear at his side with a platter and he would load it with smoking shish kebabs and, in turn, receive a tall, cool cup of piña colada, which he gulped down.

Now the room was jammed with people. Somebody had brought a ghetto blaster, which was blasting away, and dancers were leaping in the candlelight. When the meat ran out, Karp staggered toward the music. Guma was up on a desk doing the dirty boogie with Proud Mary, a 300-pound property clerk with chocolate skin and blonde hair. He had removed his shirt, shoes, and socks and rolled up his trouser legs. He was wearing a green cellophane Hawaiian skirt and Proud Mary's brassiere, stuffed with paper napkins. Karp watched hypnotized as Proud Mary's unrestrained size 46s struggled for freedom against her dress. She was laughing, a high-pitched, "hee-yuh-yuh-yuh . . . HEE-yuh-yuh-yuh" like the artificial fat lady in front of a Coney Island fun house.

"Butch! Man of the hour! C'mon dance!" Marlene Ciampi grabbed his hand and pulled him onto the dance floor. "Jesus, Butch, you look like you just finished the graveyard shift at a coal mine. What you been doing?"

Karp rocked back and forth on rubbery legs. He had stopped feeling his face a long time ago. "Cooking . . . meat," he said. He tried to think about why he was sad, but couldn't quite recall the reason. It was hard enough to keep Marlene's face, her flying black hair, in focus, and to remain upright. Grace Slick sang, her voice like copper pennies on the tongue: "When the truth is shown, to be just LIES, and all the joy within you DIES, don't you WANT somebody to love, don't you NEED somebody to love, wouldn't you LOVE somebody to love, you better FIND somebody to LUH–UH–UV!"

Karp thought this made good sense. He made a clumsy grab for Marlene and squeezed her to his breast.

"Oooof! Hey, Karp, take it easy! This is so sudden! God, Karp, what a sweathog! Yecch!" She spun away and danced around him. He stumbled after her through the whirling couples, like King Kong stalking the blonde.

"May I have this dance?"

Marlene found herself dancing with V.T. Newbury, looking elegant in a white dinner jacket.

"V.T.! Where you been?" She fingered his lapel. "What's with the getup? Trying to make the peasants feel bad?"

"Only a true peasant could have made a remark like that, my dear. No, actually, I'm coming from a wedding reception. My cousin Phootie."

"Phootie? Be real, V.T. Nobody calls themself Phootie."

"One does, if one is rich enough. Actually, there's a charming family story about how she got that name, but I'm pledged to reveal it only to Episcopalians. Good Christ! What's wrong with Karp?"

Karp's head and shoulders could be seen over the crowd. His jaw was slack and he had a curiously intent expression on his face, the kind imbeciles wear when they are trying to remember how to tie their shoes.

"I don't know," said Marlene. "I think he's drunk."

"Karp? Drunk? Impossible. Where are the networks, the cameras?"

"No, he's whacked out, V.T. Maybe we should get him to sit down."

"No that's absolutely the wrong thing to do. Keep him on his feet and working, that's the answer. Speaking of which, I have just the job. Come on!"

The two of them shoved through the dancers to Karp and led him out of the Gym.

"V.T., where are we going?" Marlene asked. Karp was docile and softly humming to himself.

"Just down the hall to the men's room."

"What! V.T., what the . . ."

"Now, Champ, you know you've been longing for this opportunity. It's your ultimate rite of passage into the closely guarded world of male supremacy. Ah, here we are."

V.T. opened the men's room door with his foot and shouldered Karp in. Marlene followed, cursing fluently.

Roland Hrcany and Denny Maher were standing in the corner by the towel dispensers, looking speculatively at what first appeared to be a pile of clothes.

"Hi guys," said Hrcany cheerfully. "We're just waiting for the ambulance. Denny called Jerry Lipsky at Bellevue and he's sending one over. The problem is, it probably isn't a good idea to have it come right up to One Hundred Centre, so we're going to have to drag him a couple of blocks away and make the pickup there."

"I'm going to start screaming if somebody doesn't tell me what's going on," said Marlene, her voice rising threateningly.

"Calm down, Champ," said Hrcany. "Look at this." He turned the pile of clothes over to reveal a face like a spilled quart of cottage cheese (large curd) attached to a corpulent, three-piece-suited body.

"Hey, it's Sheldon the Shit. Far out! Is he dead?"

"No such luck, dear," replied Maher. "My preliminary analysis shows that Sheldon, who was, by the bye, uninvited to our party, has overindulged in my famous punch."

"Yeah," said Hrcany, "I was in here taking a leak, the door crashes open and Sheldon comes in, opens a booth, gets down on his knees to puke, and passes out in the bowl. I had to save him from drowning."

Marlene said, "And here I thought you just looked like a lifeguard. Did you give mouth-to-mouth?"

Hrcany made a face. "Give me a break! But then it occurred to me that here was a God-given opportunity to help Sheldon out, kind of show him the error of his ways. And of course pay the asshole back for all the times he's left us holding the bag. Denny, for your information, Sheldon Ehrengard is generally considered the chief prick lawyer in this office . . ."

"No, Wharton is," said Marlene.

"I don't consider Wharton a lawyer," continued Hrcany, "but anyway, Debra Tiel, down in the Complaint Room, calls him the laziest white man in North America. Hey, Butch, you remember the night in the Complaint Room, when he didn't show up and we got bombed? Butch?"

Karp was swaying gently back and forth like a poplar in a gale. "What's wrong with Karp? We need him for this plan."

Maher peered into Karp's glassy eyes. "Ah, he's all right. It's merely the ill effects of years of clean living and regular exercise. The man can hardly drink at all."

"Wait a minute," said Marlene, "what's Butch got to do with this?"

"Beast of burden, dear," said Maher. "And I'm sure that

were he in his right mind he'd be glad to cooperate. As you can see, Sheldon is a considerable tub of lard."

"Hey guys, the ambulance is here, over on White and Baxter. Holy shit? What are you doing here, Ciampi?"

Guma had burst in, still in his hula outfit, but with a suit jacket thrown over his shoulders in the manner of Italian movie directors. The debonair effect was marred by the magenta bra peeking out from between his coat lapels.

"What am I doing here? You rat! You promised you were going to teach me to pee standing up. Hey, nice set of jugs, Goom. You'll blow them away at Brighton Beach this summer."

"Ciampi, one of these days . . . ah shit, let's get him out of here."

In the manner of an animal trainer, Hrcany coaxed Karp into picking up Ehrengard's elephantine legs. The other four men arranged themselves around the massive form, and with Marlene in the lead as door-opener they marched out of the building and into the night, giggling and humming the Dead March. What in any other city would have been a remarkable procession drew hardly a glance on the still-crowded streets of Chinatown. The ways of the round-eyed barbarians are inscrutable.

Once at their destination, the City Morgue, they removed Ehrengard's clothes and laid him on a stainless steel autopsy table. It was chilly in the big room, but Guma had—with his usual foresight—brought along a full bottle of Teacher's, which passed among them until it was empty.

"Great party, Denny," said V.T. "Nice place. I like the lighting." He gestured to the half dozen real corpses lying on tables for next morning's scalpels. "I like your friends, too. They're a laid-back bunch."

Maher grinned and pulled a sheet over Ehrengard's body, and tied a toe-tag to his big toe. "Thank you, Newbury. Now, who will say a few holy words over the dear departed?"

"I'll do it," said V.T. "Dearly beloved . . ."

"No, Jewish, Jewish," said Hrcany. "Let Butch do it. Butch, make this kosher."

"Naw, Karp can't do it," Guma said, "he's so fucking assimilated they revoked his bar mitzvah. He had his foreskin surgically reattached. Besides he's too pissed."

"Sure he can do it." Hrcany shook Karp gently. "Butchie. Wake up. Say something Jewish so we can get out of here."

"Joosh?" said Karp.

"Yeah, say the Ten Commandments."

"Manments?"

"C'mon Butch, say the first commandment, c'mon think! Thou shalt . . . thou shalt . . ."

"Never . . ."

"That's right, good, never what?"

"Never . . . never . . . ah . . . never pay retail."

"A-men! Ah rest mah case. Let's go. Night-night, Sheldon."

The party was still humming when they got back. The punch was nearly gone, and two hundred people were poised on the delicate boundary between total abandon and utter psychophysical collapse. But this was not lively enough for the Mad Dog of Centre Street. Guma had no difficulty in talking Proud Mary out of the key to the evidence locker. Soon the crowd had liberated a pile of films confiscated during the great Pornography Campaign. Someone was thoughtful enough to have been caught stealing a 16 mm. projector, which was dragged out and set up.

Guma stood on a chair and shouted out the titles: "Beach Boys in Bondage? Wrong crowd. No? You want it? OK, second feature, Cheerleaders in Chains, must see! OK, here it is! A Girl and Her Donkey! I'm dying! Hunk! Roll this one first. Where's the fucking popcorn! I got to have buttered popcorn!"

"Marlene," said V.T. as the film unfolded, "help me out. Do you think this film has any redeeming social value? More to the point, is she getting off with the donkey, or is it just clever acting?"

"Gee, V.T., why ask me, I'm a Sacred Heart girl. But offhand, I'd say yeah, there was a close personal relationship." Marlene became aware of a heavy pressure on her shoulder.

The tower of sodden flesh that was Butch Karp was about to collapse onto her.

"Hey, Butch, wake up! Damn, V.T., help me here!"

The two of them managed to get Karp settled in a large swivel chair.

"Drink," said Karp, his expression witless and good-natured, like that of the donkey performing on the screen.

"Sorry, baby, you've had enough. V.T. what are we going to do with this man?"

"Oh, we'll think of something. We usually do . . . what the hell!"

"ALL RIGHT YOU PERVERTS, FREEZE! THIS IS A RAID!"

A man in a long trench coat with a snap-brim fedora pulled over his eyes was standing in the projector beam, pointing a shotgun at the onlookers. The room froze for an instant, the only sound the whirring of the projector and the boom of music from the tape player. Then someone laughed hysterically: the front of the man's trench coat was covered with the projection of a dripping genital close-up. Then the gunman whipped off his hat and flung open his trench coat.

"Guma, you asshole. Get out of that cunt!" Hrcany shouted. Boos, catcalls and bits of debris flew through the flickering light. "Guma! Where'd you get the gun?" somebody yelled.

"The evidence locker. There's goddam everything there. Here take this! It's COPS AND ROBBERS TIME!"

Guma pulled pistol after pistol out of his coat pockets and flung them into the crowd. The average mental age of the assemblage was now six and dropping fast. Distinguished attorneys and grave civil servants crouched behind desks and crawled on their bellies through potato salad, shouting POW-POW! CHHSS! CHHSS! YOU DEAD, MUTHAFUCKA! at one another.

Guests began dropping to the floor, and not from the imaginary bullets. The bottom of Denny Maher's washtub was finally shining in the sputtering candlelight. Stouter physiques dragged the wounded away from the scene; toward home in some cases, in others toward offices known to have long leather couches.

Around 3:00 A.M., a group of about twenty hard cases were watching the last few minutes of "Babes in Toyland," an item that featured two teenaged girls who were being forced by a mad scientist to submit to an increasingly elaborate collection of motor-driven sexual appliances. The girls had thoughtfully removed their pubic hair to provide the last iota of lubricity.

"I can't stand any more of this," said Marlene Ciampi, yawning. "I'm not going to think about sex for a year. Goddam, look at that!"

"Yeah," said V.T., "it looks like a clam eating a Buick."

"CLAMS!" shouted Guma. "Let's go for clams! Larrupa's All-Nite Clam House in Sheepshead. Clams! Clams!"

Everyone started chanting, "Clams! Clams! Clams!" as they rose from the wreckage and started for the exit. "Pick up the guns!" yelled Hrcany, "and the films!"

The porno films and the weapons were dumped into a trash can and thrown into the evidence locker. Guma led the chanting procession down the hallway: "Guns! Clams! Guns! Clams!" He had removed his grass skirt and now wore Proud Mary's bra around his neck in place of a necktie. Somebody hoisted the tape player. Jim Morrison was asking his baby to light his fire, at 110 decibels.

"Hey, wait!" Marlene shouted. "What about Karp? Hey, guys! Wait, he's out cold. Don't leave!"

She shook Karp as hard as a smallish woman can shake a 210-pound man. No reaction. The sound of the party faded away.

"Ah, shit!" said Marlene. She was exhausted and not a little drunk herself, having been sucking white wine all evening, not to mention the Scotch in the morgue. But she felt unable to leave Karp helpless in the middle of the Gym.

Looking about for a solution, she spotted Maher's washtub. It held about two inches of icy water—the remains of the fifty-pound block that had cooled the punch—in which floated some paper cups and a pair of beige lace panties. She removed this debris, emptied a trash can, and tilted the washtub to fill the can with about a gallon of ice water.

This she poured over Karp's head.

179 —

Karp sat upright and made a sound like a breaching fur seal.

"Phooooo-ahhh! 'sall right! 'sall right! I'm fine," he said looking about wildly. Seeing Marlene, he smiled and said "Hi, Champ. Les go t'the Garn."

"C'mon Butch, we got to get out of here. Everybody's gone."

She helped Karp to his feet, and steadied his sway, like a flying buttress. "OK, Butch, one step at a time, slow and steady."

They left the wreckage behind, descended in the elevator, and staggered drunkenly, clutching one another, into Foley Square.

"Christ, Butch, where the hell are we going to find a cab? Shit, I don't even know where you live."

"Wanna go t'Manson Squa' Garn. Play basabaw," said Karp.

"Karp, you're looney. Just sit there, willya, and I'll go get us a cab. Jesus, I'm going to have to flash tit to get anybody to stop at three-fucking-thirty."

But as she turned to walk up toward Broadway, Karp suddenly leaped to his feet and went into a basketball crouch. He took the long throw from Frazier, hit the pivot and raced down court on the fast break.

"Karp! Wait! Oh, goddam it! Karp, stop!" Marlene took off after the weaving figure. Karp was naturally much faster than Marlene, but of course he had to keep the ball away from five Celtics, which slowed him down somewhat. On the other side of Foley Square Park he saw De Busschere open and whipped a screen pass over to him and then raced for the boards, which happened to be in the middle of Lafayette Street. He was just getting into good position again when somebody blind sided him with a terrific body check. Not for nothing had Marlene Ciampi spent five straight seasons as the only girl ever to make the first team on the dreaded 112th Street Rangers, the undisputed roller-hockey champions of Ozone Park. He went down on the cool pavement a few feet from the double yellow line.

"Hey, foul," he called weakly. He didn't feel so good now. His knee hurt. The game seemed to have passed him by. Where were the other Knicks? Where was the crowd? There was only a woman yelling not very nice language at him.

"Champ! Wha' you doin' here? Where's a game?"

"Game, my ass! Get up, Karp!"

He got up and allowed himself to be led to the curb.

"Oh, thank you God, here's a cab. Karp, don't move!"

There was an empty cab with its dome light on in front of an all-night diner on the far side of Lafayette Street. As Marlene approached it, the cabbie came out of the joint, picking his teeth. He was a gap-toothed man with a fringe of graying hair, not much taller than Marlene, but twice as big around.

Marlene opened the rear door and sat in the backseat.

"I'm off duty, lady."

"Your sign's not on."

"I was just gonna. C'mon lady, out. I gotta get home."

"No way. I'm in the cab and the law says you have to take me."

The cabbie sighed. "Where you goin', huh? Canarsie, right?"

"Uh ... I don't know. I mean, I'm taking my friend home."

"What friend?"

At that moment Karp wandered up. The cabbie saw a swaying giant in a soaked and filthy shirt open to the waist, with a striped necktie wrapped around his head.

"THIS is your friend? No way, lady, this guy's drunk. No way in hell I'm takin' him nowhere. Now, c'mon, get out of the cab."

"Butch, get in the cab!"

"We wanna go t' Manson Squa' Garn," said Karp brightly.

"I'm leavin'," said the cabbie. "Go play games with somebody else."

At this, Marlene leaped from the cab, grabbed Karp by the belt and collar and, before the startled driver could make a move, jackknifed Karp face down across the backseat. She

181 —

then got in herself, sat on Karp's backside, pulled his legs in so that his shoes pointed to the sky, and slammed the door.

"Look buddy," she said to the cabbie, "I don't want any trouble, but it's been a long day for me too. Take us home and it's twenty bucks over the meter. But, I'll tell you this. I work for the DA, Homicide Bureau. Screw with me and I'll have two blue-and-whites following you around for the rest of your life."

"Hey, wait a second, I got my rights, huh? I got rights!"

Karp said, into the seat cushion, "You have the ri' to re-main silen'. You have the ri' t' have a lawyer presen' durn que-sering. If you cannot afrd a lawyer you are a cheap l'il punk."

"Ah, crap, lady, what if he pukes in my cab—it's the end of the goddam shift!"

"If he pukes," said Marlene in a voice that rose into an alto shriek, "I will personally wipe up every single motherfucking drop—with my UNDERPANTS! NOW DRIVE!"

"Where to, lady?"

Marlene had to pull Karp's wallet out of his hip pocket and read his address to the cabbie.

When they reached Karp's place, Marlene opened the door with Karp's keys. He stood in the middle of his bedroom for about ten seconds, then stumbled to the bathroom, got on his knees and threw up everything he had eaten since October 1956, or so it seemed. He rinsed out his mouth, walked to the side of the bed and fell straight across it, bouncing twice. He was snoring before the second bounce.

Marlene watched him for a moment. She thought, if I could just rest my eyes for a minute, I could get myself together and figure out how I am going to get back to my apartment. She looked around. No chairs, no couch, no rug. She walked over to the bed and eased herself down across its head.

Just five minutes, she thought.

When she opened her eyes again, sunlight was streaming through the closed venetian blinds in thin, downward-slanting shafts. She looked at her watch: 11:30. She got out of the bed and stood up. After a while her brain caught up with her skull and the room stopped spinning. Karp hadn't moved a millimeter all night, was still face down, mouth open, gently snoring.

Marlene felt as if her skin were covered with glue. She ran her fingers through her hair, and started when she felt something damp. It was a bit of cole slaw. If I don't get a shower this minute, she thought, I am going to commit suicide.

She walked into the bathroom and stripped. She let the hot stream of the shower beat the garbage out of her head and off her body. Looking around for soap or shampoo she found only a double cake of Ivory. Ivory? Oh, Karp, you sybaritic devil, you! OK, she thought, so I'll smell like a dish.

Karp was awakened by the familiar sound of his shower running. The previous evening was nearly a complete blank. He remembered the phone call to his wife (Oh God, that!), the campaign headquarters, going with Guma, cooking shish kebabs—and that was it. Period. He couldn't remember ever having gotten that smashed on a six-pack of beer. Maybe he was losing his marbles. He couldn't even remember turning on the shower.

The bathroom air was nearly opaque with steam. Naked now, Karp pulled back the shower curtain on the faucet side and took the heavy spray straight in the face, as was his habit. Then he reached behind him to grope for the soap in its shelf midway up the wall. But instead of the soap, what he grabbed was Marlene Ciampi's small and pointy breast.

"Hey," said Marlene, "you could at least say 'good morning.'"

He pulled away and spun around. Marlene was standing with hands on her hips, a characteristic pose of hers when fully dressed, and trying to arrange her face into an expression suitable for the occasion. Karp struggled to do the same.

Karp said, "Marlene. Oh."

Marlene said, "Butch. Oh."

Simultaneously, their faces fell apart and they began to laugh uncontrollably, a huge, gasping, wracking laughter.

183 —

Their legs couldn't hold them. They slid down the soapy walls to the floor of the tub, with the bullets of water streaming down on them.

"God! Karp, stop it, I'm peeing in my pants," said Marlene, and this struck them as additionally hilarious, and they laughed some more.

After a while their laughing died away, and they looked each other in the eye. Both were a little frightened, which, of course, they saw in each other's eyes. Because they knew, these two very smart, very verbal people, that the Animal Train was about to leave the station, taking them both to some unknown place which they both hoped was True Love, a hope neither of them would admit for some time, having been taught that it was no longer a regularly scheduled stop.

So without thinking—for once—Karp jumped on the delicious girl in his bathtub, and Marlene opened her arms and her soapy thighs to him, also without a thought in her head and they both, as Marlene would have said, fucked like minks until they were wrinkled, soggy, exhausted, and drunk with happiness.

CHAPTER THIRTEEN

I swore, I swore, I would never get involved with anybody where I worked. I can't believe I'm doing this. I had a thing going with my contracts professor in law school. Nice guy, married, three kids. I sweated bullets in that course. I mean, we agreed that we were going to keep it separate, sex and grades. So like three people ever aced contracts since 1706, or something, and I got one. Needless to say, every pissant law-school wimp was smirking all over himself when they posted the grade. 'Of course, *she* got one, snicker-snicker.'

"I had migraines for a month. What could I do, hang the marked blue books and papers from my lip? I make law review—the same thing, snicker-snicker. Anyway, I said, 'never again' and here I am, *involved.*"

They were dry and lying side by side on Karp's bed, with a sheet over them. The window was open and a summer breeze rhythmically stirred the half-closed venetians. Bars of sunlight moved across the bed, up the wall and back again. They had both called in sick.

"What makes you think we're *involved,* snicker-snicker?"

"Oh, we're involved, all right. Do you think I'd let you ravish my milk-white body for a cheap one-night stand? I'm a proud Sicilian maiden. Betray me and my brother will cut your balls off. Then I'll dress in black and wear them forever in a little embroidered bag, around my neck."

"I thought you said your brother was a dentist."

"Orthodontist. Doesn't matter though. He's connected, heavy. The mob is queer for straight teeth, it's common knowledge. Guys who know how to fix an overbite can write their own ticket with the dons."

"You're a nut, Ciampi, you know that?"

"Maybe, but I'm serious about keeping this whatever-it-is from getting around the office."

"What? You mean I can't boast of my conquest in the locker room?"

"No, really, Butch." She was silent for a moment, then propped herself up on one elbow and looked into his face.

"I heard about your wife."

"*You* heard about my wife! Shit, Champ, *I* just heard about my wife. Who the hell told you? Oh, Christ, Guma!" He pulled a pillow over his face and groaned.

"Well, what did you expect? Tell Guma, tell Jimmy Breslin, except Guma maybe gets the word around a little faster. We could talk about it, if you want."

Karp peeked over the top of the pillow. "I don't know what to say. I mean, I feel like a jerk. I thought I was in love, I thought I knew who with, and all of a sudden, it turns out that person doesn't exist. It's amazing, this year. It starts out, I have a job, a career that makes sense. I believe in it. I have a marriage, maybe going through some rough spots, but I believed in that, too. Now, Jesus, the DA's office is heading for the garbage can, my wife is gay. I thought I got through the sixties, all that bullshit. I thought I knew the answers. You know, like an exam. Study hard, work out, clean mind, clean body. Fuck the answers—I don't even know the *questions* anymore."

"You should have taken more philosophy."

"Yeah, right, instead of basketball. If I was five inches taller I wouldn't need to know how to *spell* philosophy. Oh, well, I guess the great cosmic questions will always elude me, jock that I am. How about you, Ciampi, do they elude you too?"

"Well, I've always had some problems with 'what is the ultimate ground of being' and 'what is the meaning of "meaning."' And of course, the triune nature of the Godhead has kept me awake many a night. But right now, I believe the most important question is, 'Do you eat pussy?'"

"Me? Never!"

"What, never?"

"Well, I do drag a slow kiss through it, now and again."

Marlene threw back the sheet from their bodies and stretched luxuriously. "Then do so," she said.

Much later, there were no longer any slats of light floating in the walls, just the bluish glow of a summer evening in New York. Marlene lit a Marlboro and sent a geyser of smoke up to the ceiling.

"Karp, the soles of my feet are sweating. They never did that before. God, what can it mean? Karp? Karp are you listening?" She knuckled him in the ribs.

"Ow. Marlene, why are you always abusing me physically? You're always *punching* me."

"Because you don't give me your absolute attention at all times and do everything I want."

"Oh, well, just asking. By the way, you also drool when you pop your rocks."

"Yeah, it's true, my dirty little secret. Karp!"

"What now?"

"Karp, I just realized we haven't eaten anything all day."

"So to speak."

"No, food! I'm starving! What have you got?" She leaped off the bed and trotted into the kitchen, her buns winking in the dying light. Karp listened to the opening of cabinets and the slamming of the refrigerator door. In a few minutes she came back holding a plastic zip-lock bag.

"This is great, Butch. I can eat the refrigerator instructions and you can have the warranty card. There is no *food* in this apartment. How can you *live* that way?"

"We of the planet Zarkon have no need of earthly foods. We get our sustenance from young females, whom we lure to our dens and drain of their vital liquids." He made a clumsy lunge for her leg, which she avoided.

"Uh-uh, bozo. First eat. Marlene wants protein. Marlene want STEAK. If I don't get to Max's in five minutes, you will have to explain my shriveled corpse to the police. Let's get cleaned up."

So they had another shower, with appropriate soapings

and rubbings and tickles, until Marlene pushed him away saying, "Oh God, don't get me started again. I'm going to have to get my thing relined as it is."

"Oh, yeah? There's a guy on Coney Island Avenue does a good job. He'll do your muffler for the same price."

"Get away from me, you maniac," she said, and jumped out of the shower.

There was a full-length mirror on the back of the bathroom door. While Karp dried himself, Marlene wiped the fog from the mirror. She made Karp stand next to her facing it. At five-two, her head barely cleared his breastbone.

"Christ, we look like two different species. What a giant! If you were wearing roller skates, I could practically give you a blow-job without bending down."

"Damn it, isn't it funny how you never can find a skate key when you want one? Ahhhgh! Stop it, Marlene! I thought you wanted a steak."

Later, as they were dressing, she asked, "What happened to your knee? It looks like Frankenstein's face."

"I hurt it playing ball in college. It was sort of a freak accident. I landed on my face with my leg sticking up over somebody's back. Then a two-hundred-and-thirty pound forward came flying through the air and landed on my ankle. The lever effect. The only thing holding my leg to my thigh was skin."

"Oh, yucch, poor baby!"

"Yucch is right. My orthopedist said it was the perfect knee injury. Everything that could rip out in a human knee ripped out. He had residents from all over the West Coast coming in to observe. Didn't do a bad job, though. I can walk all right, mostly, even run a little. But big-time basketball? Finito."

"How come? I read all the time about the pros getting hurt and still playing."

"That's different. First of all, practically nobody gets hurt in basketball as badly as I did. I told you, it was a freak. Then again, they're already part of the team. They can wrap themselves up, shoot in some dope and play a couple of minutes. It's different if you're trying to break in. You're competing with guys who are in perfect shape . . . and well . . ." Karp was staring out the window as he said this, his voice dying away at the end. Marlene touched his arm.

"You still feel bad about it, huh? Were you really good?"

"Yeah, I guess. I don't have that much natural talent, and I'm a hair short for the pros, but I worked at it. I can handle the ball. I'm a dead shot from anywhere on the court. I can, I could, jump better than most white guys. I think I would have had a shot at point guard or second guard someplace. Being a honky helps, there. The fans don't like seeing ten black dudes running around. Hey, let's change the subject. This is getting me depressed."

"Fine. How come you live this way? I mean the place looks like a crash pad. No food, no furniture. Shit, you don't even have a wastebasket."

"I eat out a lot."

"No, really, Butch."

"Really? Because eating in is what you do at home, and this isn't a home. You think I want to fix a little frozen Salisbury steak every night and eat it in front of the tube? I sleep here, and keep my clothes here, period. And every so often some hot little number insinuates herself into my life and I fuck here."

"Every so often, eh? How often is that?"

"Just kidding, Marlene. The truth is, you are the first human being besides me to enter this apartment since I moved in. You have stolen the virginity of my Macy's seventy-nine dollar box spring and mattress. OK?"

"Yeah? Well, keep it that way, Buster, if you know what's good for you." She poked him sharply in the midsection, and trotted out of the apartment. He followed, happy and enslaved.

They ate huge steaks at Max's, oblivious to the glitter underground cavorting around them. They saw a movie. They talked. Karp spilled his guts; he had not talked so much outside a courtroom in years, if ever. For a loudmouth, Marlene was a surprisingly good listener. They walked. They shared an egg cream from a sidewalk stand on Canal Street near Broadway, the heart of New York's bazaar, the junction of Little Italy, Chinatown, and SoHo. There was nothing in the world, legal or illegal, you could not buy within half a mile of where they stood: dried sea cucumbers from the Sulu Sea, a World War II bombsight, a Parmesan cheese as tall as a man, an abstract expressionist painting, a gram of cocaine, a ton of powdered cinnamon, a ton of cocaine, the services of a naughty masseuse, an acupuncturist, a fortune teller, an assassin.

Karp was not in the market for any of those exotica. He thought, I have what I need. Then he thought, be careful, this is a classic rebound situation. He looked at Marlene leaning against the metal serving counter, a Marlboro clenched in her teeth at a jaunty angle, observing the midnight ramblers on Canal Street. He thought about rebounding, about rebounding in basketball. An image popped into his head, of himself jumping high into the air and catching Marlene, naked and curled into a ball, rebounding off a backboard, snatching her away from half a dozen grabbing hands. He laughed out loud. But when Marlene asked him what he was laughing about, he said, "Nothing. You had to be there."

They strolled back uptown to Karp's place. The air remained warm and not as humid as it would be later in the summer. Marlene went into an all-night emporium and bought, over his protests, a metal wastebasket with the Statue of Liberty and other New York scenes printed on it.

Toward dawn, they were in bed, pumping each other to yet another Big O. Remarkable how Marlene, filthy mouthed in the office, in deepest sex would say only "oh gosh" and "oh dear" like a barely fallen Carmelite. Now, though, she was even passed the "oh gosh" stage, sweating and flushed, her head lashing back and forth across the pillow like the tail of a harpooned eel, at which point the telephone rang. Around the sixth ring, the sound penetrated into Karp's brain. He let ten more rings go by, until he realized both that the phone was not going to stop and that he was conditioned, like Pavlov's dog, to stop what he was doing, no matter what, and answer a ringing phone.

"Sorry, I got to answer that," he gasped.

"Sure, yeah. But make it snappy," said Marlene.

He rolled off and picked up the receiver. "Yeah?"

"Karp, is that you?"

"No, it's Henry Kissinger. Who is this?"

"Butch, it's me, Sonny Dunbar. I been trying to get you all night."

"Well, you got me now. This better be good, Sonny."

"No, it's bad, real bad. Donny's dead."

"Dead? When . . . what happened?"

"They called us from Vorland about ten-thirty. He was dead in his cell at bed check. They think he got hold of some dope and OD'd. I'm over at his house—we just got my sister to bed. I still can't believe it, you know? Anyway, I thought you better hear about it."

"Thanks, Sonny. Look, I'm sorry as hell about this . . . let's talk later, see where we stand."

Karp hung up and flopped back on the pillow. He hadn't thought about Mandeville Louis and Donald Walker for some time. He was carrying a full caseload now; it was hard enough to keep abreast of current cases, not to mention the strain of the Garrahy campaign. Tomorrow he would have to pull the file and rethink the case. But these thoughts were interrupted by a small, warm hand gliding down his belly to his groin.

"Ding-dong! Remember me?"

"Oh, yeah. Where was I?"

"Right here. Just a little higher. Ahh, that's marvelous," she said. But he couldn't get Donald Walker's frightened face out of his mind. That man was scared shitless, he thought, and he was right.

At the office the next day, Karp felt sleepy and sated, and found himself staring out the window at nothing. Shortly after noon, Sonny Dunbar came into his office, looking ashen and drawn.

"Pretty rough, huh?" said Karp. "You feel like going for coffee or a drink?"

"Nah, I got coffee up the wazzoo."

"OK, what's the story?"

Dunbar told a fairly common tale, but a sad one nonetheless. Donald Walker had drawn three-to-five for his role in the Marchione killings. Because he had no record of violence—and because Karp put in a good word—he was sent to the minimum-security facility at Vorland, in the Hudson Valley, about ninety minutes out of the city.

At Vorland, he was supposed to receive therapy and rehabilitation in the company of other young men who had gotten into trouble but were not regarded as dangerous, and whose crimes did not seem to warrant a ticket to the hell of Attica.

Or so it was supposed to work. Because of the peculiar distinction the law makes between adult and juvenile offenders, many individuals in Vorland's population had half a dozen years of ferocious criminality behind them when their slates were wiped clean on their eighteenth birthdays. They may have been *adult* first offenders, but they were hardly simple lads in their first bit of trouble.

Besides that, Vorland had been designed for a high ratio of correction officers to inmates. That ratio was consumed—like so many other good ideas—by the implacable grinding of the criminal justice machine. Vorland had twice as many inmates as it had been designed for. It was better than the Tombs; it was better than Attica, but that wasn't saying much. It was also one of the easiest places in the state of New York to cop drugs. The prison dealers just got on the phone and arranged for a friend to take a pleasant drive upstate, take a stroll along the eight-foot chain-link fence that bounded the facility, and flip a package over the top at a prearranged time and place.

Apparently Donald Walker had gotten a phone call the previous evening. It was from a woman claiming to be his sister; this was later discovered to be a lie. Walker had talked with her for a few minutes and the next day had been seen walking near the fence in the area known to the inmates as the Holy Land, because of the good things that fell out of the sky. By nine that evening he was dead, his belt around his arm, an empty syringe sticking in his vein.

"The little jerk," Dunbar went on, "he was clean for most of a year and then he goes and pulls a dumb trick the first time somebody, some 'friend' lays some shit on him. Go figure!"

"You know what they say, 'when the needle goes in, it never comes out.' Any lead on the supplier?"

"Who the fuck knows? Could be anybody—a friend of a friend . . ."

"I'm thinking who might want him dead."

"Who, that what's-his-face, Louis? He's still in the funny farm, right?"

"Right. But he could have set it up."

"Come on, Karp. You been reading too many books. The mob maybe does stuff like that. We're talking a mutt, a shooter, with no organization, no record. Besides, he's still nailed—you still got the old lady and the gun, the other evidence too."

"Yeah, but Donny was the linchpin. And, you know something? I'm not so sure that Mr. Louis is such a mutt. This bastard, I don't know, he stinks, from the word go. There's wheels within wheels going on there. Look, Sonny, I think it's important that we try to find the third man."

"What third man? The other guy in the car? Give me a break, Karp. It's been near two goddamn years. How'm I going to start looking? Walk down Lenox Avenue, bracing dudes: 'Say, scuse me bro', you happen to be in a car somewheres back in Nineteen-seventy with a guy who wasted a coupla honkies in a liquor store? No? Well, have a nice day.' Fuck me, Jack! You know how many cases I'm holding?"

"OK, Sonny, don't get your balls in an uproar. Just a suggestion. We got the gun, we'll go with that. On the other hand, you stumble on something, give me a call, OK? I want this shithead bad."

"I can tell that. It'll have to be stumble though, I'm warning you. Meanwhile, I got to go to a funeral."

After Dunbar left, Karp leafed through his beautiful file on the Marchione case. He had his doubts. An old lady witness on a dark street. A gun. Some bits of glass. Juries liked eyewitnesses, despite their notorious unreliability. Sussman would tear this shit apart—without Donald Walker to weave it together.

Karp got up and stretched. He decided to go down to the evidence locker to check over some material from a case he was preparing for presentation to the bureau on Friday. Karp liked to physically handle the evidence. He couldn't say exactly what it was, but the sight and feel of the guns, knives, chemicals, and blunt instruments with which New Yorkers ended one another's lives enriched his presentation of a case. For the same reason, he forced himself to visit the morgue and look at the victims. Also, there was always the chance, however slight, that something would pop out at him from the dreadful stuff and change the meaning of a case.

In the evidence locker Proud Mary was looking glum.

"What's happening, Mary?"

"I swear, Karp, that Guma ever come by me again I better not have no gun, or no knife in my hand. It took me the whole damn day to straighten out the mess you all made. Gettin' stuff back in the right boxes, fixin' tags . . . damn, I musta been pure crazy givin' him my key."

"That, or drunk. I hear it was quite a party, not that I remember much of it."

She let out a loud chuckle. "Shee-it! It *was* a party though. Dance? I was hurtin' all the next day. But you don' wanna hear 'bout no old lady miseries—what can we do for you today?"

Karp consulted a slip of paper. "I need Veliz," he said, and read off a case number. Then, as an afterthought, he said, "Oh, and give me Louis, too." On that one he had the number memorized. In a few minutes, Mary had returned with two covered cardboard boxes.

Karp signed them out and hefted the boxes. Immediately, he knew something was wrong. The boxes were too light a load. Veliz was a razor job. But there should have been a heavy .38 in the Louis box. He tore off the lid, his heart pounding. Plastic bags, a liquor bottle, no gun.

"Mary, where's the gun?"

"What gun is that, Mr. Karp?"

"The gun that's supposed to be in this box. Look, read the box inventory. There's supposed to be a Colt .38 Airweight here. Where is it?"

Mary's mouth hung slack for a moment and her eyes were

wide with fear. "Oh, Jesus God, Mr. Karp, I don't know! I found all these guns here in a trash can, and I put them . . . I put them back in the plastic bags in the right boxes, but that's all there was. What'm I gonna do?"

"I don't know, Mary, but we got to find that gun. Look, you're going to have to search every box in this locker. I'll check with some of the people at the party."

Tears shone on Mary's cheeks. "Mr. Karp, I got twenty-five years in. I got retirement in three years. They could fire me for this . . ."

He patted her shoulder. "Nobody's firing anybody, and nobody has to know about this. Don't worry, we'll find it. Just start looking, hey?"

He nailed Guma outside of the fourth floor courtrooms.

"Hey, Butch, some party!" said Guma, leering like a gargoyle.

"Yeah, right. Especially the part with the evidence guns. Guma, I mean, do you *ever* fucking think about what you're doing? You got *any* idea of how much shit you put me in with that dumb trick?"

Guma's smile faded. "What's wrong with you, man? Relax!"

"Relax, my ass! I just checked the evidence room and the pistol in the Marchione case is gone. You remember the Marchione case?"

"Yeah, that's the guy who pulled the wacko act, the one you got a hard-on for."

"That's right, I'm a little quirky that way, I don't like seeing cold-blooded multiple murderers get a free walk."

"What walk? I thought you had an eye on that, and his buddy snitched, right?"

"Right, but the snitch is dead, and the eye is about a hundred and two. The gun is my case, man, and you fucking lost it."

Guma chewed his lower lip and averted his eyes from Karp's smoldering gaze. "OK, OK, let me think. Look it's bad, but it's not that bad. If it's not still in the Gym, then Luis and his crew probably picked it up."

"Who the fuck is Luis?"

"The head of the night cleaning crew. I slipped him fifty to come back after the party and clean up, and turn the place back into an office. You know, move the partitions and shit. We always do it after a Gym party. I can check with him when he comes on at six-thirty tonight."

"Great, Guma. Let's hope he didn't loan it to his cousin to knock over a bank."

"Hell, no, Butch, Luis is all right. In fact, he was telling me how he wanted to be a cop. He's a law-and-order dude right down the line. Trust me, it'll be OK."

"It'll never be OK, Guma—the goddamn chain of custody for the goddamn gun is blown to hell. What am I going to do, depose the goddamn janitor? Your honor, we're pretty, fairly sure we got the right gun here as People's Exhibit 1—tell 'em, Luis! Too bad he's *not* a cop—what is he, too short?"

"Nah, he had a little history of breaking and entering, but..."

"Guma, NO MORE!" Karp put his hands over his ears and backed away. "Just find it, hey? I don't want to know another fucking thing about who got it or where it's been."

"By tonight, guaranteed!" yelled Guma, as Karp vanished into the Streets of Calcutta.

But Karp was no longer thinking about the gun. He was thinking about the third man. He had to have the third man in the car, and get him with something so heavy that the guy would turn on Louis. He didn't know how to find him, or how to turn him if he did find him. All he knew was that Louis wasn't going to be allowed to slip through the cracks. He thought, at least he's in Matteawan, at least we know where *he* is.

In fact, Mandeville Louis was nowhere near Matteawan at that moment. He was in a holding pen in that very building, waiting for a hearing, trying to slip through the cracks.

The cracks were pretty big. At about two o'clock that afternoon Louis was called into Part 30 of the Supreme Court. Part 30 was a calendar court, a gritty switching yard of the criminal justice system. No trials were held there. Instead, de-

196 —

fendants were brought before a judge, asked for a plea, and, if they pleaded not guilty, the judge set bail and calendared a trial date in another part. All returnees from Matteawan were brought to Part 30.

Calendar courts handled about a hundred cases a day. Their only purpose was to promote efficient movement in the system. The ADAs assigned to Part 30 were always the youngest, the most inexperienced from the ranks of the Criminal Court or the Felony Trial Bureau. In general, they learned about the case in the few seconds between the time the clerk called it and the time the judge asked what the People wished to do.

The People today in Part 30 was Dean Pennberry, a bright enough young man, but the ink on his bar exam was still damp. He favored bow ties and sober three-piece suits, which his mom bought for him. He was just getting over acne and still got the shakes when he had to talk to a judge.

The judge was Mervyn Stein. His devoted service on behalf of the Narcotics Control Commission and several other city agencies had earned him a lifetime job on the bench. One hundred Centre Street was a small world. The same characters appeared in different roles, defender one day, prosecutor the next, judge the week after, like characters in an interminable Chinese opera.

Judge Stein did not have a distinguished bench, but it suited him. Stein liked to make deals; he prided himself also on his case flow. Part 30 was hardly anything *but* deals. He had a talent for avoiding the legal niceties—like justice, which might slow things down in his court. As a result, from his first weeks as a judge he had been known as Merv the Swerve.

"How does the defendant plead," Judge Stein asked Leonard Sussman. He was surprised to see so distinguished a defense counsel in his courtroom, surprised but pleased. Not only did the lawyer add tone to his generally undistinguished circus, but Stein was glad of the opportunity to do a good turn for someone with powerful political connections.

"Not guilty, Your Honor," said Mandeville Louis earnestly. He was dressed in a yellow Tombs jumpsuit again, and to all appearances sane as a brick.

Stein glanced over the case file before him. "OK, wait a minute," he said, "this is a two-year-old case. Is that right, Mister Pennberry? The crime was Nineteen-seventy and this is seventy-two?"

"That's correct, Your Honor, ah ... two years this past March."

"Mister Sussman, have you discussed this case with the People?"

"Yes, Your Honor. My client would be willing to plead guilty to a charge of manslaughter in the first degree, with a sentence of zero to twelve years."

This offer sounded fine to Stein. If accepted, it meant that he would get credit for a felony conviction and a twelve-year sentence. Oddly enough, it was also fine with Louis, who had directed Sussman to make it. This was because in New York State there is a thing called a Max-out Rule, which states that a convict may be incarcerated for only two-thirds of the maximum sentence handed out by the judge.

But the zero was what counted. Louis would be up for parole immediately. In most cases with a zero-to-twelve sentence, the Parole Board would insist on at least a year in prison, but here was a man who had "served" two years in Matteawan. With Sussman's help, the Parole Board might quickly dispose of Louis's case. It was, after all, under considerable pressure to relieve the monstrous overcrowding of Attica. He could be out walking in a matter of weeks. The board had its own numbers game.

Pennberry was uncomfortable, not so much about Louis walking but about how the twelve-year max would look. He swallowed hard and cleared his throat.

"Judge, this man is charged with two common law intentional murders, two felony murders and armed robbery. I think the minimum acceptable plea is zip to fifteen."

Sussman returned to the defendant's table and spoke softly to Louis: "Well, Mister Louis?"

Louis glanced over at Pennberry, who was nervously fiddling with his bow tie. "No. Stick with the twelve. I don't want a fifteen-year sentence confusing the parole board."

Sussman spoke from the table. "Your Honor, in light of the fact that the defendant has spent over two years in a mental institution, we still think that zero to twelve is a reasonable sentence."

Stein did not like the way this was going. He looked at the wall clock. He was falling behind schedule. He frowned at Pennberry and asked both counsels to approach the bench.

"Dean, let's be reasonable. This is a stale case, one, and two, this is what we usually give to cases of this type, Matteawan returnees. I mean, face it, what else can you do? There's no way you're going to get a conviction on a two-year-old case. Now go back and take another look at the file and see if we can't get a disposal on this right now." He flashed a false and paternal smile and winked at Sussman.

Pennberry trotted back to his table. He glanced at the defendant, who looked like a clerk or a schoolteacher. Pennberry thumbed through the file. He was starting to sweat. Every eye in the courtroom was on him; this was a lot worse than being called on to answer a question in law school. The file was a blur.

Then salvation swam up to him in big red letters. He cleared his throat and said in a loud voice, "Your Honor, I see here that I am instructed to accept no lesser plea than Murder One."

"What!" said Stein. "Where does it say that? Who instructed you?"

"Ah, Judge, that would be Mister Karp, of the Homicide Bureau."

Pennberry shrugged and tried a nervous smile. "I'm sorry, Your Honor. There's nothing I can do. It's Karp's case."

Stein glanced again at the wall clock. "Get Karp down here. Now!" he snapped to his clerk.

Sussman went back to Louis and explained what was going on.

Louis had forgotten who Karp was. Sussman reminded him.

"Oh, him. The big muthafucka."

"Yes, him," said Sussman, wondering how long this endless and quite unpleasant case was going to drag on. "I think we may have a little problem, Mister Louis."

Karp took the call in his office, and was standing in Part 30 three minutes later. Stein gave Karp a long, sour look. "Mr. Karp, we are trying to reach a fair and equitable disposition here. The defense has agreed to plead guilty, but we seem to have run into some problems."

"What problems, Judge? A plea of guilty to Murder One is perfectly acceptable to the People," said Karp mildly.

"The plea is to Man One, Mister Karp, with zero to twelve."

"Oh. Well *that* plea is totally unacceptable to the People."

Karp smiled. Stein glared. "Mister Karp, will you approach the bench?"

Karp didn't move. "Your Honor, everything can be kept on the record."

Stein turned his glare on the stenographer. "Karp, you're obstructing the orderly progress of this court. What is this goddamn crap about no lesser plea?" The stenographer's flashing fingers halted. There was more than one way of keeping things off the record.

Karp was unperturbed. "It's simple, Your Honor. We are ready to try this case, unless the defendant wants to take a murder plea." Murder was the one exception to the Max-out Rule. By statute, fifteen years was the absolute minimum time a convicted murderer had to serve in prison. The Parole Board liked to add another five to the fifteen, to show it was on the job, which meant that pleading guilty to murder meant at least twenty years in Attica.

Sussman explained this to Louis, not without some satisfaction. "Mister Louis," he whispered, "your current strategy seems to be in ruins. Go to trial. You can beat this in court. Can I change your plea to 'not guilty'?" Louis shook his head and said nothing, but began toying with the zipper of his jumpsuit.

Stein said, "Mister Karp, I'm sure we all appreciate your diligence, but surely you're aware that this is a two-year-old case. You still have evidence and witnesses?"

"The People are ready, Your Honor. All we need is a two-week adjournment to prepare for trial. And that's what we intend to do, unless the defendant is ready to plead guilty to the top count of the indictment." He turned and looked at Louis: "Murder One."

Louis's response to this was to stand up, pull down his zipper, and urinate onto the neatly stacked papers covering the defendant's table. "Aiiiie! They're after me! They're after me!" he shrieked in a loud falsetto voice.

He then climbed up on the table and began stripping off his jumpsuit. Two guards leaped forward to control him, trying to avoid the stream of urine that sprayed in all directions. Sussman jumped backward in panic, but not before a row of dark stains was drawn like a sash across his immaculate pearl-gray suit coat.

The guards at last pinned Louis facedown on the table and cuffed his hands behind his back. His body was still thrashing about, arched backward like a bow. His face was contorted, mouth open and drooling ropes of saliva, eyes rolled up into his head, showing only yellowish whites. Karp noticed again that Louis had somehow removed his glasses before throwing his fit.

Stein was pounding his gavel. The packed courtroom was in pandemonium, the spectators and the eternal waiters on justice delighted with this amusing break in their mortal boredom. Somebody yelled, "Shit, boy, if you hadna run out of piss, you coulda got away."

Finally, Stein was able to stop gaveling. Louis's heavy breathing could be heard above the shuffling and coughing of the crowd. "Get that man out of here," Stein told the guards and they picked Louis up by his shoulders and ankles and began to carry him across the well of the court to the holding-pen door.

As they carried him past Karp, he said, "Hey, Louis, take care of those eyeglasses, now." For an instant, Karp thought he saw Louis's eyes snap down and focus on Karp's own. Karp grinned. The eyes disappeared, and in half a minute, so did Louis.

"Mister Sussman, I am remanding your client to Bellevue Hospital, for observation," said Judge Stein. "Next case."

Karp strolled over to Pennberry and patted his shoulder. "Thanks for keeping awake, kid. I know it's hard."

"That's all right, Mister Karp, ah . . . Butch. Thanks," said Pennberry, feeling for the first time like Mr. District Attorney.

Sussman was gathering his papers, dabbing at the damp ones with a wad of tissues. As Karp walked by him he said, "Your client's quite the pisser, hey, Mister Sussman. So to speak."

Sussman looked up bleakly. "It's a dirty business, Mister Karp."

"It is that, Mister Sussman. It is that," said Karp.

"Mister Karp, if you have no more business in this courtroom, I will ask you to leave forthwith," said Judge Stein from the bench.

"Your Honor, my business is concluded," said Karp, and trotted up the center aisle.

"Sonny? Butch. I'm sorry to disturb you at home, especially now, but . . . ah . . . we got to talk."

"Sure, that's OK. By the way, thanks for the flowers."

"No, it's the least—how was the funeral?"

"The usual. Ella and my mom took it pretty hard."

"Sonny, the reason I called is, we lost the gun, the pistol in the Marchione case."

"You what!"

"It was a fuck-up in the evidence room—it's a long story, but we can't build the case on it anymore. We got to find the other guy."

"Butch, I really mean this now. This is bullshit. Let me tell it to you again, and I hope it sticks this time. We do not have the horses to find people who we *know* killed folks and are walking around on the street, much less chase around after people we don't even know if they're still in town, where we at least got the mutt who did the job locked up. We got priorities. My lieutenant got priorities. The fucking chief of detectives got priorities, and baby, this ain't one of them."

"Sonny, don't give me that jive about 'locked up!' Matteawan isn't Attica and you know it. I just came this minute from Part 30. Louis was trying to cop to Man One, zip to twelve. If I missed the call, he'd be walking by the end of the month. I got to go . . ."

"Butch, you got your problems and I got mine. It don't change the priorities."

"Come on, Sonny, you sound like Wharton. Priorities, my ass!"

"That's the way it is, Butch, sorry. Hey, let me give you a little example. At the funeral now. Your basic regular black working-stiff family. I'm sitting drinking a bourbon and ginger and listening to these old ladies jawing, right? My Auntie Jess, and her cousin Helen, and my mom's cousin Bella. They keep the books on the old neighborhood, OK? They're talking about how many of the kids they know have gotten dead off dope, *and* not only dead off dope, but dead after they killed somebody with a goddamn shotgun.

"They went through, it must have been, six, seven kids, ripped off some dude, wasted him, took the money, bought dope, shot up, checked out. OK, that's the personal knowledge of *one* goddamn family. That give you some idea of what it's like up in the ghet-to? What we got on our hands in Fun City?"

"Sonny, I work in Homicide, I know what it's like."

"Yeah, well stop busting my horns on this thing, then."

"Hey, Sonny?"

"What."

"Donald didn't kill anybody with a shotgun."

"Right, he had a buddy did the job. So what?"

"Think, Sonny! The car, the phony plates, the phone call—Louis was setting Donald up, right? OK, suppose he didn't have a brother-in-law in the cops. Suppose somebody found him dead three days with a needle in his arm and some evidence strewn around connecting him to the liquor store. What happens then, Sonny? You're the cop, what would you do? Case closed, right? Shit, Donald was *alive* and he had a hard time convincing us that Louis even existed."

"What are you talking about, Karp?"

"Sonny, what the old ladies were saying. Figure the odds of that pattern repeating itself that many times. Even in New York it's off the charts. But, Sonny, what if *it's an M.O.* He uses junkies. He runs a bunch of robberies, kills the witnesses, sticks the junkies with the evidence, and slips them a hotshot or something, and sets up the overdose. Do the cops want to clear cases? Does a bear shit in the woods? He gives you clearances on a plate, dammit!"

"Karp, that's crazy. How the hell you going to go to court with that shit?"

"That's the point, Sonny. I don't have to. I can nail this motherfucker for life in Attica with the Marchiones. He's only got the one life, hey? But I got to have the other guy."

"I can't buy this, Butch, it's too weird."

"OK, do me a favor. Run a check. Pull files. Find out how many cases in the last five, ten years match the pattern. Shotgun murder of victim and any witnesses on the scene; probably a sizable score; case cleared when junkie is found dead of OD with incriminating evidence. Maybe there'll be a helpful anonymous tip leading the cops to the so-called killer. Just do it, Sonny. I'm right, I can feel it. That son of a bitch! Crazy, my ass!"

"Butch, if you're right . . ."

"Yeah, Louis got to Donny in Vorland. That's another lead. Find out who threw the stuff over the fence, you're getting close."

"This'll take a couple days to check out."

"I don't care how long it takes, just do it!"

CHAPTER FOURTEEN

Aweek passed. Karp was in his office talking to Guma on the phone.

"Sheldon ratted on us, the fink," said Guma.

"Guma, what are you talking about? What ratted?" It was not a welcome phone call. Karp was irritated, with his life in general, with the Marchione case in particular, and with Guma most of all.

Sonny Dunbar was still pawing through records and had come up with zilch on the other guy. Karp was also getting the cold shoulder from the dons of the Homicide Bureau. They had not forgiven him for supporting Garrahy and depriving smiling Jack Conlin of what they regarded as his rightful inheritance. He got the shitty cases now; and the nastiest grilling from the bureau. Conlin himself had stopped speaking to Karp almost entirely, ever since the awful interview when Karp told him about his plan to rally support for the old man.

As for Guma, Karp was pissed that every goddam member of the criminal justice bureaucracy—and a good part of the sleazy population of Calcutta—was privy to the details of his marital problems. The other day he had overhead two pimps talking in the hallway—"See that big dude, the ADA? I hear his wife's a bulldagger"—and he had wanted to smash their faces in, but he ground his teeth and walked away, because he knew that once he started smashing faces there was no clear line where to stop.

And the gun—the gun was still missing. No gun; no witness; no family; no career. Karp felt himself sliding into self-pity and depression. He reached for a hand-hold. Marlene? Maybe. He shook himself and tried to concentrate on what Guma was saying.

". . . anyway, Sheldon did a little investigation of his own, his first one as far as anybody knows, goes to show you what the right motivation can do, and turned up a night-shift guy who saw us carrying him into the morgue. So he whines about it where he knows Wharton will hear the story, and of course the Corncob does his own investigation, about the party and all, and takes it to the Old Man, which is why . . ."

"Guma, stop! What the *fuck* are you talking about?"

"Jesus, Butch, you didn't hear a word I been saying. We're in trouble. Garrahy wants us in his office at two today. The word is he's got a royal hair up his ass. I just hope it don't give him a stroke."

"*We're* in trouble? Where do *I* come into this, Goom? I thought I was just an innocent bystander."

"Well, not exactly, Butch. I mean, you helped us drag Sheldon down to the morgue. I mean, that's what got it all started. The morgue assistant pulls the fucking sheet off him the next morning and Sheldon opens his eyes and starts hollering. It's kind of hard to keep that under wraps. I think the *News* even had a filler on it."

"And I was there?"

"Well, yeah, Butch, we needed a hand with the corpse . . ."

"And you took advantage of me while I was drunk and incapable?"

"Oh, for cryin' out loud, Butch, stop being such a prick! It was a *joke*. You know what a joke is? C'mon, even if we both get fired, it'll be worth it just to think about what happened when Sheldon woke up on the slab. Denny was there. He says Sheldon sees where he is and starts moaning. He must of had a hell of a hangover, too. The attendant yells out, 'Hey, Doc, this guy ain't dead!' but Denny goes over there and says, 'Nonsense! What you're seeing is merely a reflex reaction caused by the contraction of the musculature, it's quite common'—you know that Haaah-vad way he talks sometimes—and then he pulls out his scalpel and says, 'Watch this! As soon as I've made the primary incision, the effect will disappear.'

"With that, Sheldon starts yelling and running around the autopsy room wrapped in the sheet. It took three guys to hold him down. He kept bawling, 'I'm alive, I'm alive, don't cut me!' and meanwhile, Denny is waving the scalpel and yelling, 'You fools! That's a corpse. Look at its face! Is that the face of a living man?' I hear he's in deep shit with the M.E. But what the fuck, if you can't have a little fun with your friends, what's the goddam point? Right?"

"Right. With friends like that, I don't need any enemies."

"OK, be that way. But just for being an asshole about it, I'm not going to tell you my good news."

"What good news?"

"Say 'pretty please with a cherry on top.' "

"Guma, I'm going to walk over to Mulberry Street and give the first guinea I see a hundred bucks to blow you away. Now give!"

Guma giggled over the line. "Karp, you ever want to kill me, *I'll* do the job for fifty. I mean, what are friends for? Anyway, I got the gun."

"Great, Guma. Stick it in your ear. Look, I got to go ..."

"Butch, you're not listening. I got The Gun—the gun from your case. We found it, me and Sonny Dunbar and the skinhead, Fred Slocum, his partner. We must of hit every pawn shop in Spanish Harlem. You know what Luis said. 'Mister Guma, you wan' to trow away any more gun, joos give 'em to me. Don' trow 'em inna sheet can, they get all steeky.' "

"All right! Way to go, Mad Dog, I take back forty percent of everything bad I ever said about you. This makes my month. Where is it?"

"In its little box in the evidence locker, where it's been since you put it there, these many months. And I'm glad you're happy, Butch, 'cause you're gonna need it. See you at two."

A dozen or so lawyers assembled in Garrahy's office at two o'clock that afternoon. Garrahy did not ask them to sit down. He looked at them with bloody murder in his eyes for a long moment. They shuffled their feet and hung their heads. Then there was a shattering crash, and they all jumped in unison, like a herd of antelope startled by a gunshot. Garrahy had flung his heavy glass ashtray at the wall, something he was wont to do in moments of extreme anger. Legend had it that he once brained a defaulting assistant DA with such a missile.

"Dis-gusting!" he roared hoarsely, his face blotched red with anger. "Disgusting behavior! Using evidence for infantile pranks! Drunkenness! Showing pornographic films for your own amusement! You are officers of the court. You are supposed to be above reproach. Not only have you besmirched yourselves, but you have brought dishonor on this office, my office, and that I cannot, I *will not* tolerate.

"Let me tell you something, and I hope that none of you ever forgets it. You know what keeps the law alive? It's not the jails, it's not the police—it's respect. Without respect, this office and all that it represents to this city in terms of order, probity, and justice, cannot survive. And how do we build respect? By hard work. By honesty. By dignity. By *dignity*, gentlemen, if I can still call you that.

"A certain standard of behavior is expected of us. Aristotle said, 'The state should be a school of virtue,' and that is what I expect this office to be.

"You are the teachers in that school. In every aspect of your behavior, both in the courtroom and in your private lives—perhaps *especially* in your private lives—you are obliged to conform to a higher standard than the ordinary citizen. You must be literally above reproach.

"Do you imagine that I am ignorant of what is happening in this city, in this nation? Do you imagine that I am unaware of the filth in which you spend your lives? But let me warn you. If you do not hold yourselves to a higher standard by force of will, by discipline, that filth will wash over you, and destroy you, and destroy this great office, and destroy this city too. It will be Babylon and wolves will walk in its streets."

Garrahy had leaned forward at his desk as he spoke, his deep voice filling the room, his hands clenched, his blue eyes bright and challenging. No one met his gaze.

When he had done, a sepulchral silence lay over the room, as if his dire prediction had already come to pass. Someone in the rear of the crowd sighed out loud.

Karp thought, this is the Real, all right. It was one thing to respect the man through reputation; it was another to see with your own eyes the splendid power that made Francis P. Garrahy one of the most devastating prosecuting attorneys in the history of American jurisprudence and one of the great men of his generation. At that moment, Karp would gladly have traded twenty years of his life to have worked under Garrahy in his prime.

The moment passed. Garrahy slumped back in his big chair. He began to rub his chest in a circular motion. Then he fumbled in his desk drawer, extracted a pill, and swallowed it with some water from his desk carafe. When he looked up again, he seemed older—and surprised to see the room filled with people. He waved his hand in a gesture of dismissal, as if brushing away insects. The office was cleared in three seconds.

In the hall outside, the attorneys were hurrying back to their stations in courtroom or office, chatting nervously. It had not been so bad after all. Roland Hrcany fell in with Karp.

"Helluva speech," said Hrcany. "Made me feel real small. We'll have to be more discreet about our excesses in the future."

"Assuming there is one," said Karp. "I've got a feeling that was the last dab of whipped cream in the bowl."

"Mr. Karp!" It was Ida, the secretary, calling from Garrahy's doorway. She jerked her thumb back over her shoulder. "He wants to see you."

Hrcany said, "He must want the other testicle."

Karp went back into Garrahy's office. The old man hadn't moved. He motioned Karp to a chair.

"I'll be blunt," he said, his voice once again an old man's gravel. "I'm moving you out of Homicide."

Karp's stomach hit the top of his shoes and rebounded. Oh, shit, he found out about the pistol.

"What! You mean because of the party?" he said weakly.

"God, no! What has that to do with it?"

"Then . . . ah . . . I don't understand. You think I haven't been doing the job?"

"Of course not. You're an excellent prosecutor. But you've

got enemies there now. I see you're surprised." He let out a dry chuckle. "People are. They think I sit here and talk to politicians all day. Or that I'm drooling.

"Jack Conlin will never forgive you. I've known him for twenty years, no, twenty-five. An unforgiving, a relentless man. That's what you get for dabbling in politics, my boy. But I'm grateful to you. Not many would have done what you did. And it's time for the rewards."

"Mister Garrahy, please! I hope you don't think . . ."

"What? That you helped me out of ambition? What of it? How do you think this city works, God help it? You helped me out and I'm returning the favor. How would you like to be an assistant bureau chief?"

"An assistant bureau chief?" said Karp idiotically.

"Yes. The Criminal Courts Bureau. Cheeseborough's retiring next week. Frank Gelb's moving in, but I expect he'll be swamped with paperwork. He'll need someone to work with the new attorneys, show them how we do things around here. It'll give you a chance to shake the bottom of the system up a little bit. I've spoken with Gelb, and it's OK with him. What about it?"

"Mister Garrahy, I don't know what to say."

"Say yes. Learn to take, Butch. God knows you give enough. All of you."

Karp said yes and shook his chief's hand. It was small, cold and dry.

He was hardly back in the office when the phone rang.

"Thirty-nine," said Sonny Dunbar over the line. His voice was high and excited.

"What's thirty-nine, Sonny?"

"There are thirty-nine dead junkie shotgun killers. I'm down at Police Records. They closed out fifty-six separate homicides on them over the past five years. In each case, all the witnesses were killed with a shotgun blast to the head. Except the Marchione kid, who got it with a .38. Each case was closed when a junkie was found dead of an overdose with incriminating evidence around him. In each case, the junkie was a slightly built black male. We even had three positive ID's of the 'killer' on the slab, from people who said they saw him leaving the crime scene. And in twenty-four of the cases, the cops were led to the corpse or the getaway car by an anonymous tip."

"Holy shit, Sonny, this guy might have killed nearly a hundred people in five years. He could be the greatest mass murderer in history."

"Could be, brother, but try and prove it. He suckered us good."

"Yeah, but no more. Listen, make copies of all those files and get them to me, all right? Oh, and I'll probably be changing offices. It looks like I got a new job."

"Oh, yeah? Does that mean somebody else is going to ride this case?"

"No way, baby. This is our private war. Keep it under your hat, and find that other guy!"

"You're on. We'll get him."

That evening, Karp and Marlene Ciampi had dinner at Villa Cella. They hadn't seen each other in several days, because Marlene was involved with a major case. Some members of an organization called the Bakunin Society had blown themselves up in a townhouse in the East Sixties. The police had investigated and rounded up several of the surviving members. It turned out that they had planted dozens of bombs in the New York area over the past year, including one, a letter bomb, that had killed a federal judge's secretary. Apparently they did not teach you in revolution school that big shots have their mail opened by members of the working class. As if it mattered.

"Anyway, I'm now an expert on what they used to call infernal machines. Letter bombs. Pipe bombs. Did you know you could go into any hardware store and buy the raw materials to build a bomb that'll level a building? The pros, though, try to get military explosives—C-4, plastic. And these little shits had a load of it. They're still trying to trace where it came from.

"But, Butch, the thing that sticks in my mind about the

case is these kids—hah, I say 'kids,' but one of these guys was older than me—the wackiest thing was how sure they were about themselves, that what they were doing was right. I mean, *I'm* not that sure about what *I'm* doing and I've got the whole fucking society patting me on the back, you know?"

Karp said, "What's the problem? They're fanatics, right."

"Bullshit, *you're* a fanatic, for that matter. No, the thing that hit me about them was how weird it was for them to end up this way. One of them, the guy who was in the house when it went up, had half his face missing and an arm that didn't work anymore, but they seemed, I don't know, *satisfied.* These are middle-class people now, I mean, every advantage, care, education, the works. Not exactly the desperate poor."

Karp chewed his lasagna and considered this. "I don't know, but I think it has something to do with power. I mean, there's the criminal who commits crimes because he can't do anything else, or because everybody he knows is into some kind of hustle. But I also think there's a kind of criminal who's got a hole in him that he has to fill, who gets whatever we get from our work out of beating the squares.

"Your terrorists are criminals who get their self-respect out of killing people and blowing things up for a cause. That and keeping themselves pure. They're just stuffing in bullshit to fill up that hollow place. The cause doesn't matter, I don't think, except to give an inflated tone to the whole business. I mean, they make these incredible demands—dismantle the fascist state, and that bullshit—but if the demands were actually met, would they stop being terrorists? Hell, no. Even if they ran the whole country, they wouldn't stop eating people up. The point of their lives is to fuck people over. If they didn't get to do that, they'd dry up and blow away."

"Damn, Butch, you're really getting excited about this. You're practically waxing philosophical. So tell me, where does the hollow place come from?"

Karp was oddly embarrassed. Like many men successful in manipulating the world and its powers, he was uncomfortable with analytic thought. He also felt strange speaking in this vein to his lover. He had never discussed his work abstractly with his wife. Their after-work conversation consisted of brief assessments of how the day had gone ("Lousy." "OK." "Great.") and anecdotes about personalities or events. Also, there was the feeling, of which he was ashamed, and which he suppressed, that Marlene was a hair sharper in the thinking department than he was. This added to his discomfort. He retreated into toughness.

"I don't know. I'm no criminologist. And you know what? I don't really give a rat's ass. I'm not in the understanding business, I'm in the putting asses in jail and keeping mutts from fucking people over business. It's hard enough."

"So it is. On the other hand, I'm not sure you can survive long doing what we do without developing some understanding for the bad guys. Look at the Grand Inquisitor in Dostoevsky. He keeps his mouth shut and radiates understanding and the killer spills his guts. Case closed."

"Dostoevsky? Didn't he write *New York State Criminal Procedure*?"

She laughed. "Up yours, Karp. You're such a barbarian, I don't know why I bother talking to you."

She lit a cigarette, drew deeply, and coughed.

"You ought to quit smoking," he said.

She squinted at him through a gray haze. "I ought to quit seeing you, but I won't," she retorted. "Besides, I tried once and gained fourteen pounds in a month. Fuck the surgeon general. A size five is well worth ten years of life."

The waiter came back with coffee, American for Karp, espresso for Marlene.

"Well," said Karp, after they finished, "my place or yours, baby?"

"How romantic! You didn't even ask me what my sign was."

"OK, what's your sign?"

"Scorpio."

"I knew it," said Karp. "Let's fuck."

Later, they walked north out of Little Italy, toward Karp's place in the Village. The night was warm and muggy, and smelled of anise and frying sausage. At 14th Street they passed a TV and appliance store. Marlene remarked, "Hey, Butch, that place is having a going-out-of-business sale. Why don't you pick yourself up a TV?"

"I've got a TV," answered Karp, moving on. "And this guy's been going out of business since Nineteen Fifty-two."

But Marlene had stopped. "No, you don't have a TV. You have a rowing machine. You get much better reception with a TV set."

"No, really, I do have one. It's in storage with the rest of my stuff."

"Oh, *that* does a lot of good. Is it color?"

"No, black and white. What is this, Marlene, you having media withdrawal?"

She smiled sheepishly. "Oh, nothing. I just, you know, like to watch TV in bed. And if I don't catch the news in the morning, I get nauseous."

He laughed. "OK, Champ, I unconditionally support any activity you do in bed."

They turned to study the dozen or so sets in the window. They were all tuned to the same channel. A woman did a dance in her bathroom. They couldn't hear the sound, but it was clear from the words on the screen that she was glad that her toilet paper was extremely soft. Then a famous newscaster came on, looking grave. Then another face came on the screen.

Karp said, "Hey, look, it's the DA."

Garrahy's weathered face was replaced by one even more famous, that of the governor of New York. He was addressing a crowd of newsmen at a press conference. He looked grave as well. Then another face, not a famous one at all, appeared on the screen.

Karp caught on. "Oh, God damn! God damn it!" he cried and ran into the store. There were sets operating within the store, too, and Karp rushed up to one of them and turned up the volume. The not-very-famous face was saying, "pledge to do my utmost to carry on the great traditions of this office."

The famous newscaster came on and said, "Sanford Bloom, just appointed to the post of New York District Attorney, replacing Francis Phillip Garrahy, dead tonight of a heart attack at the age of seventy-three. It's the end of an era for criminal justice in New York, at a time when most Americans feel that crime is their most important concern. In Washington today, the president asked for . . ."

Karp snapped off the sound. He felt Marlene's hand on his arm. He looked down at her. His face was contorted with grief and miserable with unshed tears. She tried to lead him out of the store. He moved stumblingly, like a mourner being tugged away from a grave. She held tightly to his hand as they walked in silence. Finally, she said, "Butch, he was an old man . . ."

He turned facing her, pulling away, his eyes blazing. "I *know* he was old, Marlene. You don't have to tell me he was *old*. Guy that old should be sitting on the beach in Florida, playing with grandchildren. But, oh no! Butch couldn't do without his fucking hero. He had to keep him around one more term. And it killed him."

"Come on, Butch . . ."

"No, it's true. I am a total piece of shit."

"No, you are not a total piece of shit. What you are is a self-centered, perfectionist, workaholic asshole with a tendency to overdramatize. I'm sorry he's dead, too, but he was an old man, and old men also die on the beach in Florida. He died with his boots on, and that was the kind of person he was anyway. And he didn't have any grandchildren.

"OK, you convinced him to run. He was a grown-up. He knew how to call a doctor and get a physical. You want to mourn him? Fine. God knows he's worth mourning for. But make sure it's him you're mourning and not something to do with your self-image and the failure of your little schemes."

"Thank you, Marlene, dear. That was quite a little speech. I'm glad I can count on you for support . . ."

"SHIT!" Marlene yelled at the top of her voice. "You won't listen and you won't stop! You're not thinking about Garrahy. You're just thinking about yourself and your fucking guilt. Now snap out of it! Get drunk or go to church or take me home and pull my pants off, but stop this goddamned *whining*."

"Hey, I didn't start this fight," said Karp weakly.

"FIGHT! You think this is a fight? This isn't a fight. *This* is a fight." With that she slammed her fist into him just above the belt buckle. Then she dropped her shoulder bag to the pavement, snapped into a fighter's crouch and started to pound him with quick, sharp punches in the midsection.

Karp was driven back against a building, shielding himself with his forearms. "Hey, damn it, stop it, Marlene! Cut it out! I mean it, cut it out!"

But she kept at it, bobbing and weaving, ducking her head, landing punches. "Come on, you wanna fight? Come on, you big bastard, fight!"

A small crowd of half a dozen or so had gathered to watch. Somebody laughed and said, "Two bucks on the chick."

Karp shouted, "OK, you asked for it," and lashed out with his right, an openhanded blow to her head. To his amazement, she blocked with her left, ducked under the punch and threw a right cross to his mouth that rocked his head back and split his lip. He let out a yell and charged forward. He grabbed her at the shoulders and pulled her to him in a tight clinch. She was trying to work her arms up between them and break his hold, when something wet dropped on her face. She looked up and saw that Karp's chin was covered with blood.

"Oh, Butch, you're bleeding. Oh, no, I'm sorry. Oh, let me go, I'll get you a hankie."

She squirmed out of his grasp, picked up her bag, extracted a handkerchief and pressed it tenderly to his cut lip. "Please, don't be mad at me, Butch. It just drives me crazy when you act all schmucky like that." She kissed his cheek and hugged him. The crowd drifted away. The joker said, "I tol' ya. The chick by a TKO."

Karp, still a bit stunned, wiped at his lip and chin. "That's OK, Marlene. It was a little unexpected, that's all." He grinned bloodily. "I don't intend to press charges for assault."

"Thank God! I thought I was looking at six in the House of D."

"Where did you learn to box like that?" Karp asked as they walked north again, holding hands.

"Oh, from my old man. We all used to watch the Friday night fights together, and then we would all roughhouse. Girls, boys, it didn't make any difference, until the girls grew tits. Then we had to ref."

"Smart daddy."

"Yeah, really. But I guess it was the whole scene at home. My mom and dad are both really physical people, you know? Lots of hugs, kisses, and smacks in the head. They would get to fighting over something and start swinging punches. I mean he didn't beat up on her or anything, they just used to whale away at each other in the kitchen or wherever. Then they used to cry and clean each other up and jump into bed and ball. It wasn't scary or anything, the fighting, because we knew they loved each other a lot. Still do, in fact. I bet you think that's pretty primitive, huh?"

"Not the jumping-into-bed part."

"Ooh, goody. I'm hot as a pistol. Let's take a cab."

As Guma had predicted, it was a helluva wake. Flags flew at half-mast throughout the city as the mortal remains of Francis Garrahy lay in state for three days in a funeral home, guarded by spit-and-polished cops from the Emerald Society, while the great and famous and the ordinary people whose lives he had touched filed past. Then came the state funeral with its police bands, the eulogy by the governor himself, the tributes by anyone of any consequence connected to the criminal justice business, the City of New York, or Ireland.

They buried him on a sunny Saturday in June in Queens, the Borough of the Dead and the Might As Well Be, as they say in Manhattan. Karp went, as did the rest of the office, and did not cry. He was amazed to see Ray Guma wiping tears and blowing his nose like a bereaved widow.

CHAPTER FIFTEEN

O n the Monday after Garrahy's funeral, Sanford L. Bloom held his first senior staff meeting as district attorney. Karp's name had been entered as an assistant bureau chief, in what was probably one of Garrahy's last official acts, so he was on the list and he attended.

The nine bureau chiefs and their deputies took their places around the long oak table in the DA's conference room. Conlin and Joe Lerner were up toward the head of the table next to the door to the new DA's office. Conlin looked dyspeptic while Lerner looked nervous and uncomfortable. The other chiefs—all Garrahy's men, some of whom had served him for decades—appeared similarly uncomfortable, like the leaders of a nation defeated in war, waiting upon the commander of the occupying forces.

Karp sat next to his new boss, Frank Gelb, whom he barely knew. Gelb was a quiet man, heavy set, balding, with a ginger mustache. As head of Criminal Courts, he had the most frustrating and thankless job in the justice system; after only a few months in the post he looked worn.

"What's happening, Frank?" said Karp.

Gelb regarded him bleakly. "Damned if I know. They told me to show up, so I showed up. There's no agenda. The rumor is, no reorganization, and he's sticking with the bureau chiefs he's got, for the time being. I guess this'll be a pep talk, the great traditions of the New York DA's office, et cetera. Shit, Garrahy's not even cold. What is he going to do, tell the world the old man didn't know what he was doing? On the other hand . . ."

"What, on the other hand?"

"Apparently, he's been closeted with Conrad Wharton ever since the funeral. Also, I hear stirrings from my buddies in personnel and budget. There's forty new attorney positions in the budget for the next fiscal year. I hear Conrad is carving out a little empire from those."

"No way! Those are courtroom slots. They'd have to be crazy to use them anyplace else. How's he going to move cases without attorneys?"

Gelb sighed and ran his hand across the top of his scalp. "There are ways and ways. In any case we will soon see. Oh, by the way, you might as well move into the Assistant Bureau Chief Office. It's always a mistake to have empty office space when a change in regime is going on. One of the eternal verities of bureaucratic life."

Karp was about to ask what an assistant bureau chief actually did for a living, when the door to the DA's office swung open and Bloom strode vigorously into the room, with a pink and shiny Wharton trailing behind him, as if he were a painted pull toy.

Sanford Bloom was a medium-sized man with large moist eyes, a full mouth and a thin, prominent nose. He was forty-four and looked much younger. He was tanned with his brown hair coiffed over his ears in a politician's blowdry. His face was unmarked by lines of worry, which was not surprising, since he had enjoyed ease and wealth and the right contacts since the cradle. He had a softness of expression about his eyes and mouth, the suggestion being that, if seriously crossed, his lip would begin to tremble and his face might dissolve into petulance.

Bloom sat at the head of the table. There was no room at the table for Wharton, who waited politely for one of the seated men to make room for him. No one moved. After a minute he pulled up one of the straight-backed chairs lined against one wall and settled himself to Bloom's right rear, like a translator behind a diplomat.

"I suppose you're wondering why I asked you all here," Bloom began with a boyish smile, and got a chuckle in response. "Let me say, first of all," he continued, "that I had and retain the greatest admiration for the late Phil Garrahy and for this office. But as I look around at the conditions we now find ourselves in, I have to say, and believe me, it is painful for me to say it, that the current methods and procedures of the New York District Attorney's Office are totally inadequate for the modern age. Gentlemen, we are losing the war on crime in this city!"

Here he paused for effect and looked around the table. Silence and blank faces. He cleared his throat and resumed.

"The productivity of this office has not significantly increased in thirty years, while crime has increased tenfold. Our record-keeping systems are a disaster. We have no way of centrally tracking a case through the system, to find out where the worst delays are, and get these cases moving again. This is the twentieth century, men! We've got to modernize. I need new ideas. I want this office to become a leader in criminal justice system innovation."

He stared around the table again. No one came up with any new ideas. Conlin stared off into space.

"I don't intend to make any massive changes in personnel or organization, right off. I believe in giving all of you a chance to see if you can play in a new ball game. On the other hand, I have to start exerting some control over the way this office is run, and I need, that is, the Office needs, an administrative bureau on a par with the operational bureaus. I have chosen Chip Wharton here, who I think you all know, to head up that new organization. I know I can count on all of you to give him your strong support. Well, any comments? Suggestions?"

Bloom looked around brightly. After a long pause, Joe Lerner said, "Ah . . . Chief, how are we going to staff this new bureau? Is it going to be a tap on the existing resources?"

"Not at all, Carl . . . Joe? Is it Joe? Sorry. Not at all, Joe. The existing units will be held harmless. It so happens that we are expecting an increase in positions in the upcoming fiscal year, which we will use to establish the new bureau."

Jaws dropped all around the table and half a dozen bureau chiefs all started talking at once. Everybody had been expecting a share of the new recruits, so that maybe they would be only up to their necks in the shit rather than nostril-deep.

Bloom raised his hands for silence and scowled until the grumbling died away.

"I am not," he said, "going to keep pouring resources down a rathole. The legal staff you have now is working at about a tenth of the efficiency it could have with a decent system. I need the new slots to set up such a system, and enforce it. I hope that all of you will help me do that. If not . . ."

He let the statement hang. No one said a word. There was some discussion of minor administrative details after that, and ten minutes later the chiefs were dispersing to their posts.

In the hallway outside Karp shook his head in disbelief, then said to Gelb, "You were right. I can't believe it. More lawyers is throwing resources down a rathole? A rathole? He should know from ratholes, right?"

Gelb sighed and glanced around to check for big ears. "Right, and Wharton seems to have fixed himself a nice little nest. On the other hand, Bloom is a pretty bright guy, I hear. I mean, he's right, in a way, things *are* pretty fucked up."

"Come on, anybody who talks to Wharton more than ten minutes has got to be an asshole. And giving Corncob our lawyer slots for admin.? I still can't believe it. What are we going to do?"

"What's the choice? We do our jobs, the best we can. Or get the fuck out, like Jack Conlin."

"Conlin's leaving?"

"Are you serious? He had a job lined up with Whitman Brady about twenty minutes after the governor announced Bloom. I figure a quintupling of his current salary the first year. He'll cry all the way to the bank."

"Yeah, but Jack Conlin defending skells? Yecch!"

"But very high-class skells. Hey, Jack was always out for number one. If he can't have the power, he'll have the coins. Oh, well, if I had Jack's rep, I'd be off too. Christ, if I had his *hair* I would. What about you? You figure to stay?"

"Me? I hadn't thought about it much. I guess I'll stick around. It might be interesting."

"I can guarantee that, kid," said Gelb.

They agreed to meet later in the day to discuss the details of Karp's new job. Gelb left and Karp rode down to the snackbar for a coffee and a greasy doughnut to go. He entered the elevator to ride up to six and begin cleaning out his Homicide Bureau office. Someone said, "Hold it!" Karp pushed the button like a good citizen and Joe Lerner got in.

"How did you like your new boy, Karp?" Lerner asked.

"He's not *my* new boy, Joe."

"Oh, no? I would think he might be favorably disposed to the guy who iced the competition. I'm sure that will be brought to his attention. I mean Wharton and Mr. Twentieth Century there are going to need a fucking lawyer on the team, and you, whatever else you are, are a lawyer."

The elevator doors opened. Lerner moved to get out, but Karp blocked his way. The automatic door went ka-chunk, ka-chunk against his shoulder.

"Piss on all that, Lerner! I don't give a damn what you think about me or what I did. I presume you're acting bureau chief now that Conlin is out. Congratulations. I would like to see the acting bureau chief sometime today to discuss a number of cases I have been working on, since despite the recent tragic events I believe we are still in the business of putting asses in jail, ever more efficiently, of course. Now, how about it Mister Lerner?"

Lerner glared at him for a couple of beats, then pushed past Karp into the hallway. "Call the girl and set it up," he snapped.

"Maybe I should get out of this too," said Karp.

"Oh, bullshit!" replied Marlene Ciampi. Karp was sitting in her old wooden swivel chair in her tiny office in the walled-in hallway, and Ciampi was sitting cosily in his lap. It was about seven o'clock that Monday evening. Karp had just finished telling Marlene about his day, and was feeling mildly sorry for himself.

"Why is it bullshit? Move your ass, you're squashing my keys into me."

"Sorry. It's bullshit because the last thing you need is another giant upset in your life, on top of your wife and Garrahy. Give it a year with Bloom, or two. How bad could it be?"

"Real bad. Gelb's got me doing all the administrative work. I'll be an old man before I see a courtroom again. Also, I'm in charge of recruiting and training, which I've never done before. I mean how the hell do you tell if somebody is going to make a good ADA?"

"Ask them to tell you a lie. If you fall for it, they're in. Do you mind if I stroke your fevered brow?"

"No, go right ahead. OK, then I go to see my friend Joe Lerner, we're talking about homicide cases I'm handling, and I tell him I want to keep following this business with the Marchione killer. No way, he says—get this—because he thinks I'll throw the case to feed the numbers. Me! I fucking *invented* that case."

"So what happened?"

"Ah, we worked it out. A little screaming and yelling, clenched fists, tight jaws, your basic locker-room fight. He's really a good guy, just being a hard-ass because he's pissed at me from the Garrahy campaign. But he knows it's my case, and if he can get it lifted from Homicide's effective caseload for free, it's gravy to him. He saw the light.

"Oh, yeah, and this is the cherry on top—Gelb told me I have to represent the bureau on Wharton's fucking task force. Can you believe this?"

"I don't know, you might do some good. You can't slay dragons all the time. Sometimes you have to polish your sword, or whatever. Anyway, you'll survive. Between me and Corncob, this is the year you get your character built."

"Thanks, Marlene, I needed that. What was your day like?"

"Dreamy. I spent the morning with the bomb squad out at Hunts Point. Just little me and all those big, brave, macho police officers. Those guys are real men, not paper-shuffling candy-ass lawyers like you."

"Oh yeah? What were you out there for?"

"My terrorists, remember? The cops set up a demo of different kinds of explosives and devices, fuses, detonators, timers— the works. They were falling all over themselves to show me what kind of daredevils they were. I'm surprised I wasn't blown to *smithereens*. Smithereens! I've always loved that word. Maybe I was a bomber in a previous life. Look, I got souvenirs!"

She reached out to her desk and scooped up several objects. Holding up a sphere of tan puttylike material, she said, in a deep-voiced, heavy Queens accent, "This here's a genuine piece of C-4, size of a golf ball, it'd blow yer ass to Canarsie, it ever went off, heh-heh. Now this here's yer primacord. Looks like something you'd hang yer undies on, hey? You wrap a piece a this aroun' a telephone pole, set it off, wham—cut that mother right off at the knees."

"Marlene, this is real stuff? They gave it to you?"

"Shit, no! I ripped it off. It's my payment for handling five hours of patronizing chauvie bullshit with unrelenting cheerfulness."

"What're you going to use it for?"

"I don't know—I'll think of something. Oh, here's the best one. It's a fixed-time detonator." She held up a finger-long black plastic tube with a knurled end and a metal ring dangling from its side. "What you do is, you take the primacord and stick it in this little hole here, like this. Then you wrap the cord around the C-4, like this. Instant bomb. When you twist the end of the detonator, it breaks a vial of acid, which eats through a wire in a fixed time—this one is for two minutes—which releases a spring, setting off a cap, which explodes the primacord and the plastic. You can't stop it going off once it's set. Even works under water. Neat, heh?"

"Marvelous. Now put it away. It gives me the willies."

Her face broke into a fiendish grin. "The willies? I'll give you willies." With which she raised herself up, twisted the detonator, pulled Karp's waistband out, and dropped the bomb down his pants.

Karp came out of the chair like a rocket, dumping Marlene on the floor, bellowing and trying simultaneously to grab the thing by reaching down his front and to shake the bomb down his pants leg by dancing on one foot. But the irregularly shaped device had hung up somewhere in the crotch area, and Karp had to drop his trousers and pick it up. He was about to heave it over the partition toward what he prayed was a deserted hallway, when his brain started to function again, and he looked around to see what Marlene was doing.

She was still sitting on the floor, shaking in a paroxysm of silent laughter. "Oh, God," she gasped, "It's OK! I didn't . . . I didn't . . . remove the safety pin with a . . . Oh, God . . . look at you . . . with a sharp downward pull on the ring."

Karp was not amused. He put the bomb down on the desk and pulled up his pants. Then he took off his belt.

"OK, Ciampi, this is it," he snarled.

"Ahh, come on, Butch, it was just a joke. This is me, Marlene, your main squeeze. You think I would blow my favorite genitalia to smithereens? Besides, you wouldn't want to make marks on my lush, milky-white thighs, or my adorable perfectly rounded buttocks, would you?" She spread her raised knees a few inches, waggled her hips and contorted her face into a parody of cross-eyed lust.

Karp swung the belt menacingly for a moment. Then he sputtered into laughter, too, and reached his hand down to help her off the floor. She gave him a hot squirmy hug.

"Forgive?" she asked into his ear.

"Not only that, but I'm going to do you a good one. After I move my stuff down to Criminal Courts, I'll help you move yours into my old office."

"Oh goodie, a window! Is it legal?"

"Who gives a shit? Possession is nine-tenths of the law."

"Ah, Butchie, when you do lawyer talk like that it makes me all shivery inside. OK, I'll get packed up here. Then can we go out?"

"Absolutely. The usual dinner, movie, sex?"

"Yes, yawn."

"Boring, huh. How about all three simultaneously? We could get take-out Chinese and go to Radio City."

"Now you're talking, Buster!"

"Champ," he said, "some day you're going to go too far."

"When I do," she said, hugging him harder, "you'll be the first to know."

By the tail end of that summer, Karp came to realize that the new regime was both worse and better than he had expected.

Worse, because under Bloom, a brainy man with high political ambitions and no particular attachment to the notion of justice, the rule of numbers became absolute. As always, the rule of numbers meant rule by men who were comfortable with numbers, who believed that the neat boxes on their organization charts could somehow order and wash clean the screaming social chaos of crime in the City of New York. The lawyers called them data weenies.

Wharton ruled these men. He set targets for what he called "throughput" and his troops broke these out into specific targets for each bureau and for each individual attorney. Since a certain number of cases came in each week, each assistant DA was obliged to move a certain number out, and would get dinged if he came up short. This meant that plea bargaining became virtually the only way by which cases were ever *disposed*. There were of course standards governing the acceptability of bargains, based on the initial charges and the circumstances of the crime. But the way it turned out was that nobody ever got dinged on failure to meet standards, just on failure to meet clearance targets.

Trials virtually disappeared under this standards system, and so did the old guard of seasoned prosecutors who had grown up in the Garrahy era, the lawyers to whom trials were the center of their professional lives. One by one, and then in clumps, they left for private practice, the bench, the beach. Six weeks after taking office, Bloom dissolved the Homicide Bureau, thus abolishing the true church of the Garrahy religion. It was a natural consequence of the new order: silly to make a big deal about homicide, if a killing was just another occasion for a plea bargain, another felony clearance, another digit to keep the data weenies off your back. But oddly, in this unpromising situation Roger Karp flourished.

On a morning in late August, Karp was standing at the counter buying coffee in Sam's when someone pinned his arms from behind, and said, "Hey, big shot! What's going on? You don't fucking talk to your old friends, now that you're a padrone. I got him, Roland, let's punch him out!"

"Guma, you jerk! Let go, I'm spilling the coffee here."

Guma released his grip. "How'd you know it was me?"

"Stumpy arms. It could've been V.T., but he cleans his nails. How's it going, Roland?"

Between time on the new job and time with Marlene, Karp had seen neither Guma nor Hrcany much since the start of the summer.

"Sucks, as usual. I'm about ready to quit. Sit down, Butch, let's hear what you're up to."

"I can't. I got a meeting with my staff in five minutes."

" 'My staff,' my ass! Listen to this guy, Roland. We taught him everything he knows, now he gets a little rank, he gets snotty with us."

"Yeah, Karp, fuck your staff. You're the boss, let 'em wait."

They muscled Karp into a booth.

"OK, give!" said Guma. "Where the fuck you been? Getting any gash?"

"Who has time?"

"I'm cryin' my eyes out. Nah, you're getting it somewhere. It shows. Who is it? Somebody we know?"

"Guma, you think I'd ball anybody you knew?"

"Don't be so wise, Karp. OK, tell us about life in the big time. What's this guy Gelb like to work for?"

"Damned if I know. I never see the guy. He's cruising all day looking for another job, like everybody else."

"You, too?" asked Hrcany.

"No, although I thought I'd never say this. I'm having a good time."

"See, it's the gash," said Guma.

"Nah, he sold out to the weenies," said Hrcany, in a not entirely facetious tone.

"Look," said Karp, ignoring this, "they're trying to control the whole office with numbers. But you can't really control anything with numbers unless you have a sense of what the numbers mean. Which they don't. Bloom and Corncob, they don't know jackshit about what really goes on. It's like that story about the Russian chandelier factory. They get a quota from Moscow every year—make six tons of chandeliers. So they make one six-ton chandelier and take the rest of the year off.

"So what they want out of the Criminal Courts Bureau is clearances. You got to have a certain number every week, every month, based on what comes into the system through the Complaint Room, a percentage, right? The felony hearings are the choke point of the whole system—where we get the plea bargaining—so the pressure is on my guys to clear at any cost. The data weenies are calculating percentages right and left.

"Naturally, it takes about twenty minutes after Bloom's system goes into effect before every skell and every skell lawyer in town knows the score. Why should they take a hard deal, right? They know the kid ADA *has* to deal, or his own people are on his ass. Hey, my client shot four old ladies, we'll cop to simple assault and time served, right?"

"Yeah, right," said Hrcany.

"No, wrong. We got standards for cases like that, signed by Bloom in his own blood. The skell goes up for five to seven or we try."

"But how can you do that, Butch? What about the percentages?"

"Easy. We're supposed to clear a set proportion of what comes in through the Complaint Room. That's the base. And who controls the Complaint Room?"

"You do," said Hrcany, "but what does that matter, if . . . oh, I see, said the blind man. You sly devil, you, you're cooking the Complaint Room books."

Karp placed a finger next to his nose, like old St. Nick. "That's a shocking accusation, Roland, and impossible to prove. None of the weenies ever sets foot in the Complaint Room. They might see a victim and have to throw up from the degradation of it all. I *will* say that although we have a terrible crime wave in New York, we of the New York District Attorney's Office are keeping the cases moving through the system at an ever increasing rate. I quote our fearless leader."

"Amazing. But how much can you fudge?"

"Not a lot. Enough so that when we get a case that would

break our rate if we had to try it—but which we can't let the assholes just walk away on—we can hold out for a tough plea. I won't say it's winning. It's just losing slower. And it lets my guys keep their self-respect, which otherwise would be down the drain the first day. Look, it's been real, folks, but I got to go."

"But, Butch, what's the fucking point. How long can you keep it up?" asked Hrcany.

Karp slid out of the booth and stood up. "I don't know, but I'm building my character. Look, you know that old John Wayne movie, where he's got only four bullets left and he's in this cabin with about two hundred bad guys surrounding him. They figure he has to be out of ammo, so they send a bunch of guys up to flush him out. Wayne lets them get close and then, pow, he shoots one and they all run down the hill again. He can't beat them, but he sure as hell can make them keep their distance until the cavalry comes. It's the same thing."

"But how long can you hold out if there's no fucking cavalry," asked Guma.

"I don't know, Goom," Karp said with some asperity as he walked away. "I guess that's why the Duke doesn't wear a watch."

There were nearly thirty lawyers waiting for Karp when he walked into the bureau training room. Besides shafting the system, and putting at least the very worst of the asses in jail, training young lawyers was the other thing that made Karp's job worth doing.

He was a good teacher, and teaching lawyers how to win cases was not all that different from teaching kids how to play basketball, which Karp had spent his teenaged summers doing at a camp in New Jersey. His current crop of young attorneys looked to him now about as old as those campers. Karp was five or six years older and felt like the ancient of days.

Today Karp was giving what he had billed as his looney lecture. He told them about the legal doctrine of insanity, the M'Naughton and Durham rules, and the little kicker in the New York State criminal code that allowed a verdict of not guilty by reason of insanity if a defendant "as a result of mental disease or defect lacks substantial capacity to know or appreciate the nature and quality of his act, or that it was wrong."

"Now," Karp continued, "this is going to shock you, but there are people out there who commit crimes and who don't have a mental disease or defect and who still put in an NGI plea. Our job is to prove to the jury that they're not crazy. The defense brings in their shrink, we bring in our shrink. The jury is confused at all times, which works in favor of the defense, you understand. We have a social horror of convicting somebody on a capital offense if he really thought he was cutting up a pumpernickel, but it was really the neighbor. However, ninety-nine percent of the NGI pleas you will see are not like that. They're mutts trying to rip off the system. Yeah, Phil?"

Phil Dellia, an intense and studious kid just out of Fordham Law, had raised his hand. "But what about bizarre, motiveless crimes? Somebody likes to cut up redheads, or bald guys with cigars. What do you do?"

"Good question. The answer is, bizarre is not crazy, motiveless is not crazy. The issue you *have* to focus the jury on is, did he know he was killing a human being? Did he know that killing was wrong? I'll demonstrate. Let's say I don't like Mister Krier here. He's a pain in the ass, I want to get rid of him."

Here Richie Krier, the class clown, turned in his seat to face the group, smiled, and waved. Krier wanted lawyering to be like lawyering in the movies, because what he really wanted to be was an actor. He had the wit and the physical equipment—tall, dark, and handsome—and was disappointed that what he did in real life was so different from what he had been led to expect. He didn't begrudge the waste of three years in law school—it had kept him out of the draft—but he had seen the light and was now attending acting classes in the evenings, doing as little work as possible for the DA's office, and doing that sloppily.

"OK, let's say I go to say, Kaplan here, and give him five hundred dollars to shoot Krier."

Mike Kaplan, a former engineer and the best of Karp's recruits, grinned behind his wire-rimmed glasses and said, "Two hundred and fifty dollars."

Laughter. "OK, two hundred and fifty dollars. You do the job, you cut off Krier's head to show me that you earned the money. The cops follow a trail of blood to my office and we're arrested. What's the charge?"

"Murder One," said Kaplan.

"Because?"

"It was done with intent to cause death of deceased and did cause death."

"Right, and the contract nature of the killing makes it highly unlikely that an NGI would be offered. Now, in contrast, let's say you're at home, you're hungry. You feel like a salami sandwich. You cut a piece of salami and sit down to eat. OK, a visitor comes in and finds Krier's headless body on the kitchen floor. He finds you happily eating Krier's head between two slices of seedless rye. He says, 'What's that corpse?' You say, 'What corpse? That's salami.' "

"Butch, is this necessary?" Krier wailed. "I'm getting sick."

"Yes, it is. Although the flaw in the case is that a reasonable and prudent man might conclude that your head was in fact made of salami. OK. Kaplan's lawyer, let's say, offers an NGI plea. What do you do? Franklin."

Jerry Franklin, a squat wrestler from Brooklyn, who'd done well at Vermont and had spent two years prosecuting in an upstate county, chewed his lip for a moment. Then he said, "Assuming no substantive motive, right? What I'd check out first is, was there any prior history of delusion. Did he mistake people for food before? It's compelling that he didn't run or try to hide the act, and that the delusion persists. Of course, you'd have to see the whole pattern, but on the facts you gave, I would probably not waste time with a trial. Let the funny farm have him."

"Fine, that's a thoughtful answer, Jerry. You notice what he said about pattern. That's the key. I'll share a secret with you. Nobody knows what crazy is. You, and only you, are the judge of whether a defendant fits the definition of insanity in

231 —

the law, the only judge of whether the state is going to try to exact punishment for a responsible act. Look for the pattern.

"All right, here's the hard part. Killer Kaplan decides to whack out Krier because he hates guys whose names end in r, whatever. He cuts off Krier's head, mutilates the body, writes weird cult signs all over the room in blood. Then he changes his clothes, burns the bloody clothes, and slips out the back. The cops catch him and he says the R people are trying to poison his air, so he has to kill them. Mike, how would you handle that?"

"That's tough. He, or I, hid my tracks, showing that I knew it was wrong to kill. I was afraid of capture, which suggests rational thought. On the other hand, I have this delusion ..."

"Uh-uh," Karp interrupted. "Remember what I said to Phil. Wacky motives do not make insane crimes. No matter how much you hate your cousin Al, you can't make a career out of killing people who look like him. That's the most confusing thing to juries about insanity pleas and the defense will cover you with bullshit on it.

"OK, let's talk about competency for a minute. This is a different thing entirely."

Karp then sketched out the background of the Marchione case, and laid out what he thought Mandeville Louis was doing and how he intended to stop him from getting away with it.

"This is a classic case of gaming the system. The mutt can't go for an NGI. It was an obvious killing for profit, with an elaborate getaway plan. He figures to lay low in a mental hospital until we forget about the case. But are we going to forget about the case?"

A chorus of no's came from the group. Karp grinned and said, "That's it. Any questions?"

Krier said, "What about this party Bloom is having. Do we have to go?"

Karp was embarrassed. Handing on bullshit from the top was what he hated most about being in the chain of command.

"Yeah, I guess it's a command performance."

Krier held up a memo. "It says we have to pay seven dollars to come to a party at his 'ancestral home.' If he's so ancestral, why doesn't he shell out?"

Karp said, "Richie, I'm here to answer your legal questions. If you have moral qualms, see your goddamn clergyman, hey? I intend to go, pay my fucking seven bucks like a trooper, and smile a lot. And, what the hell, it could turn out to be a blast."

CHAPTER SIXTEEN

The ancestral home of Sanford Bloom was a fussy Gothic pile of red sandstone in Fishkill, New York. It had been built by Bloom's great-grandfather, who had inherited a substantial fortune made by selling beef and leather to the Union during the Civil War. The Blooms decided it was time to leave the slaughterhouse district of Manhattan and live among the patroons upstate. Fortunately, they held onto the stockyards, abattoirs, and surrounding property, which turned, with the fickleness of fashion, into Sutton Place, and made the Blooms truly wealthy.

Karp rode up to Fishkill with V.T., Marlene, and Guma in Guma's junker. When they got there, a uniformed guard waved them to a parking space with a little red flag. The day was overcast, still, and sultry even in the country.

"Hey, look who's there!" exclaimed Guma. "It's Konstantelos."

"Who's he?" asked Marlene, sliding out of the backseat, and adjusting her skimpy shorts. "Guma, why don't you have A/C in your car. My thighs are sticking together."

"The rent-a-cop," said Guma, "it's Marty Konstantelos from the old four-seven precinct. He retired with a three-quarter a couple of years ago, caught his hand in a trunk or some shit. What a character! They called him Fartin' Martin. He used to crack up the squad room during roll calls. The shift would chip in and get him a quart of chow mein or chili and then he'd stand there and let rip. Christ, could he cut the cheese! He could, like, do words or tunes—I swear to God, it was amazing."

"Mad Dog, how come only you know people like this?" asked V.T. with something like admiration. "Does he do concerts?"

Guma laughed. "I don't know. Maybe we can arrange something. Hey, I'm going to bullshit with him, I'll catch you guys later." Guma picked up a huge straw beach bag and waddled off. He was wearing an orange Kiss Me I'm Italian T-shirt, black Bermudas, black dress socks, and vinyl sandals.

V.T. gazed musingly after him. He himself was wearing a white Tom Wolfe suit, a yellow silk shirt and a plum-colored Paisley ascot. V.T. was one of the forty-three men in the civilized world who could wear an ascot without looking like a jerk.

"This is uncanny," he said. "We arrive at this Disneyland castle and the first person to appear is somebody out of a dirty limerick, the man from Sparta, who was such an incredible farter, on the strength of one bean, he'd do God Save the Queen, and Beethoven's Moonlight Sonata. Do you suppose the man from St. Clair is the butler and the Old Lady from Wheeling is the cook?"

"I want to see the man from Kent," said Marlene as the three of them set out on the graveled path to the house.

V.T. giggled. "Whose cock was so long that it bent? Stick around. My, this place is unbelievable. Bad taste married infinite riches and lived happily ever after."

They were passing through some unkempt ornamental plantings. Some of the rose bushes had died and a bank of hydrangeas had succumbed to an invasion of wild grape. Weeds encroached vigorously on the gravel path and pushed up the flagstones of the garden walkways.

"Hey, V.T.," said Karp, "you're the *maven*. How come this place looks so crummy. Is Bloom strapped?"

"No, far from it," answered Newbury. "But they don't live here and neither Bloom nor his wife have any real feeling for the old pile. They've got their place in town, of course, and a big spread in the Hamptons, where they entertain. This joint is for ceremonial occasions only, or for people who can't be trusted with the good furniture."

"Tacky," said Marlene. "Mom always told us to give the guests the best stuff."

"Ahh, but we're not guests, we're the help. Also, rich people are apt to be stingy, which is how they stay rich. Present company excepted, of course."

As they approached the house they heard the hum of conversation and the unmistakable sounds of a tennis match in progress. The path opened on a broad flagstoned terrace below the house, on which several long tables covered with checkered cloths had been set. On the near side of the terrace a short walk led to two clay tennis courts. These, at least, were in prime condition. On the far side, the terrace dropped off to a large, murky, ornamental fish pond. There were about a dozen DA staffers milling around, looking ill at ease. Black servants in white jackets were serving drinks and tending hamburgers, and hot dogs were cooking on a huge fieldstone grill.

"Fun is at its maddest, all right," said Marlene. "Let's scoff up seven dollars worth of drinks and hot dogs and split."

"I can't do that," replied Karp. "I muscled all my guys to come here and I'm obligated to stay to the bitter end."

"Besides, it's bad manners, dear," said V.T. "We have to greet our hosts, tell them how delightful it all is, get drunk, puke in the bushes, and *then* split. Haven't you ever been to a fancy garden party? And speaking of our hosts . . ."

Bloom, in tennis whites, his face flushed, was coming down the walk from the tennis courts accompanied by a woman and two other men, one of whom was Conrad Wharton.

"Aha, Newbury, Karp, glad you could come. Denise and I just slaughtered Chip and Rich here in doubles, straight sets. Got to work on that serve, Chip."

Wharton was also in whites. His normally pink face was bright red and his lank blond locks were plastered to his forehead. He smiled sheepishly and said, "Well, yeah, I've got a long way to go before I can take you, Sandy."

Bloom gave a high-pitched laugh. "You know it! OK, just make yourselves at home, kids. Plenty of drinks and food—swim if you want to, play a few sets. I'm going to change."

"I better change, too," said Wharton.

Bloom strode off to the house, with Wharton waddling after him. Ignoring Marlene, Mrs. Bloom immediately linked her arms through V.T.'s and Karp's. She was a wiry, heavily tanned woman of about forty, with large teeth, a truncated nose, and frosted dark hair. She was in a white tennis outfit with little red pom-poms sticking up over her Nikes.

"Oh, you must be V.T. Newbury and Butch Karp. Sandy's told me so much about you both. Oh, V.T., you know I think we have some friends in common. The Worthingtons have the place just down the road you know, and they keep their boat in the Hamptons all summer. Isn't that a coincidence."

V.T. allowed that the world was a remarkable place. Thus encouraged, Mrs. Bloom said, "Now, I know I can get you two handsome young men to find me a drinkie. To the bar, and don't spare the horses!" She laughed gaily and moved off with irresistible force. Karp shrugged at Marlene and let himself be dragged along.

Marlene was left alone on the path with the other tennis player. He was a tall, gangling man in his twenties, with long-ish razor-cut hair tied back in a red-white-and-blue terry headband, a straight pointy nose and close-set dark eyes. After a moment he stuck out his hand.

"Rich Wool," he said.

"Beg pardon?"

"I'm Richard Wool. I head up the data development team in the office. Under Chip, of course. And you are?"

Marlene took the hand gingerly. "Jane Eyre."

"Well, Jane, and what brings you here? Are you a spouse or one of the paralegals?"

"Actually, I'm with the custodial staff. I work directly for Mister Karp."

"Really? I didn't know Karp had any custodial responsibilities. What precisely do you do?"

"Oh this and that. Keep his tubes blown out, and all. Look, Rich, I'd love to stop and chat, but you've got to mingle and I need to go back to the car and shoot some smack, so . . ."

She turned and started off. "What? What did you say?" he called to her back. But by then she had already turned onto one of the many side paths that led off the gravel drive. She wasn't hungry and she certainly didn't feel like getting drunk with Denise and Sandy. She figured to screw around for an hour in the woods, sack out or indulge her secret taste for Regency romances, one of which she had stashed in her handbag.

The path came out onto a little clearing overlooking what once had been a horse paddock, but which was now overgrown with high grass and wildflowers.

A columned, domed gazebo in white stone, the kind of structure the Victorians called a "folly," stood in the clearing. It held two wide stone benches, on one of which sat a youth of about sixteen picking inexpertly at a guitar. Marlene went over and sat on the opposite bench.

"Nice guitar," she offered. "A Gibson, right?"

The boy grunted, but did not look up. He was slightly overweight and sallow, with shoulder-length straight brown hair, none too clean. He was wearing a black T-shirt and cutoff jeans.

"You live here?" Marlene asked. "How come you're not at the party?" Silence. "My name's Marlene, what's yours?"

He scowled and said, "Hey, lady, the party's down the road. You wanna leave me alone?"

Marlene got up. "OK, sport, but you're never going to get a good D Minor with your thumb all scrunched up like that."

The kid played another sour progression and looked up. "You play?"

"I used to. Here, let me sit down next to you on the old bench."

"You got a cigarette?"

"Yeah." She reached into her bag and handed the kid a Marlboro. He lit up and she took the expensive instrument and hoisted it onto her knee. "OK, let's see. Keep your wrist like so, and your fingers arched, like this. See? D minor, A seventh, D minor, then you can go B sharp, D seventh, and back to, There is a House in New Orleans, they, B sharp, call the Rising Sun, A seventh, and its been D minor again, see how it goes, me, go to G seventh, oh God, A seventh, am one, back to D minor."

Marlene sang the rest of the song without interruption, in a high shivery contralto; then sang a few more by Joan Baez, some by the Beach Boys, and then taught the kid an Eric Clapton riff—by which time he was in love.

He turned out to be Brian Bloom, and his father had told him that if he showed his face at the party with that hair and that filthy outfit he would definitely be sent to military school and I don't care what your mother says.

They smoked and chatted about music and families and agreed that Sanford Bloom was an asshole, the kid being surprised to find out that other adults shared his opinion of his old dad. Then Marlene began to play hard blues and after a while people from the party and people arriving from the parking lot began to drift into the clearing, attracted by the music, and sat around on the grass and the steps of the gazebo, listening. People came and went, going over to the terrace to get food and drinks and then drifting back to sit again and listen to the music.

Guma ran into Karp and V.T. at the edge of the crowd.

"Hey, Butch, look at this, a party within a party."

"Yeah, there's practically nobody left up at the house. What you been doing, Goom?"

"Oh, you know, mingling with the great and the near-great. Ate some burgers. Had a few brews. Got into a chug-a-lug contest with your guy, Butch, what's-his-name, the actor."

"Richie Krier?"

"Yeah. I should modestly add that I took both the quantity and the velocity crown." He slapped his gut. "The kid was fighting well above his weight."

"What happened to Richie, you child-molester?"

"Well, he got a little green toward the end there. Couple of guys and me helped him into the house and stuck him in a bedroom to relax."

"Maybe I better go check him out."

"Why? You're not his daddy. Besides, you and V.T. got to figure out how to present my house gift."

"You bought a house gift for Bloom?" asked V.T. incredulously. "On top of the seven bucks? Mad Dog, you shame us all. What did you get him?"

Guma chuckled. "Yeah, well, I might be from Bath Beach, but that don't mean I don't know from class. The man has everything, right? So, I wrack my brains. Then, the other day I'm walking on Fourteenth and I pass that joint that sells all that tourist crap. And right there in the window I see . . ."

"Plastic doggie vomit. The perfect choice!" V.T. exclaimed.

"Hey, they had that too, but I figure, everybody gives plastic doggie vomit, rubber chocolates, the ice cube with the fly in it. No, I wanted something really special. So I got this."

Guma reached into his shopping bag and pulled out a large package wrapped in clear vinyl.

Karp said, "A life-sized inflatable sex doll! Way to go Goom!"

"Yeah, it's pretty snazzy. All the orifices work and it comes with a tube of lubricant. Your rubber nipples. It's got the real acrylic crotch hair too. I hope he likes blondes."

"Mad Dog, this is a princely gift. I'll never criticize your taste again."

"Well, thanks V.T. Come on in the house, you can help me blow it up."

"Honored. Where are you going to put it?"

"I don't know. We'll think of something. You coming, Butch?"

"No, I think I'll hang around here. I want to talk to Marlene."

V.T. and Guma took off and Karp wandered through the crowd. He heard angry noises from the direction of the stone gazebo, and saw Bloom, now dressed in a lime-green jumpsuit, berating his son. Karp couldn't hear what they were saying, but Bloom was obviously very angry. He actually stamped his foot in rage. The boy said something and Bloom shoved him hard. The boy, his face screwed up and pale with anger, cursed shrilly and went crashing off into the woods.

Bloom began to do his har-har-har-these-kids-today rou-tine, smiling a political travesty of a smile, trying to jolly his not-quite guests into believing that they had not seen what they had in fact seen, which was a man brutalizing a child for no particular reason. The crowd around the gazebo began to break up. Karp spotted Marlene and headed toward her. Her brow was furrowed and she puffed aggressively on a cigarette.

"What was that all about?" Karp asked.

"Ah shit, I don't know. We were just sitting here strum-ming and passing a jug around and having a good time, when Bloom bursts out of the bushes and starts bracing the kid. It's his kid, by the way, poor little bastard. I gather he was bent out of shape because the kid was smoking and drinking, and gen-erally having a good time with adults, which according to the kid was a first. Apparently, Bloom keeps him hidden most of the time."

She looked around. "Looks like the songfest is over. Let's find the guys and go home, Butch. This place sucks. And I drank too much wine."

"OK by me. I think they're back by the house."

Marlene hoisted the Gibson and they joined the stream of people moving back toward the terrace. "You know some-thing, baby?" said Marlene. "I think the real reason Bloom was mad was because a bunch of people at his party were doing something spontaneous—I mean not under his gaze, or his control. He just took it out on the kid. Some shit, huh?"

"Yeah, you could be right. It's a real happy family. Denise is half in the bag most of the time. She spilled her guts to me and V.T. Apparently Bloom hates this place; it reminds him of his old man, the senator or the secretary of whatever the hell he was. But he won't sell it and keeps pretending it's his beloved country seat. We got the grand tour. The place is fucking crumbling. Half the rooms are closed up. The only things still in their original condition are the tennis courts and the fish pond. And the beehives."

"Beehives?"

"Oh, yeah. He's got dozens of them in the meadow on the other side of the fish pond. The great man won't have any store-bought honey on his toast. His big thing is giving quarts away at Christmas. He's famous for it. It's the only thing he ever gives away. Also the fish are not just ordinary goldfish, which they look like, but imperial carp or some shit like that. Very valuable and brought back at great expense by his grand-father when he went to China for FDR. Each one comes with a price tag."

"Fascinating."

"Yeah, right. I can't figure him. He practically wouldn't leave me alone. 'Have a pickle, Butch. More beans, Butch?' Old Corncob was all smiles, too. I can't figure it."

"You can't? It's plain as day to me. The office is suffering from terminal morale problems. More people are leaving than coming in. He spotted you as the natural leader of the younger ADAs, besides which you were closer to Garrahy than most. He figures he's got to co-opt you to complete his control of the office. He can fire the old farts, but . . ."

"He needs young farts like me, huh?"

"Right. Which is why you're going to be bureau chief when Gelb leaves. Then I'll love you even more."

She slipped her hand down the back of his cutoffs and goosed him.

The terrace was once again full of people. The servants were clearing away the rest of the food. Marlene grabbed the last hot dog off the grill, suddenly ravenous and light-headed from having eaten nothing and drunk a good deal all after-noon. The hot dog was too hot and she blew on it to cool it off. She was too engrossed to notice the arrival of V.T., who said, "Suck, Champ, blow is just a figure of speech."

"Oh, hi, V.T. Where's Goom? We want to get out of here."

"Wandering around somewhere. He'll turn up. Oh, oh. It looks like we're going to have a speech."

Bloom had climbed up on a wooden folding chair. Some-body tapped a spoon against a bottle and the crowd fell silent. The only sounds were those made by insects, and the hum of the motor that aerated the fish pond.

"Friends, I just wanted to tell you how much Denise"—here he glanced around for his wife, who was not to be seen—

"um, and I have enjoyed having you here. I want our office to be like a family, and you know I'm always ready to help you out whatever your problems are. I want to get to know you as people and I want you to know me the same way."

Marlene whispered to Karp. "How unbelievably pompous! Why is he doing this?"

Karp whispered back, "You were right. He's reestablishing control over the fun."

"You all seem to be having a good time. I hope everybody had enough to eat and drink?" Murmurs of assent. No one was crude enough to mention the seven dollars.

"Good, good. But no party is complete without entertainment and I . . ."

At that moment, Bloom was interrupted by the unmistakable sound of someone passing gas. But what a passer! The sound went on for what seemed like an impossibly long time, changing in tone and pitch from a high bagpipelike skirl to a profound popping bass. Scattered applause and laughter ran through the crowd.

"That's Fartin' Martin," said V.T. "Guma's been plying him with beans and beer all afternoon. He delivered right on cue. What a sense of theater!"

Bloom flushed and popped his eyes, but took a deep breath and recovered his composure.

"I noticed a little while ago that there was a young lady singing for some people back over in the bushes, and I wondered if she would come up here now and sing for all of us." He looked directly at Marlene, smiling broadly, except around the eyes. He started to clap, and others took up the applause.

Marlene said out of the side of her mouth, "Fuck this asshole, I'm not going to go up and perform for him."

V.T. clapped loudly by her side. "Come on, Champ, do one of your specials. Knock 'em dead."

"Yeah, Marlene, see if you can top Martin," Karp said.

"All right, bozo, you asked for it," she said grimly, as the crowd made way for her. She went up to the cleared space Bloom had spoken from, nodded curtly at Bloom and propped a foot up on a chair. Bloom sat down on the retaining wall that divided the terrace from the short slope that led to the pond. He had a front row seat. Wharton was at his side, as usual.

Marlene lifted the guitar onto her raised knee, adjusted the capo, and began to play. The tune was the "Wabash Cannonball," but the version she sang departed substantially from the original:

> *Don't put sand in the Vaseline, or you'll hurt the one you love,*
>
> *Sandy Vaseline will make chicken croquettes of your little turtle dove,*
>
> *So, be real kind and gentle, and use a velvet glove,*
>
> *But don't put sand in the Vaseline or you'll hurt the one you love.*

That was the chorus. The fifteen verses that follow are generally considered to be among the filthiest ever written. But funny. Bloom was not laughing, nor was his immediate court of lackeys. He substituted a fixed, unnatural smile, like a model in a cheap clothing ad. Everyone else was on the floor, screaming with laughter and joining in on the chorus.

Unfortunately, Marlene was not able to finish all the verses. At verse four—"Oh, did he call the axman, to chop off both their heads, No, he just put sand in the Vaseline and they tore themselves to shreds"—the air was riven by an immense explosion. The famous fish pond was history. A column of greasy black water forty feet high—laden with pureed imperial carp and the immemorial slime of the pond bottom—hovered for an instant above the terrace and then crashed down on the crowd.

There followed a second or two of stunned silence, and then pandemonium. Nobody was seriously injured, except sartorially. Bloom was thrashing about like one of his late fish in a puddle of slimy muck, bellowing. Marlene was soaked and stained black from head to toe. V.T.'s immaculate white costume was covered with silver-dollar-sized patches of grunge. The place smelled like low tide near a sewer outlet.

244 —

"This is the end! This is the goddamn end!" Bloom was shouting. Wharton and his other aides were fussing over him, picking bits of glittering fish scales, guts, and other detritus from his jumpsuit, which was now a dark olive drab. He shook away from them. "Stop that, you morons! Get the police! We've been bombed, can't you see that? There could be others planted."

As Wharton rushed toward the house to carry out these orders, it became clear that this was not, in fact "the end." An upstairs window flew open and Mrs. Bloom stuck her head out and began to shriek like a banshee.

What had happened was that Denise had decided to take a little nappie in the waning afternoon. She had been hitting the gin pretty heavily and thought it best to recover so she could bid farewell to the departing guests without swaying. She chose a spare bedroom and curled up under the covers on one of the twin beds.

But this was the same bedroom in which V.T. and Guma chose to deposit the zonked-out Richie Krier. Did they pull his clothes off and hide them under the bed? Of course. And did they inflate the life-sized sex doll and arrange it on top of Richie's nakedness in the classic sixty-nine position? Naturally.

So that when the mighty explosion awakened both sleepers, and Denise looked around in panic and in the dim light saw Richie thrashing around under the doll, she concluded—not without reason—that two people were performing an act that she had read about with a combination of fascination and horror, but which was as yet outside her experience—and performing it in *her* house. She shouted, "Stop! What! Wha ... Stop, who, who, what!!"

Richie was trying to put his mind back together. He seemed to have lost a considerable amount of time. He recognized the DA's wife, but not what was three inches from his nose, which was a fairly good simulacrum of the female pudenda. That is, he knew what it was, but had no clue as to its owner, never a good situation to wake up into.

He sat up, which caused the doll to flip over onto its back. Now its welcoming arms, huge, red-tipped breasts and gaping thighs were directed at Mrs. Bloom. Of course, Richie was out of bed by now, covering his crotch with a pillow and running around the room trying to find his clothes. Mrs. Bloom naturally concluded that this man, having reduced one woman to paralysis through that unspeakable act, was about to perform it on her. In her confusion, she shouted, "Stay away from me!" and picked up her most recent gin-and-tonic glass.

Richie said, "OK, lady, I just got to find my clothes," but in so saying he advanced toward her bed to search the other side of the room. She flung the glass at him. It glanced off his head, flew up to the ceiling and shattered the ornate glass light fixture. A rain of glass shards fell down on the bed and the doll, one of which punctured its skin.

With a fizzing sound that might have come from Fartin' Martin, the doll simultaneously deflated and flew across the room, a sexual gargoyle on the rampage. Which is why Denise Bloom was standing at the window screaming like a being demented. Which, at the time, she was.

Bloom was also screaming. "The terrorists have got my wife! Wharton, get the security guard! Do something, damn it!"

The security guard, who was, of course, Marty Konstantelos, burst out of the bushes brandishing his nightstick and his .38. He took several long steps on the terrace, slipped on the slimy surface, skidded twenty feet like a speed skater out of control, bowled over several people, including Wharton, and caught his head a nasty knock against the stone steps. As he sank into unconsciousness, his fabled gas reservoir let loose a cannonade that would have honored a chief of state, much less a district attorney.

At that moment an almost unidentifiable creature leaped up on the retaining wall. It was short and squat and glistening black in color, and stank. One might have guessed it was a sort of ape or a subhuman amphibioid creature that time forgot. A bottle of Scotch glittered in its grubby paw, not a usual accessory of such creatures. Perhaps an ape after all. Marlene identified it first. "Guma, you rotten son of a bitch! You stole my souvenirs!" she shrieked.

246 —

Guma—it was him indeed—jumped from the wall and raced across the terrace.

"Run! Run! It's the fucking bees!" he shouted, and was gone down the path. And in fact the shock wave from the blast had upset half a dozen of the beehives in the meadow near the fish pond. The bees were not amused. In a moment the air was full of tiny yellow bodies and cries of pain. Marlene, Karp, and V.T. raced after Guma toward the parking area. They leaped into the old Mercury, rolled up the windows and swatted bees as Guma peeled off down the drive, throwing a rooster-tail of gravel in his wake.

"Whoo-ee!" Guma exclaimed, as they roared onto the state road. "We stink like four inches up a penguin's asshole. Anybody want some Scotch?" Everybody took a restorative belt. They also soaked V.T.'s ascot in Scotch and used it to dab at their stings.

"Hey, Ciampi! You ain't mad at me, are you. For borrowing your bomb?"

"Shit, not really, Goom. I couldn't think of a better use for it actually. On the other hand, you ever go near my office again, paisan, I'll break your fucking head."

"And she will, too, Guma," added Karp sincerely.

They drove in silence for a while, and then V.T. let out a sigh and said, "Well, I guess he probably won't invite us back there for a long time." They laughed about that all the way down the Sawmill River Parkway.

Guma dropped Marlene and Karp off at Karp's place. They took showers and changed clothes. Marlene was spending most of her time at Karp's place by now, but kept her apartment—just in case.

"Hey, Marlene, why isn't the water draining out?" yelled Karp from the bathroom.

Marlene was wrapped in a towel, sitting on the bed drying her hair. It had frizzed into a near-Afro that she was struggling to bring under control with a dryer and a steel brush. "Oh, that's my hair. It always clogs. I'll get some Drāno tomorrow."

Karp walked out of the bathroom, naked. "Hair in the

drain? Drāno? Does this mean the romance has gone already?" He bent over and nuzzled her neck. She shivered. "Nah, it just means—ahh, that's so fine!—it just means we should get ready for new and startling levels of intimacy." She held his head between her hands and stared into his eyes. "We're in pretty deep and there's a lot we don't know about each other."

"Especially me," agreed Karp. "I mean sometimes you really whack me out, Marlene. I mean the stuff you pull. It scares me. You just decide to, I don't know, disappear, or join the circus or something. You know?"

"Yeah, I know. You want me to be calm, so you can admire my beauty in peace. Like this." She draped the towel over her head and struck a Mona Lisa pose. "I mean I know I'm easy on the eye. Shit, I've been hearing that since I was six. I know about the advantages of being attractive. But in a way, I hate it. It's like what V.T. says about being rich. Is it *me* that's desirable, or is it the other stuff, the money or the face? I mean, to a freak or a poor son of a bitch that's looney, right? But there it is. My innermost fear."

"It's you," said Karp, taking the hair dryer and the brush out of her hands. "Just you."

She lay back and flung the towel down. "It better be, Buster."

CHAPTER SEVENTEEN

Karp, I keep getting your mail. When are you going to tell the mail room you moved?"

Marlene had come into his office a little before noon and dropped a pile of envelopes on his desk. "I'll get around to it, Marlene. I've been really busy."

"I guess that means we're not going to lunch today."

"I guess it does."

She sidled around to his side of the desk, bent over, and licked his ear. He pulled away and gave her his long-suffering look. "Marlene, I got to do all this stuff." He gestured at the piles of forms, computer printouts, and other paperwork on his desk.

She backed away, her face hardening. "Well, *excuse me,* Mr. Boss. I beg your pardon. I guess I'll just climb back into my faucet until the next time you turn on the goddamn tap."

"Come on, Marlene, give me a break. Look, I appreciate you bringing the mail over and I'll take care of the mail room today, OK?" He glanced down at the pile of envelopes.

"Hey, Marlene, these are all opened."

"So? I just want to see what you're up to. You mind?"

"Yeah, I fucking well mind! Where the hell do you get off opening my mail?"

"Why? You've got big secrets?"

"That's not the point. You don't open other people's mail."

"Oh, no? You think it's too personal? You spent last night licking my ovaries, and I can't peek at your *personal* correspondence. If you were banging your secretary, you'd let *her* peek at your *personal* correspondence, wouldn't you?"

Karp got to his feet. "Marlene, what the hell has got into you?" he shouted. He realized she was picking a fight, but didn't understand why.

"I would explain it to you, but it turns out *I* haven't got the time." She turned and stormed out, slamming the door and rattling the glass.

Karp slumped back in his seat and made some tooth marks on his pencil. The phone rang. It was Helen Simms, the bureau secretary.

"You all right in there? Nothing broken?"

"Yeah, Helen, it's fine. Just fine."

"You want to take this call I been holding. It's a Mister Sussman."

After a few initial pleasantries, Sussman got to the point, which was Mandeville Louis.

"Mister Karp, my client believes you have a personal animus against him. I confess, for myself, that I fail to see what you gain by not agreeing to an early disposition of this case, which is going on three years old now."

"I don't agree, Mister Sussman. Your client killed two people in cold blood. I want to put him in jail for a long time. That's not personal, that's my job."

"Yes, of course. But you know very well that cases like Louis's are usually settled expeditiously. The man has no criminal record. He is mentally ill. He can't be tried. My God, can you imagine what would happen to the criminal justice system if every case of this type was blockaded in the way you seem intent on doing here? Surely Mister Bloom cannot approve. I had understood that he set quite a high priority on greasing the wheels of justice, so to speak."

"Yeah, but first of all, it's not every case. It's one particular case, and second, I don't believe Mister Louis is mentally ill."

"Oh? Have you added a forensic psychiatric degree to your credentials?"

Karp was suddenly exhausted. All at once, his little stratagems and evasions, his training sessions, his backbreaking work, seemed utterly futile. Some part of his mind knew the problems he was having with Marlene were connected with the monumental, and—said one part of him—absurd task he had set himself. He was heading for an emotional crash and burn *again*. And for what? If the law could not punish a ravening wolf like Mandeville Louis, a villain standing ankle deep in blood and laughing about it, then what was the point of it all?

Moral fatigue had dulled Karp's mind, and he did something foolish. He began telling Sussman what he and Dunbar suspected about Louis's M.O. He wanted, he needed, the sleek defense lawyer to step out of his formal role as advocate and share Karp's horror at what Louis had done and at the failure of the justice system to do much about it. Crazy, but true.

"And so, Mister Sussman," Karp concluded, in his best summation-to-the-jury style, "I am convinced that your client, far from being a mental incompetent who committed a single impulsive crime, is a cynical and extremely clever *mass* murderer who may have been responsible for as many as one hundred killings in the past ten years. He has been consciously manipulating the criminal justice system, and I have decided to put a stop to it. As long as I have any association with the District Attorney's Office, Mandeville Louis will not cop to a lesser. He can sit in Matteawan as long as he likes. Meanwhile, the police will continue gathering evidence linking him to his other crimes." This was a bluff. Karp knew he was lucky to get Dunbar to look for the third man. It would be virtually impossible to get the cops to open dozens of closed files.

Sussman, whose interest in justice was tenuous at best, remained unimpressed. "That was very interesting, Mister Karp. Now I'll tell one. Once upon a time, a little girl named Red Riding Hood lived with her mommy in the middle of a big forest . . ."

"OK, Sussman, you made your point," snapped Karp. "I don't give two shits if you believe me or not. But, you ever feel like calling me again, let me say this. If your man decides to plead guilty to the top count of the indictment, I'm all ears. Other than that, save your dime." He slammed down the receiver.

Leonard Sussman stared for a moment at the dead phone. Then he dialed a familiar number.

Louis was at arts and crafts when they called him to the phone. He was painting. Robert Fallon was teaching him how. Fallon joked about starting an atelier in the loony bin, to carry on his traditions after he departed for friendlier places. Fallon talked incessantly about escaping, about what he would do when he was free in South America. It was starting to get on Louis's nerves. First of all, he thought Fallon was bullshitting. All the fucker did was eat. He'd need a guy with a forklift to escape. Louis was putting on weight, too, on the starchy food, but he knew he would never become one of the doughy creatures he saw every day in the lounge. He wondered why there were weight rooms in prisons but not in looney bins.

Also, he didn't like hearing Fallon talk about what he had done with those girls, and what he was planning to do. Louis did not dwell on the murders he had committed. He didn't particularly get off on killing people, any more than a mailman gets a charge out of stuffing mailboxes. What Louis got off on was getting away with it.

So when he heard what Sussman had to say about what he had heard from Karp, Louis experienced a blow to the core of his being. Someone had found him out and would not let him off. Nothing like this had happened to him since the ice pick incident over twenty years ago. For an instant of blinding disorientation he was back in the yard of his family's home, trying to burn a blood-stained jacket as the police car approached.

Sussman was saying, "Mister Louis, I tell you he's clutching at straws. He hasn't a case and he's bluffing. Let me tell him you'll go to trial—he'll cave, I know it."

Louis made no answer. He was shaking and struggling for control. *Karp knew. Karp knew.*

"Mister Louis. Mandeville. Are you listening?"

"Karp knows," Louis said, in a creaky voice.

"Beg pardon? What was that?"

"No trial. Set up a hearing, just like before. Nothing's changed."

"Mister Louis, did you hear a word I said? This Karp is . . ."

"Let me worry about that, Sussman," Louis interrupted. "I'll worry about Karp."

"Hey there, Pres, how's my boy?"

Preston Elvis let out a long, desperate sigh when he heard the familiar voice on the phone. For months after he delivered the fatal heroin shot to Donald Walker he had stayed away from Louis's apartment, foregoing the delights of DeVonne, the yellow Firebird, and the easy money he got from swiping bits of Louis's pure heroin and selling it, heavily cut, to his friends. He had returned to the home of sorts he had before he went to prison, living off the welfare check of a woman named Vera Higgs. Vera, a mild and willing creature of eighteen, had borne him one child while he was in prison and was heavily pregnant with another. He was astonished that Louis had known where to find him.

"What's the matter, Pres? Cat got your tongue? Say hello to your old friend."

"What you want, Man?"

"What I want? Well, couple a things. You got a pencil and some paper?"

"Paper? What for?"

"'Cause you got to write down your orders, just like in a restaurant. You the waiter. Get 'em!"

Elvis scrounged up a paper bag and the stub of a pencil.

"What the fuck this about, Man?"

"Now Pres, baby, be cool. The first thing is, you gonna be glad to hear I got you a job. Now you gonna be able to keep that fine lady you got there and your baby in style. Gonna make your parole officer sit up and smile too."

"What the fuck you talkin' about, a job? What doin'?"

"You gonna be a paper boy, Pres. Now write this down."

Sonny Dunbar dropped by Karp's office that Friday to talk about the progress he had made in the search for Louis's accomplice. Or rather the progress he hadn't made.

"Butch, look. I'm just one guy, right?" Dunbar was explaining. "If this was a real case, we'd have people watching

Louis's apartment twenty-four hours a day, hitting the people who knew him. We'd have ten, twenty guys out. But this is just me. I got Slocum covering stuff I should be doing, but he can't do that forever. The loot is on my ass already. He thinks I'm cooping, can you believe it?"

"What are you saying, Sonny, you want to give up?"

"No, shit, I'll keep plugging. But this guy, Louis—it's weird. Nobody knows him. I mean the usual snitches. He's got no rep on the street, no contacts. I checked out that bar in Queens, Torry's, where Donnie met him. They ID'd Louis, all right, they knew him as Stack, but I drew a blank on 'Willie Lee.' "

"How about the girl friend?"

"Yeah, DeVonne. She knows shit. She saw the guy once, doesn't know nothing. One thing, she heard Louis call him 'Pres,' or 'Press.' "

"That's good! That's a name at least. You check it out?"

"Check what out? Is it a first name, a last name, a street name, a private joke? You know how many bloods are called Pres? You ever hear of Lester Young?"

"No, is he in the case?"

"Not that I know of. He was a jazz musician, kicked off about twenty years ago. They called him Pres because he was the president of all the sax players—the best, follow? OK, now if I had the manpower, I could go through every yellow sheet in headquarters and see whether we had somebody who was, one, black, two, about twenty, about six-two, two-hundred pounds, three, had a little scar on one side of his nose, and four, had some name or alias that fit with 'Pres.' Now, you want to go downtown with the shit we got and ask for ten guys to do that, and ten guys to work the street?"

"OK, Sonny, you made your point. But I got the feeling we're not being smart. Let's say the Louis connection is a dead end. We got to know something more about this other guy."

They thought for a while in silence. Dunbar glanced at his watch. He was due to meet Fred Slocum in twenty minutes on another case and spend four or five hours walking up and down stairs, knocking on doors, and talking to suspicious people who didn't see anything ever. Karp thought about punks and hoods, how they revolved like the dumb horses on a carousel, in and out of prison, on and off parole. He studied the clumsy Identikit sketch he had taped to his desk lamp, as if it would somehow yield up a name, an address. He drew idly on a yellow legal pad: a stick figure with no face, then bars across the figure, then he wrote "1970" above the bars and drew a big circle around the whole thing.

"Butch, I got to go," said Dunbar, getting out of his chair.

"Wait a minute, Sonny. Maybe I got something. You remember Donny said Louis said this guy was just out of the slams?"

"Yeah, so?"

"OK, so he's about twenty, right? It's probably his first adult offense. And it's got to be something like armed robbery, or ag assault."

"Why? Why not drugs, or rape?"

"Just a hunch. Louis is an armed robber. He's already got a junkie for a patsy. He needs a strong-arm—somebody like him—don't ask me why, but I figure it that way. OK, now the field is a little narrower. We're looking for an armed robbery, first offense—he probably got a bullet—released from prison in late Nineteen-sixty-nine or early Nineteen-seventy, that matches the other stuff we got on him."

"Butch, what if he's from Detroit or Jersey? Donnie didn't say what prison. I mean other states got prisons."

"Then we're fucked. For that matter, he could have split town. But, I figure Louis for somebody who's got to control everything. Look at how successful he's been. You think he's going to pick a sidekick who's going to split, who has any real options. No, we're looking for a local mutt, Sonny. Just a regular anonymous local mutt. Look, let's check the parole records. He's a first offender, he had to make parole, right. One of these guys ever did straight time it'd make headlines."

Dunbar looked skeptical. "This is another long shot, Butch."

"Shit, Sonny, a long shot is the only shot we got. And I was right once, wasn't I?"

Dunbar sighed. "I'll check it out," he said.

Number 563 Boynton Street was one of three apartment houses on the block still occupied by human beings. The name of the building, graven in a marble lintel, was Lancaster. In its better days it had sheltered a generation of Irish, then a generation of Jews. The other buildings had been torched by vandals, or by their owners for insurance. Some of these had their windows blocked with glittering tin sheets. Others had been demolished and turned into fields of gray and red lumps, from which sprang jungles of hardy weeds. The streets sparkled with crushed glass.

So many buildings had been cleared that Dunbar, climbing out of his dusty white Chevy, once again had the odd impression he often got in this part of the Bronx, of not being in the city anymore, but out west, among the classic landscapes of the horse opera. In the vacant plains of flattened rubble, the buildings stood like weathered buttes. It was one of the few parts of New York where you could see almost the whole dome of the sky from street level. It always gave Dunbar the shivers.

Karp had been right. There was an armed robber who had been released from Attica at just the right time. And who looked right. And who had the right name. Dunbar patted his gun, unconsciously, and entered the fetid hallway of 563, heading for Apartment 505, the last known address of Preston Elvis.

Dunbar was about to ask the girl who opened the door if her momma or daddy was home, until he saw her swelling belly and the little boy who clung to her pink housecoat. This thin child was the lady of the house. He flashed his shield.

"Police. Are you Mrs. Elvis?"

"What you want? I ain't done nothin'."

"Could I come in?"

Silently, she backed away from the doorway. Mother and child stared at him with liquid, sad brown eyes. The living room was the same as all the others he had been in. A lumpy couch—this one was green plastic—and a big color TV. A game show was blaring: a capering man was giving things away to white people.

"That's a nice new TV, there," said Dunbar. "Preston got that for you, did he?"

"Who?"

"Preston Elvis. This guy," said Dunbar, showing the mug shot. "He lives here, right?"

"No, nobody live here, jus us."

"But, he comes here a lot, doesn't he? I mean I could find out lots of ways, but it's easier if you tell me. And, shit, honey, I ain't from welfare. I don't give a rat's ass who lives here or when. I just need to talk to him."

"He ain't been 'round for a long while," she said, sullenly.

Dunbar looked through the apartment. There was a pair of men's shoes near the couch. The bedroom and bathroom were empty, but there were male clothes scattered around and in the closet, and there were recently used shaving things in the bathroom.

He went back to the woman. The boy had returned to watching TV.

"What's your name, girl?"

"Vera. Higgs."

"OK, Vera. I'll tell you the truth, now. I don't want to take you downtown. I don't want to take your little boy away. And I definitely don't want to tell the welfare that a man's been living here. OK? But all that is gonna come down, if I don't get to talk with Preston real soon? So tell me, where's he at?"

"He workin'. He ain't done nothin'."

"Right, and where does he work?"

"I don know. He never tell me shit about what he be up to. Someplace, down in the city. No lie, Mister, I don know." Her voice became shrill and tears started.

Dunbar believed her. He thought, OK, Sherlock, time to play detective. What he didn't want was to have to stake out this shithole, maybe for hours or days even, if Elvis decided not to come home for a while. He looked more closely at the miserable dwelling, opening drawers, peering into cabinets, willing something to pop out at him. There was a pile of newspapers on the kitchen table. Idly, Dunbar picked one up and glanced at the headline, something about black leaders selling out their third-world brothers in the struggle against imperialism. Late-breaking news. Then something clicked.

He showed the paper to the woman. "Who reads this paper, you?"

She shrugged. "He bring them here."

"He ever talk about a dude name of Mandeville Louis? Or Stack?" Shrug. Dunbar said, "I'll be back." He left the apartment and rushed down the stairs. It could be a coincidence that Preston Elvis had lying around his apartment twenty or thirty copies of the Claremont Press, the same newspaper that Mandeville Louis had worked for. But somehow Dunbar doubted it.

"Mister Barlow? Emerson Dunbar," said Dunbar, showing his ID. "I'd like to ask you some questions."

The editorial offices of the Claremont Press occupied a storefront on the avenue of the same name, and consisted of a small shop immediately off the street, where you could buy the Press and a selection of books and records, or place classified ads; and, behind a glass door, one large room, which held a jumble of battered desks, filing cabinets, and other necessaries of journalism. Dunbar was standing at one of these desks, talking to James Barlow, the managing editor of the Claremont Press.

Barlow, a chubby, tan man with an Afro and ferocious side whiskers was dressed in a bush jacket and a black T-shirt. He regarded the police ID with studied repugnance.

"Why don't you pigs leave us alone? The fucking FBI was here last week. I'm being followed, you know that? Two little blondies in a gray car. You see this phone? Tapped. The entire power of the fascist racist state is ranged against us, but we shall continue to speak and print the truth. Now, beat it! Go fuck with the *Times* for a change."

"Mister Barlow, I'm not trying to harass you. This is a routine investigation of a routine crime. All I want to know is, have you seen this man?" He held out the mug shot of Preston Elvis. Barlow barely glanced at it.

"No," he snapped.

"You sure? Why don't you take another look? We have reason to believe he worked here."

"I don't need to. One oppressed nigger is the same as another. And if you think I'm going to help an oreo pig track down a brother, you're dumber than you look."

"Take it easy, Barlow. I gave fifty bucks to the NAACP in 1969."

"Get out of here!"

"Honest, Barlow, I could care less about this guy's politics. And they promised me if I broke this case I'd make sergeant—don't you want to see the brothers get ahead on the force?"

"Brother, my ass! When the oppressed peoples rise up it'll be class traitors and running dogs like you who're gonna go to the wall first."

"I can hardly wait. Lookie here, Lumumba, I'd like to stay and bullshit with you about the class struggle and all, but there's this guy who seems to have aced about a hundred guys, most of 'em blacker than you, and I'd like to put him away, and this dude Elvis is gonna help me do it. Now, I asked you nice to help me, and you told me to get fucked, so what do you say, we go along downtown and I'll ask you again?"

Barlow jumped to his feet. "Oh, now the pig shows his true colors. You want to take me to jail? Go right ahead. I been in jail before." He held his hands out rigidly, wrists together. "Go head, muthafucka! Take me in! Hey, people! Uncle Tom is gonna arrest my black ass. If I get shot trying to escape, remember his face."

There were about twenty people in the large room, and at Barlow's outburst they stopped what they were doing and began to move ominously toward Barlow's desk, making belligerent noises.

Dunbar said, "Oh, for cryin' out loud, Barlow! Get real!" Dunbar knew he couldn't afford to start trouble. The crowd was obviously not going to let him take Barlow in without a scuffle, and if he called for backup, somebody was going to ask what he was doing there in the first place, which meant he would either have to lie, or get chewed out for wasting time on a dead case.

He snorted in disgust and pushed his way past the growling revolutionary cadres and out of the main office. He heard the crowd cheering as he swung past the glass door.

The detective loitered despondently in the bookstore for a while. There was a good deal on the collected works of Kim II Sung in twenty-five volumes, but Dunbar was able to restrain himself. He had just about become resigned to sitting in his car on Boynton Street until Elvis should decide to show, when he happened to look back into the office.

Everyone had gone back to work after their revolutionary victory. Barlow was dialing a number, reading it out of a small, black book. He looked around furtively as he waited for a connection. He was on the phone for no more than a few seconds of conversation. Then he hung up, put the book in a desk drawer and locked it.

Dunbar thought that was funny. Old Jim Barlow did not seem like a terse man. Probably talk your ear off about the oppressed working classes while ordering a cup of coffee. On the other hand, if he were telling somebody that the cops were after him and he thought his phone was tapped, he might be brief for once.

Dunbar *really* didn't want to sit on Boynton Street. Which is why he waited until the place cleared out that night, broke in, picked the desk lock, and copied down all the names, addresses, and phone numbers in Barlow's little book. All of the thirty-two names were nicknames or first names and initials— Chili T., Joe Q., Chingo Ray, Che M., and like that. Very conspiratorial. As he looked over the list, something almost rang a bell in Dunbar's head. He looked at the list for several minutes trying to make something happen, and failing. Then he locked everything up again and went home to Queens.

The next morning, early, Dunbar went to Centre Street to let Karp know what he had found. Karp was in court. As he left Karp's office, he ran into Marlene Ciampi in the hallway. As soon as he saw her, the bell finally rang.

"Hey, Champ. What does the name 'Chingo Ray' mean to you?"

"Chingo Ray? A.K.A. Charles Hargreaves, A.K.A. Charlie

the Bomber. He's the guy who got blown up in the townhouse. I'm prosecuting his buddies. Why do you ask?"

"Oh, nothing much. His name turned up in an address book I picked up on uptown. He's waxed, you say?"

"A probable. We know he was at the townhouse the night it blew up. They recovered a male body—in smithereens— from the wreckage. It could be him. On the other hand, he's a slippery bastard and smart as hell. It's not beyond him to have set up the explosion and leave us with a plausible stiff, to cover his tracks. Also, the bomb that blew away that judge's secretary. Very similar to letter bombs Charlie made in the past. So . . . tell me about this address book. Where did you get it?"

"Just stumbled over it, is all. Look, Champ. I gotta go detect. Catch you later."

As he walked to his car, Dunbar thought hard. He had asked Barlow about Elvis. The call made right after he left Barlow must have been triggered by his questions. He didn't think Barlow was calling out for a pizza; he was calling somebody in the book. Elvis's name was not in the book, therefore he was calling somebody connected with Elvis. Thirty-two addresses to check out. He decided to start with the late Chingo Ray, resident, according to his little list, at 351 Avenue A.

Nobody answered his knock at the apartment on Avenue A. He slipped the lock and went in, pistol drawn. The place looked like a typical East Village crash—mattresses on the floor, a sleeping bag, filthy sheets, garbage bags full of rotting stuff, graffiti sprayed on the walls, political and head-shop posters. A cheap table and chair stood in the center of the main room. The apartment was deserted, but Dunbar was delighted to see evidence of hurried flight—drawers half open, clothes strewn around, a pot of coffee, and dirty dishes in the kitchen sink.

Dunbar put his gun away and checked out the main room. The floor around the table was covered with short snippings of bell wire in different colors. On the table itself were several large manila envelopes. These were stamped and postmarked from different cities—Berkeley, Chicago, Detroit. Oddly, they were not addressed. Dunbar poked around some more. By the stinking trash bags he found more wire, some thin springs and a crumpled package of peel-off labels. It looked like somebody was going through a lot of trouble to create envelopes that could be made to look like they were coming from different places. Dunbar felt a chill run through his body. It had just occurred to him why somebody might want to take such trouble. He grabbed the envelopes and ran out of the apartment without bothering to close the door.

It took him nearly an hour to drive up to Boynton Street, running lights, cutting people off, pounding his fist on the wheel, and cursing every vehicle in front of him. His most vehement curses were reserved for himself. With the wisdom of hindsight it was clear that, once Elvis's dwelling had been located, someone should have watched it continually thereafter. Now, for some reason, Elvis had formed an association with terrorists. Who could have figured it? Stick-up artists don't usually move in political circles. The more Dunbar thought about it, the crazier it became.

He screeched to a stop at 563 Boynton, flung himself out of the car and raced up the stairs. At the Higgs apartment he yanked out his pistol and used it to pound on the door.

When Vera Higgs opened the door a crack, Dunbar threw his weight against it, knocking her to the floor. He stormed through the apartment, kicking through doors, tossing the bed, yanking out drawers. Nothing—no Elvis, no envelopes.

He returned to the living room. The TV was on and the child sat on the floor in front of it. Vera Higgs was just climbing to her feet.

"You knock me down. You din hafta."

"Right, sorry, it was an accident. Look, Vera, where's Preston? I'm not fooling now. I got to know where he is."

Sulkily, she walked slowly to the ratty couch and sat down. "He ain't here."

"Goddamn, I *know* that! Where is he?"

"I don know. He lef."

"When? When did he leave?"

"Bout an hour, somethin' like that."

"Oh, Christ! Where to?"

"He din say. He never tell me."

That figured. Dunbar pulled one of the manila envelopes out of his jacket pocket and held it up.

"Vera, did he have an envelope like this?"

"I don have to tell you nothin'. He say, you come back here, I don have to tell you nothin'."

Dunbar gave a strangled cry. He went over to the little boy, picked him up and put him on the couch next to his mother. Then he went over to the TV and pointed his pistol at "Lust for Life." He cocked the hammer.

"Lady, you don't tell me what I want to know, I'm gonna waste your TV. I swear it!" Dunbar shouted. The child began to blubber.

She got to her feet, her eyes widening in terror.

"No! Don! I got my programs comin'!"

Dunbar put up his gun and eased the hammer down. "OK, what about the envelope?"

"Yeah, he got one—it look the same, but it be real fat, thick like."

"Was there an address on it. Can you remember the address?"

"No, but, like, Pres, he tol me to write one on it, on account of I got real good handwritin'. The teacher, she be sayin' I could be a schoolteacher, I got such fine writin'. But I had to quit school, you know?"

"Right," said Dunbar, moving closer to her and trying to control his voice. "Now, Vera, can you remember the name and address you wrote on the envelope?"

"I don know. I copy it down. He done have it writ out, you know?"

"Try, Vera."

"It somethin' like Carl, the las name. And some street like Senn, San, somethin like that. It start with a C."

"Senn? Was it Centre Street, One hundred Centre Street?"

"Yeah, that it. I think."

I'm so stupid, I should turn in my potsy and be a fucking doorman, thought Dunbar.

"Vera, baby, tell me. The name was Karp, Roger Karp, right?"

She smiled for the first time. "Yeah! Thas right! Karp."

"Where's your phone?"

"They cut it off," she said. "Hey, I don be in no trouble jus for writin'? I din do nothin'."

But Dunbar was already gone.

Marlene Ciampi was looking for an excuse to see Karp again, and make up. At the same time she despised herself for wanting to. I can't believe it, she thought for the millionth time. I'm having an affair with a married man, who works where I work. It was so degrading—like the secretary screwing the boss, like a public convenience or one of his perquisites. Here's your big office, Mr. Karp, your special couch, your walnut bookcases, your leather judge's chair. Oh, yeah, you want some pussy? Ciampi, put down that case file and drop your pants.

Then again, she felt, she feared, she was truly in love. She could feel herself flush when he came near her. Her belly gave a jump even when she saw his name written. When she awakened in her own apartment, she felt empty, and it took all her self-restraint not to rush to the phone and call him.

And she couldn't tell anyone about it. Most of her friends from high school were married and had settled suburban lives. They'd think she was a freak. Her family? Mama, I'm fucking this married man. No, he's not Italian. He's not Catholic, either. Instant coronary. Her professional friends? Out of the question. That's all she needed, this story to get around the office.

She rubbed her face and tried to shake these thoughts out of her head. To work. Maybe he'd call. She turned to her brimming in-basket. Sorting through the papers, she noticed that they were still sending her Karp's mail.

Karp was in his outer office talking with some of his staff when the call came through.

"Mister Karp, there's a call for you—they say it's extremely urgent," said Helen Simms.

"OK, guys, back to work. The city never sleeps. It's probably the laundry calling, they put in extra starch by mistake."

The voice on the phone was scratchy and interrupted by bursts of static.

"Butch, it's me, Sonny. Listen, I found Pres."

"What, who? Speak up, Sonny, I can hardly hear you."

"Pres. The third man. His name's Preston Elvis, and he SKRRRCHHHH, the paper that Louis worked for."

"You got him? Is he in custody?"

"No! Look, I'm on the Deegan, they patched me through over the radio. Butch, he's got SKRCHHHWOOOWRR in an envelope. He's tied in with that guy, the terrorist. Butch, I think he's heading for you SSSSCHHHRRWOWR already called the bomb squad, they should be there any minute. So don't WOORRSCHH."

"Jesus, Sonny, what the fuck are you talking about. What's this about the bomb squad. I can't hear shit on this line."

"The third man, Butch. Louis set him up with a bomb. Don't touch any CCCHHWWOOOOWRRCHH."

"Any what? What?"

"Any mail! It's a letter bomb. The bomb's in a nine by twelve manila envelope, with an out-of-town postmark. You better get your office cleared out, too. Butch, are you there? Butch? Ah, shit!"

As soon as Dunbar said "letter bomb," of course, Karp had thrown down the phone and leaped for the door. He ran to his secretary and told her not to touch any mail. Then, with mounting horror, it came to him that he had still not told the mailroom that he had moved his office. His heart was pounding in his throat as he ran out of the office and toward the stairs to the sixth floor.

Marlene had three pieces of Karp's mail lined up on her desk. One was an American Express bill. One was a letter from the University of California Alumni Association. The third one was the item that held her interest, a thick manila envelope with a Berkeley postmark, addressed in a flowing, patently feminine hand.

Marlene turned the envelope over and inspected it. The flap was fastened, but not sealed. She had a cold feeling in the pit of her stomach. She wants him back, she thought. It's a long letter explaining her affair with that woman and how she realized it wasn't for her and how she's going to come home to New York and make a great little home for him and have kids. Or maybe she's sending back a bunch of letters he wrote to her, begging her to take him back, he'll be her slave, he'll move to California and sell insurance. Telling her he's been screwing this little guinea in revenge but that's all over, she's the one and only. Or maybe it's divorce papers.

"Oh, God!" said Marlene out loud, "I can't stand this."

She undid the clasp and pulled the flap up.

Now even in the midst of this emotional turmoil, there was a part of Marlene's mind that remained cool and rational. It was trying to send messages through to Marlene Central, but the circuits were blocked by hormones and random emotional noise. This part of Marlene knew pretty well what she held in her hand. Marlene had, after all, seen pictures of such envelopes before. Perhaps if it had been postmarked Detroit all would have been well.

"Bomb!" said that part of Marlene, as Marlene's hand came up on the flap. "Bomb!" it said again as Marlene felt the tiny tug of resistance and saw the fine wire glued to the flap. By then it was too late, for electrons were already flowing from the battery to the primer charge. Marlene knew what it was now, and sent an urgent message to her hand and arm to throw the thing away. Her hand came dutifully up, slowly, slowly, while her mind screamed in overdrive. The envelope left her hand, but now it was hardly an envelope any more, more like a hot flower. Marlene brought her arm up in front of her beautiful face as the fireball swallowed her.

CHAPTER EIGHTEEN

arp's chest hurt. He had a broken heart. He was breathing mere pints of air, and his face ached with unshed tears. His stomach was empty and his mouth was still sour, because after he had entered the shattered office and seen the scorched and bloody thing that lay behind Marlene's desk, he had vomited. After that, he had knelt by her side and tried to help, covering her with his jacket and mouthing meaningless words of reassurance, more for him than for her, since she was mercifully unconscious. The cops and the emergency team had arrived a few seconds later and gently moved him aside so they could tend to her.

Now he was waiting in a hallway in Bellevue, studying the cracks in the peeling green paint and trying to forget his last sight of her as they wheeled her past, the black and red Halloween mask on her face, blowing red bubbles. He shared the waiting with a crowd of assorted Ciampis, sitting in stunned silence on benches, pacing nervously, or—in the case of her mother—sobbing without letup. Karp didn't introduce himself, nor did they make any effort to include him in their circle of grief.

A tired young man in green scrubs came through swinging doors and approached the Ciampis. Karp watched from across the hall. The doctor spoke quietly to the family. Several of the women began to shriek at once. The mother fainted, and the family redirected its attention to this immediate crisis. The doctor saw Mrs. Ciampi settled on a bench and then strode briskly away. Karp followed him.

Once past the swinging doors Karp accosted the surgeon. "Hey, Doc, wait up. What's the story on Marlene Ciampi?"

"You are?"

"Roger Karp. I work with her. At the DA's office."

"Well, as I told them back there, she's pretty badly hurt. In fact, it's amazing she survived. Of course, she was sitting down at the desk when the explosion occurred, so there's only minor damage from the waist down. She's going to need extensive reconstructive surgery on her face, though. And the hand."

"The hand?"

"Yes, it looks as though she was able to get her arm up over the left side of her face. She's going to lose a lot of function in the left hand. And, of course, the right eye is completely gone."

"Of course," said Karp, the nausea rising in him again.

The doctor looked at him curiously. "Say, are you OK? You look like you got blown up, too."

Karp looked down at his clothes, which were caked with blood and soot. "I wish," he said. He turned away and walked out of the building.

Karp was startled to discover, on emerging from the hospital, that it was still day, the smoky yellow twilight of late summer in the city, hot and humid. He had mistakenly thought his hospital vigil had lasted through the night.

Karp began walking rapidly down First Avenue. He wanted to go home and change his clothes. He wanted to get drunk. But most of all he wanted the guy who planted the bomb, and the guy who made it, and the guy who thought it up. He had a pretty good idea about who two of these were. And he wanted them without Miranda or Escobedo. He wanted them raw.

By the time he got to 20th Street, Karp's imagination had subjected them to a series of punishments not authorized by the New York State Penal Code. Also, in the sliver of his mind not given over to rage and grief, he was beginning to understand how seductive an idea was vengeance, and how—beneath all the talk about rehabilitation and civil rights—that idea remained as the ancient core of criminal justice. Bad guys have to be hurt, and they have to be seen to be hurt. The cops' old song.

On the other hand, thought Karp, recoiling from his own fantasies, if you impaled criminals in Times Square, wouldn't that brutalize the society even more? Wouldn't that start a vicious cycle that would make a civil society impossible? What was the point of all this mindless hurting and counterhurting? Or of anything?

Karp's mind raced around these thoughts for a while and then clattered to a stop, like the little ball in a pachinko machine. His vision grew blurred and he felt sick. He had been walking rapidly for half an hour, crossing streets whenever there was a green light, and now he wasn't sure where he was. He sagged like a drunk against the chain-link fence around a playground. He wiped the sweat from his forehead and looked at his hand. It was filthy with soot and what could have been dried blood. There was a drinking fountain in the playground. Karp drank deeply from it then washed his face in the tepid water, drying himself with his shirtsleeves.

He sat on a bench, watching the slight breeze ruffle the leaves of a dusty maple tree. He watched some ants attack a Crackerjack nugget. He watched two teenagers playing horse on the basketball court, a very tall black kid in white Converse high-tops and a slightly shorter, but faster, redhead. All these were of equal interest. Everything else was on hold.

The basketball took a bad bounce off the rim and rolled to Karp's feet. This was interesting, too. Karp picked up the ball and stood. He was about twenty-five feet from the hoop. He stared at the ball for a long moment. The kids yelled, "Hey, Mister, let's have the ball, huh?"

Karp held the basketball in both hands. He saw a thin, glowing wire leading from the center of the ball to the basket. He gave the ball a little shove and it traveled neatly along the wire and through the basket, without touching the rim. The glowing wires were Karp's secret. He had constructed a network of them from every square inch of a standard basketball court forward of the foul line to the basket. He knew the right combination of push and spin from every one of those square inches to the basket, left-handed, right-handed, backward over the head. He didn't have to think about it anymore, just find the right wire and the push came from his body naturally, like breathing or walking. It had taken him only about twenty thousand hours of practice over ten years to learn how to do this.

The kids whistled and the redhead said "Hey, luck-eee!" The black kid retrieved the ball and said, "No way, man! That old dude can shoot."

"Shoot, my ass! Shit, he couldn't make that shot again in a million years. Look at him, he's a wino or some shit!"

The black kid laughed. "Baby, you wrong there. That dude could wipe his ass with you on this court."

"Bullshit! A buck says he can't make it again."

The black kid looked over at Karp, who stood motionless. "Hey, mister! This little man here say you can't make that shot again. How about it?"

Karp raised his hands silently and the kid threw him the ball and he sank the shot in a single liquid motion, one-handed this time.

"See?" said the black kid. "I told you he could play ball."

"That still don't mean shit. A fuckin' foul shot don't mean he can play ball."

"I bet he could take you apart under the boards too."

"No way, man!"

"Ask him, then. It's your ball, man."

The redhead, his face flushing now, grabbed the ball up and yelled at Karp, "Hey, you! You want to play a little one on one?"

Which was exactly what Karp wanted. He wanted to descend once again into the waking dream that had been his refuge for most of his life, the world of thump, thump, bang, swish, of trajectories and patterns, a world with no problems he couldn't handle, where there was always another shot, where violence could be stopped by a whistle, where pain was only physical, and could be borne. Yes, Karp wanted to play a little one on one.

The black kid sat down behind the basket, leaned against the fence, and watched his friend get his ass whipped. The redhead was an OK player, but then neither of them had ever seen anything like Karp, except on TV. The redhead's speed didn't do him any good, because Karp seemed to know where the kid was going before he himself did. Karp could lose half a step and then the kid would make his play and Karp would be there to snatch the ball out of the air, spin, fake, shoot and score. And he was wearing wing tips.

The redhead got madder and madder and began to foul Karp, giving him the hip, the elbow. After ten minutes, he was doing everything but holding Karp by the wrists. Karp didn't mind and didn't say a word. He could score off-balance, from either hand, on both sides. Karp was ahead, twenty to two, when he took to the air for a jumper, ten feet out. The kid was playing in his face and he went up too, not for the ball, but to swat Karp out of the sky. They collided with a beefy smack, their legs tangled, and Karp fell and landed on the black asphalt on his bad knee and the kid fell on top of him.

They heard Karp's bellow across the playground, and pedestrians on First Avenue paused and turned their heads, wondering who was being murdered—before going about their business.

Karp, his body arched like a bow and rigid with agony, continued to scream at top volume until his throat was raw and he was out of breath; then he just sobbed. Through a red haze of pain he saw a circle of faces surrounding him: young ball players, elderly checkers players, mommies, kids, crazy people, an ice cream man, and, since the midtown East Side of Manhattan contains one of the world's largest concentrations of medical establishments, an assortment of nurses, orderlies, nurses' aides, medical technicians, and a physical therapist.

This latter group took Karp expertly in hand, and, having determined that there was nothing life threatening about Karp's condition, took a brief medical history, which Karp grunted through gritted teeth, and recommended that he go straight to the emergency room at Bellevue or Beth Israel—depending on his insurance coverage.

"No, thanks, that's OK," he gasped. "I just need to get home. If one of you could call me a cab . . ."

The physical therapist was a stocky Puerto Rican with a lumpy but pleasant face and close-cropped graying hair. He had rolled up Karp's pant's leg and examined the knee, which was by now the size of a grapefruit and getting purple.

"All right, buddy, but I hope you know what you're doing. You want to get that in ice and keep it there, right? As soon as you get home. You got something for pain?"

"Yeah, I think I have some Empirin and codeine left."

The PT man rolled his eyes. "It's your body, mister. I had a knee looked like that, I'd crawl into a bottle of Demerol and stay a week."

Somebody found tape and scissors, and they made an immobilizing wrapping for Karp's knee out of a couple of newspapers from the trash. They got him into a cab and the PT volunteered to help him into his apartment. The cab pulled away, the crowd broke up and the two teenagers began playing horse again.

"I wonder who that dude was," said the black kid. "He sure could play some ball."

"Who the fuck cares," said the redhead. "Shoot."

"Hector Delgado," said the PT in the back of the Checker. Karp had his foot elevated on the folded jump seat. He was still in intense pain.

Karp told him his name and shook hands. "Good thing we found a Checker," Delgado said with a chuckle. "They couldn't fit you into one of them little ones, huh? So tell me, Butch, you always play a little basketball after work, on that knee?"

"Hector, you want the truth? I haven't touched a basketball in, what? Almost fourteen years."

"So why today?"

"Just crazy. I don't know. My girl got hurt today. I must

have gone batshit, blamed myself or something. Maybe I wanted to get hurt, too. Who knows?"

"What, you cracked up the car?"

"No, if you can believe this, some shithead sent me a bomb in the mail and she opened it by mistake. She's in Bellevue."

"Well, don't worry, she's in good hands."

"In Bellevue? I thought it was a . . . you know, where they send the poverty cases."

"Yeah, but it's also the best hospital in the city. Funny, right? If the president got shot in New York, they'd send him there. Don't worry. Look, give me her name and I'll look her up. I'll tell her you're flat on your ass for a week and won't be chasing any tail."

Karp did so. When the cab reached Karp's building, Delgado helped him out. A black man leaning against the doorway sprang forward and opened the outer door for them. Karp thought his face looked familiar. I've probably ridden on the elevator with him a hundred times and never said a word, he thought. New York, right? The coldest inhabited place on the globe. On the other hand there were people like Delgado, who would go out of their way to help a stranger.

Delgado guided Karp into his apartment, set him on the bed, took off the newspapers, helped him out of his shoes and trousers and made a cold pack with ice from the freezer and a towel. Karp thought achingly of Marlene, who had filled his ice trays for the first time. Delgado fed Karp some pills from the medicine cabinet, and Karp sank back on the pillows to wait for the codeine to kick in.

"OK, Chief," said Delgado, "you're all set. Hey, you got no food in the fridge. You just move in? You want me to bring some stuff up from the corner?"

"No, that's fine, Hector. You're a prince. You ever want to kill somebody, let me know. I work for the DA. I'll cop you a good plea."

Delgado laughed. "Hey, all right, I got a list. OK, I got to run, take it easy."

After the man left Karp felt the first pangs of utter loneliness. He reached out to the bedside table and lifted the phone onto his chest. Who should he call? V.T. was out of town. Hrcany? Guma? Yeah, he'd call Guma, who'd bring a pizza and a bottle of wine, and they'd sit around and bullshit and maybe he'd figure out what he was going to do with the rest of his life.

He started to dial Guma's number and then stopped. He didn't want to see Guma. He wanted to see Marlene. He should have let them take him to Bellevue. They could have given him a walking cast, or a wheelchair, and then he could have sat by her room at least and been there when she came around. OK, Guma could drive him to the hospital. He had just started to dial again when he heard the first sounds from the door.

Clicking, bumping sounds. Somebody was trying to get in. It couldn't be Delgado, or a friend with chicken soup. They would ring the bell. Karp heard the lock snap and the turning of the doorknob. There was nothing in the apartment to absorb the sound, so Karp could hear all the details of the break-in. Of course, he hadn't followed Delgado to the door, so the dead bolt wasn't set. The door swung open and Karp heard someone come into the apartment.

And he knew exactly who it was, because he had just remembered why the guy who had opened the door downstairs looked so familiar. Karp had been looking at his Identikit portrait almost every day for three years.

For a panicked moment Karp considered dialing 911. Then he realized that not only would the line be busy but that Elvis would hear him dialing. Karp placed the phone on the bed carefully, and slowly slid off, balancing on his good leg and clenching his teeth against the pain. The codeine was starting to work, but the knee still sent darts of fire up his leg. It was still completely useless as something to walk on.

Karp thought of all the scene-of-the-crime pictures he had seen while at Homicide. Lots of macho hard-boiled laughs about those. He imagined himself in one of them. Not funny. He imagined his own body on an autopsy table. His heart thumped audibly against his chest. A few hours ago he had fancied himself ready to die, but now—with a killer in the next room—he found himself not wanting to die at all. Instead, he wanted to kill.

The first thing to do was to get moving. Elvis was checking out the kitchen, and would be coming through the closed bedroom door in a few seconds. Karp didn't think it was a good strategy to hide under the bed. In the movies, killers always looked under the bed. Karp looked under the bed anyway. It was still a bad idea. But one of the slats would do for a cane. He jimmied it out and rose wretchedly to his feet.

He heard steps coming toward the bedroom door. An image from his childhood flashed into his mind. He had done something very bad, broke a lamp or something, and he was cowering in the bedroom listening to his mother searching the house for him. He was in for a serious spanking. He remembered what he had done then and he did it again. He hobbled over to the bathroom and locked himself in.

Elvis heard the bathroom door close and the shower go on. He smiled. This was going to go down smooth as shit. Mostly everything had been going right since his phone call from Louis. He had written it all out, under Louis's coaching, on the piece of brown paper bag that he kept in his wallet and consulted half a dozen times a day. No more forgetting stuff for Pres. He had made contact with the Claremont Press. He had talked all that political bullshit with Barlow and them, and got the names of brothers who were into trashing the system. They had been glad to send a tough kid who was ready for anything and obviously not a cop (they had checked, of course—people remembered him from Attica), to Chingo Ray, who could always use another mule. He'd picked up the bomb. He'd dropped it into a mail cart. He waited outside until he heard it go off. It had all worked out as Louis said it would.

Except for the cop coming to see Vera. That wasn't supposed to happen. OK, he could ditch that scene all right. Couple of clothes was all he had there. The bitch was getting too nosy anyway. There were plenty of people he could stay with. DeVonne, for example.

Everything was fine—except for the chick getting wasted instead of Karp. Elvis had watched the small, bloodied form loaded into the ambulance at Foley Square, and had stamped his foot in rage; damn, he had marked the damn package "personal," meaning Karp was supposed to open it himself. He had waited around for a while until he saw Karp, obviously unhurt, rush out of the building and hail a cab.

Elvis had studied the brown paper again, but got no new advice. He definitely did not want to call Louis and tell him the bomb had gone off and Karp was still alive. He only wanted to call Louis and tell him Karp was dead, that was the only way the crazy motherfucker would get off his ass.

So he had looked up Karp's address in the phone book, taken the subway to the Village, and waited. He had his piece with him for the occasion, a real Smith & Wesson .38, nickel-plated, with the four-inch barrel, that he had bought off a guy in a bar for ninety bucks. Big time. No more Saturday Night Specials for old Pres.

With this new toy in hand, Elvis flung open Karp's bedroom door and whirled into the room, in the predatory crouch he had seen in so many TV shows. You never could tell, maybe the guy wasn't in the shower yet. Maybe he had a gun, too.

OK, nobody here. Check under the bed. In the closet. OK, all clear. Bathroom door locked. No problem. Elvis pulled out the piece of steel shim he had used to spring the front door lock, popped the latch, threw open the door, and burst into the bathroom.

The bathroom was filled with steam. Elvis was inside a white cloud, lit by the light over the sink. He moved slowly over the steam-slick tile floor toward the sound of the shower. He was sweating heavily. Damn! Motherfucker liked hot showers. He cocked the pistol and pulled back the shower curtain. What the fuck . . . ? He peered into the tub. Visibility was about four inches, but it was enough to see that nobody was there.

He heard a sound behind him and turned his head, startled.

Karp hit him square in the face with the contents of his tin Statue of Liberty wastebasket, two gallons of water at 190 degrees, into which he had poured an almost-full bottle of Liquid Plumber. It was a pretty good trick considering Karp was balancing on one leg when he did it. Elvis shrieked and staggered backward, tripped over the tub and fell in. He shrieked again when the boiling shower struck him and began firing his pistol reflexively. One bullet hit the ceiling. The next hit the mirror over the sink, shattering it and covering the floor with broken glass.

Karp hopped over to the alcove behind the door where he had hidden, where he had parked his bed slat. He picked it up and started for the door. A bullet cracked over his head. The sound of the gunfire and Elvis's continuous screams were deafening in the little room. Karp was on automatic now. The drugs and the noise and the fear pumping through him made rational thought impossible. With nightmare slowness, he lurched through the fog to the doorway.

His bare foot landed on a sliver of glass and he cursed and staggered. Then his slat came down on a larger piece of glass and skidded away, and he fell.

Karp was nauseous with pain, and confused. He thought he heard Elvis screaming and scrabbling in the tub behind him. But when he looked up, there was a black man coming through the fog with a pointed pistol. How did he get out and in front of him again? Karp writhed in the broken glass and tried to reverse direction, knowing it was too late. The pistol exploded. Karp thought. Now I'm dead.

Karp actually enjoyed death. For one thing, he didn't hurt anymore. And it was quiet. He thought, This is the silence of the tomb. That made him laugh. Other people were there, too. They turned and looked at him when he laughed. He felt embarrassed. There were dead people, like his mom and grandma, but also live people. There was Guma. There was a blond girl he had a crush on in Junior High. They were all standing around in Karp's living room, which had been refurnished with white rugs and white modern furniture, white and chrome and glass. Marlene wasn't there, though. He wanted to call out to her, but he didn't want to be embarrassed again.

All the people were gathered around the doorway to the bedroom. They made a place for him in front of it. There was some kind of black hanging blocking the doorway. It was really a sort of garment, with sleeves, pants legs and a hood. Karp knew he was supposed to get into it, so he did. He leaned back and the garment yielded like elastic. He was almost horizontal, muffled in springy blackness. Somebody said, "Open your eyes." It seemed like a good idea.

"Holy shit! What a . . . what a . . . winger. Really ocean. A weird kind of blotter, hmm?" said Karp, through cottony lips.

"A little disoriented, are we? Pentothal will do that. How do you feel, Mister Karp?" said a voice in a lilting West Indian accent.

Karp was lying in a hospital bed. His left knee was in a heavy cast and his right wrist was in the hands of a brown young lady in a nurse's uniform. She was taking his pulse.

"Still a little vague. Where am I and what time is it?"

"You are in a postoperative ward of Bellevue Hospital. In New York City. And it just gone eleven o'clock."

"At night? It can't be."

She laughed. "In the morningtime, Mister Karp. You were in surgery for two hours and then you slept. And that man who brought you here has been waiting outside since seven."

"The man? Could I see him?"

"Yes, for a little bit. But don't tire you, now."

She cranked up his bed so that he was sitting up and pulled back the curtains. Karp felt twinges of pain from his face. Bandages. When he raised his hands to feel them he noticed that his hands were also bandaged.

The nurse ushered Sonny Dunbar into the room and left. Dunbar looked beat. His eyes were bloodshot and his pale yellow suit was wrinkled and dusty. He sat down on a straight chair near Karp's bed and rubbed his face.

"How you feeling, Butch?" he asked.

"Better than you look, anyway. They're working you too hard, or what?"

"No, the usual." After a pause, he continued. "I shot Elvis."

"You shot Elvis? Jesus Christ, Sonny, if you killed my witness . . ."

"No, no, relax! He's not dead. He's down in the lock-up ward. He had surgery about the same time you did. There was nothing else I could do. You were on the floor, you looked like you were half dead, he was blazing away, screaming out of his mind, blind, the goddamn place, you couldn't see shit anyway, so I shot him. In the arm, as it turned out, like in the movies. It's only the third guy I ever shot. I'm still rocky behind it."

"Oh, that was you in my bathroom. I thought I was going crazy, and Elvis was in front of me. Or somehow Louis had gotten away and was going to finish the job. Christ, you probably saved my life. What a fucking day, huh?"

"Yeah, Karp, you really know how to throw a party. By the way, Louis is here."

"What, in Bellevue?"

"Yeah. I heard from Monahan in the Bellevue Psych Ward. Your boy is sort of a well-known figure among the guard staff. He bites, he screams, he pisses."

"Shit, I can't believe it, the bastard! I'm not even cold in my grave and he's trying to slide one by me. Hand me that phone, Sonny."

Karp had a couple of conversations, promised favors, and called in chips. In a few minutes he had made sure that Louis would not be able to get his hearing scheduled until Karp was ready for him. Slowing down the system was easy.

"OK, Sonny, why don't you find me a wheelchair and we'll roll down to Elvis's room. I want to talk to him as soon as he comes around." Dunbar went out and was gone for half hour. When he returned, it was without a wheelchair and in the company of the West Indian nurse and a stocky man with large teeth and a white brush haircut, dressed in surgical greens.

"Mister Karp, I'm Doctor Hudson. I just operated on your knee, and now Nurse Simms here tells me you want to screw up my work."

"Butch, I tried, but she wouldn't let me have it," said Dunbar.

"It's just for a few minutes, Doc. Just down the hall."

The doctor reached down and picked up a bedpan. "You see this? The reason we give you this so you can perform your bodily functions in the comfort of your bed is because we don't want you to leave the bed. For any reason."

"But . . ."

"No buts. Look, young man, if you ever want to dance *Swan Lake* again, you'll stay put, flat on your back for at least a week. Your knee is stuck together with spit. It's a marvel you were able to run fast enough to fall down. Worst damn job I ever saw. Where did you have it done, Taiwan?"

"California."

Hudson snorted. "Same damn difference! All right, I'll be back tomorrow, and I want to see cobwebs on that cast. Simms, if he moves, sit on his face!" Hudson flashed a large grimace and strode out of the room. Simms took charge again. Turning to Dunbar, she said, "All right, you, visitin' hours is ov-ah."

"Simms, are you really going to sit on my face?" said Karp, after Dunbar had been hustled out of the room.

"None of that naughty talk, you. Here, take this pill! I don't want you to be achin' and yellin' up the night nurse."

"Kaplan! What's going on?" said Karp on the phone. "You're supposed to keep me in touch." Karp had been cosseted and bullied alternately for a week by Simms and the other nurses, and by the ferocious Hudson. He had to admit that his knee felt better; the bandages were off his hands, feet and face. He was going crazy with boredom, and with worrying about Marlene suffering and about Louis somehow getting away.

"Sorry, Butch, I've been running off my feet. All this stuff with Louis and Elvis is extracurricular, you know. I still got to hold the fort out there."

"Yeah, tell me about it. So what's the story? You talk to Elvis?"

"Not exactly. His lawyer was there as soon as the docs would let him talk. But he didn't talk. I mean stone wall."

"His lawyer? A Legal Aid?"

"Bullshit, a Legal Aid. We're talking Leonard Sussman."

"Oh, shit! Did you talk to him? What's the deal?"

"The deal is, one, Sussman's fee is being paid by a benefactor who prefers to remain anonymous. Three guesses who. Two, the story is, Elvis came to you to tell you to lay off his dear girl friend, who was apparently threatened by one of your minions. You viciously attacked him with lye and boiling water, as a result of which he is blinded and disfigured. He drew his gun merely to defend himself against this unprovoked attack. Oh, yeah, he will plead to a concealed weapons charge. How about that shit?"

"This is a fucking joke. What about the goddamn bomb!"

"What bomb? Just because our man is, get this, 'politically active,' we are going to try to frame him for an act of terrorism. A scandal."

"But, the girl friend, Higgs, she told Sonny that she . . . oh, crap!"

"Oh, crap is right. Vera is tight as a clam. Didn't see nuffin', didn't write nuffin', don't know nuffin'. Except one thing. Preston Elvis was warm in the bosom of his little family on the night of March twenty-sixth, Nineteen-seventy. She remembers *that,* clear as a bell. Mandeville Louis? Never heard of him, either of them. We been struck out, Chief."

"Uh-uh, baby, we're just getting started."

"What are you going to do, Butch?"

"Damned if I know, now. I'll think of something."

At ten o'clock that night, Karp cruised into the prison ward of Bellevue, showed his credentials to the guard, and rolled his wheelchair up to the bedside of Preston Elvis. Elvis's head was swathed in bandages yellow with furacin and his right arm was in a cast. Karp sat silently, and after a while Elvis became aware that somebody was in the room.

"Who . . . who there?" he said nervously.

"Don't worry, Pres, it's not the hit man, yet. It's just your latest victim."

"Who, Karp? What the fuck you doin' here? Get outa my room!"

"Come on, Pres, I'm just a fellow sufferer come to keep you company. Like a candy striper. Would you like something to read?"

"Fuck you, muthafucka! You finished, man. I'm gonna sue your ass, what you did to me. I'm gonna sue every fuckin' thing you got."

"Oh, yeah? Is Sussman going to do it for a contingency fee? Or is Mandeville Louis going to pay for that, too?"

"Fuck off! I ain't talkin' to you. I don have to talk to you. My lawyer say . . ."

"Shut up! I don't give a rat's ass what your lawyer says. I'm not here to ask you any questions because I already know what you did and how you did it. I don't need anything from you, Pres. But you need something from me."

"Fuck I do!"

"Yeah, you do, Pres. Lookie here. We got you on the weapons charge, and I think we could probably make simple assault stick. OK, needless to say, we go for the max, five years, and I'll make sure you do straight time, if I have to use every chip and every bit of pull I got to my name. Think about it, Pres. Five in the joint, blind, no face, a fucked-up arm. But they won't be looking at your face, Pres. They'll be a lot more interested in the other end. They'll be betting your tail in poker games, Pres. I raise you two smokes and you can fuck Elvis. After a couple years you'll be able to park a VW up your ass-hole."

"Shut up! Nurse! Get this bastard out of here!" Elvis yelled.

"OK, Pres, I was just going. But here's another thing to think about. Your good buddy, Louis. You think he's about to let somebody who could finger him on a murder rap live in prison for five years? I mean, you know him better than most, right? Few cartons of cigarettes is all it would take up there. What do you think?"

Elvis was cursing shrilly. Karp heard somebody coming in the hallway, and other people in the ward were yelling for quiet. He leaned closer to Elvis's bed and spoke softly, with a terrible intensity.

"I don't want you, Elvis. You're just a little piece of shit to me. But you give me him, *him*, and you'll walk, free and clear, I swear it. I swear it. *Free. And. Clear.*"

Karp did not go back to his room after this episode. Instead, he went to see Marlene, and begged the night nurse to let him spend a few minutes in her room. She was nearly as bandaged as Elvis. Only her mouth and a small patch of clear skin on the left side of her face remained uncovered. Her left hand was immobilized and suspended in a complicated frame attached to the bed. She appeared to be asleep. The room was full of flowers, from friends and relatives, and from Karp, who had ordered flowers sent every day since the bombing.

He rolled into the room and watched her for some minutes. Then he began to speak, softly, and to weep, a long, snuffling monologue. He told her how miserable and ashamed he was, and how he would make it up to her if it took him his whole life. He enumerated all the things he could have done that might have prevented her from getting hurt. He said he wished it was him lying there, instead of her. Worst of all, he told her they had the man who planted the bomb and he would give that man his freedom if he would help put Mandeville Louis away, and that he, Karp, was the lowest worm in the universe and if Marlene never looked at him again it was only what he deserved. And more in the same line.

After he had run out of steam and wiped his face on the sleeve of his bathrobe, he noticed, with some dismay, that she was gesturing him closer with her good arm. He rolled to the side of the bed and leaned over. She was saying something, but her voice was very weak. He put his ear next to her mouth.

"Butch . . ." she whispered.

"Yeah, baby, I'm here, what is it?"

"Butch, Butch, for chrissake . . . don't be such a schmuck!" she sighed, and drifted back into her drugged sleep.

She still loves me, thought Karp, and kissed her cheek.

CHAPTER NINETEEN

The remains of a giant mushroom-and-pepperoni pizza with extra cheese had been pushed to one side of Karp's bed. Guma had brought it, together with four quarts of Schaeffer, and Karp, desperate after nearly a month of hospital food, had eaten most of it. Mike Kaplan, Roland Hrcany, V.T., and Sonny Dunbar were arranged around the room, drinking beer, smoking, eating cannolis out of greasy paper, and generally helping with Karp's readjustment to life on the outside. Tomorrow he was scheduled to go home—on crutches.

Karp tried to get into the spirit of celebration, but failed. This was noticed.

"Hey, Butch, smile! It's supposed to be a party. You look like a rainy day in the cancer ward," said Guma.

"Yeah, Karp, lighten up!" said Hrcany. "Have some more beer. Hey, I'll get my projector, we'll set it up and watch skin flicks."

"No, maybe later," said Karp. "Listen, guys, let me not beat around the bush. I need some help here. Sonny and Mike are already in it, but we're not going to pull it off as a part-time thing. Especially with me on crutches."

"What, this is the liquor store case, that guy Louis?" asked Guma.

"Yeah, but let me fill you in on the details."

After Karp had done so, Guma gave a low whistle. "Holy shit! This guy Louis aced Sonny's brother-in-law, blew up Marlene, and almost killed you, *while he was locked up?*"

"I see your point, Butch," said V.T. "If this guy walks, nobody will be safe in their beds."

"Yeah, safety in bed is one of our most sacred rights as Americans," said Hrcany. "OK, you must have a plan. How do we nail the fucker?"

Karp grinned for the first time that evening. "We have to do two things. First, we have to crack Elvis. We're not going to be able to get next to him officially, not with Sussman on the case. So we're going to go after his alibi."

"The girl, Vera," said Dunbar.

"Right, but we also have to cover his movements from the time he was captured back as far as we can go. Where he went, the newspaper job, friends, hangouts. We should give Louis's place a good toss, too. Elvis may have been hanging around there. He's a skell, right? He must have done something we can bag him for."

"I'll do that, if I can get some help," said Dunbar.

"I'll come along, if I can wear a disguise," said Hrcany.

"Wear your Nixon mask," said Karp. "Mike, you go with the uptown squad, too. It's good training. Guys, be gentle with him, he's a mere child."

"What's the other thing?" asked V.T.

"Yeah, that's the hard one. We've got to bring Louis to trial, which means we've got to destroy this Ganser syndrome bullshit. Which means knocking off Werner."

"Can you do that?"

"I've been thinking about it, V.T. I figure the only way to get the kind of information we need on Werner is to get somebody on the inside, to present somebody as a patient with Ganser syndrome. Get a line on the internal politics of the forensic staff. I can't believe every psychiatrist in Bellevue is as whacked out as Werner."

"So somebody has to pose as a crazed criminal and be locked up in Bellevue, and be examined by Werner," V.T. mused.

"Exactly," said Karp, "but who?"

"Yeah, somebody would have to be crazy to pull a trick

like that." Guma laughed. Then he realized that everybody else in the room was silent and looking at him expectantly.

"Uh-uh, guys. No way. No fucking way. I mean, I'll help out and all, but I draw the line there. No way am I going to get locked up with a bunch of loonies. Sor-ree . . ."

"What's the matter, Goom, afraid they won't let you out?" said Hrcany.

"Up yours, blondie! You're so fuckin' wise, *you* do it! Sorry, Butch, that's it, that's final."

Ten minutes later Guma was sitting in a wheelchair, dressed in a Bellevue robe and pajamas. V.T. was preparing to push Guma down to the locked wards.

"I don't believe I'm doing this," said Guma. "I can't believe you had it all set up, the paperwork and everything. What if I'da said no?"

"We had faith in you, Mad Dog," said V.T. "Now start acting crazy, we're rolling."

Kaplan and Hrcany were standing outside Louis's apartment. Nobody gave them any trouble. Two white men in suits walking together in that neighborhood could be only cops.

Hrcany knocked on the door. It opened three inches on a chain and a blast of high-volume Funkadelics washed over the two men.

"Hi, DeVonne," said Hrcany. "Can we come in?"

"Who you?"

"What? Didn't Louis tell you? We got the money. All of it."

"What money?" said DeVonne suspiciously. Louis usually left her pretty explicit instructions about what he wanted her to do. He hadn't said anything about white guys and money. On the other hand Louis was sounding flaky on the phone recently, jabbering about plans and plots in a way that she couldn't follow. DeVonne liked simple orders. But maybe he forgot. Also, DeVonne was running short of cash. Elvis had cleaned out the cash box, and she was afraid to sell Louis's stuff. He could be back any time. Something didn't happen in a couple of weeks, she was going to have to go back to work.

"The money from the deal. Hey, baby, let's not stand out in the hall so all the neighbors can hear Louis's business. C'mon, let us in."

DeVonne shrugged, closed the door, slipped the chain, and the two men entered. DeVonne walked across the living room and sat on the couch. She was wearing a floor-length, patterned orange lounging robe, loose and cut to the thigh. She crossed her legs and lit a cigarette with a large silver lighter.

"You all better not be shittin' me. What kinda deal."

"Smack. You know. Louis moved some shit for us. His end is ten grand. Here it is, OK?"

Hrcany held out a thick wad of bills wrapped in a rubber band. DeVonnne saw Ben Franklin's picture on top. Her eyes widened and she reached out for the wad.

"Uh-uh, baby. First you got to sign this receipt. I don't give nobody ten grand in cash without a receipt." Hrcany held out a piece of paper and a ballpoint. DeVonne took it and signed it on the glass coffee table.

Hrcany picked it up: "Received September 10, 1973, $10,000, signed, DeVonne Carter," he read. "Real good, DeVonne. OK, here's your cash." He tossed the roll to DeVonne, who pulled off the rubber band and riffled through the bills. Her mouth opened in shock when she discovered that the hundred dollar bill covered a hundred ones.

"Yeah, baby, next time you want to count the money *before* you give the man a receipt."

"Hey! Goddam, what you doin'?" yelled DeVonne as Hrcany and Kaplan started for the door. Hrcany turned.

"Well, we thought we'd go make a copy of this receipt and give it to Louis, so he'll know his ten grand is safe and sound."

"What you mean? They ain't no ten grand here. This here's nothin' but a couple hunred."

"Yeah, well that *will* be sort of hard to explain to Louis when he gets out. On the other hand . . ."

"What?" DeVonne was frightened. She saw the best scene she ever had going up in smoke, or worse. She didn't want to think about how she was going to cover ten grand. DeVonne was not used to thinking on her feet.

"On the other hand," said Hrcany, waving the receipt, "we could have a little party. Maybe I could forget this, huh?"

DeVonne sighed with both relief and resignation. She was once again on familiar ground. She stood up and walked slowly over to Hrcany, smiling and exaggerating the roll of her wide hips.

"Make sure you do, honey," she said, toying with the belt of her robe. As she waggled toward the bedroom she flashed a standard sultry look over her shoulder. They saw the robe drop as she passed from view.

"It worked," said Hrcany in a low voice. "Let's get busy."

"Christ, Roland, what are we supposed to do now?"

"Oh, well, I'll toss this room and the kitchen, and you go in there and amuse DeVonne."

"Me? Why me? I don't get this whole scene, the song-and-dance about the money . . . why didn't we just identify ourselves and ask if we could look around?"

"Good idea, Kaplan. You think DeVonne is going to let a couple of ADA's nose around? She's dumb, but not that dumb. Also, we're not looking for evidence. We're looking for stuff we can use to beat Elvis over the head. We definitely don't want anybody to know we searched up here. It would screw up the case something fierce. Catch my drift?"

"Shit. But what should I do in . . .?" He jerked his thumb in the direction of the bedroom.

"Oh God! Kaplan, use your glands. Go! I got to get started. Oh, yeah, sooner or later she's going to use the can. See what you can find in the bedroom. Otherwise we'll have to figure out some way of waltzing her out here."

"You could tell her you can fuck only on a kitchen table," said Kaplan sourly.

"Hey, now you're thinking!" said Hrcany, and began pulling books from the shelves.

Dunbar was sitting on the crummy green couch in Vera Higgs's apartment, watching "Gilligan's Island." Her child was in his accustomed place in front of the TV. Vera Higgs was pretending Dunbar didn't exist. The last thing she had said to him, nearly two hours ago, was: "Pres say, the lawyer tol' him, if you keep botherin' me, he gonna get a coat order. He say it harassment. So you can sit there all night Mister PO-lice, I ain' saying nothin' I ain' tol' you a hunnerd times already."

And she was as good as her word. Dunbar would have left a long time ago, but he had agreed to meet Kaplan and Hrcany in the Bronx, on the slim chance they would turn up something important.

There was a knock on the door, and Dunbar got up and opened it. Hrcany and Kaplan stood in the doorway. Hrcany beaming, Kaplan looking glum and a little sick.

"You got something?" asked the detective.

"Yeah, we do. A Grand Jury subpoena and some other stuff. Where is she?"

Dunbar motioned to the woman on the couch. Hrcany went over to her. She glanced at him without interest and then turned back to the TV. Hrcany held the subpoena between her eyes and the glowing screen.

"This is a subpoena, Miss Higgs. It says you got to come downtown and talk to us some more."

"Do I got to? Pres, he say . . ."

"Yeah," said Hrcany, "you got to."

The four of them and the child rode down to Centre Street in Dunbar's car. The child pointed and chattered. Everyone else was stonily silent.

In his office, Hrcany seated Vera Higgs in a wooden arm-chair. He sat in a leather chair behind his desk. Dunbar and Kaplan stood in opposite corners of the room. The little boy sat on the floor near his mother, tearing up yellow legal paper and scribbling with an assortment of markers.

Hrcany began, speaking slowly and gravely. "Miss Higgs, I want to talk frankly to you about your situation. My name is Roland Hrcany, and I'm with the District Attorney's office. I am concerned about you, Miss Higgs. I fear that you may be the victim of a cruel hoax, one that is going to land you in a lot of trouble."

She looked at him blankly. "What you talkin' about?"

"Well, Miss Higgs, to put it bluntly, Preston Elvis seems to have convinced you to lie for him—"

"I ain' tellin' no lie! I tol' you . . ."

"Please, let me finish! —convinced you to lie for him concerning his whereabouts on a certain night in March, Nineteen-seventy, when we believe he was involved in a brutal
murder. You are also helping to cover up his involvement in a
bombing at the New York District Attorney's Office, in which
a woman was badly maimed. These are felonies, Miss Higgs,
and by refusing to help us, you have involved yourself as an
accomplice. You could go to prison yourself."

Vera Higgs said scornfully, "He tol' me y'all would say
that. Pres say, you cain' do nothin' to me."

"Yes, he would say that. But it isn't true. He's using you,
Miss Higgs. He intends to dump you as soon as he's safe and go
off with a woman named DeVonne Carter—whom he has been
seeing intimately for many months."

"You lie! They ain' no woman. I his woman! I want to go
home!"

Hrcany silently reached into his pocket and tossed a pack
of color Polaroid photographs across his desk. She looked
through them slowly, one by one. Slowly, tears formed in her
large eyes and dropped onto her hands and onto the photographs. Finally, she began to sob, crumpled the pictures into a
ball and flung them across the office. Her little boy picked one
up, examined it solemnly and put it in his mouth. Dunbar
picked one up, too. It showed two people screwing. You
couldn't see the woman's face very well, but Preston Elvis was
clear as day on top of her, grinning into the camera.

"Well, Miss Higgs. Do you still feel Preston Elvis is going
to take care of you? Or would you like to tell me what really
happened?"

Vera Higgs wiped her nose with a scrap of tissue. "I guess,"
she said. "Goddamn him. An' goddamn you, too. Goddamn
you all to hell!"

Two hours later, Hrcany was smoking a thin celebratory cigar,
with his feet up on his desk. Kaplan was slouched in a side
chair. Vera Higgs had been formally deposed of her revised
testimony about Preston Elvis, and driven back home. Kaplan
had called Karp and told him the news. Karp had been ec-

static, which hadn't made Kaplan feel any better. Hrcany looked over at the younger man.

"What's the matter, kid, you look like shit."

"I feel like shit. I feel like there's a thin crust of old turd over my whole body."

Hrcany laughed, not nicely. "A thin crust? Don't worry, it'll thicken up. A couple of years it'll go right down to the bone, like me."

"Yeah, I can tell. God, that woman! Did you get how she asked what would happen to Elvis? She still cares about that rat."

"Right, it's that Frankie and Johnnie bullshit. So what else is new? Hey, as soon as I saw that Polaroid on the tripod in the bedroom, I knew we had pay dirt. I wish I had kept some of them. By the way, how was old DeVonne, stud? Hot stuff?"

"Marvelous. I worked a chess problem in my head the whole time."

"No shit? Did you win?"

"I lost. But, really, what will happen to Elvis? Will he cop one if he gives us Louis?"

"Damned if I know," said Hrcany, grinding his cigar out in a glass ashtray. "It's Karp's case."

Dr. Werner was ecstatic. Another perfect example of Ganser syndrome. He regarded Lennie Trevio—the squat figure across the desk from him—with something like affection. He envisioned an international symposium on Ganser syndrome, an event that would make forensic psychiatric history, with himself at the center of it all.

He continued the interview. "So tell me, ahh, Lennie, have you ever had hallucinations or seizures—like the one you had in court today—outside of court?"

Guma said, "No doc, I never had nothin' like that before."

"Good. Now please go on. You say you saw the judge change into a giant chicken?"

"Yeah, right, more like a rooster. So he started squawkin' and then, and then I heard this voice, like it was coming from the ceiling, sayin', 'I will turn you into, ah, bread crumbs.' "

"Bread crumbs?"

"Yeah, you know, like the rooster was gonna eat me?"

"Ah, yes, I see."

"So I started making a fuss, y'know? So here I am." He laughed.

"Yes. Well, Lennie, I think that will be all for today. You will have to see another doctor, but I think what's troubling you is clear enough."

"Doc, will I have to go back to the trial?" asked Guma, in as nervous a tone as he could manage without cracking up.

"No, of course not. It would be inhuman. No, Lennie, you're in good hands now."

"Aw, thanks, doc, you're a saint!" exclaimed Guma.

Werner beamed. This was why he had gone to med school. That, and power.

The next day Guma sat in the dayroom of Bellevue's lock-up ward, reading the *Post* and feeling grumpy. He had breakfasted on what tasted like warm, damp clay and he hadn't had a beer or a cigar in more than twenty-four hours, a violation, in his view, of the constitutional safeguards against cruel and unusual punishment. And he was no closer to getting the goods on the docs. He had seen Werner, who was a dingbat, but they already knew that.

He looked up from his paper and glanced around the dayroom. He saw a couple dozen people, a cross section of male New York. Some guys talking to the air. One or two jerking off. A guy peeing in the corner. Most of them sitting and watching TV or playing cards. Nothing you couldn't see any day in Times Square or on the subway. It seemed only happenstance could explain why these men were here and not on the southbound IRT.

Guma noticed a small, skinny old man in a shiny dark suit wandering through the crowd. He carried a notebook and a stack of file folders. Guma watched him approach a large black man who was arguing with the ceiling. The old man argued with the ceiling for a while, too. The madman paused in his ravings and the two of them had a brief conversation. They smiled and shook hands. The black man went over and sat down in front of the TV. The old man spoke with some of the other inmates in a cheerful and conversational manner. Then he came over to where Guma was sitting and pulled up a chair.

Close up the man looked even older than he had across the room: a thin fringe of silver hair around a speckled scalp; a sallow, wrinkled face; a large, lumpy nose that looked as if it had been broken at some time in the remote past; bad, yellow teeth; and deeply sunken brown eyes with heavy grayish pouches beneath them. But the eyes were sharp and bright.

"Well, young man, how do you feel today?" he asked. Unlike the psychiatrists he had met previously, this guy seemed genuinely interested in the answer. He had a slight German accent.

Guma gave him the Ganser syndrome cover story. The old man listened carefully, occasionally making a note with a fountain pen in a cheap spiral-bound notebook. He said "mmm-ahh" from time to time, to keep the story moving. When Guma had finished, the old man sighed and pushed his gold-rimmed glasses up on his forehead. He held out his hand.

"Perlsteiner."

Guma shook hands and gave his cover name. The old man's grip was surprisingly strong. Dr. Perlsteiner looked through his files and pulled one out. He read it and let out a little snorting laugh.

"Ach, so we have Ganser syndrome again. *Ganser syndrome.*" He made it sound like the name of a cartoon character on Saturday morning TV.

Perlsteiner looked at Guma sharply, but his eyes still held an amused twinkle. "Mister Trevio," he said, "you would be surprised how little real mental illness there is in the world. And of that, how little is associated with criminal behavior. Irrationality, we have, plenty. And evil, oh my, we have enough, more than enough of that. But the poor crazy people: They suffer, you understand? They can barely take care of themselves. Plot a crime? Nonsense! They cannot do it. Oh, perhaps, in a frenzy they hurt someone, yes, but as I say, this is rare.

"You know, Mister Trevio, when I was much younger, I

had the opportunity to observe, at close hand, a great deal of criminal behavior, people being murdered and tortured, robbed, and so on. And afterward, when people said, 'This was madness, this was insanity,' I would say, 'No, it was not. Evil, surely. Hate and greed, yes, lust for power, yes, fear, perhaps. But not insane. This is a libel on the poor madmen.'

"But, you know, they don't listen. They wish to make a medical thing of evil. Madness is also such a useful metaphor, for that which we would rather not face, eh? So. I am didactic again. Forgive me. Now, you, my dear man—I see here by your record—wished for some money, heh? And you took it. Very sane. And you were caught, but you do not wish to pay for your crime, heh? Also, very sane."

Perlsteiner capped his pen, put it in his breast pocket, and got slowly to his feet. "So. I have examined you. You are sane as bread. I will write my report, which I am sure will be ignored, as were the others. But no matter." He looked around the dayroom and gestured to the inmates.

"You see, I make my examinations here, instead of in my office. Doctor Werner gives me a very small office, which is very inconvenient also. And damp. Much like a cell, you understand? So I do my examining in the open ward. We did the same in the *Geisteskrankheitshaus* in Vienna. And at Treblinka, of course."

Perlsteiner made to go and then began to pat and poke all his pockets. "My eyeglasses . . . ?"

"On your forehead," said Guma.

Dr. Perlsteiner laughed delightedly and adjusted his glasses. "So they are. Thank you very much. Carl Jung was always doing the same. Look, let me give you some advice. We don't see the delusions characteristic of florescent schizophrenia situationally, with no prior history of the disease. Only in literature. In real life, once you got them, they don't go away so easy, you understand? Roosters! Ha! Good God!"

Guma watched the old man walk away, humming. He smiled and strolled over to the payphone, put in some coins and dialed.

"V.T.? Good, you're in. Time to spring me. I think I got a lead."

The next morning Karp was back in his office, trying without much energy to plow through the piles of paperwork accumulated in his absence. Frank Gelb had dropped by, smiling, to say he had been appointed to the bench and was leaving immediately for a vacation in Europe before assuming his new duties. Karp was acting chief as of that morning.

Karp stared glumly at a set of large computer-generated charts laid out on his desk. They told a worse-than-usual story. Of the fifteen hundred cases arraigned by Karp's assistants every week, almost seventy percent were removed from the courts immediately, either through plea bargains or skips after release. Of those that got past arraignment, only three percent were ever brought to a full trial, the rest being plea bargained away.

The most depressing figure, however, was the conviction rate. Karp got out the folder that held several sheets of graph paper on which he had plotted the trial rates and the conviction rates in the months since Bloom took over. He added the appropriate points. In Garrahy's last month, ten percent of the cases passing through the Criminal Courts Bureau reached trial; eighty percent of the trials had ended in conviction, usually for the top count. This past month it had dropped below thirty-five percent. The golden age is gone, thought Karp, ring in the age of brass. Or toilet paper.

By noon, about two-thirds of the pile of papers had shifted from the in-basket to the out-basket. The door banged open and Guma stepped in, smoking a larger-than-usual cigar and holding a cardboard carton.

"All right! Lunch for the cripple. You like corned beef? We got corned beef. You like pastrami? We got pastrami. I got celery tonic, cream, black raspberry. I got dibs on the cream."

"Goom, glad to see you! I hear you're not crazy anymore."

"Yeah, well, that Werner's a helluva shrink. He's got the magic touch."

The door opened again, and V.T. Newbury walked in, followed by Sonny Dunbar. Newbury was wearing a long white lab coat with a stethoscope sticking out of the side pocket. He had a sheaf of manila folders under one arm.

"Looking good, V.T. Where'd you get the outfit? Hey, Sonny."

"Denny Maher lent it to me. The name tag too," said V.T.

V.T. leaned over so Karp could read the white plastic tag pinned to his breast pocket.

"Doctor Frankenstein?"

"Yeah. It got me into Bellevue to spring Guma. I guess that says something. And to rifle Werner's files. And make copies."

"So what did you learn? Give," said Karp around his corned beef sandwich.

"What we got is this," said Guma, pointing to the folders that Newbury had placed on the desk. "Each time Louis was examined, Werner sent up a report. His opinion is that Louis was incompetent, with a confirmation by another psychiatrist. A guy named Edward Stone. The same thing happened to me."

"So? Where does that get us?"

"Butch, I was examined by three shrinks. Count 'em, three. The third guy was this old dude, Perlsteiner. He's old but he don't miss much. He said there was nothing wrong with me."

"Little does he know," said Newbury.

"Up yours, Newbury. And, we find, on examining these records here, that Perlsteiner also examined Mandeville Louis on three occasions, and wrote reports saying that Louis was faking it. Reports that never made it into the file."

"Goom, this is great!" Karp exclaimed. "Great! Werner doesn't know we have this. We'll subpoena him for all documents relating to Louis. He'll never turn over the dissenting opinions. Witholding evidence! I'll tear him a new asshole on the stand." Karp turned to Dunbar. "What is that, Sonny? The sworn question and answer statement from Elvis's girlfriend?"

"Yeah, it looks solid. We got him good, now."

"Right. He's looking at so much time now he's got to give us Louis for a walk."

'What?" Dunbar said, his voice rising. "Tell me you didn't say 'walk.' "

"Well, you know we'll try to get the best deal we can on him, but if he holds out, I'll tell you right now, I'll walk him to get Louis."

"Let me understand this. I bust my black ass hunting down this muthafucka, who has blown up one of your people, *your* people, and killed my brother-in-law, and near killed you, and you tell me that after all that, you're thinking of giving him a free ride?"

"Come on, Sonny. Louis is the goddamn target here. Elvis is a tool. It'd be like, in a vehicular manslaughter, putting the car in jail instead of the driver."

"Don't give me 'tool,' man. I want his ass in jail. *His* ass."

"For chrissake, Sonny, the son of a bitch is blind, or close to it. You think he's going to go back to armed robbery in Braille?"

"Fuck that, man! What, are you the judge and the jury all of a sudden? You saying he's suffered enough? I thought this was the law around here. You think I sat up with my wife night after night, her crying her eyes out about Donnie, for a deal? I want his ass in jail!"

Karp was pale and his jaw was tight. Very quietly he said, "I'm sorry you feel that way, Sonny. Like I said, I'll try to get the best deal I can, but if not . . . it's my case."

Dunbar glared at Karp for a long moment, his teeth clenching. "Ahh, fuck you all!" he shouted, and strode out of the office, slamming the door hard enough to rattle the glass.

"Listen, don't worry about him, Butch," said Guma into the stunned silence. "He's a good guy. He'll come around when he cools off."

"You think so?" said Karp bitterly. "How about me, you think I'll come around? Get used to it all?"

Nobody said anything for a bit, as Guma and V.T. got to their feet and started cleaning the lunch scraps and papers off Karp's desk. Karp sighed and tried for the millionth time to scratch under his cast. "Guma," he said, "could you draw up the subpoena for Werner's records? I'm swamped here."

"Sure thing, Butch. I'll do it now."

The intercom buzzed and Karp answered it. He listened for a few seconds and then slammed it down with a muffled curse.

"That's all I needed. The Great One wants to see me, immediately."

Karp struggled to his feet and hoisted himself on his crutches. He picked up his trend charts. Maybe he could convince somebody upstairs that the system was going down the drain at an increasing rate.

"What's it about?" asked Newbury.

"They didn't say. Maybe he found out I put a criminal in jail last June and wants to know whether it slowed up the system any. Who the fuck cares!"

CHAPTER TWENTY

Garrahy's old office had changed. There was a new beige rug, some contemporary graphics of the traffic-accident-on-Alpha-Centauri school, and the obligatory row of Spy legal caricatures. There was also a new secretary; Ida had finally joined the other Ida's in the dust of history. The new one, Jerri, was blonde, and dressed for success. Mr. Bloom was on the phone, Karp was told, and he should make himself comfortable in the conference room. Did he want coffee? He did not.

Karp clump-clumped into the conference room. Conrad Wharton was there, seated in one of the leather armchairs toward the head of the table. Karp maneuvered himself into one of the chairs at the other end.

"Hello, Butch," said Wharton pleasantly. "How are you feeling?"

"I can't complain, Conrad. What's this all about?"

"Oh, I think we'd better wait for Sandy on that. I think he'd want to tell you personally."

Wharton regarded Karp with a benign expression, a half-smile playing about his Kewpie doll lips. Karp thought Wharton looked a little too much like a cat studying a mouse. He began to go over in his mind all the things he had done recently that Wharton might be able to nail him for. He was just starting to get nervous when he realized this was exactly what Wharton wanted. He made himself smile back.

"And how about you, Conrad? The ship of state sailing smoothly? All the columns of figures adding up?"

"Some of them, Butch, some of them. Our throughput is holding up nicely, and that's the important thing, isn't it? Although, I hear rumors from time to time about padding."

"Padding?"

"Yes, you know, inventing cases to make it look like the clearance rate is higher than it really is."

"No joke? That's low, Conrad, that must be really tough on your system."

"Yes, it is. But we're putting controls in place that should put a stop to it. Audit systems, and so on. Sandy is a real bug on clean data."

At that, the real bug himself walked through the door. As usual, he looked tan and fit. He was wearing the trousers and vest of a navy pinstriped suit, and his sleeves were rolled up to show his Patek Phillipe, and to show he was not above a little hard work. After more than a year of contact with him, Karp thought he was about the most completely phony man he had ever encountered.

"Well, hiya guy!" said Bloom heartily. "No, don't get up," he said, as he reached across the table to shake Karp's hand, although Karp had made no move to do so. Bloom sat down next to Wharton and opened a folder that Wharton handed him.

"Butch, this concerns one of your people, so I wanted to talk it over with you before I took any adverse action. I have here a Grand Jury subpoena for a Vera Higgs. Are you familiar with that?"

"Yeah, I am. What about it?"

"What about it! It's a Grand Jury subpoena, Butch. The witness was never brought before the Grand Jury. This assistant, this Kaplan, used a legal instrument as a . . . a convenience so that he could break an alibi and depose new testimony in a Criminal Court case."

"Mister Bloom, the use of Grand Jury subpoenas for things like that has been an unofficial practice in this office for all the time I've been here. Mister Garrahy knew about it, and . . ."

"You know, Butch, I get a little tired of hearing what Mister Garrahy allowed and didn't allow. The fact remains that

300 —

it's a serious procedural violation. I had to take a very unpleasant phone call from Lennie Sussman this morning. He was furious that Kaplan and what's-his-face, Hrcany, went out and coerced his alibi witness into changing her story, using an illegal subpoena."

Karp struggled for control. He took a deep breath and said carefully, "Uh, Mister Bloom . . ."

"Please, it's Sandy."

"Uh, Sandy. I'm sorry you had an unpleasant phone call, but the guy the woman was protecting with her fake alibi has been wanted for three years for involvement in a double homicide. He was also the guy who blew up Marlene Ciampi. And tried to kill me.

"Now as to the legality of the usage, Miss Higgs was interviewed in an assistant district attorney's office prior to her appearance before the Grand Jury. This is common practice. She had every opportunity to so testify, and can be rescheduled to do so at any time. So the Grand Jury subpoena was legit."

Bloom began shaking his head even before Karp had finished.

"Butch, it won't wash. It's obvious that your people's use of a Grand Jury subpoena was what pressured the woman to flip on this thing. Sussman will never accept it and neither will Judge Stein. I spoke to the judge at noon and he agreed we can work it out, but . . ."

"Wait a minute, you brought this business to a judge? Merv the Swerve is going to make a profound legal analysis of this crummy little procedural zit? I can't believe I'm hearing this. And who gives a shit what Sussman will accept? He's on the *other side*. What is going on here?"

Bloom's face darkened and began to reassemble itself into a pout.

"If you would let me finish. Both the judge and Sussman would be satisfied with an agreement that the Higgs testimony will not be used in the trial, and that both Hrcany and Kaplan will be privately reprimanded."

"I bet they would! Oh, crap, don't tell me you agreed to that!"

301 —

"Yes, I did. It's a good agreement. Don't you realize that your people could be cited for abuse of process at a judicial hearing. They could even be disbarred."

"For this *bupkes?* Sandy, give me a break. Uh-uh, there's no way I'm going to go along with this deal, and Hrcany and Kaplan would be fools if they did, and they're not fools. No, I want a full, open judicial hearing. I'll advise Kaplan to ask for one, and I'm positive Roland will demand one. And we're not suppressing that testimony, either. Sussman doesn't like it, let him challenge it in open court, on the record."

"I don't understand your attitude, Butch. I thought you were a team player," said Bloom petulantly.

'I am! I *am* a team player. I want my team to win. I play by the rules, but I still want to win. Look, let's carry the metaphor further. What's the score?"

"Score? What are you talking about?"

"This." Karp opened his folder and spread his charts of trial percentages and conviction rates out on the table. He began to explain what they meant, in terms of public service and attorney morale. But as Karp spoke, and as he observed the mounting annoyance on both of the other men's faces, he realized neither of these men was interested in either public service or attorney morale. He recalled what V.T. had said months ago about people who sought power for its own sake rather than as the means to perform useful or beloved work.

Amazing, he thought. They don't give a damn about this. They don't care about the subpoena either. What they want is my complicity in something stupid, arbitrary, and faintly nasty. They want to pull me away from my friends and my troops and everything that Phil Garrahy stood for. It was so simple; and what would they do once they had him? Make him dance around and gibber like an ape? Train him to flattery? He suddenly felt old.

"Yes, that was very interesting, Butch," said Bloom, when Karp stopped talking. "Chip, check this out, would you? Good. Now, I must get to a meeting. Butch, do me a favor. I don't want a messy hearing. There'll be press, it'll string out forever. Write a little note for Kaplan's file. Drop the testimony. I mean it's one case out of thousands. We got a big system to run here, right?"

Bloom shone his smile. Karp was impassive.

"No."

"What? Karp, damn it, you're being plain unreasonable. Didn't you understand what I said?"

Karp struggled to his feet and set his crutches. "Yes, I did. And I think it sucks. And there's going to be no secret screwing with Mike Kaplan, and no secret deals with Lennie or Irv. If anything like that goes down, I will jump the reservation in a New York minute. I will demand a judicial hearing. I will leak like a sieve. I will call Breslin. And I will call Alfredo Marchione and tell him the case against his brother's murderers is being gutted by the DA because Mister Bloom doesn't like a technical procedure that Phil Garrahy used every day for forty years. That ought to go down like peaches and cream at the Chelsea Democratic Club, of which Alfredo is past president and spiritual leader."

Bloom gaped like a carp. "You. You're threatening me. You're threatening *me?*"

"No, I'm not," said Karp, turning away and humping toward the door. "I have no reason to threaten you. You haven't done anything wrong."

That evening Karp took a cab over to Bellevue. Three days a week he had physical therapy from Hector Delgado, ate dinner in the hospital cafeteria, and then went up to see Marlene Ciampi. He went after normal visiting hours, because during them a tide of relatives filled the room. Hector knew the nurse, so Karp got fifteen minutes alone after she had shooed the Ciampis onto the elevator.

It was hard for Marlene to talk much, with her healing face. They were tapering her off the dope, but she still drifted in and out of sleep a lot. Tonight she was out cold. Karp sat in a wheelchair, held her hand and watched TV. This is what it will be like at Golden Age Ranch, when we're old, he thought.

It was a World War II movie. A sailor ran up to the star and said, "Captain, the Jap carrier is reported dead in the water and burning." Karp liked the phrase. "Marlene," he said softly, "you know what I did today? Don't ask, but I'm dead in the water and burning." He kissed her cheek and left. He felt light and clean, better than he had in months, better than he had since Garrahy died.

And of course he didn't get the bureau chief job. That went to a crony of Wharton's named S. Mervin Spence. Which meant the scam in the Complaint Room was off, or at least scaled way down. Which meant that morale dropped a little lower among the best of Karp's young lawyers. Who simply left. Kaplan, then Dellia, then half a dozen others. Which meant that the criminal justice system became a little more of a joke. Wharton's administrative system was in high gear. He knew exactly what was happening in every part of the DA's office. The problem was, nothing was happening. As V.T. said, "The criminal justice system is neither a system, nor just, but it *is* criminal." When the conviction rate hit twenty-five percent Karp stopped charting it.

Karp traded in his crutches for a cane and by Christmas he was walking unaided. He began once again to walk to and from the office when the streets weren't slick. Toward the end of the winter he grew restless. I'm waiting, he thought. Waiting for what? For spring. For the girl to get better. Waiting for him, for Louis, to make his move.

In March, nearly four years from the day he had murdered the Marchiones, Mandeville Louis reappeared in court. He had spent the fall and winter back in Matteawan, worrying and making plans. He kept telling himself time was on his side. Maybe the witness would die. Maybe Karp would die, or Elvis. He covered sheets of paper with carefully drawn plans, boxes and arrows, showing what would happen if this one did this and the other one did that. He stayed up late making one backup plan after another. Somehow they never seemed to make much sense in the morning and he would take his night's work and tear it to shreds.

He couldn't make contact with the perfect Louis anymore. That was what hurt the most. He had to pretend so much, to be cheerful, and not act out, not give vent to his almost continuous rage. Dr. Dope didn't like acting out. Louis's life had, of course, been one long pretense, but then *he* had been the master, that was the *point*.

He couldn't get Karp out of his mind. *Karp knew.* That was the tumor eating his brain. He had tried to destroy Karp and failed. And Elvis was ratting him out. That hurt too, after all he had done for that little punk. And he couldn't get to him. He took his yellow legal pad and wrote, "KARP KNOWS" and "ELVIS RATS" in big block letters. He drew lines connecting different letters together, trying to make sense out of it, trying for some combination that would bring back the old Louis.

Around three one morning, eyes burning, hand aching from gripping the pencil, he knew he had found it. He wrote furiously, page after page. From time to time he laughed out loud. The next day, early, he called Leonard Sussman and told him to set a hearing date.

When Karp saw Judge Yergin on the bench, he thought he had died and gone to heaven. He had been expecting Stein, and he didn't think even Daniel Webster could have convinced the old Swerve—with his elaborate political connections to the psychiatric community—that one of its distinguished members was both a jerk and a crook. Yergin looked irritated and bored. He must have been dragged in to preside at the last minute. Karp felt he was on a roll.

The players were in their familiar places: Louis looking docile, dull-skinned and tired, flabby from four years of hospital food; Sussman, unchanging, immaculate, sitting rather farther away from his client than was usual. But this time there were more supporting characters. Dr. Edmund Stone, for one, had been dragged from his research and pinned to the stand, like one of his preparations, by Karp's questions.

"Doctor Stone," Karp was saying, "I don't understand.

Are you able to tell this court today if Mandeville Louis is competent to stand trial?"

"Yes, I am," Stone answered. In fact, he barely remembered Louis. He had just done whatever Werner told him to do, and had signed off on whatever Werner told him to sign. Werner left him alone and didn't ask too many questions about what experimental drugs Stone gave to indigent patients. It was a fair deal.

"Good. I ask you again, Doctor. In your medical opinion, is the defendant, Mandeville Louis, competent and ready to stand trial?"

Stone essayed a superior smile. "That would depend."

"Doctor, you just told me you could answer the question. Do so!"

"The issue in a Ganser syndrome case, you must understand, is not the definition of 'competence' but of 'ready.' "

"Ready? That means right now, prepared, able to understand the charges made against him and aid in the preparation of his defense. So yes or no—which is it? Doctor." Karp put as much heat and venom into this last thrust as he thought he could get away with—without being accused of harassing the witness.

Stone was taken aback. He was used to more deference.

"No, no. You are defining competency. I am well aware of what competency means. Mister Louis is a Ganser sufferer. That means the issue is not whether he is competent, but *when* he is competent. Mister Louis is competent to stand trial, except when he is actually standing trial."

Yergin coughed. "Would you repeat that?"

"Certainly," said Stone with more confidence. "Mister Louis is a competent adult able to do anything that competent adults do, including understanding criminal charges and assisting a lawyer in his own defense. But once such a charge is made against Mister Louis, and he finds himself in a court of law about to be prosecuted for a crime, Mister Louis loses all semblance of competency."

"And how do you know that this loss of competence will occur when Mister Louis is tried?"

"Because he has Ganser syndrome."

"And how do you know that?"

"Because of the manifestations of incompetence at trial, of course. It's diagnostic. The principal effect of Ganser syndrome is that the sufferer becomes incompetent to stand trial, but only once the trial begins. Or, of course, if he were remanded for trial, it would be the same. The symptoms could evince themselves at any time. Naturally, we are still doing research on the etiology of this disease."

"Naturally," said Yergin dryly. He turned to Sussman.

"Look, Mister Sussman, answer me this. Is your client, in your opinion, presently competent to stand trial?"

"Your Honor," Sussman said, "it appears that my client is presently aware of this proceeding. My impression is borne out by the psychiatrists' reports, which state that he is presently competent. Our concern is for what will happen once a trial actually begins."

"Then maybe we should go to trial and see what happens," said Yergin. "I mean, if the man is competent right now, that's all I need to hear. How does that sit with you, Mister Karp?"

It sat very badly. Yergin obviously wanted to move this case, and he was playing into Louis's hands. Without a formal finding that Louis was malingering and not suffering from a purported Ganser syndrome, he could stage another bizarre episode at trial and go through another round in his game.

"Your Honor, I think it is essential that the court make a finding as to whether the defendant does indeed suffer from so-called Ganser syndrome. This is the first time the conclusions of the Bellevue Hospital psychiatric staff have been challenged in this case. I think the court will agree that if it can be shown that Mister Louis is not in fact a sufferer from a mental disease that makes him incompetent to stand trial, the disposition of this case in the future will be quite different from what it would be if we simply remanded him at this time."

Yergin got the point. "Very well, Mister Karp. You may resume questioning."

Karp turned once more to Stone. "Doctor, one last question. As the defendant sits here now, is it your opinion that he is competent?"

Stone said "Yes." Karp sat down. The judge offered Stone

to Sussman, who declined to cross-examine. The court broke for lunch, and at two Karp called Dr. Milton C. Werner to the stand.

Werner liked testifying in court. His expression was benign, his carriage confident as Karp went through the preliminaries of identification and qualifications, and established that Werner agreed with Stone completely about Louis suffering from Ganser syndrome. Then Karp began to dig the pit.

"Doctor Werner, is there anything that might possibly indicate that the defendant does *not* suffer from Ganser syndrome?"

"No, sir, this is a classic case. In fact, I have just had a paper accepted for the journal, *Forensic Psychiatry,* that uses this very case as a—how would you put it?—a diagnostic paratype of this disorder."

"But surely, Doctor, some psychiatrists might disagree. Some psychiatrists might suspect on present evidence that Mister Louis is no more than a clever malingerer."

"Well they might, but if they did I would be glad to tell them they were wrong." Werner chuckled at his little joke.

"So you would expect unanimity on this diagnosis among competent experts in forensic psychiatry?"

Werner checked for an instant before answering. "Um, yes, among competent experts, yes."

"And is this reflected in the medical records pertaining to the defendant, Mister Louis?"

"Yes."

Karp walked over to his table and picked up a sheaf of folders. "I notice, Doctor, that each time Mister Louis was examined, in Nineteen-seventy, in Nineteen-seventy-three, and just recently, all the examining physicians concurred in the diagnosis. Is that true?"

"Yes."

Karp handed him the file. "This is Mandeville Louis's file as delivered by you, pursuant to the subpoena. Please look through it, and would you confirm for the court that it contains the reports of all the psychiatric examinations performed on Mister Louis during his several stays at Bellevue?"

Werner thumbed carefully through the file. "Yes, they're all here."

"There were three stays and two reports for each stay. Correct?"

"Yes, that is correct."

"Now, Doctor, as one of the directors of Bellevue and as an official of the state of New York, are you conversant with the procedures under which competency is established under New York law?"

"Yes, I am."

"And, so you are aware that it is a violation of New York State law to suppress or conceal the results of a psychiatric evaluation?"

"Yes, I am." Werner was tense now. He had stopped his genial beaming after each question.

Karp handed Werner a sheaf of papers from one of his folders.

"Doctor Werner, would you tell the court what that document is?"

Werner paled when he read the first page of the document.

"Ah . . . it appears to be a psychiatric evaluation of Mandeville Louis."

"Very good, Doctor Werner. It *is* a psychiatric evaluation of Mandeville Louis, written by Doctor Emmanuel Perlsteiner of the Bellevue staff. But it was not included in any of your original reports to the court, nor was it included in the subpoenaed material. Nor did you choose to include Doctor Perlsteiner's other two reports on Mister Louis. Doctor, is it not a fact that you consciously suppressed these reports because they did not confirm your diagnosis, because they were adamant in their conclusion that Mister Louis was, and is, a blatant malingerer?"

"No, that's not true, he . . . Doctor Perlsteiner is, well, he actually hasn't kept abreast of modern developments in the field, and as an elderly man, he . . . ."

Werner's voice faded. Karp thought, Thank you, thank you. An invidious dig at your colleague's credentials is precisely what I wanted. You've broken the White Wall, you ass-

309 —

hole, and now *your* credentials are up for grabs, and so are Bellevue's, not to mention the integrity of your system.

Karp lifted his folders toward the bench. "Your Honor, I would like to present as evidence these psychiatric evaluative reports on the defendant, written by Doctor Emmanuel Perlsteiner. Doctor Perlsteiner is quite certain that Mister Louis is completely sane."

Yergin's brow looked like corrugated cardboard. "Mister Karp, do you mean to tell me that we don't have those reports?"

"Yes, Your Honor. Every year since his first evaluation, Mandeville Louis was examined by Doctor Stone, Doctor Perlsteiner, and Doctor Werner. But only the reports by Doctors Stone and Werner were sent to the court, for obvious reasons. This court never knew about the dissenting reports."

From the stand, Werner tried his last shot, a desperate one.

"Your Honor, if I may. It seems to me that this Mister Karp is presuming to make judgments about the competency of psychiatric staff that lie outside his purview. I must strenuously object on behalf of the Bellevue staff."

Yergin turned his massive head slowly toward Werner and regarded him as an alligator might a puppy. "I observe your objection, sir. I do not accept it. It is for this court to obtain the required psychiatric advice, and on the present evidence in this case, I believe that I no longer wish to obtain it from you or your staff at Bellevue Hospital. As for you, sir, I would suggest that as of now you concern yourself not with competency of medical advice, but with competency of legal advice, should the District Attorney's Office wish to bring a charge of perjury against you."

"Good for Yergin!" said Marlene from her bed. "What happened then? Yomm! Oh, gorgeous!"

Karp was sitting in Marlene's room with a cardboard bucket of half-shell oysters picked up from a fish store on First Avenue. Marlene's face was still partially bandaged, but she was off the dope and feeling more her old self. Every couple of sentences, Karp would season an oyster and slide it into her mouth. It was the sexiest thing either of them had done in months.

"Oh, it was quick work after that. He recessed and asked us for the names of two fresh shrinks. We got him two guys from Downstate Medical Center. After they had finished laughing themselves silly over Ganser syndrome, they told the judge Louis was as competent as he was, or words to that effect."

"So he's remanded for trial?"

"You bet. They're selecting the jury now."

"What do you think?"

"I think open and shut. Elvis and the physical evidence will bury him. On the other hand, I got a funny call this afternoon. From Sussman. He said, quote, 'Mister Louis would like to see you about a deal.' Unquote. He wouldn't say what it was, wouldn't say anything, in fact. Very uncharacteristic."

"Ah, piss on him. He just knows he's beat. By a better man. Oyster me again, big boy."

To Karp's surprise, when he arrived at the Tombs the next morning, Louis seemed positively glad to see him. His eyes glittered and he had an obsequious smile on his face. Sussman sat at the other end of the scarred table and merely nodded as Karp entered the interview room.

Karp examined Louis coldly. "OK, Louis, your lawyer said you wanted to see me."

"Yeah, yeah, I did. Hey, sit down, sit down. Look, Karp, let's cut out this jive, you know? I mean we understand each other, right? We're the same kind, you and me. I mean, I could, you know, work with somebody like you, you dig?"

Louis brandished a fat wad of yellow legal paper, thickly covered with writing. "Look, I got it all worked out. It can't miss. See, the deal is, we do franchises, but not just one thing, see. We franchise everything! It's a kind of service—somebody got a product they want to franchise, they come to us, we set it up, turn it over to them. And, look, here's the best part, we take a fee, plus, we get royalties on the franchises. Or maybe, we take over some of the spots. I, we, could work it out . . ."

"Louis, what are you talking about? I thought you wanted

311 —

to deal." Karp looked at Sussman, who merely shrugged and lifted his eyes to the ceiling.

"Yeah, yeah, this *is* the deal. It's hot to trot, man. Man, I figure you to be, ah, Mister Outside, I'll be Mister Inside. We'll have us a big office with classy secretaries, you know, fine foxes. And, like, we'll have a jet. A corporate jet. A corporate jet, man."

Karp stood up. He addressed Sussman. "This won't work, Lennie. It's sneaky, but I think you've played your hand on this line."

Sussman raised his palm. "Karp, cross my heart, this is all him. I have no idea what he's up to."

Louis was shuffling through his papers. "Hey, look at this, I got a drawing of the corporate jet. It's got a what d'ya call it, a logo, on it. Hey, Karp, what do you think, sharp, right? Hey, Karp, where you going?"

"See you later, Louis," said Karp, reaching for the door.

Louis got up and followed him. "Hey, Karp, let's, you know, have lunch. We got to make plans."

Karp turned and glared down at Louis. The man looked bad, that was a fact. His glasses were dirty, and there was a dried crust around his lips. His tan face was blotched and puffy and his hair looked greasy.

"Great, Louis. Let's make it twenty-five years from next Thursday. I'll call to confirm."

Louis's smile faded. "Twenty-five . . . ? Oh, shit, hey, that's all past, man. I mean, this is a new start. Right. I mean, I'm sorry. I really mean it. I mean if I caused any trouble at all, I am truly, truly sorry. What's past is past, though, ahh, you can't let the past hang you up, right? I mean, I said I was sorry and I meant it. Right? That's past."

Louis kept talking in this vein, in an insistent monotone. Karp couldn't take his eyes away from Louis's face. He felt a cold chill start in his midsection and crawl up his back. He shuddered.

Then something beyond Karp's understanding happened. He looked into Louis's wild, yellow eyes and he *saw* him. He saw the patently insane creature now babbling before him (hey, Karp, whadya say, Karp, hey what a deal, right? Karp? Hey, whata, whata, deal, right, hey, I'm sorry, alright?); he saw the phony madman under that, and under that the real monster, the beast of blood, and under that, under that, down beneath the rules and the laws, and vengeance and evil, he saw, and felt, a creature, a being like himself, writhing in a white-hot, ice-cold loveless hell, enduring torments so unspeakable that to release it by death, any death, would be an act of profound mercy.

Without conscious volition, Karp observed his hand reach out and pat Louis gently on the shoulder. Then he spun on his heel and left the room. He was sticky with sweat and breathing hard as he walked down the filthy corridors. He walked out of the Tombs into a bright, early summer day. He thought, ridiculously, this is the first day of the rest of your life.

A teenager in pimp clothes bumped into him. "Have a nice day," said Karp. "Ah, fuck ya!" snarled the pimplet. Karp laughed merrily and headed north. For the rest of the day he sat in Washington Square Park and looked at people. Everything looked scrubbed and new, and impossibly detailed, glowing. He exercised his compassion, and mourned, joyfully, his lost innocence.

"And the thing of it was," Karp explained to Marlene that night, "I didn't change my *ideas* at all. I mean, I didn't become a bleeding heart all of a sudden. I just was conscious, really *conscious,* for an instant, that me, and Louis, and Sussman, and shit, even Wharton, were just playing roles, and inside us there was something huge laughing at us all. Not cruelly, or mocking, but, like, 'when are you people going to wake up?' It was uncanny."

"It sounds like it. You and the Grand Inquisitor."

"Right. I've got to read that sometime. And the funniest part is, I don't care about the trial. I mean, I want him to go to jail for a long time. And he probably will, even though he's crazy as a loon. But I realized that what got me about him, what he was doing was a violation of the game. He wouldn't play the game. He wouldn't suffer with the rest of us. That's what made him a monster. And I destroyed that. Or something did. Something did." They were silent for a long while, thinking about how it had all played out.

She was sitting in his lap on a plastic couch in the patients' lounge. After a while, Karp felt her stiffen and she made a little noise.

"What is it, Champ? Pain?"

"No. I'm scared, Butchie. They're coming to show me the Face tomorrow."

"Oh, God! Do you want me to be there?"

"No! I mean, I'll need, I guess I'll need some time for myself, you know?"

"Look, Marlene, I got to say this, umm, whatever it turns out . . ."

She put her hand over his mouth. "No, don't say anything. Just squeeze me."

The next day, it was a Friday, she called Karp late, around five.

"Hi."

"Well?"

"I'm at your place. I let myself in."

"My place? Don't move, I'll be right there."

It was rush hour, and Karp had to put a body check on a distinguished elderly member of the bar to get a cab.

The door was open. Karp rushed through the apartment to the bedroom.

She was standing at the foot of the bed in a long-sleeved tan summer dress. She was completely transformed. Her ordeal had stripped the softness from her, and the planes of her face showed clear, through the taut skin. The right side of her face was discolored in patches and covered with a quilting of fine white scars. A black patch covered her right eye. Her hair was cropped short, and some peculiarity of the wounding had created a white blaze through her black hair from the forehead to the crown.

The cover girl was utterly lost. Instead, she had a face out of archaic imagination, like something painted on terra-cotta on an Aegean island or cut into bronze at Mykonos, for a hero's grave.

As Karp stood there, his heart pierced and full at once, staring, her mouth, which was perfectly still, hardened into a grim line, and her one eye flashed defiance like a hawk's eye, out of her hawk face. Her hands were clenched at her hips, in her old way, and Karp saw that her left hand was clad in a tight black kid glove.

Karp slowly raised both hands above his head. "Don't shoot," he said weakly. "I give up."

Then he went toward her and picked her up, placed her on the bed, and pinned her beneath him. And he kissed her face, starting with the scarred part, and then her mouth, for a long time. He kissed every scar and the bad eye and the good eye.

Marlene started to cry. She cried so hard she couldn't breathe on her back. She wriggled out from under him and went into the bathroom to sob great, whooping, wracking sobs for nearly ten minutes, while Karp stood outside and said her name, and she said, "Just a second, just a second."

She came out, and said, "Whoosh! OK, that's over. Christ, I think my patch shrank." She walked over and examined herself in the long mirror on the bedroom door. Karp came and stood behind her. She saw his reflection looming over her own, and suddenly she giggled.

"What?" he asked.

"Belmar. I just thought of Belmar, for no reason."

"What's Belmar?"

"It's a resort town on the Jersey shore. It's part of the ethnic Riviera—we used to go there when I was a kid. They had this severed head, it was an attraction on the Boardwalk that would tell your fortune. Anyway, there were all these blue-collar bungalow resorts, little hotels, too. Italians around us, Russians to the north, Polish, Irish.

"I just had the image of you and me walking up the Boardwalk in Belmar."

"Do they allow Jews?"

"Only with a responsible adult. Karp, let's go sometime. Jesus, I haven't been there since Christ was a corporal. We'd blow their pants off—Pirate Jenny and the Giant Jewboy. They'd be strolling the sand in their Jockeys."

"It's a deal. However, right now this minute . . ."

She turned toward him. "What do you think of glass eyes? Tacky, right?" She still had tears in her voice.

"No, I think a glass eye can be tasteful," said Karp conversationally, close to tears himself. He said, "Champ, I want you so much, I'm nauseous."

She held her hands out, palms up. "Well," she said, "here I am."